The Spectacle Salesman's Family

The Spectacle Salesman's Family

VIOLA ROGGENKAMP

Translated from German by
HELENA RAGG-KIRKBY

virago

VIRAGO

First published in Germany as *Familienleben* in 2004 by
Arche Literatur Verlag AG, Zürich-Hamburg
First published in Great Britain in 2007 by Virago Press

Copyright © 2004, 2005 by Arche Literatur Verlag AG, Zürich-Hamburg
Translation copyright © Helena Ragg-Kirkby 2007

The moral right of the author has been asserted

A CIP catalogue record for this book
is available from the British Library.

Hardback ISBN: 978-1-84408-491-3
C format ISBN: 978-1-84408-221-6

Typeset in Goudy by M Rules
Printed and bound in Great Britain by
Clays Ltd, St Ives plc

Virago Press
An imprint of
Little, Brown Book Group
100 Victoria Embankment
London EC4Y 0DY

An Hachette Livre UK Company

www.virago.co.uk

The Spectacle Salesman's Family

Chapter One

My mother is coming to rip the night apart. I can hear her hurried steps in the hall. Vera's lying next to me; she's awake but acting as if she were fast asleep, as if her night had only just begun. My sister does this every morning. She doesn't want it to be daytime. I do want daytime to come, clear and radiant so early in the morning, even if Vera does cast a familiar shadow over it with her strenuous pretence of sleep right next to me. For a while now I've been lying beside her with open eyes, silent and motionless. It's dark in our room, although the sun is shining outside. Vera has to sleep in a pitch-black room; she can only sleep when it's pitch-black, when she can see that she can't see anything any more after we've turned the light out and darkness has confronted her open eyes for several seconds. Stop disturbing me and keep your feet still, she just says, leave me alone, and I ask her if her eyes are still open, I have to ask, and she doesn't say yes or no; she just says leave me alone. Then I know that she's shut her eyes tight wanting nothing more to enter them, and at precisely this moment I open my eyes wide and let the darkness flood into me. And then things appear in greyish brown, our wardrobe, the little table, the two bookshelves, Vera's and mine – we keep our books separate – and red and yellow roses bloom on the two armchairs.

1

It's the same palaver every night. Are the shutters properly shut on the inside? Put the iron bar across so they can't come open. There's a gap, I can't sleep with the moon shining full in my face. Vera always exaggerates, and my mother jiggles the iron bar so that it's even more firmly in place, and the window-panes rattle in their mouldering wooden frames. There, she says, nothing and nobody can get in now.

I don't think she's breathing; if Vera's not breathing I'll have to wake her. Are you breathing, Vera, you're not breathing. I raise my head. The bed groans beneath me. She'll pounce on me out of sheer rage once I've saved her from dying of asphyxiation. Vera, tell me, are you breathing, I can't see whether you're breathing, just tell me you're asleep, or say good morning, Fania, just have a look whether the sun's shining. She pulls her pillow over her head, a sign of life at any rate, and I drop back down as if someone had kicked me in the forehead. I want to get out, but I'm lying in chains. Not heavy chains. They'll burst asunder once my mother comes in.

I wouldn't mind being woken by Vera in the mornings. She wakes me at night. Fania, wake up, there's a spider above my bed. And although it's pitch-dark in the bedroom, she knows there's a spider there. It's above her bed, above our bed, to be more precise, we sleep next to one another but the spider is always on Vera's side, on the wall above her pillow. I fumble for my light. A little reading light. I got it for my birthday. I turn it on, and there is light, and I can see that it's true: there's a spider above Vera's pillow.

Kill it, she screams, quick, kill it.

I can't do it that quickly, I need a hard object to kill it. I lean out of bed, down into the dark water, I fish from my raft for my slipper. Is it still there, I call above my head to her. In this precarious position I can see everything that's floating around below us. Little cardboard boxes. Inside them are my little dolls, bedded on cotton wool. They're naked and damaged. I don't know who they belong to. I found them on my way to school. Bits of fluff have attached themselves to them like algae on floating shipwrecks. Behind them I can see the book that Vera finished yesterday night, *Suzie Wong*, a love story, I don't read that sort of thing; and there's my slipper.

Get on with it, yells Vera.

I had to crush the spider against the wall with my slipper. My hand can feel its body through the sole. Then it drops down on its thread and escapes. I waited too long. Vera is furious with me.

You let it get away.

That may be true. Because it makes such a terrible sound when you squash the life out of something. The thread came out of the spider's body and the spider dropped down it, escaped without separating itself off.

What are you talking about, kill it, says Vera.

She'll go mad if I don't kill it this minute. She's already mad. The spider's under the bed somewhere, probably under Vera's bed, it seems to prefer Vera's bed. It can't possibly be the same spider every time, I've already killed so many of them.

It'll be under your bed, Vera, I tell her.

My sister doesn't always believe everything I say, but she does believe this, and she leaps from her bed onto the little club chair and into the roses. The spider might jump out from anywhere under the bed.

Switch the lights on, Vera cries to me from her chair, and fetch Mammy, quickly, quickly.

My grandmother appears in the door in her nightgown, my mother arrives drunk with sleep and immediately takes in the situation, she flicks the overhead light on, she fetches the

3

sweeping brush from the kitchen, and we all of us pull the bed away from the wall. My mother uses the brush to sweep along the skirting board. She knows where all the hiding places are, and hey presto the spider scurries out and runs for its life. Vera screams, my grandmother has her hand clasped to her mouth, I stand behind my mother, I want to know how she's going to do it. She bangs the bristles of the brush against the creature, over and over again.

It's dead now.

Let me see, says Vera.

My mother raises the broom, and my sister stares at the long black bristles between which there has to be a dead spider hanging somewhere.

I can't see it.

You're lucky, says my mother.

You're not lying to me, are you?

Take my word for it.

We push the bed against the wall, my mother and grandmother tug at the undersheets so they are taut and white, devoid of folds and hiding places. It's dead, no doubt about it. My mother holds the duvet out in readiness. Vera lies back down again and stares at the white cloud that slowly sinks down and envelops her.

Sometimes I'm awoken at night by her crying. Go back to sleep, says Vera. I fight against the force of tiredness pulling me into darkness. My sister is crying. She wants to carry on crying undisturbed, she's crying about the men she falls in love with and can't have, married men and men who are far too old for her, for example that singer from Paris. My parents have a couple of his records and if they have a party we can hear him singing at two in the morning, that's his hour. His voice makes its way across the hall into our room, an accordion accompanies him, and the laughing of the guests follows him. I want to keep them well away from Vera: she should have him all to herself. The guests sing along with him, they dance to his songs, we can hear their feet scraping across the floor. I don't like his voice; right from the start, when Vera fell terribly in love with him, with that very voice, and looked at my face for confirmation that she would be the best match for him and that he belonged henceforth to her, right from that moment I disliked him, this man with his straw hat perched at an angle on his head and his teeth all bared. False teeth for sure. Perhaps he's been dead for ages. She never stood a chance with this old Frenchman.

She became angry; she, too, bared her teeth; her face turned red. And although I was afraid of her, I watched the way she came to look more and more like a wild cat, a tiger or a leopard, not so much like a lioness, her hair is too dark for that. She narrowed her eyes into slits. Keep a safe distance from her and nothing will happen to you. Okay, okay, I said, and then she showed me again how she smiled when he sang, how she moved to the rhythm of his voice, how she combed her hair just for him.

He was a shellac record, so I looked at his voice. For Vera's sake. We had got up during the night to put him on. Our parents had gone to the Bar Celona to see the men in drag. These were special men, otherwise my parents wouldn't have gone to see them as my father doesn't really like men at all and my mother mistrusts all Germans.

I'm really not sure about the two slits in the front and back, said my mother forcing herself into her new evening dress. Maybe one would be enough. The special men in the Bar Celona would decide that this evening. The black fabric clung to her body like a second skin. What do you think to your mother, she asked us, turning to me as she spoke. The tailor had sewn the slender dress so that it fitted her body perfectly; long sleeved and with a high neckline it had a plunging slit down the back which finished where her spine ended and a little zip began. I traced it down the middle of her bottom with my index finger. My grandmother had helped her slip into her shimmering skin, and I was allowed to zip it up.

Vera wants to go with them to see the men in drag but she's not old enough, you have to be twenty-one, that's what she'll be in four years' time. It makes her miserable that she's not old enough yet. She's afraid it will all be over by the time she's old enough.

It was my mother's agitation in her skin-tight dress that made my sister and me get up in the night. We crept across the hall into the big room, my grandmother was sleeping next door, Vera put the record on. I sat on my father's wingback chair, Vera danced and cast tender glances in my direction. I didn't let her see what I really think of this schmaltzy old man, I put my left foot on my right knee, that's how men do it who are sure of themselves, my father never sits like that. Vera wanted to be like our mother; she wanted to be as beautiful and seductive as she is. The old Frenchman was singing in French, I didn't understand a thing. Vera repeated his words, she had something in common with him, and she made me know this and watch it.

What's he singing about, I asked, not that I was really interested, I wanted to do her a favour, and discovered that he was singing about love and that women were falling at his feet. This annoyed me.

You're too young to understand these things, Fania, said Vera.

You're mean. I removed my manly leg from my knee. She

6

stopped dancing. It was over. We were two sisters again and went back to our double bed.

Much too old for you, said my mother when she noticed Vera's lovelorn state, he could be your grandfather. She ripped Vera's dreamworld to pieces. And I have her tears in bed at night.

My sister ran out of the room, slamming the doors behind her, first the door of the living room; its timbers swollen by the damp in the house, it just scrunches slowly shut. You have no reason to behave like this, Vera; your parents do absolutely everything for the pair of you.

Try shutting the door on something once and for all and it simply creeps back up on you. Reproaches meant for one daughter are mostly directed at both. My parents want us to stick together, even against them; what matters is that my sister and I should stick together. The door to our room, generally known as the children's room, is a good one to slam. It crashes and shudders on its hinges, and the plaster by the door frame whispers quietly as it crumbles away behind the wallpaper.

My mother chased after Vera, you two are not to slam the doors, she says, but does exactly the same herself. My sister was lying diagonally across our double bed, our parents' old sofa bed. Vera was sobbing, her feet were in my half, and she had her face pressed into her pillow. How could she even breathe. I looked at my crushed duvet. My mother sat down quietly next to Vera and stroked her hair.

It's about time she got here. Why's she staying so long in the hall, she's picking the newspaper up from the doormat. Wolfram leaves the *Hamburger Abendblatt* outside our door every morning, he delivers newspapers before school. The Kupsch family is poor and Wolfram is the youngest and already

7

has to help to earn some money, they live beneath us, in the basement.

I love the day and its light, and my sister loves the night and her dreams. She remembers every dream she ever dreamt. She can carry on dreaming a dream right at the point where it was interrupted. Even if a whole new day has passed in the meantime, she can conjure up the previous night's dream again. She carefully lies in the same position as when she was dreaming. It was lovely, she says, when she wakes up again. In all her dreams Vera is the woman around whom everything else revolves. Nothing happens to me at night, I slide into sleep and through sleep until the next morning. Sometimes I talk in my sleep. Vera tells me the next morning that I laughed again and talked about tall trees. Nothing else, I ask. Nothing else, she assures me. I didn't catch everything you said.

I'm so glad. I have secrets that she and I know nothing about.

Vera would like me to lie still at the side of her as if I didn't exist at all. That's how it was for four years before I was born. Then I was there as someone who didn't yet exist. I loom large in unlived lives.

Today is Monday, and last Thursday we wrote an essay at school, a description of a picture. I didn't like one of the pictures, an old man in knight's armour sitting on a horse with a human skeleton next to him. The other picture showed a Spanish girl like a doll, a tiny old woman with a child's eyes, the infanta. We're getting our essays back today and the teacher will walk between the desks and give all the girls their exercise books back. I'll open mine up at my essay and will be shocked even though I know what's lying in wait for me. I will discover and not understand why everything I've described in my handwriting and written in my exercise book with blue ink is torn to ribbons by red slashes. Nothing will be as it was, and I will close my exercise book before the other girls see it. Annegret next to me will ask What mark did you get, Fania, that's what she always does, she knows I don't write the way we're supposed to write, all the girls know it, and the red ink will squirt out of my exercise book, and I will say You saw it for yourself. She will show me her own high mark. Annegret always writes everything the way it's supposed to be written.

I use both feet to push up against the duvet. You never know, a miracle might happen. That's what my grandmother says. If something goes wrong and works out differently from how it was meant to, she says, you just never know, it was all for the best, everything happens for a reason. That's what she believes. Whatever happens happens because something was and will be.

A shaft of white, the sound of a flute, strikes the floor through the large shutters of the patio door. The sun is shining outside. Vera is whimpering next to me. I sit up, taking in the air of the new day, and from last night I can still hear Vera saying You fell asleep at once, Fania, I lay awake for ages. Sitting on the edge of my bed, I reach for my glasses. Did you have any dreams, I ask, in the same tone that my mother uses when my father's reading the newspaper and she asks Anything interesting, Paul. Vera sits up.

Why ask if I had any dreams, did you notice anything, you noticed something.

What am I supposed to have noticed, I was fast asleep, you were restless, I say, doing her a favour; you were tossing and turning. That doesn't satisfy Vera. The whole bed was shaking.

I feel ill, Vera says threateningly, really ill.

She's trying it out on me to see whether she sounds convincing. I don't like it; I want to be in the light. We stare at one another silently, seeing our mother in each other's face. We hear her in the hall outside, she's rustling the newspaper,

9

she's scanning the headlines, she'll be in our room any moment now.

I don't want to go to school, Fania, hisses Vera. There's no time left for pointless words. Tell her I couldn't sleep all night. She falls back onto her pillows and shuts her eyes.

When Vera doesn't want to go to school but I do go, it's easier for my mother to decide to keep Vera at home, for then at least one of her daughters is going to school. The excuse has to be carefully considered: Vera and I go to the same school, so if she had a stomach upset or something contagious I'd have to be absent as well. I roll my eyes to one side, they look out from my face like the eyes of the ancient-looking little Spanish infanta in my essay. In those days there were things like the plague and smallpox. My great-great-grandparents came from Portugal, the great-grandparents of my mother, who is just bursting into our room with the newspaper under her arm. Vera moans and pulls her duvet over her head and I yawn and stretch. It's morning, the new day has been broached.

Children, I overslept. Her voice is thick with sleep and the many cigarettes that she and my father smoke; they start straight after their first cup of coffee and even smoke in bed in the evenings.

Every morning my mother says she has overslept, she hopes that it will make my sister get a move on, and no matter how many mornings she is proven wrong her tactics remain unaltered.

Vera hasn't slept at all, I say.

Did *you* sleep, Fania, my mother asks.

I yawn and nod.

So how do you know whether your big sister slept or not, she says, thus brushing aside what I've told her about Vera's night. You two spent too long reading; we're having an early night tonight. She walks briskly over to the patio door. Her black hair is sticking out in all directions; her green pyjama top under her open dressing gown is held together by a single button, her small breasts bounce up and down, small breasts with big, dark buds. We drank from them. My sister used to fall asleep.

Vera is getting breasts herself now, they're still small, and I'm allowed to see them; she showed them to me. Vera thinks her bust is too small, small like our mother's. Our grandmother had bigger breasts, maybe one day I'll have breasts as big as hers. There's nothing to see yet, though.

My mother takes the iron bar off the grey-painted shutters and puts it in the corner with a dull thud. She noisily folds the shutters that reach down to the floor, reeling off a stream of words as she does so.

Get up, quickly, I didn't hear the alarm, this time it's the truth, it's seven, almost half seven, you'll be late, children, come on, get cracking, I overslept, Vera, get up, you have to go to school.

The white sunlight comes crashing into the room, Vera flings herself onto her other side, moaning, so that her back is turned towards the patio door. I'm waiting for my periods to start. My undersheet stayed white again last night. Vera was already having periods when she was my age, and all the girls in my class have started their periods. Not me. Don't worry, says my mother, they'll start, it'll just be a bit later with you. Without periods I won't be able to have children; I could adopt some, ten or twelve, I'll need a housekeeper and a cook and a secretary who can write correct German for me. My mother thinks my inability to write German properly might be due to a minor developmental hitch, and that it'll be alright later on, and my father keeps encouraging me to be an architect: Fania

11

will build houses, she played with Lego even when she was very small.

Vera keeps a diary. I don't, because I write everything wrong. I don't notice it myself, but Vera might read my diary and laugh herself silly over my words, so I have to write it all in my head. For the first sentence on the first page of her new diary, Vera comes up with all sorts of different handwriting, the first page is a special page. The Diary of Vera Schiefer. In italics. Underlined twice with a wooden ruler. She shows it to me, we agree that the right-hand pages in new exercise books are luscious cream, and the left-hand pages bluish skimmed milk. Or, muses Vera, maybe it should be Dear Diary or My Dear Diary rather than My Diary. She puts her head on one side and clears her throat; even ice-cream doesn't give us as much pleasure as virgin paper, new pencils and fresh erasers.

My mother stands by the patio door holding her dressing gown together in front of her stomach. Jürgen, the son of Frau Menkel who lives on the top floor of the house next door, is already nineteen and has a pair of binoculars that his father gave him. No one has ever seen his father. His mother doesn't need to earn any money. She lies in the sun on her roof terrace, getting brown; she has her groceries delivered. Jürgen has a pair of binoculars and a father with a murky past.

The wooden floor is cold; the air outside is gentle and a different colour from how it was in March, in March it was cold as ashes, this year April is as warm as May normally is, and I've been allowed to wear knee-socks for the last couple of days. I look under the bed for my slippers, my mother opens the patio door, and the room is immediately filled with birdsong. They burst in with their news; they've been piling it up against our barricaded door since the early hours of the morning. Sparrows chatter on the parapet of the patio wall, they whirr up into the air. Towards the back of the garden a thrush swoops diagonally through the morning air with a metallic clatter of wings, pigeons coo insistently, and my mother, who doesn't like pigeons one bit, claps her hands. With a squeaky beat of their wings they flap off round the corner of the house. The sparrows stay where they are; my mother has nothing against sparrows.

What a mess you look, Fania.

I can't find my slippers; fluffy balls of dust cling to my pyjamas.

We really must give the flat a thorough clean, maybe tomorrow, Paul's out on the road tomorrow. She sits on the edge of Vera's bed. My father's out on the road every week from Monday to Friday, that's what my mother calls it, out on the road. He travels, he's a sales representative, that's his profession, though actually he doesn't have a profession at all, he never got around to training for a profession, he had to rescue my mother and her mother. Buying and selling things is what people tend to do in my mother's family, and so my father became a sales representative. If anyone asks us what our father does, we're to say he's a businessman. Don't tell anyone your father is a sales rep, people don't properly understand what a rep is, travelling businessman sounds better, the best thing is to say he's a businessman, that's simple and straightforward, your father buys goods and sells them, he's a businessman twice over.

Being a rep is shabby in most people's eyes, doorknob polishers and pedlars, that's what reps are too when it really comes down to it, and my mother doesn't want her husband to be lumped together with such men. Her husband is a special man. Women are just taken in by all the other men. Your grandmother, for example, says my mother, hasn't the faintest idea about men. And by this she means her own father too, who vanished from her life.

Once upon a time my grandmother bought something off every pedlar who rang the doorbell. It was just after the war, after we'd been liberated. I hadn't been born yet but my mother has recounted the story so often that I now remember it in every detail. The doorbell rings and my grandmother opens the door. There's a stranger standing in the doorway. He opens his cardboard suitcase and looks at her expectantly. She likes that. Stretching out her neck she carefully takes in his wares, and she always chooses something, just a little something, a bottle-brush or a tin-opener or a pine-scented toothpick. But we've already got two tin-openers, my mother says; she isn't seriously complaining, just complaining a bit, so that we don't suddenly find ourselves with five or six tin-openers in the drawer. Once she bought a tube of silver polish off a penniless war invalid. My mother was furious. Buying silver polish from a penniless war invalid, meshugge, that's what you are, they'd have kicked you off their doorstep a few years ago, just look at them, exactly the same face. And I go to the front door with my grandmother and look these men in the face. They have angular faces, ill-shaven, and they are all missing parts of their bodies, an eye, a leg, an arm or at the very least a couple of fingers off one hand. They wear long grey coats and lean their grey-coated backs against the varnished wallpaper of the stairwell. They give us a spiel about the terrible time they had in the war and after the war. My grandmother gives an embarrassed smile.

I only hope, says my mother, that you two haven't inherited it from your grandmother. She's not got a clue about men. But to be on the safe side she prefers to assume that we *have* inherited it, and Vera and I know that she will scrutinise any potential son-in-law we ever bring home to see whether he'd be suitable for us, for her, and for our family.

Vera lies on the same side of our double bed that my mother used to lie on; my side is the other one, my father's side, the left-hand side of the bed. I lie almost up against the wall, there's just a little passageway free for a stool next to my pillow. My reading light is on the stool, and next to it is a heap of books; I put my glasses next to the books before I go to sleep, and in one of the books is my torch, it's no bigger than a fountain pen and just as round. I've trapped it between the pages of the book so that it doesn't roll off the stool as the floor in our room has developed a slope. Sometimes we have no electricity, during storms for example, and even if there's not a storm, we still get power cuts. Then it's good to know where the torch is.

I'd prefer to sleep on the other side of the bed, the side that faces the room and the door leading to the patio and the world outside. Vera won't swap and my parents back her up. You fidget too much in your sleep, Fania. They've put Vera between me and the world. She's the older one, the first-born, and she'll be the one who leaves first. That's how long I have to wait: first Vera will get married, my mother said, and then you'll marry too. If I were to go first Vera might never manage it; it's possible that she'll never manage it anyway and I'll spend the whole of eternity waiting for Vera to find her way outside so that I can go too. That's what I think sometimes. When I see her body lying there all covered up, blocking my route to the outside world, then it occurs to me that this route merely leads across the terrace, down the iron stairs and into the garden but no further. No matter which side of our marital bed Vera lies on, she's in the same predicament as me, and I wonder whether we'll ever succeed in getting away. Perhaps we'll only manage it together.

My mother bends over Vera and carefully pulls her covers back, talking non-stop as she does so. Go into the kitchen, Fania, and get yourself washed; it's going to be a lovely day today.

The last few words are addressed to my sister, who is gripping her duvet as tightly as she can and refusing to open her eyes. My mother makes her voice all soft and full of promise. A really lovely day, and by the time you get back from school I'll have made you a Spring Feast. Do you want me to make a Spring Feast? You do like it so.

A Spring Feast consists of hard-boiled eggs in a white chive sauce with new potatoes and a green salad. We get the lettuces from the market and have to wash them they're so full of caterpillars, just as green as the lettuces. We could grow everything in the garden – lettuces, potatoes, cucumbers. We could keep hens, too. Then we'd never have to go out again.

What am I supposed to wear? I have no idea what to wear, complains Vera. She feels too fat no matter what she puts on. She sits and reads and stuffs herself with bread and cheese. You don't get enough exercise, says my mother, and when Vera has finished reading her book she stands in front of the mirror, puts on her shortest and tightest mini-skirt, draws in her wide lacquered belt another notch, and sobs. I'm fat, Fania, look at me, I'm a terrible sight. She wants me to contradict her, of course, but she doesn't believe a word I say. She's growing up, everyone says. Vera is suffering, I can tell. I never want this to happen to me. Fania should have started long ago as well, I hear my mother say.

I run barefoot into the kitchen to have a wash. Alien feet beneath alien voices have left their mark in the swirly brown

16

pattern of the lino: they lived here before us, and the lino is still their territory. Tiles would be nice, my mother thinks, and wants to rip out the lino during the course of this year.

We don't have the money to do it: my father isn't selling anything and my mother's borrowed money from my grandmother for the housekeeping. She's completely broke, my father's not to know about it, he's got enough on his plate already. My sister's broke as well, she's borrowed money from me. I'm sure you've got some, Fania, she said. My grandmother and I are the ones that always have a bit of money. Come on, out with it, don't be mean.

I'm not mean, I like having a little bit spare, I give her some to show her I'm not the slightest bit mean, I go to my bookshelf and pull out a cigar box from underneath *Oliver Twist*, *David Copperfield* and *The Jungle Book*, Vera peeps over my shoulder to make sure I don't keep too much of it back. You'll get it back for sure, Fania, word of honour. She butters me up just like my mother butters up my father when he comes back from one of his selling trips and has earned lots of money. They both butter him up and he sits in his armchair and enjoys it and pulls banknotes from his wallet. Vera and I get an extra dollop of pocket money, and my mother holds three, four, five or even six fifty-mark notes in front of her face like a fan, she rolls her big black eyes for him, she reels off all the things she can buy with the money – something nice to eat, some smoked salmon, a bottle of cognac for my father, and there might even be just about enough for that green wraparound blouse in the shop window at Gloria's in the Colonnades. For that he gives her an extra banknote.

I never do get back what I lent Vera. Think yourself lucky, she says, without me you'd never have got extra pocket money. I feel ashamed to be crying about my missing money. I stare and stare at her, my tears have an effect on her slanty face. We're meant to love each other not hate each other, so our parents don't get worried. You hang on to your own money, my grandmother consoles me, it's nothing to be ashamed of. Vera grins contemptuously, and suddenly I'm as old as my grandmother. My money will give me an escape route to the outside world, an escape route that will enable me to slip through my sister's fingers.

In the kitchen sink is an enamel bowl. I turn the taps on, sparks flash in the gas boiler above me, a flame bursts into life. I scoop up the water with both hands and splash it into my face so vigorously that it drips right down to my feet. I don't use the yellowish lump of soap on its saucer beside me: it's covered in varicose veins. I dry myself, clean my teeth, and tip the water on the large azalea that my grandmother has put next to the sink: water is precious.

My sister comes shuffling into the kitchen in her nightdress and dumps herself down on a kitchen chair.

I think I'm getting ill, she whispers.

With a sigh my mother fastens her dressing gown, fills the kettle, and says that yet again there's a smell of gas. She turns the main gas tap on and off, trying to tell whether it had been on or off when she came to use it for the first time that morning.

You two are not to touch the stove in the evenings any more.

Rubbish, says Vera.

That's how she starts her day today. She looks peevishly around the kitchen with half-open eyes, my mother is looking for matches, Vera notices, she hands her a box from the table. My mother, too, hates getting up early, but she just won't believe that we would ever get out of the house if she didn't wake us up, give us a kiss, get our breakfast and make our break-time snack. My grandmother would do it for her: let *me* get up, Alma, you stay in bed, you need your sleep, and I wake up early of a morning anyway and can get the girls ready for school. My mother won't hear of it. Her mother would secretly play mother-and-daughters with us. We're *her* children, for goodness' sake; she'd thought she would never have children of her own.

My children are never getting up on their own. This is important for my mother, and her voice is tinged with scorn for all the other mothers who let their children do as they like.

It was just a suggestion, my grandmother says and goes off in a huff, and I sit there in the middle, a tasty morsel that both women fight over and both need to feed on.

There are girls that come to school without a snack. They wear a key round their neck; I envy them this token of their independence, and they envy me my sandwiches, which I can't share with them because they're tokens of my mother's love.

I kept you out of school only last week. My mother breaks several matches in her attempts to light the gas: gas pours out, it won't be long before the whole kitchen explodes. Vera is sitting behind her, she has pulled up her legs and is resting her head on her knees.

I kept you out of school last week, you had gym. The gas suddenly bursts into a blue wreath of flame, tongues of which come licking out from beneath the kettle.

I don't feel well, I feel so miserable. Vera cries – not much, just two or three tears, she's putting it on. My mother and I know she's putting it on, Vera knows, and she knows that we know, and yet we take her burdensome gloom seriously and hump it around with us today like every other day because that's just the way it is: she can't help it. My mother opens the kitchen cupboard, puts cups and plates on the table, butter, milk, jam, honey, darting to and fro the whole time between table and cupboard.

The kitchen is a long, narrow room, with just enough space on one of its short sides for the gas stove and a double sink. At the opposite end is a window with a deep window sill. I push open both halves of the window, which almost bump into the railings of the outside stairway, an iron stair that leads down from the terrace into the back garden.

Don't fall out of the window, says my mother without turning round, you could break your neck.

It's impossible to fall out of this particular window, to do so I would have to climb up onto the window sill, which is on a level with my stomach; and even if I did, I wouldn't fall to the ground but instead get tangled up in the stair railings with my neck broken and my eyes bulging out. What a terrible death so early in the morning.

The kettle is boiling, drops of water splash hissing into the flames. My father comes into the kitchen, fondles his wife's bottom, gives first Vera then me a kiss, and starts making a pot of coffee. When he was a small boy he made coffee for his mother and her friends: ladies with huge hats and with little velvet bags over their arms. Tiny paper-thin coffee cups.

My father smells of Yardley's soap, he stands there at the kitchen sideboard, puts the porcelain filter on the large, pot-bellied coffee pot, folds the bottom edge of the filter bag so that it doesn't come apart the moment it's filled with water, sticks it in the filter, and pours in just a little hot water from the kettle: according to him this gets rid of the papery taste, and at the same time warms the pot. Whatever he does acquires by that very fact a special aura. While he devotes himself single-mindedly to coffee-making, my mother gets

20

countless other things done and is constantly on the move. She never rests. If the bread knife is not immediately to hand, she quickly grabs some other knife. My father makes sure that the teaspoon he uses to scoop the ground coffee into the filter is always the same one; he won't allow this spoon to be washed, and it has turned brown as a result. The coffee doesn't taste right if I don't use my special spoon, he maintains, and neither my mother nor my grandmother dares to gainsay him.

He tips coffee beans from their container into the electric coffee grinder, puts the lid on the grinder, pulls its white lead from beneath a jumble of teacloths and magazines, and sticks the bakelite plug at the end of the lead into a socket. A sudden deafening noise renders conversation impossible, communication being doggedly maintained by my mother alone, who shouts at my sister with a twisted face; my father stands at the sideboard with his lips pressed together, both hands tightly grasping the fiendish little contraption within which tiny sharp blades pulverise the dark-coloured coffee beans. Seconds later, and just as suddenly, silence descends once again.

There you are, says my father, glancing back over his shoulder with a forced smile, you can carry on squabbling now.

What do you mean, squabbling, screams my mother, I can't let her stay at home every other day.

Don't shout like that, the coffee grinder isn't going any more, says my sister coolly.

The smell of freshly ground coffee spreads in the ensuing quietness. My father sucks in the aroma through his large, fat nose while shovelling the coffee into the filter with his spoon. He gets my mother to pass him the salt, she's busy doing other things at the time, he takes a pinch from the wooden salt-box and crumbles the fine grains over the coffee, he takes some cocoa with the tip of his spoon and scatters it carefully over the

21

dark-brown powdery mound, then goes to the gas stove, where the water is bubbling away in its kettle; the water has to stay boiling, this is indispensable to the success of his coffee-making, so every two or three minutes my father strides with out-turned feet and great deliberation from one end of the narrow kitchen to the other as he journeys between sideboard and stove replenishing the filter or putting the kettle back on the heat. Humming quietly to himself and with his hands in his trouser pockets he stands waiting in front of the coffee filter until the water has almost completely disappeared, walks over to the stove, carries the steaming kettle back to the sideboard, and refills the filter. And since my mother – still arguing with Vera – is constantly toing and froing in the kitchen as she darts to the stove, the sideboard, the sink, the fridge, the rubbish bin, she skips around behind her husband and threads her dainty way amongst his galumphing, flat-footed strides.

My father is already dressed. He must have got up before us and crept through our bedroom into the kitchen. The only way any of us can wash is by using the sink in the kitchen, and the kitchen can only be reached through our room or through our grandmother's, and my father wouldn't dream of going through his mother-in-law's room. My grandmother hasn't been visited by a man in pyjamas for a very long time. It would embarrass her, and my father too. Today, Monday, my grand-mother is still in her room, sitting there on her sofa on the other side of the kitchen wall, washed, dressed, her hair all done, a magazine from the magazine rack on her lap. Monday is the day my father goes off in search of customers, the day my parents have to part from each other for five days. Until Friday. Last Monday, like every previous Monday and every other day of the week, my grandmother was sitting with us at the kitchen table, then all of a sudden my mother yelled at

22

her: you just wait in your own room until my husband's left the house.

I can't bear it when my mother shouts at her mother and packs her off to her room, none of us can bear it, including my mother, but she does it all the same. My grandmother is afraid when she's enveloped in her own silence. At night she gets up, creeps through the kitchen, opens our bedroom door a crack, nods silently in our direction, creeps back through the kitchen to her own room, leaves her door open a crack as well, then in the early morning she comes back out again, I glimpse her as I first open my eyes, she waves to me with a finger on her lips and quietly closes our door. This morning when I surfaced from my sleep I thought that my grandmother Hedwig had died and was waving to me from the Other Side. I wanted to follow her, to hold her tight, but feared that by doing so I would lose her altogether. Then I heard water splashing into the wash bowl. She's washing, I said to myself, so she can't be dead.

We do have a bathroom. It's in the cellar. We never use it. What sort of people were they who put their bathroom in the cellar? Mad or rich. Probably rich. The whole building was probably one big house once, with luxurious carpets in every room. I didn't know anything about this bathroom. In the front garden, right at the foot of the front wall of the house, I discovered a boarded-up window that reached down half a metre or so below ground level. My little rubber ball had rolled into the space in front of the window, fallen through a gaunt iron grid and disappeared into the depths. My father helped me to lift the grating and retrieve the ball with a rake. Clumps of leaves, black and mouldering, had caught on the tines of the rake, it smelled musty. What's down there, I asked my father.

Our bathroom, he answered casually.

We have a *bathroom*?! I said. I found it spooky right from the

23

start. If we had a bathroom, why didn't we use it. Everyone has a bathroom these days, or at least a shower. But not us: we have a big grey galvanised bath that I can sit in provided I draw my knees right up, we fill it with water from the kitchen, first heating the water on the stove in two large saucepans. We bathed like that when we were young, says my mother whenever Vera complains that after all it *is* a bit primitive.

We'd have to go through the air-raid shelter to get to the bathroom, my father explained, and that would be much too off-putting and inconvenient; what's more, the bathroom is stuffed to the ceiling with old bits and pieces.

Old stuff belonging to Frau Kupsch? I asked. My parents have rented out the basement kitchen and the two basement rooms at the front to the Kupsch family – Elsa and Erich Kupsch and their four children, who came from Breslau.

No, not the Kupsches. The fact that he laughed as he said this bothered me. You don't know the people the stuff belongs to, he said; they're not nice people, and it's really crazy that your parents are looking after loads of old stuff belonging to complete strangers. He was trying to reassure me, and this worried me. We've just never got around to chucking the stuff out, Fania, that's all; it's nothing that need bother you. I bounced my rubber ball really hard on the ground, it flew up in the air, well above the garden fence, then fell back down into the garden. Enjoy your game, my father called out.

My mother is standing in front of her husband. Pull your cuffs out, she says, and reaches up on tiptoe to adjust his shirt collar. My father is wearing a light-grey suit, the sun lights up his wavy hair, which he has wetted and combed back. My mother is proud of her husband, she starches and irons his shirts, no one can do it like she does. She wants him to look good, to be elegant and desirable in the eyes of all those women who will never ever get him, and to come across to his customers as a real gentleman. When he arrives at their premises with his two cases of samples, they are going to treat him as a gentleman, and with him being so neat and spruce they're bound to place an order, and if things go badly and he has to leave without having won an order, then his quality suit-material and the shirt that she herself has starched will see him through and enable him to leave the shop with his head held high.

My father pours us out some coffee, giving me the least as I'm only allowed to drink coffee with lots of milk in it; he gives my sister just as much as he gives his wife and himself: Vera is very nearly grown-up. He puts two sugar lumps in the saucer of the fifth cup and carries it through to his mother-in-law's room. We all sit silently at the table. The atmosphere created by my father's imminent departure makes my mother feel ill.

My father comes back. Go on, let Vera stay at home, he says.

You just want some peace while you drink your coffee. It's me that has the bother with her. You're never here. She has to get about. What's to become of her: she hasn't any friends, she doesn't even have a friend who's a girl, she just sits in an armchair reading and dreaming. When I think of all the things *I* did at her age!

Like what, like what? Vera chips in.

I went dancing.

Who with, who with?

With your father.

Exactly, says Vera, slumping against the back of her chair with a bitter smile. With your husband. Anyone else would have been far too dangerous for you, women as much as men.

How can you say such a thing, my mother retorts. I went to

the cinema, I couldn't count how often I went to the cinema, I just about *lived* in the cinema. I went to the tea dance at the Orchid Café, and when the Gestapo came we managed to escape in all the turmoil, your father and me, we scrambled over the tables, me in my heels, and got out through a window. Even though Paul gets giddy so easily.

My mother stares at Vera with a searing gaze. Vera lets her hair fall over her eyes. My father hums to himself: hmm, hmm, hmm.

Like Vera he's not very keen on leaving the house. My mother would gladly take his place and go off to see his customers. She has the feeling that she would land more customers than him, and he has this feeling too. But they leave things as they are. My father travels all around the region from Monday to Friday visiting opticians with his case full of spectacle frames, and every evening between six and seven he phones his wife. It's unthinkable that he would ever *not* ring her up, so my mother is at home every weekday from half past five onwards, awaiting the phone call from her husband. She waits fairly patiently until half past six; if he doesn't ring until nearly seven or even a bit after seven, she repeatedly imagines him having a fatal or near-fatal accident, as only a disaster of some sort could occasion such a delay. The telephone rings, she rushes over to the little round table, yanks the receiver up to her face, her ear, her mouth, the black contraption slips and falls, but not right down to the floor, it's dangling there, what a mercy, dangling from its cord, swaying to and fro right next to her body. The sound of his voice reaches her ear, her face relaxes, and she shovels loving words into the black mouthpiece.

My mother stands up, goes to the sideboard and opens the bread bin. There's something up with you, Vera, you aren't ill, it's something else, just tell me what's the matter. She takes out a square loaf of bread and cuts slices from it, her eyes still fixed on Vera. It's your final year at school next year. You missed loads of lessons *last* year. They won't let you sit the school-leaving exam, you'll have to redo the year, and *you* – she turns to my father – you're never here, it's me that goes to the parents' evenings and has to sit there being told that Vera is missing from gym classes, missing from music classes, dreams her way through chemistry lessons, reads poetry in maths lessons.

What do you want on it, jellied raspberry or strawberry jam? She's talking to me, she's doing me a slice of bread, I want butter and jellied raspberry, loads of it. She nods and with purposeful strokes of her hand butters the bread that is meant for me. At Elsa Kupsch's there's only margarine, and when she cuts off a slice of bread she clamps the loaf between her breasts.

I want to know how 'raspberry' is spelt. I know about 'bread', that's easy: the bread you cut with a knife is obviously different from the 'bred' that's all about rabbits.

How would *you* spell it? my father asks, grateful for the change of topic.

It has to be 'rasbry', same as 'strawbry', it's only logical.

Vera snorts with laughter. Her gloom is instantly dispelled.

Fania just needs to enjoy them, not spell them, says my mother, butting in.

I can't walk in my shoes, says Vera, the heels are too high, my back hurts.

What do you mean, too high, my mother asks. Too high for whom? You have lovely legs, you chose the shoes yourself, they've got low heels, you can walk perfectly well on them, why would they be too high? They *aren't* too high.

Because men are all shorter than me, and that's your fault, snaps Vera. I'm going to be as tall as your husband, I just can't stop growing, all because you were hell-bent on marrying him.

27

You mean your father, my lovely Paul, says my mother, caressing her husband's hand.

Every time I bite into my bread and butter with raspberry jam I make a strenuous effort not to ingest a single word of my sister's complaints; I take a bite, then study the impression of my teeth in the layer of butter.

Why did you have to marry such a tall man, wails Vera; someone smaller would have suited you perfectly well, and now I can't find *anyone* who is my sort of size – anyone who is the slightest bit interesting is either smaller than me or else married.

My mother laughs, her coffee spills over onto the tablecloth, she's relieved to see her daughter animated at last, and my sister sobs out of sheer rage. Boys of my age smell and are covered in spots; I want a man who is older – the same age as Pappy.

My father is flattered: yes, my darling, he says, and this time he doesn't mean his wife.

I leave the kitchen, I want to get dressed ready for school, I open the wardrobe in our bedroom, where Vera's things hang next to mine. I look at her shoes, these silent companions that tell me the story of my sister's tribulations: a few pairs of high heels, but most are flat-heeled, flat as ballet shoes. Vera has been going to dancing classes for the last two months.

You're a big, beautiful woman, I hear my mother say in the kitchen. Trying to talk Vera round is a complete waste of time. You have beautiful legs; I'd like to be a bit taller myself. Exactly: a bit – my sister seizes on the words 'a bit' – but not as horribly tall as I am. One metre seventy-four-and-a-half centimetres, that's a crap height for a woman. You've no idea what it's like, you with your one metre fifty.

I'm one metre sixty-one.

28

Yes, Vera screams, one sixty-one, and Pappy is one metre eighty.

Her voice breaks off. She is crying. I can hear my father laughing quietly: he enjoys it when people talk about how tall he is.

And that's why you want to stay away from school and just sit here turning into a zombie, my mother screams. You're in love with your form-master and he's married and just about the same height as me in my high heels.

Vera gives a great sob, rushes out of the kitchen into our bedroom, and throws herself crying onto the bed.

High heels. What a special pair of words. The very epitome of femininity in its most perfect, most revered and most desirable form. My mother has an entire little cupboard full of these dreamy shoes – a shoe cupboard specially made to house her high heels, screened by a dark-red curtain and crowned by a dressing table with a three-fold mirror.

It stands in my parents' bedroom, next to my father's desk. When she was little Vera used to stick her feet in the shoes and shuffle around the room. You'll wear shoes just like Mammy's when you're a grown-up lady, my mother promised her then, and I heard the same promise in my turn, I heard her fond laughter as she watched me struggle along in the shoes. You too, Fania, later on, when you're all grown up. How wonderfully certain this promise was; it was bound to come true. There was so much room in the shoes, so much space for growing up, we had plenty of time. Now, though, Vera's feet are two sizes too big, she schlepps her adolescent body around like a sack of potatoes, and her misery is plain to see. One morning she suddenly started developing, she let me see the whole lot, showed me her tiny new breasts, and started having periods. It'll be my turn soon. All the girls in my class have started their

29

periods, and their breasts flop up and down, but I'm lagging behind. Give her time, Alma, my grandmother tells my mother, who is worried about it. I hear her, though I'm not meant to, and see them both give an anxious shake of the head.

Vera keeps romantic novels under her mattress – books she won't read to me from any more. She buries herself in them, and if I ask her whether it's exciting – just that one simple question, 'is it exciting?', though actually I'd like to tear the book from her hand and hurl it against the wall – she tells me to leave her in peace. Sometimes she cries, that's when she is enjoying it the most. They're paperbacks on the covers of which a smiling young woman with a pointy nose and pointy shoes walks along the road followed by a smiling man with an equally pointy nose; the woman has a handbag slung over her shoulder, the man has a beret on his head and a pipe in his mouth. Books like these have titles like *Spring in Paris* or *Mon Petit* or *Him and Her*. They are my enemies. One of these days Vera will go off with them and I shall be left behind.

Last winter for the first time my parents took Vera out for the evening. They went to a ball. My grandmother and I listened to a play on the radio; my mother had made us little sandwiches with lumpfish caviar and egg salad. Then I went to bed – *our* bed, but without Vera. At some point I got up and rifled through my parents' bookshelves looking for company. I took out a particularly fat book bound in green and extremely well thumbed. I opened it at the beginning and was met by my father's handwriting. From your loving Paul to my beloved Little One. I climbed back into bed with the book and opened it in the middle. I was looking for bodies but found words about bodies, words that made me feel warm and then hot and made my body tingle. I put the book to one side with my head burning and my fingers all moist.

30

Come on, come to school with me. I touch Vera's shoulder, she is lying on the bed crying. It's nearly eight o'clock, I'm already going to be late and she's not even dressed. She lifts her bloated face from the pillow.

You'll grow and get bigger too, younger children usually end up bigger than their older siblings, that's just the way it is. I don't like such prophecies; I meant her well, and all she does is wish her own misfortune on me. I make a resolution to stay smaller than her. Perhaps I'll get bigger, perhaps not, I say. Who knows? No one knows. I'm going to be careful, I'm not going to tempt fate so far as my future is concerned. It makes no difference what I say, she's not listening to a word of it; even if I end up three metres tall it won't make her feel any better.

Perhaps you can have a little bit sawn off your thigh bones? She lifts up her nightie, looks at her beautiful long legs and strokes her smooth skin. My legs being that much shorter I quickly pull on my blue skirt with its elasticated waist. A summer skirt. Summer will soon be here, I won't need to wear a coat any more. An anorak would be good, but I'll never get one: my mother has bought us expensive poplin coats, despite the fact that we're short of money at the moment. You can do up an anorak with a single hand movement: pull the zip from your stomach right up to your chin, and you're in your own private cocoon. My mother dislikes anoraks, she dislikes anoraks and jolly groups of hikers and camp fires and folk songs and recorders and rucksacks. Vera scrutinises me from top to toe. Are you checking your height regularly, she asks. I stare back at her, each of us trying to outface the other. We never come to blows. We had a play-fight once: hitting and being hit. A waste of time; it didn't even hurt. She wants to know whether I've grown during the night. Stand by the doorpost and draw a line with the pencil. I put my hand on my head and draw a line at the point where my fingertips touch the door frame. Vera sits up in bed: you wobbled, your hand slipped down, you're cheating, check it again, you've grown at least two centimetres.

I yank my pullover over my head, I want to leave right now, I want to get away from Vera just as fast as I can, and perhaps I've got top marks for my essay, my instinct tells me I *must* have scored top marks. Are you going or not, I ask, but Vera flops back onto the pillow and shakes her head without a word. My mother brings me my snack, wrapped in greyish-white greaseproof paper with a strip of milk chocolate on top. I stuff the little package into my school bag. You haven't got any shoes on, she remarks. I slip into my Birkenstocks – foot-shaped bits of wood with a leather strap across the toe; they make a lot of noise when you walk, they were a present from my grandmother, I was desperate to have them. My mother hates them. They're like the clogs they had in the camp. All the girls in my class wear them, and I have to go around in normal shoes with narrow little straps.

You are not wearing those wooden contraptions, she fulminates, it's too cold. You're going to wear your ordinary shoes and knee-length socks and that's the end of it. My sister lifts her head from the pillow. Please, Fania, says my mother, don't you start making things difficult for me as well, not this morning. She accompanies me to the front door, opens it, makes to give me a kiss but suddenly freezes: on our doormat is a large package, a cardboard box with Hebrew writing on it, but with Latin script as well to make sure everyone knows what's inside. Something significant. 'Matzos', it says, 'Matzos' in Hebrew and 'Matzos' in German. Kosher matzos for Passover.

My mother shoves me brusquely aside, yanks the package

into our flat, and with deep-furrowed brow and a finger pointing menacingly towards the heavens she yells for her mother, curses those damned people, why can't they ring the bell, and my grandmother comes running and waving her arms in the air: Alma, calm down, she calls, but my mother doesn't calm down, I've told you a hundred times, she screams, they're not just to dump the matzos on our doormat, I don't want everyone in the entire house tripping over them.

The package comes from the Jewish Community, they've delivered matzos for Passover, and I hope *all* the occupants of the house have tripped over it and stumbled over each and every Hebrew character. My mother tugs frenziedly at the box full of matzos, my father comes dashing up behind my grandmother, he wants to calm my mother down, he doesn't want a row between his mother-in-law and his wife, that's enough, Alma! She doesn't even seem to hear him, she's yelling as loudly as her mother, it's the same thing every time with these damned matzos, she screams, who on earth is meant to eat them, there are far too many, and my grandmother tugs at the box in the opposite direction, she wants to carry the matzos off to her room, through the hall, through our bedroom, to the kitchen and into her own hideaway, safe from the angry looks darting from her daughter's eyes.

For God's sake, yells my father standing in the kitchen doorway, stop making such a fuss, Alma, what difference does it make, just let people see them! Vera is sitting up now, she's watching the battle of the matzos which has already reached the end of our bed. I'm standing by the door, I want to hit my mother, I squeeze my school bag against my chest.

You keep out of it, she screams at him, her face red, the veins in her temple protruding violently, it's none of your business. He turns pale. Jewish stuff of all things: is that really

33

none of his business? My grandmother has let go of the matzos and is gazing in consternation at her son-in-law. My mother, grappling with the box and hunched over the matzos, doesn't have to look my father in the eye. The kosher spirit has quit the cardboard box and is in amongst us. We stare at her: my mother is grappling with a dead thing. Oh my God, Paul. Still bent over the box, she slowly straightens up. I didn't mean it like that. And speaking just as slowly – they speak with one voice – he says, I really must go straight away.

Chapter Two

I get back home at about half past one, my essay on the little infanta in my school bag, torn to shreds by a mass of red marks, and skip up the driveway bordering our front garden. I'm desperate to wee, really desperate. I wrote that it's just not true. He'd said that the little infanta mocks the dwarf and treats him just as a plaything. It's not true. I know it's not true. They don't know anything. My words are such a weight on my shoulders. My hands hang right down to my knees. I am the dwarf, carrying home his infanta's school bag, I clutch at her knees, I clutch a bit higher, then higher, then higher again, my hand stemming the flow within. That feels so good.

They don't know anything. She was just pretending, in fact she loves him, but that wasn't allowed. That's how it was, and that's what I wrote. They laughed. I'd got it all wrong. The teacher let them laugh, he joined in at first, then told them to be quiet. Annegret banged her exercise book on the table and a load of Bs came tumbling out. She always gets Bs, I sometimes get Es and sometimes Fs; this time it's an F+.

Our house is hidden behind trees and bushes. It is a haven of peace. No other house in the whole street is surrounded by so much greenery; I can't be seen from any of the windows of our flat on the upper ground floor. They can see me from the windows above, the ones on the first floor and the top floor. I can feel their eyes on me. My entire abdomen is full to bursting, a glittering ball of water, I balance it on the tip of my tongue. A special trick to please the infanta. As the cat says in the *Witches' Kitchen*: Such is the world – all ups and downs. Vera read me *Faust* in bed, it's by Goethe. At home I won't be punished for wetting my trousers. At school I can never go back into the toilets again, back into that yellow-tiled room with its frosted-glass door, black footprints everywhere, the floor all wet and slippery and strewn with crumpled green paper hand towels, the stink of liquid soap. Several pans are blocked. Shrill screeching and the slamming of doors. What a filthy mess, I'm not going in there, but they push their way in and the door bangs shut behind them, three girls in the next-door toilet, nothing between us but a thin partition. They whisper to one another and open the door again. The mid-morning break is over, bells are ringing throughout the building, they've even put one here in the toilets, above the swing door.

Those are Annegret's shoes, she's standing in front of my door, I don't recognise the other shoes. They're giggling and whispering. Why don't they go away and leave me in peace. Three pairs of shoes altogether: Annegret's and probably Gerda's and another pair with little brown tassels dangling from the ends of the laces. The three pairs are all pointing at each other, so close that their toes almost touch. I could flush the toilet, I could be someone else, some other girl at the school who's finished and immediately tears the door open. They'd be startled into running away and I'd be able to get out.

Fania, is that you in there? It's Fania, Fania's in there. They start kicking my door. Bet that's Fania skulking in there. It's their voices, Annegret's and Gerda's, I don't recognise the third one. Liquids pour out of me: tears flood from my eyes, saliva drips from my mouth, my body doubles up and evacuates my bladder. They'll stare down at me over the top of the partition, they'll see me squatting here on the toilet, why don't they go back to the classroom, the next lesson will be starting any second, I've got stomach-ache, their smirks and giggles are above my head, boring into the back of my neck as I sit there with my trousers round my ankles.

On the blackboard are words taken from my essay, the teacher keeps adding more and more of them, dismembered chunks, random fragments of a once whole body that had its own story to tell, but is now so broken to pieces that even I can no longer say what fits where, and I feel ashamed to have spawned such words, words that simply don't exist.

Who on earth is supposed to read this, who on earth is supposed to understand it, asks the teacher, and carries on writing my words on the blackboard exactly as I had written them myself, and the giggles and whispers of the girls continue unabated. He has my essay in his hand and looks at it over the top of his glasses. He's Wilhelm Bobbenberg, the teacher my sister is in love with. Vera has him for German, too, and she loves German, it's her best subject – and my worst. A strand of brown hair falls down across his face and brushes the edge of my exercise book.

Astonishing, he says, it's truly astonishing, Fania, that you managed to write the word 'infanta' without making a single mistake, I think it's the only word in the entire essay that you spelt correctly.

Perhaps that's because it's not a German word, I reply, and he stops writing, his hand poised in the air and his eyes boring into me. Is that some kind of joke, Fania, he asks, then carries on writing, his eyes alternating between my exercise book and the blackboard. He rubs a letter out: he'd copied my word wrong, making it correct rather than correctly incorrect. This irritates him, I'm causing him trouble, and without looking at me he repeats the question that the entire class has already heard. Because it's not German, Fania: is that some kind of joke?

Vera's got a crush on him, at lunch one day she said how well they get on. Bobbi – that's what she calls him – can be so wonderfully ironic, she says, and they joke with each other during lessons. No, it's not a joke, I reply, it's only in German that I seem to get everything wrong, my spelling's fine in English.

What about other languages, he asks, his tone hardening. He wants me to cry. I don't want to cry – though it's no bad thing to cry, quite the reverse, as my mother's always saying, in our family *everyone* cries, even your father's not ashamed to cry, that's something you can both be proud of, there'll never be anyone like your father.

Spanish, I say. I don't mention Hebrew.

Go on.

Is just the same, I say. My voice is still audible.

The same as what, he asks.

The same with the spelling, I say. I always get it right in Spanish, and we've only been doing Spanish for four weeks, first period on Wednesdays, so there's still hope. My voice dries up.

Hope? Hope for what? he asks, copying even more words onto the board from my exercise book – German words, I haven't spelt them quite right, generally just one letter's wrong, one too many or one too few, or one that crept in by mistake from somewhere else, even though I know for a fact that as I wrote I thought I was spelling everything properly and I thought the same when I read it all through, I had plenty of time to read it through because I finished it so quickly I didn't need to think about it, just write it all down, I know all there is to know about the secret story of the infanta and her dwarf; reading it through, giving every single word a thorough going-over, I was certain that this time I had nothing to be ashamed of and people would be able to read it and they'd understand the whole thing and be impressed by the story.

I tell him there's hope in the fact that my spelling is alright in Spanish and English. I really do think this offers some hope, but he's not even listening. If I can spell alright in these other languages, then – and my voice is becoming more animated – I might be able to spell in German as well one day.

So we all hope, he says. There are giggles from every corner of the classroom.

He points at the blackboard, at my words written there in his hand. Read them out.

I read them out. It's strange to encounter my words in his hand. Because he's written them himself you might almost think they were correctly spelt, but in fact they reveal my glaring deficiencies. The way they're written, they just don't work. I feel ashamed, but I stick by my words and give them voice. I read them out loud. The first word is 'speak', then 'dwarf' immediately below it – the dwarf that has to speak and speak on the little infanta's birthday to make her laugh, but she can't laugh, and nor can he. I wrote down every word exactly as it was spoken and exactly as I heard it, I absorb everything I hear, I store it away and remember it exactly as it was said. It can't come back out of me any differently from the way it went in.

Just spell the word out for us. Wilhelm Bobbenberg is speaking to me, and the corners of his mouth are trembling with suppressed laughter. Please, Fania, spell it for us, letter by letter. I have to do it. 'Speak'. I single out the letters and say their names one by one: S, B, E, E, C, 'sbeec'. The word is complete: it has left my mouth and is off on its own. Behind me in the classroom there is silence, the silence of forty-two mouths and eighty-four eyes.

I expect there are other ways of spelling it, I say, just to be on the safe side.

A gale of laughter bursts forth, swirling and echoing around the room, raining down on my back like so many blows, my eyes feel too hot within my skull, I raise my head with difficulty and see that my teacher is grinning, Vera likes the way he grins, she says that Bobbi looks especially good and especially manly when he lifts one corner of his mouth and lets the other droop.

His lips are moist, he is chewing on his saliva. Forgive me, Fania, but this is something quite unique in my experience. How come your big sister is the best in her class in German – he gazes at the girls behind me; it's true, Fania's sister is the best in German in our entire school – whereas you (he addresses this to me, his eyes sparkling with delight), you most certainly are not.

I hate him for bringing Vera into the picture, but at the same time the other girls do need to know that my sister is better than everyone else at German.

Vera had rolled her eyes: Oh Fania, you're going to have Bobbi for German, he's so fantastic, everyone thinks he's fantastic, he's simply brilliant, completely different from all the other teachers, you'll see, he can take a joke, all the girls are in love with him, and most of the female teachers as well.

I can see my own words on the blackboard: Wilhelm Bobbenberg has moved to one side and so left them in full view, they are greeted by a storm of laughter, forty-two gaping mouths, incisors bared right up to their owners' noses. I try to laugh along with them, I smile, perhaps it really is funny, I don't know how it happens, I can't explain it. He's so incredulous at what I've written that he feels impelled to add even more words from my essay. I was accepted into this middle-school class two months ago. My mother put up a fight on my behalf, thanks to her persistence they let me take the exam, even though my spelling was said to be atrocious. You have to judge Fania differently from the way you judge the other girls, my mother told the headmistress. You simply disregard spelling in your assessment. You can't ruin her entire future just because of that. Perhaps it's just a passing phase. It would be awful not to give her a chance.

I'm not stupid. I've always been good at arithmetic, and I learnt to read very quickly – quicker than everyone else. I was bored at school. We had Herr Timmler for reading in Year 2. He wanted me to carry on reading aloud from where another girl had stopped, and I didn't say anything. My mind was elsewhere, so I didn't say anything. Nor did he. I'd been reading further on in the book, the bit that had little stories. I looked up. In front of me, right in front of my desk, stood a large grey lump of rock at the very top of which were two watery blue eyes darting about in a shiny sphere. Your turn, Fania, said Herr Timmler, and I read out the words that were in front of me but shouldn't have been, the bit where the grandfather tells his grandson about the old days when times were hard, but everything had been lovely all the same on their farm in Silesia.

Stop! The command issued forth from the looming rock above me. Herr Timmler laid the tip of his pointer on the lines in my book. Now read the whole lot backwards.

41

I hesitated. Needless to say, reading backwards is no big deal. My sister can talk backwards. She was teaching me how to do it, and told me one supper-time how we needed a secret language so as to keep our mother in the dark, whereupon my mother immediately declared that *she* knew a secret language, one she'd used in her childhood with other children – and a cascade of syllables came tumbling out of her mouth, a salad of words that tasted of grated carrot.

Where? Who with? I asked in disbelief. You haven't got any brothers and sisters. Who on earth else would she have needed to talk to in a secret language.

With the other children in the street, of course, she replied.

My mother was a street urchin; I know this, but keep forgetting. And Vera and me, we're confined to the garden. My God, I want to play in the street as well, I said. You know why we can't let you, replied my mother. And my grandmother chipped in too: you're not to say 'God'; if that's who you mean, say 'Adonai'. That wouldn't do much good though. You used to let your daughter play in the street, but just look at us, for Adonai's sake, we're stuck in this garden and can never get out or our parents will kill themselves.

That's just the way it is, said my mother, and Vera and I looked at each other and started learning how to talk backwards. My mother tried to keep pace with us, but we were quicker at getting the hang of it. 'Vera' turned into 'Arev', 'Fania' became 'Ainaf'. Read backwards, we turned into males. Arev and Ainaf – two names that could have come from my grandmother's Hebrew prayer book; Arev and Ainaf, two amongst ten men who gather together in her book to pray. There have to be at least ten men, or Adonai doesn't listen. Why ten, I asked my grandmother. Why not, she retorted. I had no answer to that. Questions that remain unanswered go back into the ground, back into the rich, fertile soil, and carry on growing. Nothing gets lost. What happens to the answers, I asked. They go up into heaven, she replied.

What if the answer's untrue, enquired Vera.

Depends whether it's deliberate or out of ignorance, said my grandmother.

Vera went red, my big sister doesn't often go red, she is pretty skilled at deception; Vera wants a boyfriend but doesn't have one, her friends all have boyfriends, she'll never find one in our garden.

When my grandmother first showed me her book, I was amazed to see that she opened it at the back, and I asked her, why at the back? and she said she opened it at the back so she could start at the beginning. Everything that is past reaches back to the beginning, she said; the end lies ahead of us, somewhere in the future. My grandmother washed her hands before picking up the book and opening it, and the first thing that she read was the words 'Seder n'tilat yadayim shel Shacarit'. With her head bowed down over the book she looked at me with raised eyebrows over the rim of her glasses. A foreign language was issuing from her lips, a language that belonged to her and me, a language that was now and had always been my own just as much as it was hers, even though I understood not a word of it.

What does that mean, I asked her raptly.

It's about the washing of hands, she said; it's a blessing we recite when washing our hands.

I was surprised to hear that this momentous book required its readers to wash their hands before entering upon its many pages. Fania, wash your hands; have you washed your hands; you must wash your hands first. I decided that in future I would regard hand-washing as a task full of significance.

My grandmother put her index finger beneath every word, sliding it from letter to letter. The letters threw their arms and legs to left and right, some looming steeply upwards as though to lick the heavens, others clawed at the earth, and with a good wind behind them they were pushed steadily on, further and further, infinite in their repetition, Baruch ata Adonai, the same today as thousands of years ago, tomorrow and tomorrow the same as today.

Even unto the Last Day, said my grandmother, when the Mashiach will come.

Won't be a man for Vera. Vera needs a man right now.

The last day of mankind is the first day of a new order; every beginning is the end of something past that expresses itself in the new. I can think logically even if I can't spell, and I've still not started my periods, even though I'm already thirteen and a bit. I'm expecting to start any day now. Your periods will come, say my mother and grandmother. And perhaps I'll be able to spell once my periods have started, it's quite possible, let's wait and see, we won't even mention it just in case it stops this miracle from happening.

She laid her prayer book on my lap, my grandmother guided my stumbling progression from letter to letter. I made a real effort, I was full of zeal, and I felt important because my grandmother bestowed importance on me. You can do it, she said, shut the door. I stood up, shut the door, and sat down again by her side, where the open book awaited me with its black, strong words.

Who was I shutting out if not the outside world. I shut my mother out, I shut my father out. My mother's in favour of Jewish stuff and not in favour; she doesn't want her daughters to have too much of it, only as much as she herself can control, and that's a great deal less than the knowledge possessed by her

44

mother. For Hedwig Glitzer attended the Israelite School for Girls. She knows it all. My mother knows bits and pieces, a smattering of Yiddish, but Hebrew is a foreign country to her. What my mother rejects is not the Jewish religion, but God.

Personally I don't believe in him, she says. Personally she doesn't believe either in her mother's God or in her husband's, who isn't the same as the Jews' one. She doesn't believe in God at all, and her father didn't believe in God either, nor did he believe in his daughter Alma or his wife Hedwig. One day he disappeared out of their lives and never returned. My mother doesn't want to talk about God, and she also doesn't want to talk about her father. Don't get me wrong, she says, lighting another cigarette with the one she's just finishing, something she doesn't do very often, don't get me wrong, I'm proud of being Jewish, but spare me all that nonsense about our dear Lord. God and her father: these topics are taboo for her. My father is the only man my mother doesn't fight against.

For many years my grandmother has been a woman without a man, a woman who carries with her in her handbag the prayers of pious men as well as her building society passbook, her passport, a small flask of 4711, a handkerchief, a powder compact and her front-door key. And within herself she carries a whole world – a world that has more of death about it than of life.

Once each month her six friends come to visit us. That makes seven women altogether, and me, Vera and my mother would make it ten. But it doesn't work with women: Adonai only listens to men. Women do things differently. My grandmother Hedwig and her friends Ruchla, Olga, Emilie, Wilma, Betty and Lotti whinge, moan, eat, drink liqueur, play cards, sing, cry and squabble. None of them is over seventy, and all of them look as though dead and resurrected. Aunt

45

Emilie wears nappies inside her trousers, Aunt Wilma has to sit on a rubber ring, Aunt Ruchla is fat and heavy and walks with sticks, Aunt Betty has nothing but gold teeth in her mouth, Aunt Olga is almost bald, and Aunt Lotti has a jewellery shop on the Reeperbahn and a number on her left forearm; she's skin and bone and sweats all the time and therefore drinks loads and loads. I call all of them 'Aunt'.

They call themselves the Theresienstadt Circle. When they play cards I'm allowed to count the money in the pot. All of them want me to sit next to them, I bring masl, I was born with a good-luck caul on my head, says my mother, it nearly suffocated me. But it's usually Aunt Lotti who wins, Aunt Lotti with the number and the jewellery shop, whereupon Aunt Olga shakes her hairless head, Aunt Betty runs her tongue over her gold teeth and asks Aunt Lotti to touch her and so transfer a bit of masl, Aunt Wilma shuffles on her rubber ring and says to Aunt Betty 'You certainly need it', fat Aunt Ruchla says 'No wonder, eh, the devil always shits on the biggest heap', my grandmother does several quick taps on the pot to make sure it comes to her in the next round, Aunt Emilie shrugs her shoulders and murmurs 'So what'. With a steady hand and watched by all, Aunt Lotti drags the mound of coins towards her with her gold bangles jingling and her diamond rings sparkling. And now give our little shnorrer a penny or two, says Aunt Ruchla. The shnorrer is me.

The fact that her daughter Alma neither knows nor cares very much about Jewish traditions causes my grandmother pain, a pain that is always with her. It permeates the entire store of Jewish knowledge that she has within her and means to pass on. When she showed me her book I wanted to be a good granddaughter to her, better than her own daughter had been. And so we shut my mother out. Shutting my father out was different. He's not a Jew. There's nothing we would have needed to shut him out of. He's just not part of it. He would have been delighted, touched, moved to see us sitting with the book in front of us and hear his mother-in-law reciting Hebrew. We didn't shut him out: he was shut out already. And that's why I had him with me but kept my mother out of it, so that I could get what is mine.

Baruch ata Adonai, read my grandmother, then recited it again: Baruch ata Adonai eloheynu melech ha-olam. A wind began to sigh in her voice, Baruuuch ataaa Adonaiii, a wind familiar with the heat of the desert and capable of igniting a mighty fire. My grandmother told me what it means in ordinary language: Blessed are you, Lord, King of the universe. This was rain, dripping from a roof.

Hurry up, Fania, read it backwards. Herr Timmler struck my desk with his pointer, and I read backwards, letter by letter. It was difficult: German doesn't lend itself to being read in this way, the consonants shoved and stumbled, trampled all over each other, and crushed the vowels. Once again Herr Timmler banged his pointer down, this time on my head. Stop, he said, we can't understand a single word.

No one is allowed to hit me on the head. Herr Timmler doesn't know this. You mustn't put up with it, Fania, do you hear me. If anyone hits you on the head or in the face, then you tell them your mother said it's absolutely out of order, then you tell me, and I'll go and make a big stink and give them what for.

Backwards, Fania. Quick. Get on with it.

I looked up from the book. I'd done what he asked, for goodness' sake, and it certainly hadn't been easy.

Blows from his stick rained down on my head. You're to read backwards word by word, not give us that gobbledygook of yours.

47

On his lips were streaks of dried froth, bubbles of saliva sprayed from his mouth and dropped onto the letters. The next word was dehctap. I left the c and the h in the middle as 'ch': h-c might have sounded like Hungarian or Polish, I thought.

Herr Timmler slammed his stick onto the desk, my hand was right by it, I snatched it away. He'd taken careful aim no doubt and wouldn't have hit me, I got a fright, that's all. Don't say anything at home, I thought. She'll never let me out of the house again. Or she'll have a go at him, and then he'll have a go at me.

Stop, he ordered. You're too stupid, Fania. He turned to Annegret, sitting next to me. You read, he said, Fania's too stupid.

Annegret read, and I listened. It was just as terrible as it had been at the cinema a few days earlier. Someone had run the film backwards. A man was sitting at the table while his wife came stumbling backwards from the door holding an empty plate, which found its way onto the table in front of him together with its knife and fork, whereupon he leant over it and proceeded to pull chunks of meat from his mouth with the fork; his knife reconstituted a big fat sausage slice by slice until it lay there pristine on his plate and he leant back in his chair with a contented grin.

And now you, said Herr Timmler, who had retreated to the blackboard with his grey bulk of a stomach. I obeyed, and as I read the sentences backwards, word for word, I felt certain they must all think me mad for being so incompetent when they had cottoned on straightaway when he first gave the order. Word for word, backwards. Utterly pointless. I think that was the moment my spelling went to pot.

Fania is an excellent pupil, my mother had said to the headmistress. She is good at everything – except German

48

spelling. We don't know why that is. She can read. In English she's good at speaking, reading and writing – she's just not good at writing German. She's good at sums and maths in general – just think, she does her older sister's maths homework. At this point if not earlier the headmistress gave a placatory wave of her hand and said she really didn't need to know all that, they were faced with a mystery themselves and perhaps it really was just a congenital defect.

Yes, said my mother, a congenital defect, that's what it'll be, it's not her fault, you could even say it's *my* fault – I gave birth to her.

When my mother arrived home after her discussion with the headmistress we all sat down in the living room so she could tell us all about it. It was a Thursday, my father had returned from his sales trip the previous evening, two days earlier than expected, business had been bad, scarcely any orders this time, why prolong the agony, he'd come back home, he needed cheering up.

Right, said my mother, and she sat down on the sofa, crossed her legs, took a cigarette, put it between her red lips, gestured to her husband to light it, and drew the first lot of smoke deep into her lungs; three teachers will be giving you your exam, Fania, two women and a man, I'll talk to them all first, the man won't be a problem, I'll have to play it carefully with the two women though, one of them's called Nelli Kohn, she teaches English in the middle school.

I leant against the chest of drawers that isn't actually a chest of drawers, but two old mahogany seamen's chests stacked on top of one another. My father inherited them from his father. That's what they look like, anyway, and you'd readily believe it. 'An old heirloom': that's how we describe them sometimes. The truth of it is that my father was thrown out of the house by his father. Because he'd fallen in love with a Jewess, Alma Glitzer.

I leant back against the old heirloom that wasn't. I was holding a plate in my hand, I'd spread quark on a slice of black bread then cut it up into small pieces. I ate while they talked about me.

Nelli Kohn, repeated my grandmother, you can certainly talk openly to her, Alma, she's one of our lot.

I'm not so sure about that, said my mother.

Of course she is, my grandmother shouted, Kohn, what can a Kohn be other than a Kohn.

Alright, alright, Mum, don't yell so, replied my mother, out-yelling her mother, the window's open, do you want the neighbours to hear, talk to *me* about 'our lot', they're just as touchy about these things as we are.

My grandmother rocked back and forth; nebbish, she said, and she's got to do an exam, the poor child. They all looked at me. It would come to nothing again. It would all be fine again. Everything was a jumble. I didn't know the right words to describe everything properly.

Don't you worry, my little sweetheart, said my mother, your mother will sort it all out for you, I promise, you'll go on to the high school just like your sister, you'll see.

Who's the other female teacher, asked Vera.

Someone called Fräulein von der Höhe.

Sport and History, said Vera; hair in a bun and crêpe-soled shoes.

I get the picture, said my mother.

I know her, I said.

What d'you mean, you know her, snapped Vera, sounding just like my mother. They weren't going to let go of me that quickly.

I chewed slowly on my black bread and quark; Fräulein von der Höhe, I said, I have her too, she teaches PE. She takes us swimming and is always trying to teach me how to swim.

My father can't swim, my mother is an excellent swimmer. She tried to teach me how to swim, but in a lake that had sharp stones on the bottom. I was eight years old, I couldn't stand up, I couldn't swim, I couldn't rely on her keeping me afloat, I was so terrified of drowning that I screamed and screamed. She was disappointed, but she accepted the situation and took me ashore. She swam, and I fastened my arms around her stomach. I was proud of her for getting me ashore. Learning to swim without my mother would mean I'd have to find someone else. Vera can swim. I think she could swim right from the start.

And why can't you do it already, my mother asked.

Why on earth was she asking – she knew perfectly well. I told Fräulein von der Höhe that I wasn't allowed into the water until I could swim, so she lets me sit on the side and I wait until the lesson's finished.

They laughed. I couldn't see anything funny about it. My mother bit her lip. I grabbed the last bit of bread and quark from my plate and threw it at her. It hit her in the left eye. Everyone fell silent. My mother fixed me with a one-eyed stare. I expected an outburst and quaked in my shoes, but didn't feel I'd done anything wrong. I floated away out of the window and hovered above the house, invisibly tethered.

My father, the non-swimmer, brought me back in. He directed his laughter at his wife, with his ringing tenor voice he threw up a protective wall around me, all shiny and silvery, he directed dazzling shafts of mirth at his wife's one good eye.

Alma, your daughter's just like you, his words were dancing on the surface of his laughter, go on, just think, how often did

51

you chuck your engagement ring in my face. Once he deliberately made her retrieve it herself. You never did it again after that.

An expression part love part guilt spread across my mother's face. She took off the lump of black bread masking her eye and a pool of tears trickled down her face.

My father leapt up, his glass fell over, red wine spilled out. Who cares, he called to the glass, and leant over his wife. He wanted to kiss her. Leave me alone, she said, leaning her head against his chest. He pressed his mouth into her hair.

I'll be having swimming again in four weeks. You'll have learnt how to do it by then, my mother promised me, swimming is easy.

The next afternoon we took the train to the Kellinghusenstrasse swimming pool. The smell of chlorine assaulted our noses, by the side of the pool stood the swimming instructor, an athletic-looking man with an enormous moustache. He was sizing me up. My mother started speaking. She spoke from the very first instant and kept him completely pinned down. She said how she herself had been a real water-baby as a child but her husband couldn't swim at all and was it possible for someone of his age to learn.

I never fail, said the instructor. He was looking at my mother, who had commandeered all his attention as if to distract him from his prey.

I wanted to learn how to swim, I wanted to be able to do it as well, I *would* be able to do it, I just had to get the man with the moustache to turn his attention to me.

I'm not so sure in my husband's case, said my mother. Would you believe, he kept it secret from me for years, we were already engaged and I still didn't know, then we went to the beach and he said, you go in the water, I'll come in a minute, but he never came, he just lay on the sand and read the paper or claimed he'd forgotten his trunks and I said, Paul, you can't swim, come on, just tell me the truth, and he said, of course I can swim, my brother can swim, my father could swim, even my grandfather who went off to sea could swim, and I believed him.

The man was almost ensnared in the web of her words, then his moustache gave a sudden jerk.

Right, then just step aside for a moment, madam, he said with a frown.

My mother pursed her lips and gave me a look. She gave me a look because he was diverting his gaze from her, because his attention was focused on me, because she had no choice but to hand me over.

He took a good look at me. I can teach anyone, I can, he said, including you, my lass, so in you go. He lifted me bodily by grabbing the back of my swimsuit and lowered me into the deep water. A sort of broom hung just in front of me, and I clung to it for dear life. If I drown, at least my mother will be here, I thought. By the seventh lesson I was swimming without the aid of the broom, and at the end of four weeks I was ready to do the swimming-test bit of the entrance exam under the watchful eye of Fräulein von der Höhe.

The enormous pool was empty, its surface smooth and impenetrable, Fräulein von der Höhe, my mother and I were the only people there. My mother who insisted on being present while her daughter passed her swimming test, and Fräulein von der Höhe who objected, and my mother who dug her heels in, and Fräulein von der Höhe who kept looking at her watch and was anxious to go home, and me, who was desperate to get the whole business over at last: all three of us went to the edge of the pool.

You begin the test with a dive, Fania, said the teacher.

Why does she have to dive, asked my mother, no one's ever mentioned diving.

It's part and parcel of the swimming test, replied Fräulein von der Höhe, stepping ahead of us to the top end of the pool where four small stone plinths were ranged, tiled in green and blue and decorated with fishes. I'd often watched children leaping off them into the water with complete abandon.

Is it really necessary? My mother came jostling along behind me, overtook me, and in her tight dress and slippery bathing shoes slithered her way towards Fräulein von der Höhe.

It's part of the swimming test, Frau Schiefer, it's nothing, just a dive, that's all. Come here, Fania.

I didn't budge.

What's the matter with you, said Fräulein von der Höhe impatiently, you're doing your swimming test, Fania, you can do it easily, we all want you to get into the middle school, diving and a 15-minute swimming test are part of the entrance exam, come on now, hop up onto this starting block, then afterwards your mother will buy you an ice from the ice-cream man outside.

I know that ice-cream man, my mother said frostily. He's been here for twenty years and more.

A whistle dangled on Fräulein von der Höhe's chest. Chop chop. Your mother will be proud of you.

No, said my mother, why should I be proud of my daughter throwing herself into the water. She won't dive.

And why not, asked Fräulein von der Höhe, putting her right foot on the first of the four plinths.

In our family no one dives, said my mother. Something had dropped from her face into a timeless realm, and I bear the image of her within me.

The face that my mother's face turns into seeks sense in the mayhem, loudly and quietly by turns, and questions pour out of me. Where have I come from, where am I, where shall I be when I go. I'm losing my way. You'll be taken away. I'll be taken away. You're losing your way. I'm losing my way. You know which way I have to go. I know which way you have to go. I hope nothing happens to you. I hope nothing happens to me. Past the house, past the old villa. The Gestapo house, the Jewish villa. No one knows the streets I've lost, the streets I can't find. Taken away from there. Taken away on foot. That's your house, from there to the Gestapo place, through the streets in handcuffs, the daylight departs as well, the night is bright. I walk through streets, they form a ribbon, a cutting between yesterday's houses, we live there today. Two hours from there. The same streets. You buy an ice-cream, a two-groschen ice-cream, in the same street. It's not my mouth. You're released, a visit home before they come and get you. No period for months. You pick me up. Two groschen for an ice-cream. To the Gestapo man I'm told you said Lend me two groschen for the tram can you please I can't walk just look at my feet and my legs all swollen from the cells I can't walk home like this it's a two-hour journey. I'll bring you the money for sure. For sure. You wait there. I'll pick you up. For sure. He hands over two groschen, typical Jewish chutzpah, he says. For the tram. You walk, and I walk through streets that are yesterday's places, I walk through my own time that is bereft of place. There are streets within me that know what's what. My mother for two groschen. Your beautiful hair. From the Gestapo to home. An ice-cream for two groschen. On foot for your life, on foot for an ice. With five hundred women in a single room. Your hair full of lice. My beautiful hair. No period for months. And you walk. And I walk. Beneath my feet her

55

life in the beyond. The street brings her street towards me. I expect to hear her footsteps, familiar yet destroyed: this was her territory, she knew her way around. Beneath my feet: traces of her, her life itself. I don't want to surrender my life to her. It was hot. It is hot. The same street, the same man. He sells ices for two groschen.

My teacher removed her foot from the plinth and with her lips narrowed to a thin line she said 'Fania, use the ladder'. I used the ladder, lowered myself into the water rung by rung, and swam. Perhaps diving was like flying. If diving was like flying then I'd have been able to do it. The two women walked along the edge of the pool with Fräulein von der Höhe in front shouting You can do it, Fania, come on, come on, you can do it, and my mother behind her shouting Oh Fania, my darling, can you do it, can you do it. And I did it, smack between the two of them.

The bell shrills. The school shudders. The door to the toilets opens and slams shut. The three girls have gone from my door at last. I'm the only one left. Outside, the voices of five hundred schoolgirls grow fainter. They're going into their classrooms. I wait. My body doubles up with fear, an agreeable sensation of pain courses through the hollows of my knees, saliva collects beneath my tongue, between my legs a second heart beats and a second mouth vibrates, pushing out waves of warm white wetness, I foam and froth, I'm there, and the tiled walls are flattered by my sighs.

Lessons have long since begun. I walk down the long hall, right to the door of my classroom. All is quiet behind it. Simply carry on down the hall, past the caretaker's office, into the street, then home. I could do it, but can't do it. I can't be in two places at once, both at school and at home, and if I'm halfway between the two and they notice I'm missing and ring

56

up, either I will go mad and she will die of fear, or I will die and she will go mad.

Never go off with anyone else, not even your Aunt Mimi. If Aunt Mimi's standing by the school gates and tells you she is collecting you to buy you an ice-cream or take you home, then you say No, we're waiting for Mammy, Mammy's collecting us, and even if Aunt Mimi says Mammy's given permission, you still mustn't go with her because I'd never do such a thing without telling you first that Aunt Mimi's collecting you just for once, do you understand, you must promise me or else I'll be so afraid it will turn me mad. Aunt Mimi complained to my father, Who am I for goodness' sake, I'm no criminal, I'm your sister and your daughters are my nieces. My father shrugged his shoulders. You just have to understand, he said to his sister, our children matter more to us than anything else, they're our most precious possessions.

I open the door without knocking. Their heads are lowered, they are reading quietly. Wilhelm Bobbenberg is sitting at his desk, my words have been wiped off the blackboard, he looks up at me crossly, he wants to say something. I turn away, I have nothing to say to him, I go to my desk, pick up my school bag, put in my exercise book, and leave the room. I have to do it. I'm going home.

The narrow driveway is skirted on one side by a tall hedge as neat as brickwork. In summer the scent of jasmine from our garden hangs sweet and heavy in the air and blossom-clad branches droop down over the rusty garden fence. Neighbours regularly complain to our landlord that the leaves brush against the roofs of their cars, and Frau Schmalstück claims that we're letting everything turn into a wilderness; she might be attacked in our driveway and no one would even notice.

No bad thing, says my mother, but we get the old stepladder

out of the cellar all the same and set it up in the driveway. My mother in her close-fitting skirt with a lighted Gold Dollar in the corner of her mouth and a large pair of shears in her hand climbs the narrow treads on one side of the ladder right to the top; I hold it steady from the other side, I want to do the same as her and climb on to the first tread, the second, the third.

Stay at the bottom, Fania. She hands me her cigarette. Here, hold this. One blossom-decked branch after another comes crashing to the ground, and each is followed by a comment from me: Not that one. Why that one. Leave that one. My grandmother collects up the prettiest samples for the big dark-green vase. My sister and I once peed in this vase. It was a prank. Perhaps not even that. My sister had encountered the word 'lustful' in one of her romantic novels, and we were on the lookout for some means of discovering what it felt like. That's what it was. The vase began to stink, and my mother and grandmother had a row about who had forgotten to empty the water after the last lot of flowers.

Eyes peering from the house drive me onwards. I'm being watched. I can't take a single step without being watched. I could squat down somewhere. Perhaps I'll do it. At a stroke every window in the house will be thrown open.

I slip into the cool stairwell. To the right is the stairway leading down into the dark cellar. The door at the top of the stairs is open, the narrow wooden treads are badly worn. The Kupsch family are out at this time of day. Erich Kupsch works in the shipyard, leaving at five in the morning and returning home around four in the afternoon. Elsa Kupsch does cleaning for other people, her sons Kurt and Michael work on building sites, Elisabeth helps her mother do the cleaning, and Wolfram is probably playing truant and hanging about on a street corner somewhere.

58

To the left are the stairs leading up to the various flats. Our toilet is on the first landing, behind a locked door. Seven steps further on is our flat, and immediately to the right of it the stairs curve round on their way to the other flats above us. On the first floor are Hermann and Eva Hainichen. The building belongs to him, he runs a removal business, the yellow tarpaulins of his thirty trucks say House to House with Hainichen. Whenever he parks one of his leviathans in our street no other vehicle can get past, so people have to drive their cars onto the pavement or else sound their horn and wait until Hermann Hainichen comes down with his white shirt open at the neck and wiping his hands on his brown corduroy trousers. Tall and stocky with a chest like a randy cock-pigeon he climbs up into the cab and starts the engine. Rumbling and roaring the enormous truck quivers beneath him, Hainichen backs it into our narrow driveway, branches are ripped off, first the acacia branches, which snap with a loud crack, and his truck pushes its way in. Hainichen leans out of the side window, grins, and shouts that it's not the end of the world, it'll all grow back. Eva Hainichen, his wife, has golden blonde hair. I've never before seen a woman with such golden blonde hair. Is that woman a princess, I asked my grandmother who was holding my hand as I stumbled down the driveway. I was learning to walk, being much worse at it at the age of two than I was at talking. Frau Hainichen came towards us, said hello and slipped quickly past. I didn't know she was Frau Hainichen, I didn't know she lived in the same house as us, the house I had been born in two years earlier, and I didn't know that the house was not ours but hers. She hadn't bent down to look at me and stroke me, and this was quite new to me. People beamed at me, carried me in their arms, swung me through the air, cuddled me and kissed me, I was so fat that I put off walking until the very last weeks of my second year of life, or so I've been told.

Frau Hainichen's unremitting reserve is the same as ever it was. She glides through the years, friendly but remote. He's cheating on her, says my mother, Herr Hainichen is unfaithful, but your father isn't unfaithful; Vera and I aren't unfaithful either, we are loyal to our mother. She constantly feels it necessary to make sure about this, she has to know what things were like at birthday parties and whether the other mothers do everything as wonderfully as she does. No, nice enough, but not wonderful, not as wonderful.

My sister and I call our mother 'Mammy'. Not a single girl in my class calls her mother 'Mammy'. They say 'Mum' or 'Mother' or 'Mummy'. We regularly make fools of ourselves whenever outsiders hear us say 'Mammy', and of course because we say 'Mammy' we also say 'Pappy'. My mother would feel offended if we called her 'Mum' or 'Mother' or 'Mummy', she'd feel we didn't love her any more, or at least not with the total devotion we showed when we were babies. And even though my mother calls her own mother 'Mummy', she insists on us, her daughters, calling her 'Mammy'.

Frau Hainichen is a fake, according to my mother. Her hair's dyed, you can bet your life on it – but say hello really nicely, do you hear, and give her a curtsy, at your age girls should still curtsy to grown-ups. Vera doesn't do curtsies any more and grown-ups have started calling her 'Fräulein Vera' and sometimes even 'Fräulein Schiefer'. Or may we still call you Vera? After all we know you so well and you used to be so little. No one's ever been 'so little', at any rate not outside their mother's womb.

In the attic flat above the Hainichens lives Frau Schmalstück, a war widow a bit younger than my grandmother

60

who'll be celebrating her sixty-fifth birthday on the sixth of June. Frau Schmalstück has a lodger called Sturmius Fraasch, a tall, thin man, even taller than my father, an old Nazi, but a poor devil all the same, according to my mother. Sturmius Fraasch is a journalist and has a wooden leg. He drinks a lot, and quite often gets visits from men; one of them has pink-varnished fingernails, his hand was resting on the banister in our stairwell, my grandmother hurried me past it and said a curt hello. The pink nail varnish made the rest of the hand look coarse; the man who was attached to it threw us a timorous glance. My grandmother couldn't be a threat to anyone, fear is ingrained in her very skin.

Not a sound in the stairwell. It would be a help to me if someone were to appear: my bladder would be startled into shrinking. No one appears, and I stand by our front door incapable of ringing the bell. My left hand has to stay where it is, and with the other I cling on to my school bag. I'll have to wait around hopping up and down until someone inside wonders where on earth I am and my mother tears open the door to rush off down the street in a frantic search for me, she'll come storming out and knock me over and I'll burst like a water-bomb.

For the last eight weeks I've been allowed to come home on my own without my sister, ever since I started at middle school. Usually my sister and I do come home together, but I didn't see Vera at school at all today, so she must have stayed at home. It's not very far, just a ten-minute walk. There's no scope for dawdling, and absolutely no chance of buying ten pfennigs' worth of raspberry drops at Finke's grocery because Herr Finke takes ages hunting through all his jars to find the right one, transferring seven sweets into a paper bag with his silvery little scoop, then weighing them out. He's very short and a hunchback so we both have to stand on tiptoe so that I can hand him the money and he can hand me the sweets above the mounds of goods stacked on the counter. You always get seven sweets for ten pfennigs, so if there are only six in the bag when I get outside and look, I know he's cheated me. I don't check inside the shop whether there are seven sweets: he can cheat me if he likes, but I don't want him to see that I know I've been cheated. Buying something at Finke's grocery is only possible on the way to school in the morning, it's out of the question on the way back home; getting to school late is better than getting home late, then once I'm back I'm confined to the garden.

Annegret and Gerda think I'm meshugge, they say I'm crazy, you're completely crazy, they say, just come in with us, your mother won't kill you. Of course my mother won't kill me. My mother will kill herself. They can't understand this, they exchange glances and go into Finke's grocery, and I carry on on my own, quicker than before, I don't want them to catch me up. I have to get home. I don't need a watch, I can already tell that I'm a few minutes late.

Clutching my school bag in my right hand I try to reach up to the bell push, the bag is all corners and bumps into the wall, the contents of my bladder nearly spill out, like a plate of soup put down at an angle. Dancing up and down on the spot I let my eyes wander around the stairwell. How about the cellar. I could creep down and wee into one of its dark corners, by the coal hole or behind the door leading into the air-raid shelter. At this time of day none of the Kupsches could catch me by surprise down there. The wee has risen right into my mouth, my tongue is swimming in it, my lips are shiny wet. I turn away light-footed and liberated. My mother might tear our front door open at any moment, I want to go down into the dark

62

cellar and yield to the tingling urge inside me, I want to squat down in a dark corner and squirt my wee into the forbidden realm through one of the legs of my knickers.

The front door of the building is slowly being pushed open. Dressed in black coat and black hat, Frau Schmalstück struggles in with the aid of her walking stick. Small and thin, like a starving rat. Despite the early summer warmth she is dressed as she always is throughout the year: I have only ever seen her in black. My whole body tenses up at the sight of her. She comes up the stairs, her stick in her left hand, her right hand clutching the banister, her black handbag banging against her leg at every step. I stand silently by our front door watching her come up towards me. I wipe my left hand across my face. I can smell my urine. Climbing two more steps she reaches our landing, I step aside a little, do a little curtsy and say Hello, Frau Schmalstück, as always she says nothing, gives a jerk of her head, and her little black hat bobs up and down on her sparse hair. She walks stiffly past me, and no sooner has she turned the bend leading to the next flight of stairs than I press our doorbell.

My grandmother opens the door, which means that my mother's not in. Where is she. Why didn't anyone tell me she was going out. If she'd been in, no one could have got to the door before her.

Isn't Mammy there, I ask.

But of course, replies my grandmother. Alma's there.

I give her a kiss on the cheek, and she glances over my shoulder at Frau Schmalstück. That was Frau Schmalstück, wasn't it?

Yes, I say.

Come in.

I'm bursting. Could you give me the key.

She gives me the chunky key to the toilet. It's tied to a bit of wood together with a key to our front door.

Fania, the whole time you've been at school you've kept it in again, it's just not good for you.

I drop my school bag on the floor without a word, slam the front door shut behind me and leap down the stairs to the toilet, a small room with the dustbins under its window. There mustn't be any hitches now. Stick the key in the lock. Turn it round. Pull it out. Tear the door open. Slip inside. Shut the door. Fasten the hook. Lid up, skirt up, knickers down. Safe at last. It gushes out. I fold my arms over my knees and rest my head on my arms. The big washbasin in front of me disappears and is replaced by my bed, in the other corner is my bookshelf and in front of it, at a slight angle, the doll's bed with Paula and my old teddy and the other Steiff animals, right next to where I'm sitting a little round table appears then a rug underneath it and a rocking chair with a reading light and two candles on the window sill. Why didn't my mother open our front door? Something must have happened.

They're sitting at the table in the kitchen, my mother, my grandmother and Vera, she's still got her nightie on, the breakfast things are still on the table.

Come and sit down, says my mother, she's holding an unfolded letter in her hand, this is really important, we need to plan everything carefully.

We have to talk Pappy into it. Vera's already in the picture.

Would you like some cocoa, my mother asks me, then before I can reply she asks my grandmother if she would please make me a cup of cocoa. She speaks as if I were my father and she were getting my grandmother to pour him a glass of cognac. Vera is chomping on a roll filled with Cheddar cheese; she's been feeling alright for hours.

This letter – my mother points up at the kitchen ceiling, above which Herr Hainichen and his wife live – this letter is from him up there.

Are we going to have to leave, I ask.

Absolutely not. She rocks to and fro on her kitchen chair. Hainichen wants to sell the house, this lovely old villa of ours, and as we're his tenants he has to offer it to us first. The house is worth less with sitting tenants than if it's empty. If none of us buys it he'll want us all out as rapidly as possible so he can get a better price. He wants fifty-six thousand marks for the house including the land – the two big garden areas. We don't have the money, that's for sure, at any rate not ready to hand right here and now, and the building's in poor condition. My mother is trying her arguments out on me. In really poor condition, she says emphatically, the damp's creeping up the walls, you only have to look at the wallpaper, and we have to air all the clothes several times a year. It's true, she's not exaggerating there, our things stink of fustiness. We can't store things in the cellar, they go mouldy. Erich Kupsch has insulated the walls down in the cellar, but it's made no difference. It would have to be done by specialists. In every room of our flat the wallpaper's peeling off somewhere, particularly in the big room. We can pull the wallpaper straight off the wall in our bedroom, says Vera, and there's heaps of mould behind the wardrobe in my grandmother's room. There too! My mother spells it all out to us. If we owned the house we'd have to renovate it from top to bottom. Fifty-six thousand marks is a lot of money, but a reasonable price for a property like this, and it'll quickly increase in value, this is a good part of town; once we've bought the house we'll leave it as it is for the time being, then if it starts falling down around our ears we'll have another think, we'll send the Schmalstück woman packing, the Hainichens will leave

65

anyway, it says in his letter that he wants to move his haulage business to Berlin, he'll save on taxes, though of course he doesn't mention that here, Sturmius Fraasch can carry on living upstairs so far as I'm concerned, perhaps the Kupsches will want to take over the Hainichens' flat, it'll all sort itself out, we need to borrow the money, perhaps we can get a mortgage from the bank, perhaps we can raise the money ourselves. We'll have to talk it all through with Paul, we'll have to handle him carefully so he doesn't shy away from it right from the start.

My mother is on fire with enthusiasm. The whole house with its two big gardens would be ours, we'd be able to live here for ever.

Oh children – she jumps up with jubilation in her voice – it would be so wonderful, too wonderful to be true, we deserve it, we do, we really do. She stands there in the kitchen pressing her hands against her cheeks, so bursting with energy that she seems about to explode for sheer joy tinged with irrepressible sorrow. We stand too, my grandmother and Vera and me, and my mother hugs all three of us at once.

Perhaps, says my grandmother, I can ask the ladies in my little circle. Lotti has just had a bonanza from Reparations, and perhaps Ruchla and Wilma will lend us a bit, and whatever I've got in my savings account he can have, fine man that he is, such a fine man, my son-in-law is such a fine son-in-law.

My mother wipes her eyes. We'll give the whole flat a really good clean, we'll rearrange the big room, we could fry some steak when Paul gets home on Friday, it doesn't take long, with onion and potato, he likes that. And my grandmother suggests something he likes even more: beef olives braised with lovely big onions and a touch of garlic accompanied by tender French beans in melted butter, and followed by vanilla pudding – my father loves vanilla pudding with chocolate sauce. Brilliant

66

idea, says my mother, you cook it, Mummy. My grandmother nods and beams with joy from head to toe.

There's just one small problem, says my mother, gathering up the breakfast things with much clinking and clattering, and my grandmother says You haven't any money.

My mother takes on a slightly shy, embarrassed air and starts fawning on her mother, and my grandmother tut-tuts disapprovingly whilst feeling delighted that her daughter needs her, then gets up from her chair and goes into her room, leaving the door slightly ajar.

Do you want me to come and help you look, Mummy, calls my mother. She is suddenly one of us, a daughter amongst daughters.

No, shouts my grandmother from inside her room, stay there, Peter.

Why's she calling you Peter, asks Vera.

Oh – my mother sweeps her hand across the table, sweeping Peter out of the way along with the breadcrumbs – that's what they sometimes used to call me in the old days, her and my grandparents.

She pushes a slice of salami into her mouth. Beyond the door we can hear her mother rummaging about. My grandmother keeps little stashes hidden all over her room, just in case of emergencies.

Were you meant to be a boy, asks Vera.

No. My mother is immediately indignant. Just a boy that never happened.

My grandmother returns with shining eyes and carefully, solemnly places four banknotes on the table in front of her daughter, two green twenties and two blue tens, smooth and serene, they look brand new.

Why don't you manage on your housekeeping money, Paul gives you plenty of it after all.

Ask me something easier, Mummy, says my mother, or tell me instead who you're hiding your money from, I hope it's not from me, your own daughter; and so saying, she takes the notes, folds them over several times, and sticks them under her foot into her shoe. This amuses Vera, but not my grandmother: her poor lovely banknotes. Go on, lose the whole lot, she grumbles, but with the sole aim of warding off any such misfortune. What sort of example are you setting your children, what a way to treat money, where on earth is your purse.

My mother laughs, her laughter dances its cheeky way through the kitchen and over the fence, right out over our garden fence.

I don't hide my money under the carpet.

My grandmother turns red: her most cunning hiding place of all has been rumbled. She looks with love and disquiet at her daughter – a certain Peter – as she wanders over to the sideboard, commandeers pencil and paper, and returns to the table. I can't give it you back until next week though. Vera uses exactly the same tone of voice.

No need, Alma. That's my contribution to the plan. My grandmother slides her hand across the bit of the table where moments earlier her savings had lain, four impressively shiny banknotes, now creased and squashed beneath her daughter's warm foot. I hope it works out. It sounds like manna from heaven.

My mother starts to write a shopping list. Have we got any scouring powder left. We've plenty of floor polish. We'll do the kitchen last. We'll start with our bedroom, then do the sun room and the big room. Shall we rearrange your bedroom, my mother asks us. My grandmother suggests making new net curtains for the kitchen. The doorbell rings and we all freeze.

Did the doorbell ring, my grandmother asks; that was the doorbell, my mother says. Their nervous voices interweave with each other. Vera and me, we don't budge, we never just go to the door when the bell rings.

My mother jumps to her feet. I'll get it. The words come out like bullets. She's already halfway there. Whenever the doorbell rings her body jerks as though hit by an electric shock. Whether she's reading or sleeping or eating or in the middle of a conversation, the ringing of the doorbell or the phone instantly tears her out of one existence and thrusts her into another, an existence that brooks no rivals, an existence that she has known before and that she can never stop fighting against. She needs to know at once what's coming.

Vera, my grandmother and I remain motionless in our seats, our mouths half open, our ears on my mother's heels.

Oh, it's Frau Kupsch. My grandmother stands up, fetches a clean cup from the cupboard, and puts it on the table. We breathe again.

My mother hustles the considerable bulk of Elsa Kupsch into the kitchen, Frau Kupsch, embarrassed, attempts to resist, protests that she doesn't want to be in the way, and no, she doesn't want to sit down, and no, she really doesn't want a cup of anything.

You're not in the way at all, Frau Kupsch – my mother repeats this again and again, then tells us with a knowing look on her face: there, you see, Frau Kupsch has had a letter too, from whatsisname upstairs, from Hainichen.

That's right, says Elsa Kupsch, at any rate my 'usband 'as, look, there it is, To Herr Erich Kupsch, and I said to Erich, I said, Erich, wouldn't that be just wonderful if Herr Schiefer could buy the 'ouse.

Chapter Three

We shall soon be the owners of this old villa. It's the shabbiest house in the street, its fine façade is crumbling away, damp's climbing up the cellar walls, and the pipes burst as soon as there's a frost – but it's in a good part of Hamburg, close to the Alster, we live on the upper ground floor with a sun room at the front and a terrace at the back and two big gardens. My parents reckon it's something along the lines of poetic justice. After all that's happened, who'd have guessed, said my mother, amazing how much fits into a single life, and how many lives fit into a single era; there's no breath big enough to say it all, no voice loud enough to get it heard. All the same, there isn't heating in every room, just in the living room and my grandmother's bedroom; the toilet's down a flight of stairs, and each winter once the pipes have burst we put a heater next to the loo. It's especially in winter that my mother moans about our situation: she doesn't like the cold, she belongs in the south where the sun turns her skin a deep dark brown, the heat doesn't bother her. My father likes the Hamburg rain: his skin turns red and peels in the sun. That's why we stayed. We could be in America or in Israel; we could be living there. My mother tells us what it would be like if we lived there. She says she'd have a business in America: toys or clothes or fabrics or leather goods – no matter what it is she can buy it and sell it.

But you don't speak a word of English, says Vera.

Then I'll learn it; Paul speaks English.

But we're here all the same. In Israel my mother would open a restaurant. Just a little snack bar to start with, then when the business takes off – and my mother's business will inevitably take off – she'll extend her snack bar into a restaurant.

Once they've tasted my chicken soup, says my mother, they'll all be queuing up for it.

Chicken soup's what all women cook in Israel, Vera says. And my mother replies that her chicken soup is better than theirs. She got her chicken soup recipe from her grandmother, Marianne Wasserstrahl née Nehemias, and we will get it from her. In Israel too the sun is hot. My mother can't imagine her husband in the desert. And so we're staying here.

In winter we sleep in unheated rooms. There's a hot brick for our feet, and we wear hats and woolly gloves to read in bed. In summer the house is pleasantly cool. We squirt one another with the hosepipe in the garden and we have a table-tennis table. We're the only people in the whole area with a table-tennis table, so there are often as many as twenty children here, most of them unknown to my sister and me, Wolfram brings them in from outside.

What you doin' bringin' a horde of strange kids in 'ere, says Elsa Kupsch slapping her son on the back of the head.

My mother won't hear of it. On the contrary, Frau Kupsch, we're delighted when Wolfram brings children into the garden.

But we want to get out. Vera and I are dependent on Wolfram. He's our helpmate, our link with the outside world, he keeps us posted with news from beyond the garden fence. His bits of news are monosyllabic grunts, insufficient for my

71

sister and me. In winter we want to know whether the Alster has frozen over, and Wolfram just says Yeah or Naah. That's not enough for us. Can you go on the ice, does it break, where are the ducks and the swans, are they stuck in the ice, they'll be marooned on the bank, someone's got to smash a hole in the ice so that they can dive in and out. Go and bloody look for yerselves, says Wolfram, it'll only take yer five minutes, bottom of the back garden, down the road from the British Consulate to Harvestehuder Weg, and you're there, I'll take yer, you can see yer house from down there, yer mother won't notice and you'll be back in a flash.

So we can be seen from down there, from the Alster; our house can be seen but we can't see a thing, not even the people who can see us. The rear wall of the back garden is high, it's the end of our world. And Wolfram is our sub-tenant, that's why he says it's our house, even though our house isn't ours at all. He's the poorest child in the street but because he shares our house he shares our paradise. No other child from outside can come and go the way he does. We're something unusual in his eyes. He stands there in front of us, in his threadbare short trousers leaning against the fence, now on the inside but soon on the outside. He can't make us out, his brain churns away behind his angular brow, a slight grin plays around his dirty mouth. Maybe our unusualness is nothing to be proud of; after all he's so daring and gets beaten by his father and slapped around by his mother and that's not at all unusual, whereas we're never beaten and never dare to do anything, not even to walk the few steps to the Alster.

I bet your mother wouldn't mind. He said this off the top of his head, but he's not far wrong. Wolfram has something in common with Alma Schiefer, they're both street urchins, my mother would have done exactly the same, he wouldn't have

72

had to talk her into it. How are we supposed to explain what keeps us imprisoned here, we can't explain it to anyone, least of all outsiders. He has to go on thinking we're unusual: we still need him. You ain't babies any more, he says. He mustn't see us in these terms. We have to stop him thinking about us. What colour is the Alster? Does it make any noise? Wolfram shrugged his shoulders, that's asking too much, he doesn't know, questions like that make him feel uncomfortable. It gurgles, he says after a while. Yes, Vera and I are happy with this piece of information, we can make sense of it. Sometimes it stinks, he adds, getting into his stride. When it stinks, it stinks really bad, like rotten eggs. We ask Wolfram whether it's difficult to roller-skate and ice-skate. Yeah, he says and grins, then he says Naah. Vera and I know we'd break our arm or something if we tried ice-skating or roller-skating, and we know without ever having laid eyes on it what the Alster looks and sounds like: in summer it whispers along between its banks, and in winter its crust of ice grates and grinds.

Wolfram shins over the garden gate, see yer! We go into the sandpit, we can hear his footsteps beyond the bushes, he kicks the gravel, snaps some twigs off our hedge, we call out 'Bye! – we want him to know that we can still hear him, that we still exist. The sandpit is small, Vera and I grew out of it long ago, we sit on the edge and put our feet in the yellow sand; have you ever heard of Orlando, asks Vera.

I've never heard of Orlando.

Orlando's a woman I think. Vera's not exactly sure. Anyway they go ice-skating on a lake in England, there's a river that leads off into the countryside, further and further and further. I make waves in the sand with my fingers.

We give Wolfram our old newspapers, my grandmother saves them up in a cardboard box in the hall. Wolfram tells us how much he gets for a kilo of newspapers from the scrap-paper man, this is of great interest to him as it's his only source of pocket money. We get pocket money from our parents, my sister gets a bit more because she's older, and every month my grandmother gives us ten marks each out of her reparation money. On the first of every month she gets a small grant that's been awarded to her by the Reparations Office. On the official notification form it says compensation for Hedwig Glitzer, née Wasserstrahl, on account of persecution, wrongful imprisonment, denial of career opportunities; words like these are as much common currency in our household as trading stamps. After every shopping trip my grandmother sits herself down at the kitchen table, takes her hat off with both hands, puts it on a chair next to her, not on the table: a hat on the table provokes an immediate row. She sticks trading stamps into a special booklet.

Bet old Frau Schmalstück gets a bigger pension than you. My mother's sure on this point, because old Schmalstück was killed in the war, on the Eastern Front. We know this for a fact from her lodger Sturmius Fraasch, who told my father, and who also admitted that he himself hadn't lost his leg at the Front but at the corner of the street: someone ran over it while he was home on leave and he was very unhappy about this.

My mother has grilled some plaice, and a lemon sole for me because I don't like plaice. Aunt Mimi, my father's sister, is eating with us. Her boyfriend spends Sundays with his wife, his name is Hubert Arnold Zinselmayer and he's a chartered engineer. Aunt Mimi writes his letters for him and she's also his mistress. She can't be more than that because his wife is rich. I do understand his position, my aunt tells us. Why should he let his inheritance slip through his fingers, he's put up with the old cow for such a long time, really she ought to have died ages ago, she's got cancer.

But she hasn't died, says my mother spitting bones on to her fork, and my aunt says, Alma you're spoiling the child, lemon sole just for Fania, such an expensive kind of fish. Why, wonders my mother, expelling a delicate fan of fish bones from her mouth, should Fania eat plaice when she doesn't like plaice but does like sole and I want her to eat fish because fish is good for her. When Fania eats sole she's happy and I'm happy so we're both happy. My aunt doesn't look very happy. The man on the radio tells us the prevailing water levels on the Elbe, the Saale and the Weser, it'll soon be children's hour – the second instalment of a drama serial. Vera and I want to listen to that – we're already familiar with stories about Hubert Arnold Zinselmayer. He pays for my aunt's flat, and the furniture's his as well. Aunt Mimi pointedly remarks that they're all antique heirlooms. My mother isn't the least impressed by this, for my mother has seen stuff being dragged out of houses and auctioned off right there in the street at dirt-cheap prices, furniture, carpets, pictures, silverware. My aunt is keen to impress my mother and tries another tack.

Hubert Arnold Zinselmayer's older brother never returned from the Russian Front, she says. My mother looks up briefly; I'm sorry to hear it; her brow is furrowed. This is not enough for Aunt Mimi. He was killed and never came back.

How could he come back if he was killed, giggles Vera. My father puts his hand on his sister's hand. Don't take any notice of Vera, he says quickly. But Aunt Mimi is determined to take notice of Vera, she gets all upset, her voice becomes strident with indignation, we're so badly brought up, so disrespectful of others' misfortune; my mother daubs horseradish sauce on her beautifully buttered potato and says very calmly, Don't give us your grieving widow act, you never even met his brother, and my father picks up the wine bottle and Aunt Mimi holds out her glass to him.

75

Some of us never came back either. Selma and her daughters. They dragged Selma away by the hair, and there were jackboots and loud voices too. You two must never do that, never pull each other's hair, never hit each other in the face, you must be kind to each other. The holy commandments of my mother. Vera and I know Selma only from a photograph – a woman in a picture frame on the display cabinet in my grandmother's bedroom. She's sitting at a table, a small, fat woman with an enormous chest across which lies a white lace collar; she's resting her head on her hand and gazing at her daughters, and I'm gazing at her. Selma was the younger sister, like me, my grandmother's little sister, and Selma's youngest, three-year-old Paula, lies cradled on the lap of her oldest, Lilly, who's nineteen; Margarete and Edith have bows in their hair. Departure from Falkenried 6pm Friday 15th May 1942, Sabbath Eve, Selma and her four daughters Lilly, Margarete, Edith and Paula, one suitcase per person, not more than twenty kilos, Edith and Paula were too little to merit twenty kilos, three twenty-kilo suitcases instead of five, from Falkenried to Moorweide on foot – I wouldn't have the faintest idea how to get from Falkenried to Moorweide, where on earth *is* Falkenried, a street around here somwhere – and from there to the station and onto the train to Riga.

We were sitting in the train. The train to Sylt. It was making its way across the sea, my father was going to follow us at the weekend, the waves were crashing down close to the carriages, my grandmother was sitting by the window, and the ticket inspector came in, and she needed something to drink, and my mother was going to pass her the thermos flask and couldn't find the tickets, and my grandmother's face turned a blotchy red, and my mother got upset about the upsetness of her mother, don't upset yourself, Mummy, she said, then finally she found the tickets in her handbag between her lipstick and her little pot of rouge and her powder compact, the inspector checked the tickets, you must listen to the wheels, my mother said to Vera and me, they're whispering something, more and more clearly, Vera and I both knew what was coming, but we pretended to be surprised. Far-to-go-but-oh-so-slow, far-to-go-but-oh-so-slow. She laughed, we took the train wheels' words from her lips and mimicked them again and again with our own mouths, but she had already disappeared in search of her mother who had wandered off and couldn't find her way back.

Selma had had the photo of herself and her four daughters done to send to her husband Leon in Palestine, and she'd given a copy to Hedwig as a present. Here you are, from sister to sister, do you want it, do you like the picture, I've had a copy made for you. Leon had already left for Palestine to get everything ready for the family, Selma was to follow later on with Lilly, Margarete and Edith. That was the plan. There was no Paula then. Paula arrived in 1939, and couldn't have been Leon's. In the picture it looks as if Paula were Lilly's child. Leon in Palestine might have wondered the same thing.

That's what your mother looked like when she was little, says my grandmother pointing at Paula. My grandmother tells me about Paula and her sisters, and I repeat their names. Margarete and Edith and Lilly with two Ls; everything that's left of them is so important, even the extra L in Lilly. There's nothing more that can be said about them. Perhaps Paula and Mammy share the same father, Vera says to me later, wouldn't that be something.

Who are Aunt Fanny and Uncle Robert though, I ask.

Aunt Fanny is my aunt, says my mother. She's my father's sister, and Uncle Robert is her husband.

What's their surname then.

My mother looks at me in surprise, and since my mother is incapable of being surprised without also being suspicious, her look is one of suspicion as well as surprise. Surely you know that already, Fania. Why do you ask.

No special reason.

Aunt Fanny and Uncle Robert are called Freundlich, as well you know.

I do know, I definitely know, I can't possibly not know, yes of course: Freundlich.

Same as Rosa.

Who's Rosa?

Rosa, for goodness' sake, Rosa Freundlich, my cousin, Aunt Fanny and Uncle Robert's daughter. You know who Rosa is, she comes and visits us sometimes, I could give her a ring, we haven't heard from her for ages. She talks to her mother about Rosa and how she should have rung her long ago and Rosa never gets in touch, and with a start I realise for the first time that Rosa is the daughter of parents who were taken away. My father says nothing. He has no place in these stories.

We Jews believe that the souls of murdered Jews remain among the living until their allotted time is up. My grandmother told me this. A secret and potent form of magic. Submerged in dark water and with my face pointing towards the surface from the deepest depths I ask how Rosa and I are related.

She's your first cousin once removed, says my mother, delighted to have found me such a thing; her face hovers above the dark water oscillating gently, the corners of her mouth float up and down. My mother loves Rosa like a sister, but she's afraid of her.

Wolfram had one of his teeth knocked out at school and they injured his left eye so badly that he can't see very well with it any more. We tie the newspapers into bundles in the garden then stuff a flat stone into the middle of each one to make it heavier. Wolfram piles them all into a little cart that he fixes to the back of his bike. A heavy load.

He pedals away, down the drive and away, I look at his calves, I look at his feet in their ragged gym shoes. 'Away' is the end of the driveway, the point where he hits the road and disappears round the corner. Vera and I perch on the closed garden gate. He breaks through a sound barrier, but we are shut in. We wait. All of a sudden Wolfram is back, we haven't any idea which way he went or which way he came back.

We'll share, says Wolfram. We refuse. He accepts gratefully and asks if we want Tarzan instead. We do. He fetches us Tarzan in black and white and Mickey Mouse in colour. They smell musty and the pages are all dog-eared, having passed through the hands of countless children. My mother discovers them under my pillow and throws them in the big rubbish bin by the main entrance. I'm not to read the speech bubbles in those awful comics, your writing's bad enough already, Fania.

Wolfram liberates Tarzan and Jane from the bin and sneaks them back to me in the coal cellar. I've come down to stack the briquettes that we get delivered cheap in the spring. Take more care of them, he growls, and tells me my mother told his mother that Wolfram's got to stop it and his mother told him you better not do it again, and his father took his belt off and gave him a good hiding.

I sit on the pile of briquettes in the coal cellar with a light bulb dangling from the sloping ceiling and gaze at Tarzan with his black quiff, he's coming out of the jungle and cautiously approaching a village. Tarzan has muscles everywhere and is wearing a leopard-skin loincloth. That's all he has on, but no matter how bold his leaps are you never catch sight of what lies concealed beneath his leopard-skin covering, though I've caught sight of Wolfram's, I looked up his trouser leg when he was sitting in the sandpit and could see what was dangling against his leg and he never noticed. I think I'd find it a nuisance, I told Vera later.

The bright sunshine comes streaming in from outside.

Wolfram and some other boys have put the table-tennis table up. The two leaves are supported by four trestles, the net is taut, the garden is full of children; bats are being tried out to see whether they fit in the hand nicely and whether the rubber is stuck down properly. Wolfram stands by the stove in the cellar kitchen boiling two table-tennis balls in a bubbling pan of water to get the dents out. He's best of all of us at table tennis. There are nineteen of us and we dash round the table hitting the ball in turn and anyone not getting the ball back over the net has to drop out until only two players are left and they play a one-point decider. We call this 'playing Chinese'. I'm the smallest but I keep my end up really well, Wolfram has taught me how to smash and slice.

Elsa Kupsch watches her youngest with coy pride in her face. She's standing at the cellar window in her button-through dress, with her plump arms thrust beneath her heavy breasts.

Come out into the garden, Frau Kupsch, calls my mother carrying a wicker chair down the terrace steps, and Elsa Kupsch duly comes out but refuses point blank to sit on the wicker chair or one of the deckchairs, instead bringing out her own wooden stool.

My mother and my grandmother bring a tray from the kitchen with home-made biscuits and three big jugs of juice. We break off from the game, take a glass of juice and reach for the biscuits with our sweat-covered hands, the other children say thank you very nicely, the girls curtsying and the boys doing a little bow. The same children that laugh at my sister and me because we have such anxious parents are now glad to be at our house, things can be so lovely at our house and we're happy for them to join in. Annegret and Gerda are standing in the driveway outside looking through the fence, and I walk over to them. Could they come in, asks Annegret. Gerda says nothing; Gerda usually says nothing. I open the garden gate a little way and they slip inside.

Chuck them out, whispers Vera, standing behind me; why on earth did you let them in in the first place?

In the school playground I make sure Vera doesn't get at them; if Vera interferes it just makes things worse for me. I have to indulge their every whim. That's the only way I can exert any control over what they do to me. I run up the terrace steps and into the kitchen and plunge my hot face into cold water until it is right over my ears. I dive down into the depths and hear the gurgling of the sea all around me. Oh to stay like that. I feel the hand of my grandmother on my shoulder, she's standing next to me. She thinks it's possible to drown in a kitchen sink. So do I. Yesterday we read Kaddish together, yesterday was the day her sister and her sister's daughters were taken away. A candle was burning in her room: this day and this night and for ever and to all eternity.

Back in the garden they've started again without me, they're running round the table-tennis table with whoops and shouts, I dash down the steps, I'm too late. Next game, Wolfram shouts across to me. I want to play. It's our garden, it's for us to say what's what, and Annegret and Gerda are running round the table too. So is my mother.

You're mean, I shout.

Let the little one join in, yells my mother running full pelt and barking the words out, she's running to try to win the point, she's playing the game for all she's worth, she adores the game. I bite my lip, I don't want to be her 'little one' in front of all the others, but whatever happens I mustn't cry, God help me if I cry in front of Annegret and Gerda. My mother takes her eye off the little white ball for a moment, looks across to me and blows me a kiss, I try to smile, she mustn't see that I'm crying, she dashes round the table-tennis table, most of the boys are already taller than her, one of them hits her on the backside with his bat to make her pay attention, she's about to miss the ball that's flying towards her. She gives a yelp, hits the ball over the net and turns round, it's blond-haired Hans-Jürgen behind her, she waves me into the circle, I shake my head, having just cooled myself down I'm getting hot and bothered again. There's no way I'll join in now, that would make me seem even littler, she should stop looking at me, where's my sister, Vera's a good player, a calm player, Vera's right out of the game, my mother's still in the game, we are on the sidelines and she's right in it, she's one of them, a child from outside, a girl that goes ice-skating in City Park and plays marbles in the gutters. Vera and I have no idea how many streets there are between our street and City Park or whether we'd have to turn left or right or which tram would be the right one. It's the same city and a different city.

Where actually was it where you used to play in the street, I ask, and my mother reels off the names of the streets forming the shortest route from here to there, the same now as then, the same city and a different city. She knows the streets off pat, but we don't. You can go via Mittelweg and Rothenbaumchaussee, then Grindel, Schlump and Fruchtallee, or else you can go down Osterstrasse – she's forgotten that I'm not allowed to – or better still Gärtnerstrasse, Unnastrasse, Heussweg, Am Weiher; that's where Dr Braun, our doctor, lived when the Nazis tried to knock his house down in March '33, he and his wife were away on a skiing trip, his wife played the piano so beautifully, and his patients protected his house, they all gathered in front of it, working-class people from Eimsbüttel, and sent the Nazis packing, he treated people who didn't have any money for free or else traded his skills for theirs, he and his wife got away to Palestine before it was too late.

The game is over, my mother has won, in the final one-to-one she beat Hans-Jürgen, the oldest of all the children in the garden, he's almost a young man and already wears long trousers; when he arrived in the garden he slipped my sister a tightly folded piece of paper. He grabs hold of my left hand and left foot and whirls me round, faster and faster. I open my eyes, the garden is whizzing round my head, a narrow band onto which everything else is firmly glued – the house, the trees, the children, the anxious face of my mother. My mother has numerous heads.

Ask Wolfram where Hans-Jürgen is, says Vera. It's table-tennis time again. So I ask Wolfram where Hans-Jürgen is and why he isn't coming any more and Wolfram shrugs his shoulders. Dunno. Bring someone else instead, I tell Wolfram, but he brings back two not one, a couple of brothers. You can have the younger one, says Vera. She's only interested in the older one. Now that she's made her choice I find the older one nicer too, but he's already my sister's property. You can't really complain, says my mother, the garden's always full of children. We're often alone in the garden, my sister and me. We read books, including books we already know, they're our special stories and we recount them to each other again and again.

I'm woken in the night by the sound of Vera crying. What's the matter, I ask, but I know what's the matter.

I hate her, sobs Vera.

I don't need to ask. She means our mother, who trails behind her a long black train in whose folds the story of her survival is indelibly inscribed. I slide swiftly across the join between our mattresses into Vera's bed and beneath her duvet, I want to stem her floods of bitter tears, she's turning to liquid and melting away and leaving me behind, I reach out for her, for her body, for her bones, for her hard white bones. We've been through all the bones in biology, ulna and radius, sternum and costal arch, I skate over Vera's soft stomach and put my hand between her legs onto her pubic bone – mons veneris, my mother calls it; I rub my foot against her tibias and fibulas and her femurs – skelos in Greek, hence the word skeleton, or so it says in *Humans*, our school textbook. There are altogether two hundred and forty bones in a skeleton including thirty-two teeth and six auditory ossicles. The crying beneath me eases a little, my fingers are sticky, her thigh is sticky. Vera begins to speak, she stammers out syllables between her sobs, her voice catches in her throat.

I just wish they were all dead.

I've had the same thought myself. Once they're dead they won't need to be afraid for us any more, and we'll be able to go off on our own. Once they're dead I'll be free. It's the only hope we've got.

Vera pushes me away. I couldn't care less whether or not they're afraid for us, I want to get out of here, I couldn't give a shit about their fear. Nothing will ever kill that off. She laughs, her mouth trembles.

Before we went away on holiday we put our dolls into deep, death-like sleep. We didn't want them to be frightened to death without us, we didn't want them to know we were going without them. Our return breathed new life into them.

I'm afraid of being left behind. Vera mustn't leave without me, she's hell-bent on going, and now she doesn't even give a shit about our parents' fear. Don't leave me here on my own, I say. Don't be silly, Fania, and I can tell that in her thoughts she's already somewhere else, I hang on to her and weigh her down, I haul her back behind the fence, she's not to leave without me, not even in her thoughts. Vera too wants to be yanked out by me and carried along, I know how heavy she is and I know my own strength, strained as it is by the burden of her. This time I'm heavier than she is, I have my mother with me.

Vera was leaning against the clothes-line post and our mother hit a smash and won the point against Hans-Jürgen who smiled and bowed to her. In his boy's eyes she was a special mother, he didn't have a mother like her, none of the children did.

She suddenly put the bat down on the table. Go on, Frau Schiefer, play with us some more, the children chorused. She looked across at Vera. My father was lying on a deckchair gazing dreamily at the blue sky. She walked over to him. She's got that from my mother, I heard her say to him, whenever I wanted to enjoy myself she was all hurt and started crying. My father pursed his lips into a kiss. His mother-in-law was sitting in a wicker chair on the lawn next to Elsa Kupsch knitting a red woollen blanket. His older daughter was leaning against the clothes-line post, Vera, a young girl, the same age as Alma was when he first met her. Vera was gazing at our mother with a look of hatred, he looked across at me, beseeching me with his eyes to go over to Vera, he wanted his peace and quiet. Why don't you go and play table tennis with your daughters, said my mother. I looked at his backside sagging down in the deckchair, he pulled his wife onto his lap, she tried to get away, he held onto her, they both laughed, their voices came over to me as though through a keyhole. That's enough, Paul, I heard her say. What's the matter with you, he said.

They'd all left at some point. Vera had stayed leaning against the post the entire time, smiling with narrowed lips and fighting back her tears. They drip onto my face in the darkness. We swear never to leave each other, we'll stick together, and when they're all dead we'll travel round the world.

The very same night I steal out of the house without Vera. There's a hole in the fence behind the currant bushes in the back garden. Wolfram showed it to me. I've got my little blue cardboard case with me. How did that get into my hand all of a sudden? I didn't even know I still had it. It's probably been in the cellar for years. I open it and look at my treasures: freshly sharpened pencils, a red india rubber, blank sheets of paper, a doll. It's Paula-Two. Her soft body is filled with yellow cotton wool, her lovely cool head is made of china, her blue eyes are made of glass, and her small, half-opened lips are the same cherry red as my mother's fingernails. I call her Paula because I can't think of any other name for her. Vera has a doll of the same name, she looks just like my Paula, you could almost say that they're as much alike as Selma's little Paula and Hedwig's little Alma. If they had the same father, then which of the husbands was it, and if it was Hedwig's and not Selma's – but Vera interrupts me, she wants to know what I've called my doll, Paula, I say, her name's Paula. No it's not, you can't call your doll Paula, that's my doll's name. Think up some other name. Nothing else occurs to me. I don't want to call her Margarete or Edith or Lilly with two Ls. I want to call her Paula: she's my youngest. Tears drip from my eyes into my ears. You can call her Paula-Two, says Vera magnanimously. I take Paula-Two out of the little blue case, kiss her on the nail-polish-red mouth, and climb out through the hole in the fence.

Chapter Four

In the kitchen my grandmother fills two buckets with water, pours powdered green soap into them, mixes it in with a long wooden spoon, then I carry the buckets across the hall and through a couple of rooms until I get to my mother, who is standing on my father's desk in order to get the net curtains down. The scarlet nail varnish has flaked off her long fingernails and she has tied back her black locks with a headscarf.

What happens if old Frau Schmalstück buys the house, wonders Vera, what happens then?

Frau Schmalstück won't buy the house, says my mother, I'll strangle her with my own hands if necessary.

We invent a game called Housekeeping School to stop us getting bored with all the cleaning. My mother is the strict Head of School, but also wants to play the part of the Popular Teacher who enjoys the trust of the pupils, who are, after all, her own daughters. But Granny can be the Popular Teacher, suggests Vera; of course she can, says my mother. But Vera and I make rude remarks about the strict Head, stupid cow, did you see those shoes she's got on, laces and crêpe soles, then Vera thinks up lots more insults, so my mother soon gets fed up with the game and decides to have a cigarette instead.

We go into the kitchen where my grandmother is in the process of putting bed linen and masses of lace curtains into the galvanised bath to soak; on the stove last week's underwear is on the boil in a massive grey saucepan.

My mother sits down on the window seat with her cigarette, beyond it on the outside is the iron ladder, between the ladder and the window is the abyss in which I could easily break my neck; she pulls up her legs and makes herself comfortable. We've got plenty of time before Paul gets back on Friday afternoon, by then we'll have finished the four rooms, the sun room and the kitchen. She counts it out: we've got today, or what's left of today, then Tuesday, Wednesday, Thursday and half of Friday. Paul's aiming to be back by late afternoon, that's four days altogether, so in fact we could repaper the living room, the old wallpaper's mouldy and smells of cellar. Fania, pop downstairs to Elsa Kupsch a bit later and ask her when Erich will be getting back.

We're bursting with energy. We four women can do it, my mother's sure of that, this house is going to be ours. My grandmother considers it highly unlikely but hopes for a miracle that might just happen, you never know, and which would help her daughter and son-in-law to buy this semi-derelict old house – something that would benefit her as well, she's desperate not to move into the Jewish Old People's Home where all her friends live, there's plenty of room in this house for her.

This house has always been ours, says my mother, no one appreciates it like we do, and as soon as it's legally ours, all signed and sealed, we'll clear all the muck out, first and foremost we'll smoke out that old biddy Frau Schmalstück. It's a matter of great importance to my mother that we share her hatreds, any grudges we bear must match her own, especially when they have anything to do with the old days.

The old days, when your father and I couldn't even dare to hope that we would ever have children. She reaches out to grab me, and I surrender before I can turn into her prey, I hold still and send forth my soul to watch what happens. My mother is off and away. I see her speechless. How long? A good while. I move my hands, my lips.

Then the bathroom, I say.

The bathroom, repeats my mother, astonished.

Yes, the bathroom in the cellar. Once we've cleared Frau Schmalstück out we'll clear out the bathroom – you know, beyond the air-raid shelter doors – all those old papers dumped in the bath, I want to know what's underneath me in the house when I'm asleep.

What do you know about those papers, asks my grandmother, but my mother immediately cuts her off: oh yes, of course, all that clutter in the bathroom, that'll go too. She gets up from the window seat, picks up the full ashtray, walks over to the rubbish bin and chucks the cigarette stubs onto yesterday's potato peelings. Not today, she says; another time. The steel door bangs shut. Locked and sealed.

Vera comes into the kitchen to tell us that Hainichen is in the front garden.

We creep between piled-up furniture, rolled-up carpets and buckets full of soapy water into the sun room – which with its bare curtainless windows exposes us to the gaze of anyone who happens to be looking. Thank goodness my father's not here, he's driving along some country road in his car, he hasn't got muscles like Hainichen, even the fat on Hainichen is made of hard rubber.

We stand pressed against the wall peeking out through a crack round the sun room door: it's closed but its thin wood is swollen and warped and it doesn't fit properly. Stone steps lead down into the front garden, I've often gone jumping down them. With Hainichen in the garden they don't belong to us any more. He's tramping through the overgrown grass in his black wellies, he's stuffed his trousers into the top of them, he's carrying a large wooden sign on a long pole over his left shoulder and a spade in his right hand. He walks over to the garden fence. My mother could tear the sun room door open and call out to him. We watch him in silence. He smashes his way into the dense array of bushes, we stand and watch, it's his house and his garden, we have no say in the matter, he kicks out at the branches with his boots so that they snap and splinter, jasmine, lilac and snowberry are all thrust aside then close up again behind him, the tops of the maples and acacias sway despite the absence of wind. Struck dumb, we stare through the bare sun room windows at the green branches and their unnatural motion. We hear the sound of scratching and scraping.

What's he doing, asks my grandmother.

Hainichen rams his spade into the ground, cutting through the roots below; the leaves above him tremble, they will age prematurely and fall off within days. Amongst the bushes by the fence Hainichen is digging a hole for his sign. My mother says nothing, gazes out, pulls on her cigarette, draws in her cheeks and inhales deeply, then lets the smoke out through her mouth and nose. She'll think of something we can do to thwart that man out there.

Give me one too, says Vera.

Vera has never said this before.

Wordlessly my mother hands her her cigarettes and matches. Vera's been smoking in secret, though not for long. I know, I'm her accomplice. She blushes for sheer joy, she's proud to be allowed to enjoy a cigarette with her mother in our presence – and I'm no longer her accomplice, Vera has surrendered something we shared. All of a sudden I feel empty and prematurely old like the leaves on the bushes that Hainichen has butchered and that will no longer wilt gracefully but shrivel up in their prime and look wrinkled and aged like my grandmother whose face stood still when she stopped living in this city and disappeared into the ground.

My mother calls Hainichen a war profiteer and calls his long black boots SS boots. We won't move out of here even if it kills us. She says this in a loud and penetrating voice, all the doors and windows of our flat are wide open to let out the dust that we're beating out of the mattresses and upholstery. She likes voicing her opinion. So does my father, but he doesn't get much opportunity. If friends come to visit my parents my father's not allowed to talk about politics: please, Paul, just for once this evening don't bother our guests with talk about politics. Why on earth not, Vera says then, and my mother leaps from her chair: you keep out of it. Vera's intervention only makes things worse, as she well knows, but she does it all the same, she's bolder than I am, I'm frightened that it will tear my mother to pieces. Calm down will you, bellows my father, I can't bear this, I want to be able to speak my mind in my own four walls at least; my mother screams back, then shut the windows first and just think who you're going to invite here, just tell me who we can really trust amongst our friends, go on, who. My father takes his glasses off, hides his face behind his enormous white handkerchief and ceremoniously blows his large fleshy nose; he's probably thinking hard, he's probably trying to come up with two or three uncontentious names, he probably can't think of a single one.

Who. Go on, tell me: who. My mother dances in bitter triumph around her own question. No one, absolutely no one.

We should have gone from here in that case.

91

Yes, she nods. She has calmed down now.

Why don't the pair of you ask a few girls round that you're friends with. We were all sitting together in the sun room and my mother said: Vera, the two of you should join in with the others more, you should approach them, talk to them; some of the girls have brothers, how are you ever going to find a husband otherwise, you'll never find a husband. This was aimed at Vera. I'm not in the firing line yet. Vera immediately started crying, and my mother immediately launched into a list of Vera's virtues: you're pretty, you're clever, you can bring your friends home, you've no need to feel ashamed of your parents, invite some of your friends round, I'll put on a spread, what would you like, you can have whatever you want.

Just leave me alone, hissed Vera.

My mother recoiled in astonishment. I don't understand you. Do you understand your sister, Fania? And I said, Yes I do understand her.

Alright then, let's see how you cope on your own. She flounced out in a huff. We looked at one another. We knew we wouldn't cope on our own. There's spotty-faced Dörte Lückenhausen, said Vera, perhaps I could invite her, she lays her breasts on her desk during lessons, she's really big-bosomed, you'll see. Yes, ask her, I said. And Freigart Bölitz and Monika Meyer. Freigart's tall and fat, taller than me – Vera looked pleased with herself – her father's an old Nazi, and Monika Meyer has dandruff and wears thick-rimmed specs, though she *is* a bit smaller than me.

My mother is worried about what's going to become of her daughters, she shuts us in, she keeps her eye on us, she always comes to collect us, and she's afraid she'll never get rid of us. Follow my example, she tells us, just look at your mother, I don't find it difficult to approach other people. These people need to be forewarned about her: she smiles at them but doesn't trust them, she approaches them bent on attack or retreat.

Vera invited the girls, my mother bought some dainty little cakes, my grandmother baked strudel, there was tea and juice, they were to go short of nothing. My mother put out five cups, not four.

Why five, asked Vera.

For Fania, replied my mother.

Why's Fania included, asked Vera.

Why shouldn't she be included, said my mother. She's your sister, you're supposed to do everything together. Vera pulled a face, and I felt like my grandmother, who always wants to be in on the act when my parents celebrate anything and who extracts from her daughter's life what she was cheated out of in her own life as a woman.

My mother was disappointed by Vera's choice of friends. She appeared in the sun room saying she'd only come to check that we had everything we needed. In truth she had come to exhibit herself to these as yet unknown daughters of other mothers, she had dressed up for them, and they blushed with delight when she addressed them as 'Miss This' and 'Miss That' and unctuously begged her to call them by their first names. My mother stuck to surnames: no, no, she said, it was only right and proper in her opinion, as a young girl she detested the fact that people still kept calling her by her first name. 'Still' she said – and was suddenly the young girl she used to be. She gave Vera a look: why did her daughter have to drag along these three spotty lumpy drears, all made-to-measure for the Hitler Youth? It's neither here nor there whether *you* like them, declared Vera later.

After saying her hellos my mother disappeared again. A

good entrance requires a good exit. She sailed off with a bewitching laugh, leaving her young guests flushed and excited.

She's great, your mother is, enthused Dörte Lückenhausen with her chest heaving. Dead chic, said Freigart Bölitz, and Vera shook her hair and stood up to pour more tea, trying to make each and every movement dead chic.

Vera and her friends started to talk about French kissing, their eyes flickered salaciously and their lips grew moist. I sat there pretending to be the innocent little sister while relishing their burgeoning bodies. The girls were nowhere near as ugly as Vera had made out. I know all about kisses and kissing, I'm familiar with kisses of every sort, kisses are common currency in our household. We get going first thing in the morning as soon as we're up, even before we've had breakfast, we blow kisses in all directions – making-up kisses, calming-down kisses, kisses as a mark of agreement, kisses to welcome back someone who's been lost in thought; my parents feed us on kisses and we feed them in return, licking their worries from their faces. I find my mother's kisses in lipstick on my school sandwich wrapper; none of us can leave the house without kisses, they are the stamp in our passports: come on, you haven't given me a kiss yet, and before we've even got through the door of the flat everything tumbles to the floor – satchel, shopping basket, brolly, handbag, car keys – and we're hugging each other, one kiss turns into countless kisses, a whole shower of kisses, regardless of the fact that we'll be back together again within an hour or so. You never know what might happen, a hurried kiss might be just the thing to provoke a disaster of some kind, so kisses must be firm and precisely on target. Go on, kiss me properly, smack on the mouth, that's it, you can go now. When my father gets home from his trips and turns into the drive we can hear him sound his horn, he gives us a signal, we know he's due back because it's Friday, and anyway my mother's had a feeling for the last two hours that he'll be back earlier than the time he told her on the phone the previous evening; and there he is, driving into the back garden, we've opened the gate for him, solely and exclusively for him, my mother dashes towards him, he climbs out of his car, she calls his name, he stands with outstretched arms by the open car door, then there she is, wrapped round his neck, they kiss, and my grandmother, my sister and I all stand on the terrace, spectators of this ritual happy ending to the week. Then the pair of us run over to him as well, Vera and I race each other and I win: my sister's afraid of the iron stairs, while I can bound down them in great leaps, though I don't do it any more. I hold back all the same, it's as clear as day that my sister has turned into a woman second only to my mother, she strides towards my father, smiling and calm, not tempestuous like his wife, she shows him the other woman, the woman that embodies his own languor. I walk round his car until they have finished. My grandmother is the last to arrive: which of the two of us do you think he wants to see first, said my mother to her mother. My grandmother and I lift his sample case out of the car, my sister takes his coat and carries it as though it were carrying her, I take his briefcase containing his blank order forms, his advertising material, and the orders that he has hopefully secured during his trip. Hugging each other tightly my father and my mother walk ahead of us up the terrace steps and into the house. I'm so glad to be back with you all again – and shaking off the dust of the outside world he also shakes off its alien atmosphere. My mother turns round to me: shut the garden gate please, Fania.

The only one who really can leave the garden via the gate is my father in his car. It is for him that we open it then shut it, for him that we reopen it five days and four nights later. I push the two halves of the garden gate together, two decaying wooden frames clad in rusty wire netting. The lower hinge is broken so the gate hangs from the upper one alone, and each time it is pushed open or shut it scratches a perfect quadrant in the greyish-yellow sand, a narrow groove that rainwater trickles into before draining down into the lower depths and running off into the world beyond. While digging the rose-beds in the front garden I found an enormous ants' nest and poked around in it. The ants scuttled away then suddenly stopped, kissed one another, and scuttled on again, telling each other that they had survived. Just like us. I bent right down to them and nodded my head to them: I'm sorry, I just wanted to see what it's like.

Come over here, Fania, said Vera. I went and sat next to her, they were still on about French kissing. Right, so you stick your tongue in their mouth, Vera said once again. Dörte, Freigart and Monika giggled. Vera put her hands on my shoulders and turned me round to face her, planted her mouth on mine, pushed her tongue between my lips, my teeth parted to let it in, and without taking her mouth from mine she squinted across at her friends and asked in a strangled voice: is that right, is that it, and then added, Fania don't slobber like that.

She can do what she likes with my mouth, I let her in without demur, we're dependent on each other, our discoveries come from mutual exploration. But no outsiders had ever been allowed to watch. That's why I'm angry with Vera. It happened without her inventing one of her stories. On previous occasions we were at a party dancing with each other surrounded by strange voices and laughter and champagne, I was the moustachioed man with a louche smile and she was the object of everyone's desire who wanted to be desired by him alone. This time she hadn't thrown her head back like my mother when she dances, and I hadn't leant right over her. I was simply a convenient mouth that Vera could poke about in with her tongue, and Dörte, Freigart and Monika squealed with excitement, their lascivious eyes feasting on Vera's antics, Monika cried to Vera to move her tongue round and round, Freigart told her to flick it up and down. Vera tried everything she could think of. She let go of my shoulders and told the other girls it wasn't up to much and answered their questions and I wiped the saliva, hers and mine, from my chin.

Vera needs me. Whenever she is invited to a birthday party she takes me with her. Beforehand the same row always takes place between my mother and Vera. Vera doesn't want to go, she'll be bored, she won't know what to do, she'll feel spare and out of place, anyway she's too fat and her hair's all greasy, and my mother stands face to face with Vera and gets worked up and pleads with her daughter to go to the party, you'll never get to know anybody by reading books and daydreaming. Vera cries; she can't possibly go like this, her nose is red and shiny, her eyes are swollen. Just because she has no desire whatever to go to a birthday party she obviously hasn't the least intention of forever forfeiting the chance to find her future husband lurking there amongst the other girls, though finding him would be a major miracle given that he'd have to be like my father and there'll never be anyone else like him. But Vera mustn't give up, we can't live for ever in the garden, and my mother wants loads of grandchildren. Every invitation to a birthday party is yet another awkward step in Vera's journey to her future life with an as yet unknown man and without any of us.

With much grimacing and floods of tears she finally agrees,

but on two conditions. First, my mother must buy a book that Vera hasn't yet read that she can give as her present once she's rushed through it herself; second, Fania must come with her. Although I've not been invited, Vera takes me with her, and it is expected of me by my mother that I will go with Vera, stay with Vera, accompany Vera; we are to be as loyal to each other as our parents are. I do go, I even look forward to it a little bit. There'll be cakes and whipped cream. If my father's at home he takes us in his car. Standing in front of the unfamiliar front door he tells us he'll collect us at seven that evening, he presses the bell, the birthday girl opens the door, welcomes my sister, glances at me, I offer her my present – an extra, unexpected one, the girl's mother hurries over from the sitting room and is thrilled by my father's charm, she thinks it so sweet that Vera takes her little sister with her wherever she goes, do come in for a cup of coffee and a piece of birthday cake, Herr Schiefer, the mother, a complete stranger to us, dashes over to a fancy display cabinet and fetches a plate and a cup, but my father can't spare the time, he must get back to his wife. Cup and plate go back into the cabinet. An extra place-setting is brought out for me – but not best china, that's for grown-ups.

I sit at the coffee table, in front of my plate is a place-card depicting a rose with the name 'Vera' inscribed on its stem in copperplate writing. My sister is standing in front of a bookcase belonging to the other girl's parents. Vera doesn't like cake, only the chocolate sort that my mother or my grandmother bakes for her birthday. She's leafing through a book while putting on an air of utter composure the better to abash these alien people who duly refrain from intervening despite not liking the sight of Vera pensively surveying the titles of their books. The older girls sitting next to me take no notice of me, immersed as they are in a conversation about a class test they have not yet had back. Tonight in bed Vera will tell me what she read – that's our pact.

At other children's birthday parties there are always lots of adults. I used to wonder what all these strange people were doing at children's birthday parties, now I realise they're all members of the family. They sat at a different table in a different room and made even more noise than the children. Some adults gave money instead of presents and I used to count this money – I like counting money – while the birthday child's mother kept a watchful eye on me.

One hundred and fifty marks, I told my mother later, that much! She laughed, ran her hand through my hair, then through her own hair. There shouldn't be adults at children's birthday parties, she said, however nice it is to be given money. Children's birthday parties are for children, adults have no business there.

In the wake of this pronouncement I went down into the back garden and plucked great clusters of snowberries from the bushes. I let the small, white, round berries drop to the ground in front of me, I stamped on them in the sand, they exploded beneath my feet, I filled my skirt pockets with them and swirled them around, all that money, lots of shiny silver fifty-pfennig pieces and golden groschen, even a few five-mark pieces, all clink-ing and tinkling in my hands under the watchful eye of the birthday girl's mother who then checked the amount: I hadn't taken anything. I would have liked to, though. What a lot I would get if all my relatives came to my birthday party instead of just a couple of girls and Wolfram from downstairs. There'd be my grandmother and Aunt Mimi, my father's sister, and Rosa too, my mother's cousin, I can't think of anyone else, my father has an elder brother who is married to a woman we don't like, they have two sons. My father doesn't want to have anything to do with them, though very occasionally my mother says But Paul he *is* your brother after all.

I tipped the snowberries out of my skirt pockets, a shimmering trail of white droplets, step by step I picked my way across the all-encompassing horizon, sunshine turned to darkness. I wasn't supposed to be here but something was drawing me to this spot, the passageway by the house, the barbed wire. Beyond were steps leading to a door into the cellar. I threw in a handful of snowberries. They went skipping and tumbling down the steps. The cellar door was torn open. A man was there. His face was dirty, he was holding a shovel. He stared at me. I was transfixed. Cursing and swearing he came leaping up the steps. The white snowberries tumbled out of my hands in front of his feet. He slammed the shovel-head against the barbed wire. With trembling knees I bolted down the dark passageway towards the bright-green radiance of the lime tree in the front garden. I could hear my mother calling out in the distance, Fania, Fania, where are you. She was shouting down into the back garden but I was in the front garden not daring to run back through the dark passageway and calm her fears. I was there, right there, I still existed, even though she couldn't see me. I ran up the steps to the sun room. The door was locked. At night in my sleep it opened all on its own and I tried to shut it, the door frame disintegrated as soon as I touched it, the wood turned to pulp. I ran on round the house to the side gate that opened onto the drive, its iron bars are coated with rust. I stood before it and imagined myself leaping over the gate into the driveway, then in through the main entrance, there's the door to the flat, ring the bell, my mother would tear the door open and I'd be able to calm her down – all this in my imagination. There was a padlock on the gate. This gate must stay locked, have you got that both of you,

you might go running into the driveway, we might go running into the driveway, not a thought for bad things, not a single thought, and at that very moment the car will arrive that is permanently on the verge of running Vera and me over, that's why the key to the padlock is always kept in the drawer of my father's desk. My mother shouted my name, I didn't shout back, I didn't want her to know that I'd gone down the dark passageway or that I'd seen the man. I tried to climb over the side gate. Fania, where are you for God's sake, Fania, Mamma, Fania's gone, Mamma, she shouted 'Mamma' not 'Mummy', Mamma, Mamma, have you seen Fania. Tears welled up in my eyes, I wept with her for the child she had lost, and I was so heavy with fear for myself that I couldn't heave myself over the gate but instead fell back into the garden and cut my knee. To spare her I had to run back through the passageway, there was no alternative, I was frightened of the horrible man but he would give ground, get out of my way, my mother's worried to death, he would snarl his way back down the steps to the cellar. I was just on my way when my mother tore open the sun room door, she had dashed from the kitchen and across the hall, right from the back of the flat to the front, she came leaping down the steps and sank to her knees in front of me, she wrapped her arms round me, sobbing and asking in strangled tones Where were you, where've you been, you're not to run off down the passageway, I can't see you in there.

Have we got any aunts beside Aunt Mimi, I asked, tipping the last few snowberries out of my skirt pockets. You've another uncle, she said, your father's elder brother, and he's married. We'll invite them round sometime soon.

Really, Alma, whispers my grandmother, I don't think it's right that you let Vera smoke, it's not good at all. Vera throws her head back and looks at her mother out of the corner of her eye in just the same way that I look at Vera, a fickle friend whose loyalty can never be relied on.

It's better this way don't you think, we don't want her smoking in secret; my mother's eyes are glued to the spot where Hainichen is bound to re-emerge from the bushes. Vera steps on my toe, not wanting me to betray the fact that she already smokes in secret. How can Vera possibly suppose I would give her away? It's hurtful, and it makes me want to cry that Vera has moved that little bit away from me. We've always been given the same soft toys to stop us being jealous of each other and only the two of us can tell them apart. Now she's smoking and I'm not.

We carry on staring out of the window at the dense patch of bushes that conceal Hainichen and his digging activities; I suddenly feel such hatred towards him that it makes me feel ill. I'm of no importance to Vera any more; her facial expression, the way she's holding a cigarette: she's imitating my mother in everything she does, and she'll pull it off, I'll be left all on my own.

What's he doing down there, Alma, asks my grandmother.

He's putting up a sign, Mummy, just use your eyes. My mother stares into the undergrowth. 'House for Sale', that's what he'll have written on it. Go on, put your sign up, but tonight as soon as it's dark we'll knock it over.

Vera puffs blue smoke from the depths of her body at the windowpane.

Are you already inhaling that deeply, my mother asks. Vera doesn't answer, she's gazing at Hainichen who minus the sign and with his spade over his shoulder is making his way through the garden towards the house and us. We stand at the window without moving a muscle. He greets my mother, putting his right hand to his forehead and clicking the heels of his boots, she nods her head and gives a frosty smile. He grins and offers the selfsame greeting to Vera, and Vera feels flattered.

The bedroom and sun room are both finished by the evening. We do my parents' bedroom first. It's a matter of special importance to my mother to put this room back to rights straightaway. Snow-white net curtains, freshly ironed by my grandmother, reach down to the floor, there's fresh linen on the bed, the floor is all polished, the wardrobe tidied, and Vera has enthusiastically taken care of my mother's dressing table, polishing the three-fold mirror and reorganising all the things on the glass top – nail varnish, perfume samples, lipsticks, pots of face cream, hairpins, mascara, eyeshadow, curlers, brush, comb – sorting and polishing the imitation jewellery in the drawers, rolling up all the nylon stockings, and finally pulling out the high heels from behind their dark-red curtain and cleaning these thrilling objects with their red lacquer and soft black suede and slender straps before lining them up again in neat rows. Just as we're collapsing into bed close to midnight Vera mentions that we've forgotten Hainichen's sign, and my mother yawns that we'll do it next week, this isn't a good time for it anyway, Hainichen will be on the lookout.

When my father's away on his trips my sister and I share the marital bed with my mother. She can't sleep on her own, she's just not used to it. As a child she slept with her mother on the side her husband had occupied before he left them. Later she lay in the same bed with her lover, Paul Schiefer; she was the same age as Vera is today, and he was only five years older. My grandmother gave them two gold rings and let them have the double bed in order to make her Jewish daughter's relationship with this young goy decent and respectable in her own eyes. It was no longer permissible for them to marry. It would be an offence against the racial purity laws. From then on Hedwig

Glitzer slept on the sofa in the kitchen. Her daughter Alma, who all of a sudden had a man with her in her parents' bed instead of her mother, changed sides and slept on her mother's half: she didn't want her lover lying where her mother had lain, but where her father had always been before getting up one day and leaving never to return.

From Mondays to Fridays when my father's on the road with his cases of samples my mother climbs into his side of the bed each night while my sister gets into my mother's side and I sleep in the middle with the gap between the mattresses plugged with blankets. Yet again Vera doesn't want to go to school in the morning, she's whispered this to me, above us hovers the face of my mother who is trying to give us our goodnight kisses, she rests her body on mine to kiss Vera, then she kisses me, darkens the light on her bedside table with a red scarf, picks up her book, and within minutes her eyes start to close and the book droops in her hand.

I can't sleep until I know what's happening about school tomorrow, whispers Vera. My mother's heavy eyelids snap open again, she's heard every word in her sleep: you can both stay at home and carry on with the spring-cleaning. Vera is cock-a-hoop, I'm pleased as well, it's only later in the dark with sleep creeping up on us that I'm beset with anxiety: perhaps it's not right to stay in when they're meant to let me out so that I can go to school.

Next morning Erich Kupsch appears with a long painter's ladder over his shoulder and his beer gut hanging down over his waistband. With my mother he paces around the room inspecting the three-metre-twenty-high walls; above the skirting boards grey, gossamer-thin strands of mould stick out from the walls wherever the furniture normally stands, massed round the edges of creamy-brown patches of damp. Nicotine and coal dust have turned the ceiling brown. Every tap on the wallpaper is answered with the gentle rustling noise of something crumbling away inside.

It's all gotta come off, growls Erich Kupsch.

My mother, standing next to him, shakes her head. Out of the question, Herr Kupsch, the entire house is held together by the wallpaper, and until it belongs to us we don't want to spend too much money on it.

Erich Kupsch signals his agreement by a single nod of the head, chews on his stub of a cigar, fair enough then, fair enough, Frau Schiefer, if that's the way it is, best slap on a coat of paint.

He goes off and returns with three buckets of milky-white paint, and by evening the job is done. Our big room, the one in which our family life is played out, is displaying its innards, which resemble the inside of a sick stomach. The walls now have a greenish tinge.

Erich Kupsch takes his leave. Needs to dry first, be white as white, you'll see.

My mother nods and offers him a banknote, which he declines; don't want nothing, he growls. All he'll take are the two packets of cigarettes that my grandmother offers him and the last bottle left in the beer crate. He gives a sly wink: it's fer me Elsa; then turning to my mother who's standing next to him all spattered with paint he says Don't you worry, Frau Schiefer, we'll talk to that Herr Schiefer when 'e gets back, and he nods his head towards the ceiling.

Hainichen, you mean Hainichen, says my mother, and once again Erich Kupsch gives a single nod by way of agreement. She takes his hand with both of hers: all we have to do is to persuade my husband, Herr Kupsch. She says this in a pressing, almost pleading tone: perhaps even this alcoholic manual labourer from Upper Silesia can help to achieve the near and perhaps completely impossible and persuade her husband to buy the house. Erich Kupsch shuffles out of the room with the bottle of beer in his trouser pocket.

It's late. We mop the floor, tip floor polish all over it, rub it laboriously into the dark-green lino, then buff the floor with the heavy polishing brush until it gleams; we clean the windows, shrouded on the outside with the blackness of the night; the clock is creeping towards midnight, we drag the furniture back into the room, Norddeutscher Rundfunk's Third Programme is just finishing its final programme of the day, someone has been reading something that none of us listened to, but the rhythm and flow of the voice have kept us going, the dirt of the house lies thick on our skin, we wish you goodnight says a male voice on the radio, we survey what we have achieved, the room smells of paint and floor wax, the loudspeaker suddenly emits a continuous high-pitched tone, I turn the right-hand button anti-clockwise, the radio falls silent.

Vera thinks the painted-over wallpaper looks as if someone's been sick on it.

My mother bursts out laughing, she laughs so much that she clasps her stomach, crumples up and collapses onto the floor, we collapse next to her, doubled up with helpless laughter, we are exhausted, we're hunched up in the very innards of this house with its ulcers in full view and are quite certain we must stay put to restore it to health, to retain this place for ourselves, for we can't imagine a lovelier one. We still have our room to do and my grandmother's room and the kitchen. That'll be tomorrow; tomorrow is Wednesday.

Wednesdays always make the week feel very long for my mother. Every Wednesday she says This week is never-ending, almost another three days until Paul gets back. But Wednesday is also the day that Elsa Kupsch comes to clean for us at eight in the morning; this week we're doing the cleaning, so today Elsa Kupsch is going to do the ironing – bed linen, table linen, teacloths. Breakfast first, though. My grandmother makes scrambled eggs, there's cheese and home-made raspberry jam, my mother produces cocoa with cream – 'Queen's cocoa' she calls it.

When I was little I often sat on Elsa Kupsch's lap, on her enormous thighs; I'd lay my head against her large, soft breasts and hear how her voice vibrated inside her while she chatted about the neighbourhood in her broad throaty Silesian accent, changing all the vowel sounds in just the same way that Yiddish does.

Let's have breakfast first, Frau Kupsch, says my mother, who wants to hear all the fresh gossip about people in our street. Elsa Kupsch wants to pay her rent before she sits down, it's the middle of the month today, she has a small blue rent book in her hand together with a ten-mark note. Frau Kupsch enters the amount herself, she's not used to writing, she sits hunched over the rent book, panting heavily, and with the tip of her tongue licks her stump of a pencil which, moistened by her spit, writes purply-blue figures that can't be rubbed out. My mother initials the entry by way of a receipt and opening the top buttons of her smock Elsa Kupsch stuffs the rent book down the side of her left breast, orangey-pink material comes briefly into view – the voluminous cups of Elsa Kupsch's bra – then her dark-coloured smock slips back down to conceal her treasure.

Elsa Kupsch is a hard-working woman, and everything about her is round – her face, her hands, her heavy body. She gets up every morning at half past four because her husband has to be down at the shipyard by six o'clock, four days a week she does cleaning jobs both morning and afternoon, on Fridays and Saturdays she does her own housework, on Sundays Elsa Kupsch attends the local Catholic Church, and afterwards makes dumplings and bakes a cake to have in the afternoon.

One morning soon after the war – my mother had emerged from her hiding place and looked like a starved cat – there was a ring on the doorbell. Could Frau Schiefer do with a cleaning lady? My mother could indeed, she asked Elsa Kupsch to come in, asked a lot of questions, showed interest in all aspects of the Kupsch family, and Elsa Kupsch recounted her story. She'd managed to get over from Breslau, she didn't have a residence permit for Hamburg, at night she hid in bombed-out houses, she wasn't just looking for a job but also for a place to live – but without a residence permit no job, no job without a settled address, no settled address without a residence permit; her husband was sitting it out with the children on the other side of the border, waiting for news from her.

My mother went down into the cellar with Elsa Kupsch and showed her three rooms plus the big cellar-kitchen: you can live here if you like, she said.

There was one other thing she should mention, said Frau Kupsch: we're Catholics.

So what, my mother said.

But everyone's Protestant around here, said Frau Kupsch.

So they are, replied my mother, but Catholic, Protestant, it's all the same to me; I'm neither one nor the other, and if you're happy with that, Frau Kupsch, then you're very welcome.

Elsa Kupsch didn't seem altogether happy with that, but what really mattered was the flat in the cellar, so the next day the two women went to the Residents' Registration Office. My mother told the official that Elsa Kupsch was her home help.

Forms, stamps, signatures. Both the mouth and the parting of the man behind the desk were as straight and as thin as a razor blade. So terrified was Elsa Kupsch that her eyes began to roll.

They don't frighten me, said my mother, I know all about ugly mugs like that. I'll never forget this, Frau Schiefer, I'll never forget what you done for me; Elsa Kupsch sobbed and kissed my mother's hands, she rushed off to her church and lit a candle in front of the mother of her God. A week later Erich Kupsch arrived with the three Kupsch children, Kurt, Michael and Elisabeth. Wolfram wasn't born then. Nor were Vera and I.

There are plenty of prosperous people in our area who can afford a cleaner several days each week. This is a boon for Frau Kupsch. I don't want to tell no tales, says Elsa Kupsch – but this is how she always begins, my mother nods in agreement, and my grandmother, Vera and I all focus intently on our scrambled eggs so that without any further inhibitions Elsa Kupsch can tell us all the things about our neighbours that she doesn't want to tell us.

Well yesterday I was doin' the washing at Frau Stierich's; my mother gave another slow nod to indicate that she was fully in the picture: Magda Stierich, wife of Admiral Friedhelm Stierich (retired), spends her days and nights hobbling stiffly around her richly appointed flat with the help of sticks.

Elsa Kupsch takes a morsel of bread and forces it between her scarcely parted lips: she is so embarrassed to be eating with us that she can hardly bear to open her mouth.

Don't let your scrambled eggs get cold, Frau Kupsch, says my mother with her mouth full and with another forkload all ready to go in, while Vera and I discard our knives and forks and eat our egg and bread with our fingers, and my grandmother dunks her buttered bread roll in her coffee. Elsa Kupsch thus remains the only person at the table eating with a knife and fork like a well-brought-up lady and politely dabbing her lips with a napkin after every mouthful.

So was he with that woman across the road, asks my mother, and this sets Elsa Kupsch's tongue wagging.

Admiral (ret'd) Friedhelm Stierich, a boozer ever since he lost the war, spends his days and nights shuttling back and forth across the street between his wife Magda and his mistress Katjenka Nohke, a Russian married to one Alfred Nohke of Nohke Bros, the clothiers in Mönckebergstrasse, formerly Silbermann & Co. Going out of a morning to get milk from the milkman one or other of the two housewives has occasionally found the admiral fast asleep in the gutter, his head resting on his carefully folded jacket.

Ooh no, Frau Schiefer, I mean yes, there I was just washin' his underpants, and 'e gets back 'ome from Frau Nohke's, back to his Magda, and didn't she just, she bashed 'im one and bawled at 'im, words like I can't bear to tell yer, can't bear to think about.

My grandmother drinks this all in; oh how can he do it, how terrible for his wife. My mother immediately pounces on her mother: what do you mean, terrible for his wife? I can well understand why he cheats on that old bag – but Katjenka doing it with him, I just don't get it. Katjenka Nohke, and doing it for years, how can she, she's Russian, how can she do it with him, with him of all people – but do go on, Frau Kupsch. My mother had chosen to bite her tongue.

What you mean, how can she do it? Vera wants to put her oar in too. After all she did it with Nohke as well, and he's just as much of a . . . Yes, alright! My mother snatches the word from her daughter's lips before it's even spoken: she doesn't want Frau Kupsch to know that in our eyes Friedhelm Stierich

110

and Alfred Nohke are both Nazis; Stierich was an admiral in Hitler's navy, Nohke was Deputy Chief Bookkeeper at Silbermann & Co. He bought the Mönckebergstrasse clothes shop for a tiny fraction of its true value. We know that, I know that, my mother tells us that every time we go down Mönckebergstrasse on our way into town. I think of the Silbermanns every time I see Alfred Nohke in the street and curtsy to him. Clothier Solomon Silbermann and his sister Sidonie had boat tickets to Argentina, and had to hand over to the German state the full value in gold of everything they took with them by way of furniture, pictures, crockery, clothing, jewellery – thus paying all over again for whatever they had bought, and at a price many times higher than the original one. 'Silbermann & Co.' was written above the shop in italic script, but not a single pane of glass was smashed: Alfred Nohke had planted himself in front of it to protect his future property.

And how far on is Frau Schulze-Edel, asks my grandmother, reckon she'll be having that baby seven months after her wedding.

So I believe, so I believe, nods Elsa Kupsch. She's finished her scrambled eggs and wipes her plate clean with a slice of bread. Mention of Frau Schulze-Edel, her hurried marriage to Herr Schulze and her seven-months-after baby at the age of nearly forty rather sours the atmosphere in our kitchen. Elsa Kupsch carries on wiping her plate with her bread.

And what about the Kütings, have you been at the Kütings', my mother asks. The Kütings live in the big house next to ours, the house belongs to them, you can tell by looking at their house that ours must once have been lovely, it's exactly the same as ours only the other way round, their bay window with the balcony on top is on the right and the adjoining sun room is on the left. The driveway from the street through to the back gate of the British Consulate lies between the Kütings and us. Professor Werner Küting is a well-known cancer specialist and Ada Küting is an interior designer. Every Sunday in summer she has a great horde of grandchildren to visit and on sunny days she reads to them in the garden. On such occasions she sits in a comfortable deckchair holding a book by Astrid Lindgren or Charles Dickens, Mark Twain or Edith Nesbit, a glass of sherry close to hand, and sprawled by her side and at her feet a gaggle of boys and girls from her extensive family, silent and bewitched for a full two hours.

Before starting to read, Adolfine Küting calls to us in her resonant alto voice across her neatly trimmed hedge and the driveway and our jungle of bushes: Frau Schiefer, if your girls want to pop over, I'm going to read now. Vera and I push our way out of our garden into the driveway. See you later, my mother calls, take care, adding – to make sure we come back to her – I'll do you something special for supper. We cross the driveway, quit our own world and crawl through a gap in the hedge into the world of the Kütings' large family. No sooner have we arrived in the other garden, separated from our own by a ten-metre-wide driveway, than we hear my father's ringing tenor voice just checking that everything is alright and we call back Ye-es to reassure him that we're safe and sound. He does it for his wife and he does it for his own sake. He has stayed with her, and we shouldn't leave him on his own either.

The Professor 'as cancer, says Elsa Kupsch.

Nebbish, says my grandmother shaking her head in dismay; and does he know?

What a question, interjects my mother, he's a cancer specialist!

That's just it, says Elsa Kupsch, 'e won't face the truth.

We are all upset at this tragic turn of events in Professor

Küting's life. And he always greets us so politely, says my grandmother, always doffs his hat.

At lunchtime when Elsa Kupsch has finished her ironing she knocks on the open door.

Frau Schiefer, there's summat else I wanted to mention.

What's the matter, Frau Kupsch, says my mother, is anything wrong with the children.

Elsa Kupsch's face is blotchy, and my mother takes her into the bedroom and shuts the door. After a while we can hear indignation in her voice and the sound of Elsa Kupsch sobbing.

You mustn't put up with that, Frau Kupsch, cries my mother vehemently, I'll come with you and give him a piece of my mind. The bedroom door flies open, my mother's fighting spirit is well and truly aroused, Frau Kupsch becomes invisible behind her, frightened and worried yet flushed with hope.

When's your appointment, my mother asks; fortnight today, the doctor said.

Not for a fortnight! The earlier he sees you, the better for you. I'll ring him up.

Elsa Kupsch goes to the door, more diffident and distraught than I have ever seen her, walks silently into the stairwell, and disappears; we stand there straining to catch the sound of the door closing. Has she gone, or is she still outside. Vera goes to look: Frau Kupsch has gone.

My mother raises her hands and her eyebrows, my grandmother makes tut-tutting noises with her tongue, and Vera nods her head sagely. I'm completely at a loss, I feel rejected, I don't know what they know, I float away from my mother, my sister, my grandmother, I float away under the garden gate, my body is being dragged away, sucked out, they are losing me, I want to get back in, I'm clinging to the wire, I won't let go. My entire existence depends on my being here.

Vera and my grandmother say nothing and look at my mother: it's for her to decide whether I'm allowed to know.

I want to know. You all know, so why can't I. You can't do this to me, I'll have a screaming fit. They have to tell me, right now, anything else is sheer betrayal.

My mother gives me a quizzical look and puts her hand on my forehead, have you got a temperature, Fania, calm down or you'll get a temperature, nothing to worry about though. She takes my hand, we sit down. It's just that you mustn't say a word to anybody, Frau Kupsch wouldn't want that: Frau Kupsch is having a baby.

Ohhowlovely I say without conviction, still fully aware that Frau Kupsch didn't look at all happy; I say ohhowlovely because that's what my mother says whenever she sees a pregnant woman. She liked being pregnant, giving birth was no big deal, she always says; the main thing was that it was happening at last.

It's lovely when a woman's expecting a baby. Her face doesn't light up this time. Frau Kupsch already has four children, Kurt, Michael and Elisabeth are already grown-up and Wolfram's still at school, and you know, Fania, Frau Kupsch's legs look awful, all those big fat varicose veins, and some of them are ulcerous. Frau Kupsch wears button-through frocks in dark blue, dark grey and small check so people can't see the stains, and they've been washed so often that they're almost falling apart. Over her fat thighs the material is stretched to bursting.

The baby in her tummy is still tiny. My mother makes a face as if it were already dead. Imagine it dropping out of its nest like a baby bird that still can't see.

I don't want to imagine anything. You're to tell me the truth, I scream at her, just tell me the truth, tell me everything,

114

I want to know everything. She remains calm, she doesn't shout back at me.

Alma, pleads my grandmother, that's enough, it's too much for Fania.

My mother carries on. It's not a proper human being yet, Fania, it still doesn't really exist. It has to be aborted, that'll be better for Frau Kupsch, it'll be taken out of her tummy before it's come properly alive and turned into a human being. You mustn't talk about it to anyone at all.

I nod quickly, she's to carry on, she's not to stop, it isn't too much for me, I know all about it. They'll cut Frau Kupsch open. There was this goose on the kitchen table with its legs splayed out, I was standing on a stool to get a better view, and my mother reached into its body. There, can you see, these are the intestines, we carefully strip the fat off and turn it into lard. Vera and I peered into the sliced-open carcase of the goose. My mother pulled out an egg, bigger than a fat grape, the yolk surrounded by a strong membrane, all slippery and shiny and still without a shell. Ooh, a baby, Vera and I cried dramatically; nebbish, said my mother and dropped it into the waiting rubbish bin. Next came the stomach and heart, which were put in the soup; the liver was fried in butter and given to Vera and me.

Frau Kupsch won't be cut open, I hear my mother say; it's like a miscarriage, the baby comes out, but it doesn't happen all on its own, the doctor has to help, and by then it's already dead. But not yet, I say; no, not yet, she says. But then it is, I say; yes, then it is, she nods. There is something comforting about the finality of death: it brings suffering to a close for ever and to all eternity.

Frau Kupsch will feel much better afterwards. My mother is to leave me alone now. That's enough.

115

What do you think, shall we change things round. My mother's eyes dart around the room. How about having the couch with its back to the sun room, just give me a hand. Vera, my grandmother and I move the couch, shifting the couch means the chest of drawers can't stay where it is. Everything is in the melting pot, the familiar order of things dissolves, pieces of furniture move away from the wall, turn their backs on each other, get in each other's way, we retreat to the sofa and ponder the rearrangement from there. My grandmother goes into the kitchen and brings back a tray of hot vegetable soup with semolina dumplings and bread. We eat squatting on the couch and the floor, we are strangers in a rocky landscape camping in a clearing and slurping their soup, I scoff twelve dumplings and get another two from my grandmother.

Paul's wingback chair could go in that corner there, suggests my mother. The furniture is arranged anew and brings new perspectives into our lives, intimate tableaux involving the wingback chair, a side table and a picture of a Provençal landscape, or green upholstery and the yellow table lamp plus radio and record player. We try it all out from different vantage points. The round dining table is moved under the large mirror with the chest of drawers quite close to it against the wall, the big bookcase goes opposite it, we have to empty the shelves to shift it, there are mountains of books all over the floor, my mother and I put them back with the novels in alphabetical order, the detective stories grouped together on their own on the lower shelves, three dozen red-and-black-striped paperbacks claiming on their back covers that Edgar Wallace is irresistibly gripping.

My mother is quick at this. In her hands the books are thoroughly compliant, they take on the air of attentive listeners that are collectively silent yet all have their very own story to tell. Do you want to read to us, she asks, and standing on her ladder she hands a dog-eared book down to Vera. We've reached M, M as in *Buddenbrooks* and *Gone with the Wind*; I put Margaret Mitchell onto the shelf and Vera retreats to the newly positioned wingback chair with Thomas Mann. While we quietly carry on with sorting the books, Toni Buddenbrooks runs up Mengstrasse to the Town Hall to find out whether her brother has been elected a senator – it would be such a boon for the family's reputation after their long succession of failures.

In less than two days my father will be back. We stand jostling for position in the doorway: we are in the same place as ever yet it seems a different place.

Vera and I do our room on our own while my mother and my grandmother clean the kitchen. Our books take most of the time, with each of us hunched in front of our own bookshelf. How are you going to sort them? This ever-present quandary opens the door to a magic realm; we sit on the floor and throw each other familiar titbits from our books, some we've meanwhile forgotten and others that we remember and often quote at each other. I gaze at my books, thrilled to bursting point by the prospect of what awaits me there, all the familiar things that can be mine again and again, a different life in each and every book. I shall pick seven books and put them on a special shelf above my bed. Vera thinks it's a brilliant idea.

By Thursday evening everything is done, except that we've forgotten the hall. The hall usually does get forgotten. That's where you go out of the flat, it's gloomy, lit only by a low-wattage bulb. Let's at least wipe away the fingerprints, says my grandmother, and she grabs a soapy cloth, wrings it out, cleans the varnished wood and puts the chain on. Done.

On Friday morning Vera and I go to school, though Vera protests, claiming that it won't be convincing if she doesn't stay ill on Friday and Saturday and right over the weekend with its expected fine weather. On my way to school I look forward to school; I feel as if I've returned from a journey to foreign parts and have lots to report.

Foreignness awaits me in the classroom. I have failed to do something here – I have failed to occupy my seat. Annegret and Gerda look at me and pretend to be surprised that I still exist. They don't talk to me. Annegret takes my new ink-rubber. I share a double desk with her, she spreads herself out, her elbow protrudes far into my half of the desktop.

At half past twelve I come home from school on my own, Vera has lessons until two today, my mother opens the door, her hair is wet, she's wearing her dressing gown. Barefoot she carries on ahead of me into her freshly cleaned bedroom, the galvanised bath that's used for doing the washing on Mondays is standing on the floor and she's having a bath in it, on a stool close by is a plate with thin slices of cucumber which she places on her cleavage, her face and finally her closed eyes.

I have to think about how I'm going to tackle Paul about this house business. Leave me on my own now.

Chapter Five

My grandmother puts six beef olives in a cast-iron casserole, cuts five large onions into quarters and adds them to the pot together with five cloves of garlic, a few juniper berries and some peppercorns; she doesn't use the bay leaves but pushes them to one side. I watch her. Was your hair black once, I ask. She looks up as if I've caught her doing something wrong. She carries on stirring the pot. You already know the answer to that question.

I've never seen you with black hair; you were already white by the time I arrived. I suddenly realise I don't actually know this for certain and I'm seized by a violently painful sensation: there's lots I haven't noticed, I have lived my life without retaining anything, what will I be able to recount later on? I know so little about my grandmother. What were you like as a little girl? She doesn't laugh. I was very solemn, she solemnly replies.

My grandmother will die before I do. She stands at the stove stirring time into her casserole; I look at my watch: two minutes have passed. She opens the oven door. I'm sure she could tell that I was thinking of her death. I didn't want to trespass on the span of her life.

We learnt a lot of poetry, I heard her say to the oven; she puts a match to the gas and burns her fingers. What's the poem called that you've got to learn, she asks.

A ballad. I'm to recite it in front of the whole class next week. There are three avenging goddesses in it, I really like them. For really bad crimes they wreak unmerciful vengeance. How lovely, says my grandmother. It's quite a long ballad, I chose it because of the three Furies. They're called Tisiphone, which means 'avenger of blood', Alecto, 'the implacable one', and Megaera, 'the jealous one'.

Are they Jews, asked one of the girls in the class. What a peculiar question, said the teacher. I was instantly electrified. That word. There it was at last. And I had to keep a careful check on what they did with it. I was under orders from my mother to take all necessary preventative steps. That word: I looked around me. Vacant faces. It was my mother looking through my eyes. These people were her enemies and mine. With my mother within me I wasn't afraid of them. At last I too was experiencing it. Our teacher said nothing. Nor did any of the girls. If they carried on saying nothing then the word would dissolve into the air and disappear. As if it had never been there. As if this word had never existed. Jew. Jews. The word was slowly evaporating above the heads of the girls; another half a minute and the teacher would be able to carry on where he'd left off. My heart fluttered beneath my tongue. Words arose in me, an uprising of words. I heard myself from several angles. I spoke. I heard my mother's voice. Jews. Vengeance. His voice intervened, he had no business to interfere. One moment, Fania, he said. Why was he interrupting us, we could provide the information, we knew, I knew. Where to start, how to start to ensure that they listened to me and understood at last. How boring and stupid they were, how pathetic just sitting there gazing into space, we were special, I was special, and I hated them, I could destroy them all with what I knew about them, me, Alma Schiefer's daughter, granddaughter of Hedwig Glitzer, great-granddaughter of Marianne Wasserstrahl, née Nehemias. He had lowered his head so far that a strand of hair lay on the poetry book. He was hiding his face from me. He looked up. Pages rustled all around me. What were they doing, why all this rustling. They were talking about a certain Otto Ernst and a certain Nis Randers. Obscure men, German men.

The rest of you are learning *Nis Randers* by Otto Ernst, I heard the teacher say to the rows of bent heads in front of him, and Fania is doing Schiller's *Cranes of Ibycus*. He nodded to me, he grinned, the left corner of his mouth going up and the right going down, chair legs grated on lino. I walked past him. He'd stayed sitting at his desk, he said I could have until Monday. It was almost as if he brushed against my arm.

Rhythmically speaking I already know the lines. Dee-dum dee-dum dee-dum dee-dum, by Friedrich Schiller. To enter the contest of songs and chariot / That joins the joyous tribes of Greece / On Corinth's narrow spit of land / Came Ibycus, the gods' belovèd.

Dark drumbeats, the swish and swirl of heavy cloth, the dance of the Furies. Vera says you have to read *against* the rhythm if you want to hear what the poem is trying to say. She's interested in the theatre at present, she wants to be an actress, my parents insist that she's got to finish school first and then learn typing and shorthand so that she can earn a living later on if she doesn't make it on the stage. Vera didn't argue and my mother said You can't fool me – your father, perhaps, but not me. My mother would like to have gone on the stage herself. She would have been a dancer, Expressive Dance was her thing.

I lay my hand on the page and raise my head, I stare at the opposite wall, the opening lines are before my eyes, I open my eyes – and my mother comes rushing in. That shameless rat Hainichen, in the stairwell just now, he'll see what I'm made of, her voice is trembling with passion, she goes to the stove and peers into the casserole, is he really trying to tell me – I've only just put that on, says my grandmother, hurrying from table to stove to rescue our lovely supper from her furious daughter. My mother turns from stove to table, is that what's left, she asks, eyeing some coins that my grandmother had put in a saucer on her return from market. Lifting her skirt and pulling it up over her left knee and thigh to the point where her stocking ends she chooses a fifty-pfennig piece as a replacement for a missing suspender button, shoves it under her stocking then pushes the suspender eyelet over the coin.

That Frau Schmalstück has made Hainichen an offer, the old biddy wants to give him sixty thousand for the house. My mother looks at me, at the kitchen table, at my grandmother, her fingers under her skirt know exactly what to do. He'd better prove it, I want to see it in writing. She lets go of her skirt which slides down her leg. My grandmother peels potatoes, my mother starts trimming the green beans, suddenly my father's standing there in the kitchen doorway, Vera's standing next to him, his name proclaims itself from my mother's mouth as though from the Oracle. Paul.

Only moments earlier he had been a total stranger, I'd seen him in the doorway before he was actually there, a merry wanderer free as a bird puffing happily round the corner to join in the contest of song and chariot. We weren't expecting you so soon, says my mother. But we *had* been expecting Vera for ages, more specifically for the last three hours: her last lesson ended at 2pm and it's now 5pm, and you'd think for all the world that she'd been out on the road with my father and that they'd come back home together.

My father is beaming with delight, I got loads of orders, my mother throws her arms round his neck, her foot kicks up at the thrill of his kiss – a dream couple, a dream woman with her dream man. I make to ask Vera where she's been, she sees my mouth about to open and signals to me to keep quiet.

Two hours later we're still sitting round our familiar table having our first meal in the newly reorganised living room. Everything's a bit crazy. My father is amazed by what we have accomplished. He looks for his wingback chair and is disconcerted to find it has moved. Do you like it, my mother wants to know, and he sits down and tries it out to see what view of us he gets from this particular vantage point. He lifts his head from the backrest: how on earth have you managed to do it so quickly. My grandmother lights two candles, my mother puts her freshly baked challah on the table. We sit down, my father opens a bottle of red wine and serves us all – even I get half a glass – he sniffs the wine, he sniffs the bread, he undoes the top button of his shirt, then sighs contentedly.

Is it all right, my mother asks, her eyes anxiously scanning our plates; we haven't eaten a single mouthful yet. My father is bent over his well-laden fork, he looks up at his wife and grunts of pleasure resonate from somewhere deep within his chest, Vera and I nod approvingly, my mother is a brilliant cook, and my grandmother congratulates her on the gravy, which in fact she has made herself, and then she laughs: it was me that made the gravy, quite true, says my mother, Mummy cooked the whole meal, you're a brilliant cook too, my father pats his mother-in-law's hand. He chews very slowly.

Suddenly all is quiet. Like a blank page in the middle of a book. My mother racks her brains for something to say. She doesn't want to let on yet about what's really on her mind – her house-buying plans; it would be premature, it's important that her husband finish his meal in peace and quiet first. Our mouths are sealed, we chew, we swallow, our thoughts start to wander along their own particular pathways, my mother chips in, by the way have I told you ... she says, and at the very same moment he says Out with it, you lot, you're hiding something from me. He couldn't stand it any longer either.

My father lifts his glass to his lips.

Happy Sabbath, says my grandmother.

I only need to look at Hedwig, you're up to something, out with it, what's up, come on, Alma, tell me. He drinks some wine.

My grandmother's face is turning red, she hides it behind her napkin. His gaze transforms her into a little girl. She is harbouring a secret. You could never be sure that Mummy wouldn't blab and the streets were crammed full of Germans, men, women, people in uniform, I can hear my mother saying this, it was one of my worst fears, you've got to lie to them even if they look just like decent people.

You just enjoy your beef olive first; my mother puckers her cherry-red-lipstick lips. My father loves the white, braided bread with its touch of sweetness, he mops up his gravy with it, the challah is as much a part of Friday evenings as the candles and the chatter: how were things his past week, what went well, what went badly, we haven't seen him since Monday, he was out on the road, how did it go for him, how did it go for us, bringing it all together until our various experiences of the alien, outside world have been sufficiently gone over and taken in. Such is our Sabbath Eve.

Vera announces that she's got an A for her essay on Goethe's *Iphigenia*, jolly good, says my father, and an E in Maths, adds my mother, well it's only Maths, says my sister, and my father says jolly good to that too, he says jolly good to everything, he wants his peace and quiet, he doesn't want any arguing, not at table, he strokes Vera's hand, I was never any good at Maths either, she's sitting on his right, my grandmother's on his left, then there's me, and between me and Vera sits my mother: my parents sit opposite one another at the round dining table.

Vera recounts the story of Iphigenia. Artemis, goddess of hunting, told Iphigenia to kill all the young men who came to visit her in the temple. Iphigenia having died, Artemis had given her her life back and now wanted her to be her priestess for ever. No man was ever to possess Iphigenia. Vera looks around at everyone with a scandalised air. My mother, whose mind is on fifty-six thousand marks, narrows her eyes in suspicion at Vera's tone of indignation; my father meanwhile is slicing his beef olive into cartwheels. Two young warriors arrive on the scene, and Iphigenia recognises one of them as her brother Orestes; of course she doesn't want to sacrifice him to her goddess.

Why are you looking at me like that, says my mother, carefully cutting a green bean in half with her knife and fork.

I'm not looking at you at all, says Vera indignantly, looking straight at her mother.

Of course, says my father, of course she doesn't, I mean why would a sister want to sacrifice her brother, and anyway all of you, isn't this food just so delicious.

But his wife is now deaf to such gambits: her food still unfinished she folds her napkin and launches into accusations. It was the *father* in the first place that wanted to kill his daughter Iphigenia, at least that's what I saw on the stage, and I must say if he'd been *my* husband I'd have given him what for. No need for details: the meaning of 'what for' is clear to us all. My father needs to save his hypersensitive stomach, as a

125

precautionary measure he tries a laugh, he doesn't want a row about the problems encountered by ancient Greek families, he reaches for her hand, Greek history would have taken a quite different course, he says with an ingratiating smile, no Trojan War, Alma.

Leave me alone, she says. My mother can't bear it when she hits the buffers. Whatever the topic she has to know it all, she wades in on subjects she knows little about and any counter-arguments give her a sneaky opportunity to garner knowledge and squirrel it away. Perhaps this is typically Jewish, I think to myself, perhaps it's what others see as typically Jewish.

My mother casts around for a name, what *was* that name. Whose name, asks Vera. Agamemnon, suggests my father, poor old Agamemnon. No no, Paul, my mother shakes her head, this is not the time for silly jokes, she is really cross, I don't mean him, I don't mean Agamemnon. Menelaos perhaps, he explains, Agamemnon's brother; poor Menelaos who had to go to war because of his beauteous Helen. My father attempts to be poor Menelaos and succeeds at once, I don't like seeing him in this guise, he reaches once again for the hand of his beauteous Helen, just stop that, Paul, she says, I mean the daughter, I mean Iphigenia, I mean the actress, who was it played her, we were both at the theatre together, her voice is growing louder and louder, last year, you were there too, Vera, or was it the year before last, and Vera's voice grows louder as well, Agamemnon *didn't* kill his daughter, screams my sister, biting vigorously on her fork, but he wanted to, screams my mother, he *didn't* screams Vera, just get it into your head at last, he didn't know, he didn't know she'd be the first to approach him, Vera shoves every word into my mother's face.

But he could have known, then suddenly she says in a quiet voice, her name was Maria I think, wasn't her name Maria, she stuffs a piece of meat into her mouth, Maria, Maria, oh what was her surname, she was Iphigenia, she always wanted to be the first to welcome her father home from his travels, she was the first to approach him every time. My mother nods her head in confirmation of her own words. Vera has tears in her eyes. She wanted to save her father, says my sister, her voice is choked by her tears, she continues speaking, we have to put up with her tear-choked voice, she spells out the family's secret: Iphigenia's father had sworn an oath so that Zeus would let him return home alive, he didn't want to die, all because of Helen.

My mother cuts her beef olive in two. My children would matter more to me than some god, I can't be doing with such nonsense, I totally reject family set-ups like that, he sacrificed his daughter and at the very last moment this goddess whisks his daughter from under his knife. You mean Artemis; Vera emits the words through tightly pursed lips. That's what I said, says my mother. No one else is eating. She eats on regardless, why shouldn't she eat, it proves the truth of what she's saying, her knife and fork scratch away at her plate. She shovels the meat in piece by piece. Vera looks at her enraged, then suddenly the thin line of her mouth resolves. Becker, she says. It was Maria Becker who played Iphigenia.

Thanks. My mother smiles, puts her knife to one side and stretches her hand towards Vera. Thanks, that was really bothering me.

So were you me. Vera doesn't take her hand, she carries on talking. The daughter wanted to free the father from his oath, otherwise he'd have drowned in the sea, he'd promised Zeus that if he let him return home alive he'd sacrifice the first and dearest creature he encountered on land. Vera looks at her father wanting him to look at her as his first and dearest. My

127

father is careful not to oblige, devoting his entire attention to his beef olive and his potatoes. He chews and swallows.

What did I say, says my mother triumphantly, was he thinking of his daughter, was he willing to sacrifice her, yes or no, yes he was.

Vera shouts out, brandishing her knife in the air, it could have been his wife.

My mother laughed, she knew her old man, and wasn't Iphigenia humane towards her brother, more humane than her father, and didn't she disobey her goddess, but her father slaughtered her, his very own daughter, just because he'd sworn an oath.

This tastes so delicious, says my father, asking his wife for a second beef olive.

So glad you like it; my mother's voice still carries a ring of triumph at the victory she has won against her daughter and Agamemnon.

I don't know why you're getting so worked up, says Vera.

Why shouldn't I get worked up, says my mother, getting even more worked up. *You're* getting worked up, you're getting worked up about everything this evening, what on earth's the matter with you, come to think of it where were you the whole time after school, that's something I'd very much like to know.

I look at Vera: I'd like to know too. She gave me a signal in the kitchen earlier on that I wasn't to ask where she'd been, a signal that was also a promise that she'd tell me later.

I'll find out, just you wait, warns my mother. She smiles as she says this: Vera is supposed to pack it in now. But Vera can't pack it in, she has to fan the flames anew. Fathers slaughtering their children because some god or other tells them to do so, she says, that's not the sole preserve of the ancient Greeks:

128

Abraham was quite willing to kill his own son just because God commanded him to do it.

My grandmother shudders from top to toe, she covers the challah with her napkin, a loaf of Sabbath bread, its cut end meek and white, she has to protect it, please don't quarrel, she begs her daughter. Her lovely food, the lovely Sabbath.

My mother bursts out laughing. And do you really think your mother's going to excuse Abraham just because he's a Jew. Believe me, if I'd been Sarah I'd have chucked him out before he ever had a chance to touch my son, I'd never even have married him in the first place. My mother shoots sharp glances in all directions, they cut through the air above the table, we keep our heads well down.

My father fixes his eyes on me. It's my responsibility now. He can't think of any other solution. I'll smother the fire at the table with my excoriated pages on the little infanta and her even littler dwarf. I've written an essay too, and this time I didn't get an F, I got an F+. They laugh with relief and seize on my dreadful mark.

F+, there's no such thing. My mother shakes her head. What on earth is the point, such nonsense. Typical Bobbi, says Vera cheerfully. And I can see him in front of me, praising my sister and holding my red-spattered essay in his hand. I don't tell them this, it completely shatters me. My mother rests her hand on mine and tells them about my Maths test: I scored an A. Algebra and geometry are stable systems, I can move around in them as freely as I like. My father gives a slow nod of the head and turns the corners of his mouth down to show his approval. I don't like him doing this.

Fania's got that from Julius, says my grandmother, her eyes sparkling with pride and delight.

There's a second man at our table and I have something good in common with him. Who's Julius, I want to know.

We can count ourselves lucky if that's *all* she's got from him, says my mother with a bitter laugh. My grandmother falls silent. The blow has hit home, and I feel it too without knowing what it's for.

My father carries on eating, slowly but steadily shovelling in the food. He mustn't get in a state or his stomach will tighten up, he needs to conserve his energy so that he can eat away in peace, his womenfolk are otherwise engaged, I've taken them off his hands, he methodically mashes his potatoes, a golden-yellow flowerbed takes shape on his plate, he gives it a good raking then waters it with dark-brown gravy.

Go on then, tell her who Julius is, says my mother to her mother, grinning unexpectedly. She is grinning in exactly the same way that she grinned earlier on when talking about 'that shameless rat' Hainichen, and now my sister is grinning too, and my grandmother encourages these cheeky dinner-table grins: she sits straight down, uncovers the Sabbath bread with her left hand and, blushing happily, declares that Julius was Alma's father.

Your former husband you mean, says my mother to her mother as if her version were incorrect. My grandmother is cross, her brief delight at the presence of her husband at our table instantly swept aside by her daughter. Anyway, Alma, your father, that's who he was, Julius Glitzer. My grandmother presents him to us in her upraised hands.

We've got a grandfather have we, says Vera, so where is he. We don't know, says my mother quickly before her mother can reply.

So he was murdered, says Vera. Amazing the way she says it, the way it simply pops out of her mouth, as though she were just talking about Agamemnon and not about her mother's father.

I don't know, says Hedwig Glitzer. All of a sudden my

130

grandmother is a wife, and I notice for the first time that she doesn't wear a wedding ring even though she'd have every right to wear one. He's gone, declares my mother with a tone of finality, he'd gone before any of that happened. I don't ask about the ring.

So you got an F+, says my father, smiling at me, I imagine that's better than an F.

No idea, I reply, I think it's just a stupid joke on Wilhelm Bobbenberg's part, he shouldn't have bothered. Vera instantly leaps to her Bobbi's defence. That's exactly it, she exclaims, you haven't got Bobbi's point, Fania – and I can already taste the bitter humiliation she's about to dish out to me. He gave you an F+ because your essay's right off the scale, I mean honestly, Fania, the way you spell, you know very well yourself it sort of exceeds an F.

That's quite enough, says my mother indignantly, putting a protective hand on my arm, and my eyes want to tip a torrent of salty rain all over the wasteland of potatoes that my father is busily tending on his plate, I'm determined not to cry, my mother and my sister exchange pleading looks. Fania's spelling isn't all that bad, the plus next to the F means exactly that: it isn't *horrendously* bad, says my mother; she is desperately trying to build some confidence, and suddenly Vera's completely on her side, that's just what I meant, if you'd only let me finish what I was saying; my sister – making up for wounds received – is feasting on my misery; the table starts to sway, I am somewhere else altogether, a camel is carrying us through the desert, at every step its flat feet stretch out across countless grains of sand, its bulging lips pluck green beans from a wasteland of potatoes, its long-lashed eyes throw sideways glances at the circling horizon. What I mean is that content-wise Fania's sort of brilliant, cries Vera in my direction, that's

131

what Bobbi was trying to convey, he was saying there's no right mark for an essay like yours, Fania, just as there's no such mark as F+, of course the plus is a positive thing.

Good, then everything's sorted out, says my father all of a sudden into the glaring desert sun. He has finished, he leans back in his chair and wipes his mouth with his napkin, his plate is empty.

Plus or minus, no matter which, we need to start doing dictations again. My mother looks dejected. And as for you, Paul – her eyelids start flickering – you've done lots of business you said, we can use the money.

The big moment has arrived. My mother has grasped the nettle, she no longer wants to have to hide her house-buying plans from him. But my father is never in any hurry to find out about secrets. On the one hand fair enough, on the other hand he'll hear all about it soon enough – soon enough for his liking at any rate; whatever it is, his wife will be wanting something from him, effort at the very least and in most cases money too.

D'you have something in mind, he asks her, are we going to have visitors or would you like to go out; he puts his knife and fork together and takes his cigarette case out of his trouser pocket; my mother quickly manufactures a smile, oh yes, Paul, let's have a night out, let's go and see Chérie Grell at the Bar Celona, we bumped into him the other day, Fania and I.

You saw Chérie Grell, yells Vera, why you and not me, and her eyes latch onto my face like limpets to suck up any last remains of my sighting of this strange creature, Chérie Grell the artiste, the cellar-bar transvestite, I saw him, so she's seeing me as him, the man in drag.

Chérie, look, there's Chérie Grell, exclaimed my mother. We were standing in Herta Tolle's fish shop, she was dressed from her neck to her wooden clogs in white rubber, her wet face was covered in scales, behind her misshapen back big fat fish and little thin fish were swimming around in four yellow-tiled tanks, as yellow as Herta Tolle's sparse hair.

What can I get you, Frau Schiefer, said Herta Tolle, her mouth all wet, in her hand an enormous gutting knife. A fish flapped its tail behind her, drops of water flew through the air. Her customers took fright, but not Frau Tolle. Stop yer splashing, you'll get yer turn.

Suddenly all agitated and wanting Frau Tolle to start descaling the fish, my mother hurriedly told her she wanted twenty herrings for frying and pickling, not too big, then grabbed my hand, called over her shoulder that she'd be back in a jiffy, rushed outside, and threw her arms round a total stranger.

The man had a bald head, a large stomach and an embarrassed smile. I looked him over mistrustfully. My mother introduced me to him. His eyes lit up. My youngest, she explained, then turning to me she said, Fania, you remember don't you, we've told you about the nightclub, the Bar Celona, this is Chérie, Chérie Grell, yes Chérie, I'm so sorry, I'm afraid I don't know your real name. And all shiny with sweat the man put his large puddingy hand in mine and spoke his name in a soft cracked voice: Arthur Pampuschke, he said. I gave a curtsy.

Vera is wallowing in a sea of longing: I want to experience some life for a change, just take me with you to the Bar Celona.

Oh Vera my darling, says my mother imploringly, your parents don't wish to deprive you of anything, we'll let both of you experience whatever you like, we really do love you, but you'll have to wait two more years at least. My mother takes a cigarette from her husband's cigarette case, you're still so young, Vera, she strikes a match and puffs out a cloud of smoke, you've got your whole life in front of you.

I want my life to start *now*. Promise me that afterwards you'll tell me every single detail of what it was like at the Bar Celona. Promise.

I always tell the pair of you every last detail, says my mother.

Vera pulls a face and takes herself a cigarette, now she too is raiding my father's cigarette case. He doesn't notice.

Does your father even know yet that you've started smoking. My mother laughs apprehensively.

Mammy lets me, blabs Vera.

Then we'd better increase your pocket money, says my father.

Fania's too, my mother is making sure I'm not left out, and while we're on the subject, Paul, I'm broke and Mummy gave us sixty marks.

My grandmother brings the vanilla pudding and the chocolate sauce. For you, Paul, she says. My father loves this kind of pudding. He puts some in a little bowl and gets up from the table, keeping hold of his trousers as he does so: he loosened them while at table, his stomach's hurting, he carries his pudding over to his armchair. His voice comes back to us from there, thin and shadowy.

What's up, Alma. Sitting with his back to us he can't bear another moment's delay.

My mother stands up from the table and walks over to him.

It's good and it's bad, Paul, Hainichen wants to sell the house.

I thought so, says my father, who always knows everything already. He swallows his first spoonful of pudding. I saw the signboard outside. Having an extremely nervous disposition he is careful not to be taken by surprise.

Just as I thought, says my grandmother to her daughter.

What do you mean, just as you thought. Did *you* realise about the signboard.

How much does he want.

Fifty-six thousand, looks like it's gone up a bit in the meantime, but I'll get him to bring it down again.

The sum is out of the bag, and claims its place in our living room. My father shrugs his shoulders; he's holding his pudding bowl in his hands. It's not a bad price, Paul, the land alone will soon be worth more than that. It would be lovely, sighs my father, but I don't have the money; if I did I'd buy it for you, Alma. His smile is an iron barrier, his wife can't advance a single step further and turns away in dismay. Paul, she says slowly and insistently, Paul, we should buy it. Her voice is that of a prophet who knows his advice will be ignored.

Who else has she spoken to about it, he wants to know.

Nobody. Erich and Elsa Kupsch have talked to me, they want to lend us some money.

How much, he asks. He knows what amounts might be involved, and none will be sufficient.

Perhaps ten thousand, she says. We can talk to the bank, we could raise a mortgage, Mummy can make us a loan. What about Lotti, cries my grandmother. Certainly not Lotti, says my mother, she's too mean, but Olga or Betty or Wilma might be willing, poor Ruchla, nebbish, has almost nothing to her name, anyway we must leave no stone unturned, we have to make our minds up quickly or else it'll be too late. Or else. The words gouge their way through the room leaving a furrow behind them.

Hainichen claims that Frau Schmalstück has offered him sixty thousand, I think he's just trying to put pressure on us, though it's possible of course, says my mother.

135

My father interrupts her: so you've already spoken to Hainichen as well.

Paul, what's the matter with you. Yes, he stopped me in the stairwell earlier on, before you got home.

Earlier on, repeats Vera, rushing once again to take my father's side, *when* earlier on.

Good God, earlier on. My mother is puffing vehemently on her cigarette, earlier on, that's all, before the pair of you arrived, you weren't even there, Vera, you were somewhere else, so what does it matter to you when I spoke to Hainichen. Don't get so worked up. Vera has turned pale but my mother cold-shoulders her, she's not important right now, what's important is to keep hold of her husband, a heavy stone that longs for the peace of the abyss.

What about the extra costs, Alma, says my father, this beautiful villa is a complete wreck, we'd have to spend a stack of money on it.

Hainichen spends nothing on it and just pockets our rent, says my mother rebelliously. He lays his head back and slowly, doggedly repeats his point: don't forget the extra costs, he sighs, I can't afford them any more.

We all stay silent.

A smile flickers across his face. I'm not up to it any more.

My mother glances across at us with furrowed brow. No point trying now. Don't press him. Not now. And faced with his nakedness she lowers her head.

My grandmother gets up from the table and quietly begins to clear the plates away with Vera and me helping her. The three of us go into the kitchen, my grandmother washes and Vera and I dry, we put the crockery away in the cupboard, the cutlery in the drawer, the saucepans remain on the stove. We sit down at the kitchen table.

136

I don't think he can do it, says my grandmother, he won't take the risk, Alma might possibly bring him round, but I don't think so. I said to her back then that he's too weak, you mustn't involve him, you'll endanger us all. She wipes the table with a damp cloth. His energy's completely exhausted; there's far less at stake this time, but he's just not up to it any more, what a crying shame, the house and the plot it's on would be such a good investment.

We decide to go to bed and leave the two of them alone in the living room. We can lie in tomorrow: every other week Vera and I don't have any lessons on a Saturday; at some point Saturday school will be abolished completely, says Vera, but it'll be after our time.

No sooner has my head hit the pillow than I fall asleep.

I float away with unknown memories echoing around me. A prince comes up to me, a prince that isn't me, and wants another kiss from the sea. Autumn leaves come rushing along from the west and lament the springtime of their final days. At that the tree rises up and uproots the earth. But I am lying in my parents' bed, I have cut the soles of my feet to ribbons by dint of running, my flesh is all gaping wounds in which all sorts of things that I've trodden on have become embedded, there are hazelnuts from the path, they don't burst open but keep their secret, there are teeth from my comb, they turn into worms, my foot hurts, my poor foot, I roam through the copious hair of the night and recover my senses in the depths of sleep, I recognise myself, and stumble and fall in front of the blackboard on which it is all written. When I wake up, the words have disappeared.

Turning up for breakfast in the sun room my parents are amorous and high-spirited, and we are filled with new hope. Both garden areas are resplendently green, the trees and bushes have bountifully opened their leaves, the lilac with its large green flowerheads reminds us that it will soon be in full bloom. We don't ever want to leave this place.

How did you actually come to live in this house, asks Vera, crunching her teeth into her toasted bread roll. On the low coffee table lies a pink tablecloth with hem-stitched edges that I made myself out of Gminder linen, a material with a very pronounced weave. In our craft class at school we were all given a small sample of Gminder linen and told to get three metres of it to bring to our next lesson. At home my mother repeated the words again and again: Gminder linen – so typically German. She hammed it up and I laughed because that's what she wanted, but I didn't enjoy it. She went into town with me where a saleswoman in the fabric department of a large store laid out several bales of fine and coarse Gminder linen for us and I chose a fine-woven one in pink. The saleswoman skilfully pushed the heavy roll of material away from her along the counter while she measured out four and a half metres: I wanted to sew some napkins as well to go with the two-by-three-metre tablecloth.

Sure you're not taking on too much, darling, asked my mother while the saleswoman waited with her huge scissors at the ready.

No, I'll manage alright. I tried to look harmless, casual, sort of normal. I was ill at ease. It was the way my mother wrinkled her nose at the words 'Gminder linen'.

That'll be it then, she nodded, and the saleswoman laid her long rule back on the fabric and started cutting.

I can't do sewing at all, I heard my mother say. The saleswoman took no notice. My mother didn't give up. Do you like sewing, doing all those little stitches gets on my nerves. The saleswoman didn't oblige with one of those friendly shop-assistant smiles. But then, my mother continued, you work here and that's completely different, my daughter's doing it for school and says she enjoys it, don't you, Fania, you really like doing it. I nodded. Or are you only doing it because the craft teacher wants you to, that wouldn't be a good enough reason, if you don't want to do it you don't have to.

But I *do* want to.

Gminder linen – my mother rolled the words around in her mouth. You like the material, Fania, that's what matters, but how much is it a metre and what's the discount for quantity, well we'll see won't we.

Turning her mouth down and deliberately not saying a word the saleswoman handed my mother the fabric and the bill to take to the cashier and turned away, giving us just a glimpse of her disparaging smile.

That saleswoman won't talk to us, remarked my mother in a voice loud enough for all the customers in our vicinity to hear. Thank you very much, miss, she shouted to the assistant, now three counters away. I took her arm. I wanted to get her out of there. She snatched her arm away. Pesky ponim. That's what she said. She said it out loud. Who except for us would understand what 'pesky ponim' meant. Nobody.

The assistant turned round: did you want something else.

Leave her be, I begged.

Let go of me, she hissed, let go of me, Fania, stop holding my arm, your mother doesn't have to take this sort of treatment these days.

Other women were looking at us, greedy for more. In that case I don't want the material any more. I hoped this would stop my mother. The saleswoman was walking back towards us.

What nonsense, Fania, you were so pleased with it. None of her words were aimed at me. She was focusing all her attention on the saleswoman, she could see that other saleswomen and

139

customers were converging on her. She was raring for a fight; the issue wasn't worth it and nor was her antagonist.

The saleswoman had planted herself back behind the fabric table. What did you call me? What am I? That word you used, I heard that word as clear as anything.

It's a word you certainly aren't acquainted with, replied my mother with such a cheeky expression on her face that for a moment I felt quite elated.

A pesky Pole you called me, screamed the assistant, I heard it clear as anything, pesky Pole, I don't have to put up with that sort of thing, not from the likes of you.

You ought to be grateful, but if you really want to know, what I actually said was 'ponim', not 'Pole'. She took my arm at this point, wanting to leave. Everything was alright now so far as she was concerned: she'd given vent to her feelings and that was the end of it.

And what does that mean, you just tell me, I'm really curious to know, said the saleswoman getting ever more worked up. She looked around at the other women enlisting their support. Come on, why don't you say. Just say that word, unless of course it's an insult of some sort. And although I called out It means face, it means face, my mother exclaimed with a dogged expression that My daughter hasn't the least idea.

It's Jewish, somebody said. It's Yiddish, that is. The voice piped up from somewhere in the crowd. Its owner seemed to know about these things. I couldn't make out who it was – but you could tell from her voice that all things Yiddish were repellent to her. All the same I was thrilled to hear the word, to hear it from someone else's mouth and not just our own. For the first time ever it had come to me from the world outside and was now winging its way up into the high-up dome of the department store. It hit my mother like a stone. She'd worked as a salesgirl herself, she screamed, and I enjoyed being a salesgirl, unlike you, we treated our customers differently and people liked coming to us, believe you me, and they went away happy, that was in the days when this department store still belonged to the family that founded it and would still own it if people hadn't taken it away from them, and you know that very well. My mother had addressed this to everyone. Her voice was shaking, but not out of fear. The phalanx of women remained silent.

Let's go, I said quietly. My mother nodded.

A discount, said the saleswoman, she wanted a discount. This isn't a bazaar for God's sake. The women murmured their agreement. We're in Germany here, not among cheats and crooks.

My mother wheeled around. Bazaar, did you say bazaar.

Her voice had darkened. These women, who didn't really mean anything to her, were party to a terrible hurt. I didn't dare look at my mother. I took her hand. We hurried to the tills. They might attack us from behind, I felt them breathing down our necks, all those bovine faces, all those huge scissors ready to hand on the bales of fabric. I took a green banknote out of my mother's purse and handed it to the cashier. Her face was still jerking in the taxi. A thought suddenly occurred to her: Have we gone and left the fabric behind? No, I kept hold of it. She squeezed my hand and quickly turned towards the window, she didn't want me to see her tears, I saw her quivering lips.

Where can I take you, asked the taxi driver.

You tell him, she sobbed, squeezing my hand again. I named our street. This was the first time I'd done so in a taxi. And I suddenly realised that I knew where we were, and knew the way home.

141

My grandmother found some pink cotton in her sewing basket that matched the material and placed the cotton reel in my hand. Lovely fine material, she said approvingly, Gminder linen, nicely woven, just the stuff for hand-sewing, I often used it in the old days, I even used it for a little pinny for Alma when she first went to school, do you remember, Alma, you used to love wearing it, come and look, Fania, this is how you pull the threads out. Threads needed to be pulled out along the entire length and breadth of the two-by-three-metre piece of material and a feeling of immense satisfaction flooded through me. Channels ran straight as a die through the finely woven linen, narrow channels with tightly packed cross-threads. Using a needle and pink cotton I then caught three of these slender threads at a time and looped them into tiny bunches forming a three-fingered shin. The Hebrew letter shin. Three flames, representing the number three hundred. Catch three threads, pass the pink cotton around them, form a loop, tighten it carefully – after doing this three times I had already reached the number nine hundred, and thus it continued along the narrow channels of threads: one thousand nine hundred, two thousand one hundred, three thousand six hundred, nine thousand nine hundred, fifteen thousand three hundred. I wanted to be rich, I wanted to have a hundred thousand marks in the bank when I was older, I'd be able to live off the interest, modestly but very comfortably, I knew this from my arithmetic lessons at primary school. The teacher, Frau Löblich, had a beaming, dimpled face, and explained it all to us girls. Women needed to know how to handle money, she said. We were doing percentages, we sat at our tables in twos and fours, Annegret had her hands folded, we were always supposed to keep our hands folded on top of the table, I refused to do it, it looked like praying at church, and then Frau Löblich stood by the blackboard. Now if you put your one hundred thousand marks into a savings account and get a good rate of interest, let's say seven and a half per cent a month – she drew a line on the board with her chalk then wrote the amount underneath it – that yields the agreeable sum of seven thousand five hundred marks.

I saw at once that this would enable me to feed me and my parents, my grandmother, my sister, my entire family, and also that there'd be no need to get married, a woman could work and earn her own money, and with a bit of care she could save one hundred thousand marks within a few years in order to live comfortably and pleasantly off the interest.

I wove all these considerations into the tablecloth and gave it to my mother as a birthday present together with seven napkins. She was pleased, so I made her an identical set of a hem-stitched tablecloth plus seven napkins in white. My daughter made them for me, she said at every opportunity to Aunt Mimi and Aunt Mimi's lover, to Rosa Freundlich, to Herr Bohn the vegetable man who delivered our purchases to the house, to Frau Küting from next door when she came over for tea. Elsa Kupsch washed and ironed these two table-cloths with special care, and one of them was always put on the table for the Theresienstadt Circle, together with the seven matching napkins. Lotti, Wilma, Betty, Emilie, Olga and Ruchla felt the fabric with expert fingers. Gminder linen, they nodded with satisfaction, examining the tiny rows of hem-stitching with their now highly presbyopic eyes. Your daughter made this did she, Alma, even though Fania's such a wild child. Am I wild. This is news to me. I often feel so hot, that's all.

On this particular Saturday morning the pink tablecloth is lying on the table in the sun room, we've put out the pink crockery, my grandmother gave it to her daughter and son-in-law as a present last Christmas: side plates, tall cups and an imposing big-bellied coffee pot with a rosebud on its lid. Our table is small, and not having any other side tables we've brought in the two stools from the kitchen and covered them with white napkins as there's not enough room on the table for all the delicious things we're having – boiled eggs, several different kinds of cheese, a large piece of calves' liver sausage with little chunks of liver in it, prawn salad, various preserves bottled the previous summer – raspberry jelly, strawberry jam, apple and cherry conserve – plus honey and a golden-yellow lump of butter straight from the churn, and finally toasted bread rolls, pumpernickel and the challah left over from the previous evening.

My grandmother and I are already dressed: my grandmother would never sit at table in her nightdress, and I'm going in the garden after breakfast, I want to dig, I've got a real yen to do digging today, I want to push my hands deep into the earth. My sister has wrapped herself in a woollen blanket, my parents are in their dressing gowns, sitting next to each other today. The sun is shining playfully through the windows. The pattern of the leaves turns its light into dancing lacework.

How did it happen back then, how did you ever come across this house, asks Vera. Her question isn't a question, it's the familiar key that unlocks our parents' story and how they managed to survive it all, a wonderful story that my life-history and Vera's will never be able to touch, by comparison with our parents we will never really have lived.

We've told you so often, my mother begins. Before we ever came to live in this beautiful villa with its beautiful gardens *so* many things happened, so many unbelievable things. She takes her husband's hand.

It began, says my father looking across at his mother-in-law, when I moved in as your lodger; I was twenty, my mother had just died, and I liked you right from the start.

My grandmother nodded in his direction. She often remains silent. The memory of it all seems to strike her dumb. Without her daughter and her son-in-law she'd never have got through it; it would have been easier for them if they hadn't had her. This weighs on my grandmother. She carries the burden of it all the time.

We found the previous lodger's party badge on top of the wardrobe, it was hard getting rid of it, and then you moved in, recounts my mother, her eyes resting on her husband. We didn't know anything about you or whether you were just like the others, and I didn't know anything about you, adds my father, I stayed in my room and I sang with the window open, and then, adds my mother, the neighbours rang our doorbell, they wanted to know which station we were listening to on the radio, but we didn't have a radio any more, we'd had to hand it in.

Listening to them I lose track of my questions. Where did they have to take their radio, who was there to take it off them. How come their neighbours thought the Glitzers still had a radio to listen to. People never gave it a thought, obviously they knew we were Jews, they never gave it a thought. I am faced with my parents' story. They anticipate all my questions. We'll tell you everything there is to tell.

I kiss your hand, Madame, and dream it was your mouth: my father sings, the windowpanes vibrate in their frames. Richard Tauber, says my grandmother dreamily. He sang better than Richard Tauber. He was one as well, says my grandmother; was he, asks my mother; yes, says my father, he was one as well; well I never knew that he was one, says my mother, is that

145

really true; of course he was, says my grandmother, trust me; one what, one what, asks Vera through gritted teeth, she's all on edge, she hates it when the story takes unexpected turns; a Jew, I say; ah, says Vera letting her butter-and-prawn-salad-laden roll hover in front of her wide-open mouth, Richard Tauber a Jew, how on earth do you know, Fania, and I reply When they talk like that what else could he be.

That's my girl, exclaims my mother excitedly, she reaches out her hand to me, palm upwards, and I blush, I blush with pride. That was Jewish, I was being Jewish, I *am* Jewish, my mother has seen that I'm Jewish, I may not have curly black hair like her, but I'm Jewish all the same, it came out of me just like that, it's within me as it's within her, it's within me just the same. I am Jewish because of her. I don't want to be more Jewish than Vera, I just want to be Jewish; I need Vera, I mustn't lose her, I need to stay close to her so that we can sleep next to one another at night. My sister was there first. She wants me to look the other way when she quarrels with her mother, no more harm must be done to our mother, strong and fearless though she is, it would kill her, or me, or both of us. Vera doesn't seem to mind that I and I alone am my mother's Jewish daughter. This gift from my mother is one I can't share with Vera, and I wouldn't want to even if I could, I need it all to myself, my mother's words glow all around me like ruby-red drops of pomegranate juice, I'm her Jewish daughter, I want to rejoice and be glad and not think of my sister as being in the shadows.

You'd fallen in love with me, says my mother.

Yes, says my father, crying and reaching out for her hand. My mother cries too, her tears cascading to the floor in front of him. He went through that for her. She went through that with him. Love and guilt combined in a place that no longer exists.

My grandmother cries and says what she otherwise never says: Oh God, she says, oh God, the poor children.

Vera and I are true dependants, we are dependent on this story and shall bear witness to it all the days of our solitude.

My mother laughs, we're crying because we're so happy, says my father.

Vera and I sit there before them crying and laughing and it's such hard work that it's as if we were being paid to do it. It's always the same film. My mother's the narrator. It's a big, big story that no one can really believe; when people hear your parents' story, says my mother, they say Go on, that can't be true. It ought to be told to someone who could make a film out of it, she reckons; it would become a Hollywood blockbuster, just as beautiful as *Gone with the Wind* – even more beautiful, adds my father, because in our case they get each other in the end. God protect us, says my grandmother. As if it could happen again with a different ending. In reality our parents never talk to anyone about it. Only to us.

We weren't allowed to marry.

Why not.

Because of the race laws.

There they go again!

You didn't know that we weren't allowed to marry. No I didn't know. I was afraid to tell you. Yes. In case you left me. Then I came home from the shop, Diamants', toys and prams, I liked working in the shop, they gave me a free hand, the other sales assistants were grown women, unmarried ladies, and I was still more or less a child.

My mother, best pupil at the school yet without a school-leaving certificate; my mother, the youngest girl in the shop, dresses the windows; my mother sells the stock that wouldn't ever sell; my mother gives shop-soiled toys to poor children in

147

the locality; my mother gives advice to married couples, young women, already pregnant – for them quite legal. Don't buy this brand-new sporty pram, it's much too expensive, buy last year's model, I'll give it to you half price. My mother, the customers' favourite salesgirl, my mother with her notice in her hand, my mother taking the Diamant sisters to the station. There's a sign on the door of the shop: Temporarily closed: business transferred into Aryan ownership.

I rang the bell and you opened the door, it was normally Mummy and suddenly it was you standing there, I was frightened to death, I thought they must have taken her away, and you gave me a hug, I couldn't let you see how scared I was, I wanted to go into the kitchen, I needed to know whether they'd taken Mummy away, and you said, I said Dearest little one, I know everything. I'd come out of my room and gone into the kitchen, I said Frau Glitzer I love your daughter and your daughter loves me, what's wrong, why won't your daughter marry me, tell me the truth. And then – says my father to his mother-in-law – you told me.

But what, what. I want to hear the word. The bad word. The special word. The precious word.

That we're Jews, says my grandmother, and her daughter cries.

Go and make some more coffee, Paul.

What's the time.

Don't we need to do some shopping.

The shops will be shutting soon.

We've got everything.

It's so cosy.

Go on, carry on with the story.

Make some fresh coffee, Paul, and bring some cigarettes with you.

148

I think we've run out.

Don't do this to me.

I need chocolate. I've eaten two rolls and an egg and calves' liver sausage on challah, three slices altogether – a spicy, meaty taste on mild-flavoured bread. I wanted to go in the garden really and do some digging after breakfast, but I'm still sitting here. Everything will happen again, everything will repeat itself, I shall be tremblingly apprehensive that something is going to happen that never happened to them in the story they tell us, I shall fear its advent and feverishly wish it upon us so that at last it may come to an end. When it comes, I will know. I won't want or need to know anything else, and at last I shall know where my life starts, where I begin.

My father goes into the kitchen to make more coffee, my grandmother goes with him. Vera also gets up and goes out.

My mother and I stay sitting in the sun room. I watch her. Her eyes dart across my face, I'm not what she is looking for. I take her apart and examine her carefully. My mother is racing through an exuberant jungle of memories, they are closing above her head, she will find a path through them, it's always the same path that she must then clear and clarify before she can walk along it in full view of her daughters with her head held high. She notices me and smiles. I have caught her in the midst of her preparations. She knows I've been rummaging through her mind.

I smile back. She doesn't want me to see the path. She runs her hand through her hair, through her black curls, I climb out from under her skirt, we're not alone any more.

My grandmother reappears in the sun room carrying a saucepan of water, she has put on her apron and is using it to carry potatoes which she's going to peel for our lunch, she sits herself down in her armchair, moving it a bit further into the sunlight.

My sister comes in and puts a bar of milk chocolate on my lap. Where did you get that, I ask dumbfounded, and it's this dumbfoundedness that conveys my gratitude: I don't know where she got the chocolate from, I just need it. I saved it for you, she says. I greedily rip the packaging off and take a bite, hard lumps of chocolate dig into my tongue and my palate and make my cheeks bulge, no one takes any notice, it doesn't matter any more, saliva escapes from my lips which I can barely manage to close, sweetness fills my entire mouth like a balm.

Vera puts cigarettes on the table, two unopened packets with twenty-four cigarettes in each. Yours, asks my mother. Vera nods. My father comes in with coffee but without cigarettes. Ah, what a good thing that we've got another smoker in the family, says my mother, and my father looks at Vera's two full packets, what a blessing.

Have you ever smoked, Vera asks my grandmother; she nods and is suddenly twenty years younger. I broke the habit specially for them, she says. For her daughter and her son-in-law.

Cigarettes were so expensive, says my mother, and the cigarettes we didn't exchange for food were all saved for Paul, let me have a puff, Paul.

The curtain opens again, my sister and I sit there expectantly, Vera with a cigarette, me with chocolate. We are separate yet together. We're not looking at one another. At this particular juncture neither must mean anything to the other. We won't be able to maintain this state of affairs for very long. Both of us know this. Free of the fear of having stolen from each other, free of the fear of having to kill or be killed, each of us is on her own. This is why we aren't looking at one another. We don't move. We're breathing quietly. What we are

150

supposing to be life is perhaps a form of death. I'd like to ask Vera whether everything's okay, we're sitting in creaking wicker chairs in the sun room, the sun is shining, are you there, are you breathing alright, is your heart beating, is your hair growing, I'm choking on my chocolate, the sugar's biting my neck.

And then when everything was over, says my mother, two ashtrays are cram-full, it's nearly half past two in the afternoon, I've eaten the last strip of chocolate, your father brought me to the front of this house and said Would you like to live in this lovely villa here, and I said Paul, you're meshugge, how could you ever manage it in a posh area like this, and go on, Paul, you tell your daughters . . . What's the time, we've been sitting here talking for five hours, we must just quickly tell you the rest of the story. Anyway that Schmalstück woman who'd denounced your parents for 'defiling the German race', she lived here, and your father saw to it that she was arrested, and we were allocated to this villa as main tenants by the British.

What a victory, what a triumph, much too scantly and speedily recounted. My mother's got a slight migraine, my father's got mild stomach-ache, my grandmother's short of breath, Vera and I are completely exhausted, my arms and legs feel like lead, my head is empty. I do still remember that I wanted to ask a question that I thought was important, it probably wasn't important at all, if it had been important I would surely have remembered it, and anyway I couldn't cope with the answer any more. Vera is still just about capable of opening her mouth, but her lips make the words stumble. Frau Schmalstück, says Vera; my mother looks up, there are dark shadows round her left eye, she can't take any more, least of all questions about Frau Schmalstück, Vera can see this but behaves as if she can't, she takes on my mother's pained expression, not so much as a deception but more as a disguise enabling her to get close to my mother without being perceived as an enemy. Both are resting the soles of their feet on the edge of the low table, both have slumped back in their armchairs.

How come old Schmalstück is still living here, asks Vera, pushing every word out through her lips without moving her jaw. My mother replies. We're the main tenants, she says, we've got it in writing, Hainichen inherited the house and let the attic flat to Frau Schmalstück.

I thought she was arrested, says Vera.

My mother nods – but carefully, to ensure that her head doesn't fall off. She was released the following day, allegedly for lack of evidence.

That's enough, says my father, go and lie down, Alma, he's concerned about her, I'll close the curtains; no, she says, crying, I don't want to be alone, and he leans over her: her husband, a motherly father, puts his hand on her forehead, she stretches out her legs so that he can massage the soles of her feet; my grandmother brings her daughter two migraine pills and a glass of water. They're so big and so bitter, she wails, he talks quietly to her, holding the pills in his hand, he's to make them smaller, he cuts them into quarters with a knife, she watches him, now she has to swallow eight times instead of just twice, an unhappy child keeping its unhappiness on the go because of its infinite need to be comforted.

That evening in bed – we've already turned our reading lights off – I ask Vera where she went after school yesterday.

You must promise me you won't talk to *anyone* about it. I promise. Vera wants my word of honour, with knobs on. I give it to her. Silence reigns, the air buzzes with bluish-black attention.

I went to Hainichen's, she says with a dusty voice.

Hainichen's! How can Vera have been there. Why. What for.

Do you want me to put a light on, Fania, are you scared, I shouldn't have told you.

No light, I say.

Why was Vera at Hainichen's. Because we want to buy the house, is that why.

That's one reason, yes, says Vera. Her words have a hollow ring. She's making no great effort to pull the wool over my eyes. When I came out of school the other day Hainichen was standing there with his truck. She falls silent.

And what did he want of you, my voice has a brusque, hurt ring to it, it's my mother speaking, at any rate it's her voice asking the question – sharp, mistrustful, hurt.

Vera laughs quietly, a laugh of excitement. I don't like her laugh, she's using it to inveigle me into something.

Well, you know, Hainichen's been flirting with me for quite a time now. I've not responded, obviously.

Obviously, I say, once again it's my mother within me snapping at my sister. Vera mustn't go on, I can't bear it, but I have to know the truth. Vera could bring disaster on us all. It's dark, I'm lying under my bedcovers, I feel paralysed, Vera's voice is a snake darting about above my head, I must bite its head off. She has fallen silent. She's probably thinking about what she can tell me and what she can't. I have to know everything, she mustn't hide anything from me, she needn't tell me anything more, I already know everything. I'll have to pretend, she must go on talking, my voice mustn't betray my murderous rage. I let my mouth utter only two words.

What happened, I ask; it sounds quite harmless, my paralysis is easing, I can carry on talking in this kind of tone, my hatred is not detectable.

What do you mean, asks Vera.

I mean, what happened. What did he do to you. I find Hainichen utterly disgusting. He's a fat, greasy Nazi pig. Surely Vera thinks the same.

For goodness' sake, Fania, flirting's flirting, you can't exactly describe it, she says, but actually she's bursting to describe it very exactly, she's had an experience now, so now she can tell me all about it, she turns on to her side with her face towards me, I can feel her breath, I mustn't turn away, she'd spot my hatred. I can smell Hainichen in her mouth, he grabs hold of her with a grin, he's to let my sister go, Vera's enjoying it, I can see it exactly, she's on fire, she lets him kiss her, he bends her over backwards, now they're falling over, just as I thought, he's too fat to bend my sister backwards in an elegant sort of way, he's tearing Vera's clothes off, he's to stop it at once, he's tearing them to pieces, he's tearing Vera to pieces, my head falls to one side, what am I doing, what are they doing to me, I don't want to have to look, he's thrown himself on top of her, he's buried her beneath his vast bulk, where's Vera, I can't see her any more, there's one of her feet, sticking out between his podgy calves, is she still alive, yes indeed, she *is* still alive, she's moaning, I know her moaning, she's sitting on his fat, hairy stomach, he's a bristly pig, I know everything, I already know everything and Vera has only got as far as flirting, what on earth will I have to put up with later on. She says it was in the stairwell, that's impossible, people are coming and going in the stairwell all the time, ah there's Frau Schmalstück, choosing the right moment for once, and there's her lodger Sturmius Fraasch with his wooden leg, click-thud, click-thud: louder, louder still, I don't want to hear anything else, just this click-thud, click-thud, it's my heart beating, my mother mustn't come, not under any circumstances, I couldn't do this to her.

Vera says she went up the stairs in front of him, how far for goodness' sake, as far as our front door or all the way up to his place, I won't ask her that, I'll keep quiet and wait and not interrupt her, wasn't his wife there, come on, Fania, as if I'd go into his flat with him. She's lying, she's trying to spare me, too late, I've gone to pieces, I can't do anything. Perhaps Vera just chatted to him for a while, no harm in that.

She's carrying on with the story, she still hasn't finished, apparently she met him in the street once, that was a coincidence too, she was on her way to a dancing class, he was standing behind an advertising pillar and suddenly popped out on her. She gives a quick laugh, it gave me a real fright. How can she laugh, that wasn't a coincidence, it was an ambush. After the dancing class he brought me home, are you still listening to me, Fania. Did you go to the dancing class at all, I ask, and Vera giggles as if she were being tickled; to be honest no I didn't, but don't tell Mammy, in fact you mustn't tell Mammy *anything* about it. Within me my mother already knows, she's listening to the whole conversation, there's nothing I can do to stop her, but I mustn't let on to Vera: who else can Vera confide in besides me.

We went and had a slap-up meal.

Tears roll down from the corners of my eyes, it's dark, she can't see them, she'd only be able to tell – if at all – from my voice. I don't need to say anything else. Vera starts talking and just doesn't stop. They went to a French restaurant in Rappstrasse, near Grindelhof, she's beginning to know her way around, near where Aunt Mimi lives, she already *does* know her way around. And what about Bobbi, I ask, what does Bobbi have to do with it, she says, completely taken aback, she was just reeling off a list of all the food Hainichen had ordered. No prices were shown on my menu, Fania, I had the ladies' menu, and Hainichen speaks really good French. Scarcely believable, a coarse brute like him. Aren't you in love with Bobbi any more, I deliberately say Bobbi and not Herr Bobbenberg. Oh, Bobbi, says Vera, Bobbi's my German teacher, that's different, completely different. I like him and we respect each other, I'm his favourite pupil, that's all, but with Hermann, with Hainichen, it's different. I can't believe they're on first-name terms. So you call that man Hermann. My voice ought to be more indignant, I'm tired, what's happened to my murderous rage. We've moved on to first names, Fania, of course we have, though naturally he called me Fräulein Schiefer at first. Have you kissed each other; I can't not ask, and the fact they're on first-name terms makes the question easier, it might just have been a peck on the cheek. Vera is different somehow. Not the same as she is when she goes all weak at the knees over her romantic novels. She really has experienced something, something forbidden. But why with him, why with this swine of all people, why does she have to do this to us.

I'm floating down the river in a red oval rubber dinghy, the sides of the dinghy are so beautifully swollen, and Vera has given me a little push, her voice is lapping against the outside of my dinghy: who are we supposed to fall in love with, where on earth are there any Jewish men, we're not even in the Community because Mammy's against it, we'd be able to get to know some there. Vera's right, she's right isn't she, where are we supposed to get to know any Jews, other Jews, not just Aunt Lotti, Aunt Wilma, Aunt Betty, Aunt Ruchla, Aunt Olga and Aunt Emilie, young Jews, Jewish girls and Jewish boys, are there any at all in our neighbourhood, Esther Fingerhut and her little sister Miriam used to live in the white house at the end of the driveway but they moved away, Esther used to sit next to me at school until Year 3 and then they moved away.

They celebrated all the Jewish festivals, to please Esther they ate kosher, Esther took everything seriously, she only laughed out of embarrassment. We both cried when they separated us. Since then there've never been any Jews in our garden except Vera and me.

Or are we supposed to get to know absolutely no Jews at all, are we supposed to forget that we're Jewish; I run to the phone, my index finger is too big for the holes in the black dial. I force it into the two and can't get it out again, I'm bleeding, four four three zero six two, that's our number. My mother answers. Schiefer sounds exactly the same as Glitzer really. My mother can't make out what I said. Schiefer sounds just as Jewish as Glitzer, I say again. My mother has dropped the receiver, I'm dangling head downwards between heaven and earth. I'm looking for my name, I poke my index finger in amongst rolls of paper, they tumble all over the place. I can't read a word, I know them all. I pick up my school bag, I want to go, it's too light, there's something missing, I look around, there's my bag all over again, I pick it up and put the two bags together, their weight is familiar to me, where's Esther. You're talking in your sleep, says Vera; yes, to Esther, I murmur. She strokes my forehead, there were huge trees, very tall, standing amidst damp foliage, I started digging there, and under the ground I found a grey-lit room, a big room, its ceiling flat, its walls rough, bare concrete everywhere, heavy doors, no windows, where was the grey light coming from.

Sleep well, says Vera. I feel her lips on my closed eyes. They roll away.

157

Chapter Six

We're standing on the terrace waving, my mother, my grandmother, Vera and me, both leaves of the garden gate are open. The old rotting gate is not reassuring. When it's closed you can see it would be easy to get in from outside, anyone could do it, a dog, a passing stray; I'd like to have a dog by my side, he's big and he growls and he pushes his nose against the back of my knee. My father is driving his car out of its wooden shed, along the driveway below us and out of the garden gate, he sounds his horn by way of goodbye, we wave, he brakes, gets out, and there he is again. We'd said our goodbyes and he's already back. It was a dress rehearsal. My father shuts the garden gate from outside, putting both hands through holes in the decrepit wire netting to tie the two halves of the gate together with a short length of thick rope to make sure they can't come open again. We watch him as he shuts us in, he smiles up at us. The engine's running, the car is trembling quietly. He straightens up and blows us kisses over the fence and up onto the terrace, we blow him kisses too, kisses waft to and fro, the four from him bring him sixteen in return. Goodbye, we shout, drive carefully, look after yourself; neither he nor we would ever at this point say 'ta-ta' or 'so long' or just 'see you' – or even 'bye' without the 'good' on the front: any such abbreviated farewell would be read by my father as an omen portending some imminent loss. Goodbye. Good-bye. It is a solemn vow whereby all four of us are sworn to live our as yet unlived lives together. After a clearly defined period of time we shall be reunited, we shall arise again for one another, we can influence the omnipotent powers of existence by reciting both syllables of the word Goodbye. If we chanced not to be reunited at the end of this coming week we would still have said everything it was necessary to say, 'Goodbye', and we would be reunited somewhere else instead. To live on without being reunited would not be tantamount simply to death but to being ripped to pieces, no one would be what they previously were but instead would be a disembodied fragment belonging nowhere, a word so damaged as to be indecipherable, an elision within a sentence. My father inscribed it in my skin with his finger, I can feel the three phalanges of his little finger encircle my wrist, I've grown too big for it now; that's how I used to hold onto you when you were little, he says, really tight. My tiny hand completely disappeared in his enormous one, and in addition he curled his little finger round my wrist, round the soft little arm of his youngest daughter. His prisoner, for safety's sake. He had slammed the bolt home. The pain was part of the reason he let go of me in the end, enabling me to run away from him, wailing and rubbing my wrist.

Not so tight, Paul, said my mother, Fania's still so little. He immediately felt deeply sorry, caught up with me with a couple of his long strides and bending his face right down to me from on high he apologised, Pappy only did it because he loves his little Fania so much, then he quarrelled about it with my mother: it wasn't too tight, he was being really careful, Fania's so wild, a proper little tomboy, just like you, she's uncontainable, the same as you are. He needed to watch over me, he said, he could see me lost, smashed, broken, destroyed, damaged; I was running across the grass to the sandpit, I tripped on a clump of turf, not a disaster, just a minor fall, a brief delay in my journey to great fun, I picked myself up and lurched and stumbled on my way, drawn forwards by the weight of my heavy head, there in front of me the source of all the fun. The sandpit. Isn't she delicious, she said to him, our sweet little creature with her plump little bum, I'm so glad she's walking at last, and he said I can't bear to look, she could fall head over heels into the sandpit and break her neck.

Sometime around then I found my first doll somewhere, the same size as his index finger, she was naked, her head had a dent in it, one leg was missing, her blue painted-on eyes stared down into the ground. I picked her up and made her a bed of grass and leaves. But it's all broken, said my mother, but you've got all your lovely dolls, said my grandmother. I didn't let up until my mother gave me one of the little cardboard boxes my father gets through the post when one of his customers sends in a spectacle frame for repair. I put the nameless invalid into the box on a layer of cotton wool and pushed it under my bed, it was cotton wool from the bag on my mother's dressing table, cotton wool my mother uses when she has her period, Fania, I need that cotton wool, you can lie your broken dolls on paper. It had to be his little cardboard boxes and her cotton wool. Other dolls followed, a whole little hospital of badly wounded naked creatures, I found them under the bushes along the fence and in the dark passageway between our house and the one next door. Unless they'd popped up out of the ground someone must have put them there. I never played with them, they needed looking after.

Take care, we shout, and my father nods, you too, look after yourselves, I'll ring this evening. And this of course is nothing new: he rings every night when he's out on the road.

But when, says my mother leaning out over the terrace parapet.

Around six, between six and seven, he promises.

My mother nods, that's lovely, Paul, she calls down, goodbye my darling, now off you go; she can't cope any longer with the fact that he's still down there, he needs to leave now, the weekly process of being torn gently apart needs to be over and done with.

As soon as it's happened he'll be sitting at the wheel of his car with only himself for company, and we'll be on our own without him, and we'll go back into the kitchen where the resonant silence will still be replete with what had gone before – we'll eat bread, we'll drink coffee – and where our future comes upon us with slow little steps along with our daily tasks reminding us of what the present demands of us.

Right then, he calls, goodbye; he looks up at us, we're standing in a row along the terrace parapet, he looks first at his wife then at all four of us and we look at him, the four of us look at him, my gaze slides away from him to his car, his metal box, his means of being at once on his own and on the move. Now it really matters, the moment of separation has arrived, each of the four of us shouts her own goodbye, he is being borne into the world outside by an echoing polyphony of female voices, he now stops looking up at us, puts his hand on the handle of the car door, opens it, climbs in, sits down, his position's uncomfortable and he braces his abdomen against the steering wheel and heaves his body up so that he can sit more comfortably. I never like to see this but I look every time. He pulls his trouser legs up to stop them being stretched, with his right hand he feels for various familiar items, yes there they are, cigarettes, peppermints, glucose tablets, with his left hand he shuts the car door with a hefty pull. My own hands are

161

resting on the parapet minding their own business. His head floats around in profile behind the car's side window, he's looking forwards, and I watch as he goes off into the outside world, something I'm not allowed to see for myself. He carefully looks left and right and disappears into the driveway, little yellow clouds of sand puffing into the air behind him. We lower our waving hands. He is no longer visible, the sound of the tyres crunching on the sand and negotiating the bend onto the road has dissolved into the air.

That's it then, says my mother.

He's gone, we're there without him, the fence should be mended straightaway, says my grandmother with tears in her eyes, the garden gate will be dropping off its hinges before long, she goes into her room leaving the door open behind her; I can hear her talking to herself: it really doesn't look nice, what are the neighbours supposed to think of us. As it's still early in the morning Vera, my mother and I sit down at the kitchen table, the period of time before he gets back has already started to reduce but at present it's still long, and my mother tells us her plans for the week, all the things she has to do, the house has to be bought, Frau Kupsch has to have an abortion, the bookkeeping has to be done, I'm months behind, Paul hasn't noticed yet thank goodness, then her eye falls on me, we have to practise, Fania, only half an hour, give me your essay again so that I can look at the words. Why tell me that now, just before I have to leave for school, how am I supposed to manage it if I'm dragging my flat-footed bandy-legged words along behind me.

You haven't even signed my essay yet.

Give it here. She opens my exercise book and signs her name against my F+, Alma Schiefer, every letter perfectly vertical.

162

We're the ones left behind, my father's mind was focused on his travels. He poured white coffee into his thermos flask, picked up his packet of sandwiches, two ham two Dutch cheese, put them in his lunch box, then stashed the thermos and the lunch box in his briefcase. I watched his hands, his fingers as he slowly and carefully carried out his routine, each moment carrying him further away from us until finally the locks on his briefcase snapped shut. His provisions, his eats, accompany him every Monday when he drives off on his travels. His sample cases full of spectacles were already in the car. Only yesterday we cleaned every single rack with soft leather cloths, polished every tiny hinge on the frames for ladies and frames for gentlemen. For ladies, frames shaped like butterfly wings and decorated with fake gems, for gentlemen, formal box-like frames, business-like, dark-coloured, rectangular, and on one wing of every pair a tiny price tag. We sat on the floor in the big room with the open sample cases ranged around us. The fire crackled in the stove: my mother had felt cold around the house.

Carola wants to come and choose herself a pair of glasses, she's not to pay for them, said my father.

Why shouldn't she pay for them, asked my mother, she earns a lot, she's a successful businesswoman, we can take fifty marks off her.

Her glasses would be worth three times that, replied my father, but Carola is a friend, she's Ruchla's daughter, I don't want any money for them.

One hundred and fifty, one hundred and fifty, my mother savoured the sum; Carola will be very happy to get such an expensive frame at such a cheap price. Has she ever given our daughters any jewellery or me a jar of face cream or Mummy a packet of bath salts, even if we don't have a bathtub. You're

163

always so big-hearted, all of them have had reparations and we've had nothing, only Mummy, and that wasn't much, Ruchla and her family had a worse time than we did, we were spared quite a lot and I'm thankful for that, but I just don't see why you want to give Carola the glasses for free.

My father said nothing. He said nothing and polished his spectacle frames and swallowed and cleared his throat.

Where does Carola get all that stuff from, asked Vera, jewellery and make-up and bath salts and such like, and my mother cut in as though chucking the things away: what difference does it make, from Israel.

Israel, repeated Vera in astonishment.

Yes Israel, and why not.

Vera looked at me. She was spoiling for a fight, but I certainly wasn't. I crouched down over the masses of lensless glasses.

Carola buys jewellery and cosmetics in Israel, continued my mother trying on a succession of ladies' frames which she picked out with her slender fingers from their well-cushioned homes in rectangular compartments, four by five compartments to each display board, three display boards on top of one another, total sixty frames in each sample case. She put a pair on, looked at herself in a hand-mirror, showed her face to us, took the glasses off and put them back in their place; my father took them out again, unfolded one wing and polished it with a piece of soft leather, unfolded the other wing, pursed his lips, breathed on the metal, polished some more, folded the frame together again and returned it to its compartment in the display board.

Carola sells the stuff in Germany, the Germans bite her hand off to get it, they think it's Arabian jewellery, in fact it's made by Yemeni Jews but of course she doesn't tell them that.

164

Does she go to Israel often, asked Vera. My mother didn't answer. We ought to go to Israel sometime, said Vera.

What on earth for, exclaimed my mother.

Well honestly, said Vera indignantly, for one thing your daughters could meet some other Jews.

We carry on polishing. Frames for ladies, frames for gentlemen.

Do you want to live in a kibbutz, do you want to keep chickens, said my mother all ruffled, do you want to water the desert, you're not even any good at raking up the leaves in the garden.

What have you got against Jews, asked Vera, seeing you're Jewish yourself.

Nothing at all. I'll get *rishes*. We carried on polishing spectacle frames. Silence. My mother was agitated. Her face kept changing. Inwardly she was carrying on the argument. Why shouldn't Carola pay something for her glasses, I just don't get it. She was letting us listen in again. At fifty marks she's still getting two-thirds off. Just because she's a Jew and spent time in a concentration camp you don't want to take any money off her.

My father pressed his lips together but she carried on regardless. It's exactly the way I say it is, and that really gets my goat, I know it's well meant, Paul, it's too well meant, they'll reckon you don't think much of the glasses.

I don't want to give her the glasses because she was in a concentration camp, I want to give them to her in order to give pleasure both to her and to me. He glanced at his daughters looking for trust in his good intentions and finding only doubts.

What a load of nonsense, Paul, laughed my mother, give both you and her some pleasure *and* take fifty marks off her, just think of that gold bracelet she was wearing recently, solid gold and as wide as a tank track, she put it on my wrist, it felt as heavy as if I'd been clapped in chains. She's not expecting you to give her the glasses for nothing, she wouldn't do it in your shoes either, business is business, what's so bad about that.

My father silently polished his spectacle frames.

And quite apart from that Carola's always been stingy; my mother was examining all the little price tags on the frames. Even as a child Carola was always a taker and never a giver. She didn't get that from the concentration camp. He remained silent. She was floundering.

Can't you raise some of your prices a bit, Paul, I mean we do need the money for the house, we do want to buy it.

No I can't do that, said my father with a shake of his head, his face bent low over his furiously polishing hand; he cleared his throat.

I know, continued my mother, Ketteler sets all the prices; you could put them up a bit and then offer the opticians a discount, they'd buy more off you and think they were getting a bargain, am I right, you bet I am.

Ketteler can't be trusted, said my father, Ketteler's spies are everywhere, he's the manufacturer. If he found out, Alma, I'd be done for, I'd lose the contract, I'd have to make penalty payments, and I'd be taken to court as well.

Leave him alone, Mammy, snarled Vera, Pappy will end up in jail thanks to you. Tears were pouring from the outer corners of her eyes.

Thanks to me, screamed my mother, your father in jail thanks to me.

My father put his hand on Vera's hand. I looked at it. My sister was enjoying his placatory hand; I would have shaken it off. Let the pair of them sit there in happy harmony polishing spectacles: I surreptitiously ordered the car to the front door. If my father's in jail with Vera because of Ketteler then my mother and I can go on selling trips. We'll make loads of money, we'll buy the house, we'll enlarge the business. Carola will be our agent in Israel, we're driving along a tree-lined road in the sunshine, I'm at the wheel, no my mother's at the wheel, she can't drive at all but she's driving very well, she stops, we get out and have a picnic in a meadow with cows and horses grazing in the background, but actually you can't have a picnic in a meadow with my mother, she thinks there are snakes everywhere, there's the clinking of crockery, I snatch up the cloth, we quickly fling everything into the car, once inside we slam the doors shut, she points at the windscreen wipers and screams, snakes have entwined themselves around them, I turn the wipers on.

There are no snakes in Israel.

What gives you that idea, Fania, said Vera, of course there are snakes, sand vipers for instance, they're especially poisonous.

Spiders too, my mother added, tarantulas.

That's it then all of you, let's stay here, there are no snakes or tarantulas in Hamburg. My father wanted to end the discussion and my mother was willing to oblige – but in return wanted to make just one further small point.

Paul, you should find yourself a new manufacturer, he's screwing you and us, and if he's screwing us then we can screw him too.

My father laughed his silvery all-polishing laugh and called his wife his sweet little Yid, and behind her butterfly-shaped fake-gem-encrusted spectacle frame she put on her coquettishly rascally Yid expression, and he kissed her.

Vera screwed up her face in rage.

What's the matter, asked my mother.

Nothing, said Vera.

My mother should just be allowed to get on with it. My father doesn't like doing what he has to do, and does it only half as well as his wife could do it. Selling. She's never once asked to do it in his place. Vera and I sometimes fear she might in fact ask, then he wouldn't be able to do it at all any more, and sometimes we hope she *will* ask because we fear he's not really been able to do it for a long time. But she thinks it's good for him to go off on his regular trips, away from her and away from us. It keeps love fresh, she thinks.

When he gets back from his trips he unburdens himself of all the things he's had to put up with from his customers. Anecdotes about old soldiers' reunions and about how the Jews are already doing too well again. My mother gets upset, he gets upset, what am I supposed to do, I have to earn a living after all. I understand his point of view, I let Annegret walk all over me to stop her doing anything nasty to me, she does things anyway, perhaps she'd do it even more if I didn't give in to her.

Then we should just have emigrated, says my father as if it were some piffling little opportunity that we'd thrown away for ever. Yes, retorts Vera, to Israel for instance.

My mother never wanted to go to Israel. They only wanted to go there when they didn't know where else to go. After the liberation. They'd already closed the borders in America, there were already so many Jews there. So let's go to Israel. But only Jews were allowed to go to Israel, and my father isn't a Jew. If my mother had married a Jew it would have been easier for us – for Vera and me. Thus we harbour within us a kind of latent separation, either separation from him or separation from her; if I had to choose I'd always go for her side: being Jewish is better than not being Jewish, especially if you're German, and

German we are, on top of everything else. Complex creatures that we are, Vera and I consist of three bits, one Jewish, one non-Jewish, and one German.

My father understands those Jews that don't want him in their country, but it makes my mother completely enraged and her words come flying out like bullets, like the time she let rip at the Jewish Aid Society man who wouldn't let my father in, and it was the same when she unleashed a barrage on our boiled potatoes. We were sitting having a meal. I could never have been able to forgive myself, she said, never ever, if I'd stayed in the Jewish Community. My mother walked out of the Jewish Community. She did it for her husband. But the fact that she walked out exercises her a lot. From our very earliest days Vera and I have been used to eating and talking at the same time, but faced with a barrage from my mother we couldn't even open our mouths to shove in a forkful of potato or a bit of calves' liver and fried onion. She and her mother both owed their lives to her darling husband, she exclaimed, and here was this Jew telling her to forsake him, a husband who'd constantly risked his life for her sake and for sheer love of her, risked his very life again and again, he'd been arrested because of it, they'd been arrested as well of course, she and her mother, but they were Jews after all, but *him* – my mother chewed and chomped and swallowed, her knife sliced through the liver causing pink juice to trickle out onto her plate. He'd been in prison because of her, for heaven's sake, he'd never have been in there otherwise, solitary confinement for month after month, tortured and maltreated by the Gestapo, put in the dock, humiliated – and my father caught her darting, knife-wielding hand in his own: it's alright, my darling, it was my own choice, he said, she pulls her hand free, come on, Paul, eat up, your liver's getting cold, and such lovely calves' liver,

169

aren't you enjoying it, I chose calves' liver especially for you, you haven't eaten any of it yet, and you never thought of leaving me.

No, he said.

Ooh, she threatened, I would have . . . and my father laughed and went red. If you really had left me, she said, you'd have been dead as far as I was concerned, I'd have made no attempt to get you back. He was clinging to the edge of the table. Then she rescued him. You stuck with us, you saved us, and that's why I walked out of the Jewish Community. You're no better than the Nazis, she screamed at the man from the Jewish Aid Society, and she bellowed it out between the calves' liver and boiled potatoes, the word *rassenschande* came hissing and rattling out of her mouth. No better than the Nazis. She found the sentence painful. Get my paperwork sorted out, she told him. He had suffered her verbal assault in silence and – irritated by her demand that he sort out her papers there and then: which papers? – he had asked her with some curiosity So you do want to go to Eretz Israel.

My mother looked up from her calves' liver with a smile. What I meant of course was that he should do the paperwork for me to resign from the Jewish Community, but he thought I meant for going to Israel. That's when I walked out. That's your mother. For me a threshold had been reached, a very particular threshold, and once that threshold is reached, it's finished, it's over.

Every word was painful to her, and she made us feel the pain. We must stick by her, we are her daughters, we must stick by her and likewise by him. There's no alternative. Otherwise it's finished, it's over. They did everything right, they survived. Something occurred to my mother all of a sudden, her tortured face grew calm. Your grandmother remained a member though, and she turned to her mother: You belong to the Jewish Community, Mummy.

Yes. I didn't resign. That was your decision, Alma.

I'm glad you didn't resign, says my father to his mother-in-law. She nodded to him, and you didn't go over to the other side. Exactly, he said contentedly. The two of them understood each other.

And what about us, asked Vera, are we in it, Fania and me.

No, replied my mother, because I'm not in it any more.

And could we join without you.

Yes, said my grandmother, you're Jews, because of your mother.

I don't count. My father laughed. It doesn't matter. I understand.

So I could join tomorrow, asked Vera.

Why do you want to join, flustered my mother, you haven't a clue about anything Jewish.

Because you don't want us to, that's why your daughters haven't got a clue, my grandmother knows it all, she learnt all about it at the Israelite School for Girls. Just let your mother have her way, screamed Vera, we could celebrate all the Jewish festivals, we do Passover sometimes, why don't we do it other times.

Go to the synagogue, shouted my mother, go and get yourself a blessing, eat kosher, we can celebrate the Jewish New Year and Yom Kippur so far as I'm concerned, but no one's taking my Christmas away from me, no one celebrates Christmas as beautifully as we do, that's true, Paul, isn't it. I'm a Jew. That's what I am. I don't need to be in the Community and I can enjoy my prawn salad just whenever I like. I can't help it if prawns aren't kosher. I've nothing against prawns. I don't care how unclean they are. I like them.

171

Vera pressed her lips together. My father muttered that we should spare a thought for his stomach. Stop quarrelling, said my grandmother, what about Paul's stomach.

After the meal we cleared the table, my mother stayed sitting on her chair and asked her husband how his stomach was doing and whether she should make him a nice warm poultice to put on it. He wanted to go to bed, he wanted a long afternoon nap, and he wanted her to join him. Don't wake us before five, he said. Then the two of them disappeared into their bedroom.

My grandmother, Vera and I went into the kitchen. During the washing up Vera asked whether we actually had any relatives in Israel. Your mother doesn't like me talking about it, said my grandmother with her arms up to her elbows in dishwater.

We've a right to know, replied Vera.

You both have to promise not to give me away.

What's his name, asked Vera. She automatically assumed it would be a man, and so it was.

Leon Wasserstrahl, said my grandmother.

Wasserstrahl is her maiden name. Hedwig Glitzer, née Wasserstrahl.

He's my cousin and my dead sister Selma's husband, said my grandmother.

That's pretty close, having a relative as a husband, surely the husband has to come from outside the family. Is that permissible, asked Vera.

It's essential, replied my grandmother, if there aren't enough Jewish men in the town or in the locality. Selma married a year before I did, my grandmother gave us a meaningful look, Selma was two years younger than I was.

I didn't look at Vera. Vera put the dried plates in a pile, I put

172

them away in the cupboard, we'd both heard what she'd said, younger daughters can marry before older daughters.

We both liked him, continued my grandmother, but Leon chose Selma and they had three daughters, first Lilly, then Margarete two years later, and Edith arrived ten years after Margarete, a year before he went off to Palestine; the fourth, little Paula, wasn't his, he'd already been gone three years by then. If Lilly were alive today she'd be roughly the same age as your mother, just four years older.

Poor dead Lilly the same age as our mother. That surprised us.

These dead people, so far away in time, their lives cut short, I can't imagine them as being any particular age, to think that Paula was only three, perhaps four, perhaps she lived for another year after they took her away, she'd be a young woman of twenty-eight now, and Edith was just seven, the age I was when I first went to school, in my mind they are senile children, ancients in infant guise, you can't even say that they died, they simply don't exist any more.

Lilly, our Aunt Lilly, we'd have called her Aunt wouldn't we, Vera asked cautiously, and my grandmother nodded, and Vera cautiously exercised her right to say our Aunt Lilly, and Lilly could have had a son of my sort of age, perhaps a bit older, and I could have married him the way Selma married your cousin Leon.

You certainly could, said my grandmother, you'd be far enough away from each other in the family tree. Leon's surname nowadays is Silon, and Silon is the Hebrew word for Wasserstrahl.

We've got a relative in Israel. Vera was euphoric.

Not me. What's the use of a relative in Israel if my mother doesn't want to see him.

He lives in Jerusalem, recounted my grandmother, he's got a little shop there selling cigarettes and newspapers. Leon wanted to bring Selma and the girls over, but by the time he had enough money it was too late, they'd already been taken away. Her voice choked, to carry on speaking she had to really force herself. And she did carry on speaking. Leon had paid a lot of money for a guide who was to take Selma and the four girls to Sicily and then on to Haifa by ship.

Why has Mammy never talked about Leon, asked Vera, why don't we visit Uncle Leon, why doesn't he come to Hamburg sometimes.

She said 'Uncle Leon' just as if she'd sat on his knee as a little girl. We discovered that she *had* sat on his knee, he'd been here in our flat, Vera and I were still very small then, I wasn't yet one, he'd sat in the sun room, eaten boiled ham, and talked about Israel; he'd been desperate for ham after twenty years without it. Leon had kissed Vera's golden curls. Vera and I looked at each other. How little we knew.

Your mother can't forgive him for not helping us after Selma and the girls had disappeared, said my grandmother.

And you, asked Vera, did you expect him to come and fetch you.

Well what could he do from Palestine, it was already too late. Alma's father could have helped us perhaps, we'd been divorced for ages, he'd disappeared, we never heard anything from him again.

Did you look for him, asked Vera.

My grandmother wrung the dishcloth out then wiped drops of water from her face with the back of her hand. There were lots of things we did in order to survive, and lots we didn't do. Fanny did see him once more before they took her away, Fanny Freundlich, the mother of Rosa, Alma's cousin, your first cousin once removed. My grandmother was reciting the names of her relatives, it did her good to count them off. Rosa survived, you know Rosa. She's coming to my sixty-fifth, I've invited her, I really must talk to Alma about the invitation list. She turned to face the stove, her back was bent, she wiped the splashes of fat off the cast-iron pan supports. She had closed the curtain on her history.

Rosa would be coming for my grandmother's birthday. I resolved to pay special attention to Rosa. Perhaps she knew the way to Leon Wasserstrahl.

Vera sits on the floor in our room, puts a shoebox between her outstretched legs and covers it with paper napkins. She puts two candles on it and next to it she puts a fat book. She lights the candles and picks up the book, one I don't know.

I'm going to read to you from Joseph and his brothers, she says, sit down on the other side.

You have to wash your hands first.

Why, she asks.

It's what Jews have to do.

How do you know. Vera stands me up against the wall and frisks me to see if I'm hiding any other Jewish knowledge. I don't reply, I fetch her some lukewarm water in the enamel bowl and fold the tea towel over my arm ready for her to use. This act of giving appeases her, she dips her hands ceremoniously in the water, lets the surplus water drip off, takes the tea towel, and then reaches for the book.

It's not the Torah, she says. Thomas Mann wrote this book, but it's the same story, the story of Joseph and his brothers.

None of the ten men in my grandmother's prayer book would recognise Vera's shoebox and our attendant actions as Jewish ritual. But so what.

I'll just start in the middle, says Vera. Joseph, a handsome,

175

clever, fine-limbed youth, very nearly a man, is sitting with his little brother Benjamin, who adores and admires his big brother, and Joseph is telling Benjamin all about a dream he had – Joseph has lots of highly imaginative dreams, just like me. Vera looks at me, I don't protest, I assume the role of Benjamin, who also wouldn't have protested. What page, I want to know, what page is that on.

Why.

No special reason.

Page three hundred and thirty-nine, the chapter's entitled The Dream of Heaven.

Three times three is nine, times nine is eighty-one, eight minus one is seven, seven is a good number, I say.

Joseph says that as well at some point, Vera looks at the book and then looks up again to tell me something important.

Joseph and Benjamin say Mammy too, by the way.

I find this incredible and Vera has to show me the word. She turns the big fat book round and holds it out for me between the two candles on the shoebox. And there it is: Mammy's cheeks were exceedingly delicate.

And a few lines later there it is again: But I know it is Mammy that he loves in me.

Joseph says this about his father Jacob, known as Israel. Perhaps it is also true of me and my father that he loves Mammy in me. Although I'm the younger child, not the first-born, Joseph wasn't really the first-born either, there were brothers before him, born of Leah, Rachel's older sister, Jacob's first and by no means favourite wife, Vera is not the first-born either, there were miscarriages before her while they were in hiding during the persecution years.

Vera begins reading: This dream came to me, began Joseph; everyone around us has fallen asleep, my grandmother in her room, my parents in their bedroom, the others are all dead, we know of only two who are still alive, Rosa and now this Leon, Leon Silon. Vera is seventeen and I'm thirteen, and we're only gradually beginning to get a proper picture of our Jewish relatives, all the people who belong to us and dwell amongst us without actually being with us, without knowing us, without our knowing them, dead or alive. A mountain of stories. I'm uncovering them layer by layer. My mother is a storyteller, she paints pictures in my ear. I stop my heart beating in order to hear the beat of hers, I feel my way silently to her secret life.

He might have killed someone, my Uncle Leon, he fought with the English against the Germans in Africa, then later in Palestine he fought the English, and today he sells cigarettes and newspapers in Jerusalem. My father was never a soldier, he claimed to have stomach ulcers and they didn't want people with stomach ulcers, now he has them for real. He'd kill for his wife but not, he says, for a fatherland. I went for a walk with him, Vera and my mother hate going for walks, I went along with him so I could have him to myself. We walked side by side. I had to spend a few weeks in a punishment battalion before they declared me unfit, they gave me a rough time.

How terrible, I said. We walked left down our street to the end then left again down to the Alster, past the naked lady kneeling on a patch of grass with dangling arms and a fixed expression, round the next corner and along Harvestehuder Way, past the British Consulate, just the two of us, he'd put his hands behind his back, his palms half open.

He looked at me. Yes, terrible, but I'm still all in one piece, as you can see, and I was one of the lucky ones, other people had far worse things to put up with.

How terrible. I wanted to know the details. His face took on a tormented air. It was a torment for me not to know *exactly* how terrible it had been, and while his torment lay in the past mine was active there and then, *how* awful, tell me the details, I was pressing him hard, my voice was tormenting him, and it was a torment for me to torment him so. Come on, tell me. I took a kick at a stone. He began to speak, slowly and deliberately, his words carefully measured for my benefit. He had had to stand in a cell with his rifle for many hours constantly presenting arms, up and down, up and down. I tried really hard to see how awful it was lifting a rifle up and down all the time. After a certain period he had collapsed unconscious on the floor, and the queers in the punishment battalion had given him water and massaged his torn body and got him back on his feet. The queers in the punishment battalion, he said, were the best comrades anyone could have had.

Sturmius Fraasch upstairs in our house, old Frau Schmalstück's lodger, he's a queer, I suddenly remembered, and he was a Nazi.

Sturmius Fraasch, poor devil, said my father, yes, he's a queer and he wasn't the only queer among the Nazis. People aren't just one thing or the other, Fania.

I wanted to understand everything he was saying, I wanted to be his all-comprehending daughter, like Vera only a bit different, and walking beside him as he paced along I felt somehow significant. I now liked his slow pace and flat-footed gait.

Cars were coming towards us, more than was usually the case. It was a late Sunday afternoon, on the far side of the road lots of people were walking in Alster Park. My father and I weren't over there amongst them, we were walking alone together on the pavement, along the street, past the gardens, there were villas in the midst of these gardens, shaded by tall trees.

Many of these villas belonged to Jews, I heard my father say, now they house the Customs Headquarters or the Institute for Forensic Medicine or simply families, different families, and if you carry straight on along here, up Harvestehuder Way, you'll get to the villa that belonged to Salomon Heine, Heinrich Heine's uncle. We could walk there together. My father looked at his wristwatch. Mammy's expecting us back. We'll go some other time. Our shoes carried us past the houses. Some other time. I'd never get this far.

If Alma were to die before I do, he said, that won't be for ages, Fania, don't let this worry you, I mean when we're really, really old, but if she did die before me, I'd put an end to my life, you understand that don't you.

And what if you die before her, I asked.

Well, he sighed, I'd much rather she died before me, at the end of a long and lovely life, so that I know she's safe.

And you'd kill yourself straight afterwards, I asked.

Yes, he said.

The pavement became too narrow for us to walk side by side, I let him go ahead, he was holding his hands clasped behind his back and I looked at his half-opened palms, I saw his drooping shoulders, we walked up the narrow lanes of Milchstrasse with our bodies hunched forward.

But if I *were* to die before her – and I thought to myself, then he'd shoot her first, but turning to face me he said: then I'd like to feel sure you'd look after her, you'll promise me that won't you.

And I gave him my word. He could die without worry, I would turn into a million ants and carry his body past me and my mother so that he could see for himself how well I was looking after her, I would schlepp him slowly along, sometimes his feet would go first, sometimes his head with its large nose.

179

We walked past the Music Academy. That villa too, I asked. He didn't know. Probably better if they hadn't all belonged to Jews. We turned the corner by the postbox and walked back side by side along our street.

The veiled goodbye smile that my father sent over my head on the morning of his departure was supposed to make me believe that going off on his obligatory travels is a sad and painful business. For him it is indeed sad and painful – but not only that. He smelt of eau de Cologne, his starched shirtcuffs were sparkling white, my mother put his white handkerchief into his breast pocket and arranged it so that two white corners stuck out in dashing fashion, then she stepped back and admired her handiwork. My husband. And she brushed his shoulders with the clothes brush, standing on tiptoe to do so. She likes doing that. He is her big man, and she is the little woman. They gave each other a deep, wild goodbye kiss, and we all watched, Vera and me and my grandmother. He planted his lips right over her mouth, I wouldn't have wanted it to be my mouth, but she seemed perfectly happy about it when they'd finished.

Can't you take me with you some time, I asked my father, and he said Perhaps when you're a bit older, Fania, but then you'll want to go off on your own, not with your old father.

Have a think about it, Paul, my mother suggested, you could take her with you during the summer holidays sometime, and my father smiled and refused to commit himself.

We won't be going to the North Sea coast this year: if we want to buy the house we can't go on holiday as well. My father doesn't want to buy the house. But he quite likes using it to put his wife under a bit of pressure, to corral her a bit. My mother's going to keep a domestic accounts book, he hasn't asked her to, but she has promised all the same. That's for sure, Paul, I'll start it today, I'll see which items of expenditure are completely unnecessary. None of us believes that my mother will consider any part of her expenditure completely unnecessary.

It's still early morning, only just after seven, the air still has a night-time chill, I'm cold, the warmth of the kitchen is inviting. The actual separation having finally occurred, feelings of happiness mingle with sad ones. And the impending future has not yet arrived. Interim feelings of happiness with a cup of hot milky coffee in my hands. My mother has countersigned my F+ and is taking another look back through the preceding pages of my exercise book. What does this mean, Fania. Where, I ask, and look at her red fingernail which is jabbing at a word that I don't understand any more either, a word in my handwriting, but now alien and incomprehensible, a random string of letters. No idea, I say and turn away. She tries to speak the word. Reading out loud can make it easier to understand what I've written down in scrambled form, using her lips, her tongue, her breath she attempts to make sense of the letters.

Just leave it, says Vera.

Dwarf, I say without looking. It's supposed to be dwarf.

Today I'm having half coffee half milk, in fact rather more coffee than milk whereas previously I've always had much more milk than coffee. Isn't that too strong for you. She puts my exercise book to one side, I shake my head. I don't want to answer now that I know about Vera and Hainichen; now that I know about it and *because* I know about it I want coffee with some milk and not milk with some coffee.

Why should that be too strong for her, says Vera. She wants to show me that she's on my side so that I won't betray her, she's always afraid I'll betray her, I've never ever betrayed her, what good would it do me if I betrayed her, no good at all.

Whatever secrets she entrusts me with I just have to schlepp around with me; if anything comes out my mother will feel deceived not only by Vera but also by me. Perhaps I should have a chat to Hainichen, muses my mother, gazing at her coffee cup, what do you all think, what do you reckon, Vera, and Vera, after wondering for a moment why Hainichen all of a sudden, says Hainichen, you want to talk to Hainichen, why not, give it a try.

Do you think it's a good idea, asks my mother. Vera affects indifference, and my mother carries on with her musings. Why shouldn't I go and talk to him, perhaps . . . though why should he pick us rather than anyone else, he might be cooperative, why *not* pick us rather than anyone else, we pay the rent on time, we're a nice family, we get on well with all the neighbours, people like us, they really do, and he's letting everything go to rack and ruin, but the rent's not high for this huge flat with gardens front and back, I expect he was in the SS, I'm sure he was in the SS, if we go by that we might as well pack up and emigrate straightaway.

Perhaps, says Vera tentatively, perhaps he was one of those people who just joined for a bit of fun, SS Mounted Brigade, horses and stuff, he took part without ever thinking about it.

He looks the part, says my mother indignantly, I bet the SS welcomed him with open arms, he's the right height, and more.

Your husband's the right height too, says Vera.

My mother freezes, she fixes a steely gaze on Vera's face, the face of a stranger that has stolen in amongst us.

Paul, my husband, your father, says my mother emphatically, her voice trembling, the veins on her neck swelling, would never have joined the SS, never ever, even if I hadn't come

182

into his life, tears begin to trickle from her eyes, he would never have been one of them, never, I don't understand you, I can't begin to understand how you can put your father in the same category as that man. And you a daughter of mine.

All three of us stare down at the table.

I didn't mean it like that. Vera is afraid of the sweet Mammy from the tents of Jacob, the raging Mammy from the deserts of the past.

I don't care what you meant. My mother is trembling; it begins in her face and then spreads through her chest. She's shaking Vera off. She can't do that, we belong together, once separated from us Vera will burn up in space.

You yourselves told us once that in Poland Pappy got hold of riding breeches and boots and a white shirt so the Germans would think he was a top Nazi.

It worked too, says my mother as though Vera had been there at the time, he needed a stamp on our fake identity papers. Her gaze wanders around the room, she's not back on friendly terms with my sister yet.

Yes, exactly, Vera offers up each word to her mother with gentleness in her voice, his height, that's all, because of his height, that's all I meant.

Yes, ah yes, my mother is lost in thought, and the Poles too, they were meant to think he was someone important, if they'd realised we were Jews they'd have betrayed Mummy and me to the Germans straightaway, and him as well, his life was just as much at risk as ours by that stage.

Vera and I exchange glances. It's worked again, Vera is back in our world and breathing our air.

Up until yesterday – my mother comes back and turns to Vera – up until yesterday Fania still drank milk with a little bit of coffee, that's right isn't it, Fania.

183

But as of today she's drinking coffee with a bit of milk, says Vera, Fania is getting bigger too, she's thirteen years old.

Over thirteen, I added.

So she is. My mother pats my hand. I forget that my baby's getting bigger too.

I'll never confront her with a husband. No such man exists. There's only my father, and men like Hainichen. I hold my cup out to her, she pours some more coffee into it, and the next mouthful tastes bitter. It's true, I'm already over thirteen. People who don't know this think I'm ten at most, and people who do know like to forget that I'm actually three years older. I'm still not allowed to go swimming on my own or go to the cinema on my own or visit Alster Park on my own or go into town on my own on a number-nine tram. No, no, no, oh Fania you know I'd die of worry, stop tormenting me like this.

I exist solely inside myself, there's nothing of me visible on the outside, I've still not had a single spot, I've still not started my periods, my hair's not greasy, I've still got no breasts, there's still not a single curly hair in my armpits, not a single curly black lock on my mons veneris. Sometimes there's an itchy, prickly feeling in my skin and I scratch at my labia until they're on fire.

She was always careful to put lots of cream on her baby, I hear my mother say, what on earth's made her think of that. 'My baby' means Vera and me, regardless: babies are babies. The skin is so important, a beautiful skin, especially for girls, her daughters, two beautiful women with beautiful skin. She had her baby vaccinated under the right breast not on the upper arm. Why disfigure the arm of a woman-to-be, I simply don't understand it, she says getting all worked up, and we agree with her wordlessly, how can people do it, marking the arm like that, it's only German doctors that do it, no one does it in other countries, only here in

Germany. I look at Vera's watch. Hainichen's hand is resting on my sister's arm. We need to go to school.

I never fed you by the clock, says my mother, if you cried I was there at the very first sound, the first tiny whimper, I gave you a bottle straightaway, at night-time too, no baby of mine was going to go to sleep hungry.

Has she forgotten that we have to go to school, on this particular morning she's not keen to be stuck at home alone with her mother, she looks from Vera to me and from me to Vera and we smile reassuringly, well-fed babies with an already well-developed maternal streak.

Are you up to something you two, you are, I can tell.

No, nothing, really, nothing at all.

You can't fool me you know.

To take her mind off Vera I ask her whether German mothers feed their babies any differently, and I don't even need to finish the sentence. Puffing on her cigarette my mother casts her eyes up at the ceiling and spits out a stray bit of tobacco: they do it with a stopwatch, five times every twenty-four hours, the babies are hungry and crying and the mothers get no sleep. The midwife I had then, Frau Vielhacke she was called, I'll never forget that name, a real Nazi, she said to me . . . And Vera and I know what Frau Vielhacke said to my mother, in due course we'll hear about Vera's first taste of spinach, she spat it in my mother's face, her eyes were plastered with green goo; she'll laugh, and at some point she'll mention with a downcast expression that she couldn't breastfeed either Vera or me, that her milk flowed alright but without anything in it, she was skin and bones herself, she just couldn't put on weight. I gave Vera a bottle right from the start, but with you, Fania, I let Frau Vielhacke put pressure on me and you nearly starved. She looks at me like she always does when she gets to

185

this point, her chin quivers, her lips go all moist, her eyes are full of tears, I have to find her a way out, she couldn't help it, you couldn't help it, I say, she cries, I have to go to school, I have to extricate myself from her pain, her love. Vera unpeels her from my neck, my arm, my chest. Vielhacke, says Vera wrinkling her nose, no wonder with a name like that.

That's all she needs to say, my mother turns towards her at once in deep gratitude. She hadn't a clue about looking after babies.

Vera asks her why she didn't just chuck her out. I can't ask, I was a baby.

I don't know, she says, I was so thin and my baby nearly starved to death, my God I didn't want that to happen, I really didn't.

All is quiet in the kitchen. We're exhausted. I put some sugar in my coffee and stir it around, my mother smokes in silence, we can hear my grandmother making her bed in the next room, my sister throws me a questioning look, are you still there, asks her look, is everything okay with you, once again that was too much – for you, for me, for her, for all of us.

You two are up to something, says my mother, but this time she says it just to show that she's herself again.

You'd do better to start thinking about your housekeeping book, suggests Vera.

Just to please Paul, sighs my mother, it'll reassure him, I've absolutely no desire to do it, I'm already fed up with bookkeeping, and she shouts through to the next room, what do you think, Mummy, can you help me with it, I bet you learned how to do it at your Israelite School for Girls.

Vera gets up from the table. We have to go; she nods to me to signal that we can leave now. Kisses are dispensed, my mother accompanies us to the front door.

186

I probably won't be here this afternoon, she says, I'll be in the hospital with Frau Kupsch, I hope everything goes alright.

Walking side by side Vera and I take our familiar route, at the end of the driveway turn right and go along the street, at the corner at the top turn left, across the road at the traffic lights, past the thick undergrowth, behind it right next to the school is the playground that we've never visited, never once in all the years we've lived here, whose climbing frames we've never dangled from nor ever will dangle from as we'd be bound to break our necks there according to the predictions of our parents. We know this playground as a place that is not for us.

We say goodbye by the caretaker's office, we do so without a kiss and look at one another to check that today as on other days we both regard not kissing as a special favour that each bestows on the other. If despite this understanding Vera or I should happen to need a kiss, then it's no big deal, we know where that comes from. Vera goes off up the stairs to the left, I carry straight on down the corridor.

Vera will marry first, then you will marry, Fania. For my mother it's quite unimaginable that I could marry before Vera does, I don't want to marry yet, perhaps I'll never want to marry. As Vera only ever falls in love with old married men I'll have to wait for ever anyway. Girlish laughter and shouting pour out of open classroom doors into the long, empty corridor. Every entrance awaits a teacher, and following their arrival the noise dries up as the door closes behind them.

Somehow I ought to get young men into the garden for Vera. Wolfram hauls in plenty of good table-tennis players but he pays no attention to their height and they need to be taller than Vera or else there's no point. I could keep my ears open in my class to find out who has an older brother and how tall he is. I go into the classroom and forget about my sister's future husband. I'm a bit late, the teacher isn't there yet, the girls are sitting on their desks, they have restless eyes, they're slumped into their bodies with their shoulders bent forward to disguise their breasts, all topped off with their heads of greasy hair. They already have all the attributes appropriate to their age. Some of them are wearing nylons. A few look over their shoulders at the door, peering through long strands of hair, their mouths tight shut: I could have been the long-awaited teacher. The fact that it's only me communicates itself even to the girls who haven't turned round. The cauldron of whispers immediately bubbles into life again, shrill giggles cut through the stale air. No one deems my arrival important, no one calls my name, I don't call anyone else's, I insert myself into the gelatinous mass which swallows me up as something of little significance and slink to the double desk that I share with Annegret. She's already there. She sees me and turns her back, she regards it as an insult that I sit next to her. I try to be friends with her, better friends than enemies, my parents have nothing but friends and don't trust them an inch. I hang my school bag on the little hook on the table leg, sit down, and feel around with my hand in the compartment below the desktop, I can't go peering in to see if there's something in there, something really vile, because if it isn't anything vile then I just make myself look ridiculous with my constant suspicions. There is something stuck to my hand that looks like bird shit. Annegret giggles. I leave my books and things in my bag, pulling out with one hand only the stuff I'll need for the lesson and putting it on the desk in front of me.

Fräulein Kahl, our geography teacher, comes into the room, her dark-brown skirt has a tear in the pleat at the back. Her first name is Brunhilde and she's in love with the music teacher, Frau Regula Hahn. I know this because my mother told me, and my mother knows because she's on the PTA.

The girls sit down, Annegret folds her hands and put them on the desktop in front of her. She does this at the beginning of every lesson, folding her hands and poking her face in the air. I hate Annegret, and I hate myself for being scared of her, what can she do to me after all, she's stupid but I'm scared of her, it's about time she stayed down for a year and then I'd be rid of her. She notices that I'm looking at her, my gaze slides away from her, she grins, turns to Gerda and taps her finger against her forehead. Nausea wells up below my tongue.

Ugh, she whispers, you've got something on you.

What, I've got something on me, perhaps she's being a bit friendly after all, what have I got on me then. Behind you, she says, and my eyes swivel round. Annegret grins, tell me what it is, I beg her, she just stares at me, please tell me, I plead with her, she turns away, I'm being a nuisance, I give Gerda behind me an ingratiating smile, have I got anything on me, Gerda giggles and gives Annegret a signal. The teacher hasn't noticed anything, she's moving her big pointer over the map, this all belonged to Germany once. I'm hungry. I pull the packet with my snack out of my school bag with my sticky hand. Perhaps my mother has included a paper napkin, she does that sometimes, then I could wipe my hand clean. A hard-boiled egg and a note. Love and kisses, Mammy. Eat it all up my darling. I'm on the verge of tears. I wipe my hand on my mother's little note.

I hear Fräulein Kahl's voice ring out above me in a malevolent sing-song: Fania will stand outside the door for five minutes. My heart misses a beat, I am startled to death.

Well, how much more of our valuable time are you going to waste, get out, stand outside the door, you're to be back in your

189

seat in five minutes precisely. I walk past the seated girls and out into the corridor, my face is burning, could I get to the loos and back in five minutes to wash my hand, I want to go, that's Annegret's anorak hanging there. All is still. I wipe my hand on Annegret's anorak. The playground is bathed in sunshine. Further along at the end of the corridor a group of people are coming out of the staffroom door. A woman, two men and a girl. They pause for a moment in uncertainty and then start coming towards me. I go and stand by the window, I could look out while they go by. I have to acknowledge them: I can see it's our headmistress, Dr Liselotte Schmidt, and Bobbi and another man and this girl with copper-coloured hair. I curtsy, nobody speaks, Bobbi would say something if the head weren't there, as she's the head it's for her to speak, she smiles and puts her head at a crooked angle. The girls dislike her because she's on first-name terms with Wilhelm Bobbenberg, she calls him Willi and he calls her Lilo. It sounds like something we shouldn't be allowed to witness.

Why are you out here and not in your classroom, asks the headmistress, with her mouth all aslant and distorted and her head on one side.

Fräulein Kahl sent me out, I answer, because I stopped paying attention for a moment or two.

Really, says Dr Schmidt, so you stopped paying attention for a moment or two, well you won't learn very much out here either, we'll take you back in with us. She opens the classroom door and at a signal from Fräulein Kahl the whole class stands up for me. Or so it seems. I go to my place and sit down.

Be seated. The head waves the girls onto their chairs with a nervous jerk of the hand. You've all become so dreadfully big. I'm bringing you a new classmate, what was your name again, Sirena, say Sirena all of you, well done; Sirena, says Dr

Schmidt again, an unusual name and such lovely hair, where would you like to sit, Sirena, you're new, choose yourself a seat.

Proceedings are interrupted by Fräulein Kahl: what about the rest, she asks, Sirena what. Bechler, says the strange man, our name is Bechler.

I'd like to sit there, says Sirena pointing at me.

Annegret's already sitting there, remarks Fräulein Kahl.

Sirena twists her hair round her finger. She shows no willingness to opt for any of the spare seats, and the headmistress shows no willingness to intervene – she has put her hand on Bobbi's arm, Willi and Lilo are whispering to each other. Pop into my office afterwards. We can all hear it. The girls giggle and exchange glances.

Very well, says Fräulein Kahl sourly, you are new, Sirena Bechler, so you shall have your way on this occasion, be so kind, Annegret, and sit next to Monika.

Making a great effort to appear kind Annegret furiously stuffs her books into her school bag. Inwardly jumping for joy I bend right down over my school bag as if I too were having to pack my things and go, but I am staying put, the new girl wants to sit next to me, she's saying goodbye to her father, she gives him a kiss on the cheek, she offers the headmistress her hand, at the same time moving her left leg very slightly backwards, that can't really count as a curtsy.

I'm Sirena, I hear her say quietly beside me, she smells of peaches, she brushes her red hair to one side so that I can see her face. I whisper my name. Fania. She nods. How lovely, I think the two of us have the loveliest names in the whole class, who on earth wants to be called Annegret.

I'm afraid to let her see how thrilled I am. Her bosom is round, not a single girl in my class has such a well-rounded bosom. Let's go off somewhere together afterwards, suggests

Sirena. The sixth and final lesson of the day has begun. I don't know where she lives, but wherever it is I won't be able to go with her, I have to go straight home and I feel ashamed about it, I'll lose Sirena once she discovers that there are so many things I'm not allowed to do that other people *are* allowed to do.

I saw you this morning, she said at the end of the lesson, you and your family, it *was* your family wasn't it, you were standing on the terrace and your father drove away.

As simple as that. For her that's all that happened when our family was torn apart this morning.

We live in the white house at the end of the driveway, she says, a family called Fingerhut used to live there before us, funny name, Jews according to my father, we're Catholics by the way, my mother always says I should come straight out with it just in case people have any objections.

She takes hold of my arm and hooks it into her own, the back of my hand brushes against her breast. Together we follow my normal route home.

When I get to our flat my mother opens the door. She pulls me inside, quick, come in, she peers anxiously over my shoulder into the stairwell.

What do I do if Sirena turns up on our doorstep after lunch wanting me to go to the pictures or the roller-skating rink with her, it's not a good thing that she knows where I live, and I don't know how to roller-skate, and I'm not allowed to go to the pictures on my own, and going with Sirena would be the same as going alone or even worse. I'm not in the slightest bit interested in what's up with my mother, what's bothering me is the question whether I touched Sirena's breast by accident or whether Sirena drew my hand along it on purpose. She wasn't wearing a bra.

192

I've just come from the hospital, my mother goes ahead of me into the kitchen.

Why, are you ill. I sound like Vera: thoroughly uninterested.

Rubbish. Because of Frau Kupsch and her abortion. My mother clatters around with plates and saucepans and gives me a searching look – searching and dissatisfied. It's normally Vera who gets such looks.

My grandmother is draining the rice. We can eat straightaway. We're having fricassee of chicken.

And where is Frau Kupsch now.

Downstairs, says my mother, the doctor discharged her straightaway even though she's not doing at all well, she bled heavily, let me through. She pushes me aside, goes to the kitchen window and opens it, and all of a sudden we can clearly hear what previously had been muffled rumblings from beneath the floor. Where's Vera for goodness' sake, she's not here.

Shh, says my mother. A man's voice is shouting loudly. I can't make out a single word.

That's the old man, says my mother to her mother. Both women nod and listen. That's Erich Kupsch, he's drunk.

Something falls over, a chair perhaps, but the bang is too loud for it to be a chair. There are loud voices, voices of several men, and Elsa Kupsch yelling in the midst of them. Her voice is high-pitched. It comes echoing up to us through the floor. My mother starts to rush towards the door.

Don't interfere, Alma, says my grandmother horror-struck, there are three men down there, and as if this were just the cue she had needed my mother tears off her apron and dashes through the door in her high-heeled shoes, through our bedroom, through the hall to the front door, into the stairwell, and down the cellar steps to the Kupsches. Her stiletto heels make a drumming noise on the wooden stairs.

193

Why three men, I ask my grandmother. We're standing by the open front door listening for noises from the stairwell.

Friends of his, of Erich Kupsch. She cups her hand round her ear. She's anxious about her daughter but simultaneously curious to know what kind of stink her daughter will kick up downstairs amidst three men. I concentrate on listening out for my mother's voice. I'm not really afraid for her, I'm not afraid that the men could do her any harm, I'm afraid that she won't be able to contain herself.

Herr Kupsch, I hear my mother bellow, you leave your wife alone.

Damned black bitch, he bellows in his turn. He obviously means my mother.

What did he say to her, whispers my grandmother, she's banging about behind the curtain where the cleaning things are stored and reappears dragging the metal floor-polisher behind her, which she can scarcely lift. I'll whack him over the head with it.

I nod and utter a quiet prayer: dear God, don't let Pappy get back right now. If he were to unexpectedly arrive home he'd be certain to go down there, he's not like those men, Herr Kupsch would throw a punch at him and knock him flat on the floor.

If you hit your wife once more, yells my mother, you'll have me to deal with, now just get out of here, you can do your boozing somewhere else.

I can see her in front of me and a great wave of delight goes coursing through me. Her honest, furious face. I hear stumbling footsteps coming up the cellar steps, two tall, heavily built men stagger out into the stairwell.

Karl, Otto, bellows Herr Kupsch from downstairs, the two men are already in the driveway, the main entrance door snaps shut behind them. Down below things have quietened down.

I can hear my mother talking to Frau Kupsch with Kupsch growling sullenly in the background.

She's coming up now, says my grandmother.

We can hear my mother's footsteps but can't see her yet, she's stopped on the cellar steps again to say goodbye to Frau Kupsch. You go and lie down and I'll bring you a plate of chicken fricassee right away. We hear her coming up the wooden stairs, she stops in the doorway at the top, she shouldn't be stopping there, she should be coming straight over to us, turning and looking back downstairs she says And as for you, Herr Kupsch, think yourself lucky I haven't called the police.

He roars. You black cow, he roars, then he comes rushing up on all fours and grabs my mother's leg by the ankle, he'll yank her downstairs, but using her other foot she stamps on his hand with her stiletto heel, he screams with pain, lets her go, and stuffs both hands in his gaping mouth.

Are you going to call the police now, I ask. No point, says my mother, the police – they wouldn't do anything anyway.

In the kitchen she picks up the brown tray, spreads a white cloth on it, fills a soup plate with rice and chicken fricassee, puts a spoon, fork and white linen napkin next to it, picks a strongly scented tea-rose from the vase, tucks it into the napkin, and having thus prepared the tray starts carrying it towards the door.

Alma, warns my grandmother, if he sees you he'll go berserk, let me do that or send Fania, he won't hurt a child. That was the doorbell.

It's the magazine man, says my mother, open the door. My grandmother opens the door, and my mother is already on her way, past the man in the brown leather jacket with a piece of shrapnel in his skull and a pack of magazines under his arm,

195

good day, Frau Schiefer, all the world's news, thank you, Mummy could you take them please. My grandmother has already put the previous week's magazines ready, she signs the receipt and gives the man two groschen. My mother totters downstairs on her high heels with the tray in her hand while I follow close behind.

You don't need to be afraid on my behalf, Fania.

Am I afraid for her, or do I want to see Frau Kupsch lying there; it's the wild man I want to get close to while under the wing of my mother, he's lying on the sofa snoring, his mouth agape, a trail of spittle across his unshaven chin. Frau Kupsch is lying on their bed with the covers pulled up to her chin. She's just as fat as she was before. I thought she'd come back a little bit slimmer. I have to bring the wooden stool from the kitchen so that my mother can put the tray with the food down next to Frau Kupsch's bed. I walk past Erich Kupsch and his snores and stand in the darkness of the hallway.

Has the bleeding stopped, I hear my mother say. Yes, Frau Schiefer, sobs Elsa Kupsch, how can I ever thank you, and my mother says Let's have a look now. I hear the rustle of the bedcovers.

Upstairs in our flat Vera is sitting in my father's wingback chair with her legs crossed leafing through the new magazines and smoking a cigarette. She's behaving as though she were somebody else. She's not interested in what we've just been through, it never occurs to her that we might have been through anything at all. The only important things happen in her own life, she is becoming a stranger to me, an adult of some sort, like a woman I don't know, her soft cheeks are my sister Vera's cheeks, her delicate chin is also my sister's, but something alien has crept in round her mouth, and her eyes are ready to connive at any lie. She looks up from her magazine and lets Farah Diba sink into her lap. I can still just make out the Persian Empress's face, only the outline of her head actually, the huge black egg of the piled-up backcombed hair. The Shah of Persia and his wife are coming on a visit to the Federal Republic, she's his second wife, my grandmother preferred the first, she had to go because she didn't produce any children, the second is younger, she could be his daughter.

What *do* you look like; my mother's standing behind me; what do you mean, says Vera, just the same as always.

What *have* you done with your hair.

Vera looks like Farah Diba. Everyone is doing it now, backcombing their hair. Her hair looks like dark-brown candy floss. My grandmother goes and extricates the two saucepans from my parents' bed, I hope the food's still hot enough, she sighs.

We sit down and eat. With gingerly fingers and extreme disgust Vera pulls yellowish skin from a chicken wing.

I took all the skin off, says my grandmother at once.

No you didn't, says Vera giggling and tugging at the limp yellowy skin. I thought she'd be sick at the very least, but she's squealing and cackling and now my mother's giggling as well, and my grandmother's blushing, come, come, she says trying to calm things down, not while we're eating, though what she really means is not while there's a child present – namely me. It's something filthy, I know for sure, but I don't know exactly what. For Vera it has to have something to do with Hainichen, which my mother doesn't realise, yet both are sharing the same joke. I sit there motionless and angry, I'm an old spinster, I'm not going to cry, I want nothing to do with whatever they're laughing about, I shall leave them at once and for ever. My mother tries to stifle her laughter and rice comes squirting from her mouth across the table as far as Vera's plate, Vera, shrieking with laughter, throws herself back in her chair, tears of laughter stream down my mother's face. Then I pick up the ladle, my grandmother gives a loud scream, and I slam it into the chicken fricassee. A blob of yellow sauce lands on Vera's backcombed hair.

Are you crazy, you stupid cow, she hisses.

Don't start quarrelling, says my mother. Vera gets up from the table in high dudgeon and goes out to clean up her Farah Diba hairdo, my grandmother asks whether any landed on her as well. We can hear Vera giggling in front of the mirror outside.

We'll leave this all right here, says my mother bracing her hands against the table. It's new-magazine day today. My grandmother just wants to put the food away, she can't walk away from a meal-table with everything still on it. You don't need to clear the table, Mummy, says my mother ensconcing herself on the sofa and reaching for a magazine. Vera holds out a different one for her, try this instead, Farah Diba's in it, she looks so sweet.

I take a magazine as well, lie down on the floor with it, and open it at the back. I always do this. There are cartoons on the last few pages. I don't find any of these cartoons funny, but in every cartoon there's at least one full-bosomed woman. Her breasts are swollen, her lips are swollen, her backside is swollen, and the men in them are either lecherous or frightened, the lechers wear check jackets, and have huge teeth and a greased-up quiff, the frightened ones are small, fat and bald. I feed my eyes on the protruding breasts, I lick my finger and then with my wet finger I flick the page over. Don't ruin it, says my grandmother.

Dreadful, I hear my mother say.

What is, asks Vera lowering her magazine.

My mother doesn't want me to see the pictures, I want to see them, women and children are running along the road weeping and screaming. They look as if they are in rags. One girl is completely naked, she hasn't a stitch of clothing, not even enough to cover her howling mouth. I turn over the page to make it go away, I turn back to the same page and she is still there.

America, says Vera.

My mother nods.

Your liberators.

Yes, says my mother, our liberators, and the English too, they saved us.

Not me they didn't. How simple it is for Vera to say this. My mother looks in surprise at the debris of her fallen idols and then at Vera, whose tower of hair is still intact. My liberators are your liberators, she says in a cool, calm voice; she is trembling with rage and almost in tears over the fact that Vera can be so hurtful to her, then a thought occurs to her: you two wouldn't exist if the English and the Americans hadn't liberated your parents.

Vera grins, she seems determined to leave the holy garden of our family, she's kicking cheekily at the fence which we all know to be rotten. I'm not as far down the path as she is. I'd planned to mend the fence this afternoon. Behind the jasmine bushes the rusty wire netting is holed in several places and the wooden posts are rotting away, every time I try to hammer in one of the rusty staples the wood falls apart even more. I've bandaged the posts with parcel tape to stop them falling apart and to stop the staples dropping out that hold up the wire netting. The tape is too thin, too weak. The slightest impact could make everything fall apart.

Don't make a face like that again, says my mother with flared nostrils and a cutting voice, and Vera stares straight ahead and flares her nostrils and makes exactly the same face as her mother.

That evening in bed I ask Vera. In the dark. Have you done it with Hainichen. We're lying next to each other.

Why do you ask. Vera's lying on her back; I can't see her, but I can hear that she's lying on her back. I'd like to tell her how pleased I am about this discovery. I can hear what position she's lying in. I don't need to ask anything. I ask all the same. Whether he hurt her.

What a weird imagination you have, I hear Vera say. I didn't want to really, we were in a hotel, a really posh hotel, I'd drunk champagne, he tried it on with me, and I said Alright, Hermann, give me one hundred marks.

I don't know what irritates me more – the fact that Vera calls Hainichen by his first name or the fact that she asked him for money. If she asked him for money it wasn't love, and how could it be love given that it's Hainichen.

Why are you so quiet all of a sudden, lambkin, I hear her say.

'Lambkin' she called me. Because she's scared. This fills me with mad delight. If Vera's afraid, she can't have left yet; perhaps only one of us will be able to go and not the other. Vera knows this too. She knows it every time she stands on my shoulders to look over the fence that both of us want to cross: perhaps only one of us will succeed. If she goes, whose shoulders will I be able to stand on.

Why the money.

Why not, I hear her say.

I thought you were in love with Hainichen.

I thought that too at first when he was so keen and kept putting more and more pressure on me, then this business with the house came into it as well and he told me he'd let us have it at the lower price.

200

The house at the lower price in exchange for my sister. She's made that up. She makes everything up.

He just pulled the hundred marks out of his wallet, there they were in his hand, ten tens, I thought what a pity I didn't ask for even more, his signature on a contract for the house perhaps, but then it would have come out that he and I had . . . You do realise don't you, Fania, you must never let on, never in your entire life or in mine, give me your word of honour, swear by all that's holy, Mammy must never find out about it.

Never.

I think she'd go to pieces, says Vera.

My poor mother. My poor sister. Poor me.

Do you have the faintest idea what I'm talking about, my little love.

I feel like hitting her in the face. She's close enough. I can feel her breath. So you're still a virgin after all.

Nonsense, my little love. With a tinkling burst of laughter Vera throws herself on top of me.

I push her away. I've never pushed her away before, not while in our bed. Our game: she disguised us as players in her stories, I was someone, I was him, I was Passion. Passion locked the door first so that nothing could happen to us, so that we didn't get caught. Vera never worried about being discovered, she worries about *not* being discovered. She turns her back on me. We're both crying. I want to fall asleep like this but can't. I feel her hand reaching out for me, and I reach out for her.

We haven't managed to do it.

Doesn't matter, says Vera.

She dries my eyes with her nightie. We'll still get out of here, don't you worry. What have you done with all that money, I ask. Thirty marks went to the hairdresser for her Farah Diba hairdo, the rest went into her savings account. This is good news. My sister has never been sensible with money, but instead of chucking it all away she took it to the bank. She's getting grown-up.

Next day, shortly before five in the afternoon, the doorbell rings. I'll go, I shout to my mother who is sitting at my father's desk wrestling with receipts and invoice duplicates. It'll be Vera. Hainichen is standing outside the door.

Well, little missy, he says grinning and holding out his hand, which I don't take. That hand has been all over Vera.

What do you want, I ask icily.

I hear my mother's footsteps, she's following me to the door, who is it, Fania, she calls, then she sees him, ah, Herr Hainichen, why didn't you ask Herr Hainichen in, do come in, Herr Hainichen. She sends me into the kitchen to make coffee, I'll put prussic acid in his coffee, he'll fall down dead, I'll be arrested and put on trial and I'll tell them everything, everything, everything, I carry the tray into the living room with two cups, the coffee pot, milk and sugar, my mother is showing Herr Hainichen the damp patches behind the sofa, both of them are leaning right over with their backsides in the air. I could give him a kick.

That comes from the cellar, says my mother, that comes from the foundations, Frau Schiefer, he replies, it's all gone rotten, it would all need to be drained and dried out but I don't have the money, I've got to sell. Buy the house and turn it into a nicer one, or better still demolish it, it's only the land that's valuable. I'd sooner let you have it than old Frau Schmalstück, don't tell her I said so, nor you, little missy; he grins and flops down in my father's wingback chair.

Fania, I hear my mother say, you're dreaming, Herr Hainichen just asked you something. What right does he have to ask me anything, I run into the garden, I run into the old

202

shed. That's where my father's car lives at weekends. The shed is empty. I want to clean up the old shed. I pick up a yard broom and sweep the floor, Hainichen had shed dandruff on his jacket, dust invades my eyes, my nose, my mouth, I push the door wide open and gulp down the fresh garden air, I drop the broom, pick up the spade and put it over my shoulder. I want to dig. I want to dig amongst the bushes next to the back garden fence. I'll start at the top by the garden gate and dig my way right through the jasmine, the snowberry, lilac, rowan, bridewort and foxglove all the way to the back wall where the currant bushes are.

I set the spade on the ground and step on its upper edge, the metal blade cuts into the earth, I heave out a great clump of soil, turn it over, and put it back in its hole, I make the next cut and the next, my back hurts, I shovel the soil, the branches scratch my face, my bare legs. The hot sun makes the scratches sting. The weight of the soil makes me puff and pant. It smells musty. I throw large worms behind me then hear a flurry of wings on the ground. I peep between my legs and see the blackbird. I wipe my mouth, I chew on earth. I hack my way through resistant roots. I shall see which of them I cut off from the juice of the earth and condemned to wither. I dig and dig. My mother calls me, she's standing on the terrace calling my name, aren't you going to stop, Fania, and I dig and hear her and carry on digging. Don't you want to come in for a coffee, Vera's here too, there are cakes.

No, I scream. I don't want her near me. No.

Isn't that too strenuous, the ground's so wet, she calls, isn't it turning too chilly, the sun will be going down very soon.

The shadows have grown longer. I look at them between my legs. To my mother it must look as if I've tipped forwards into the ground. She has put her hands on the parapet of the wall

203

and is looking at the sky and across at the pear tree near the shed.

Please yourself, I hear her say, I'll go in then, but don't stay outside much longer.

She shuts the terrace door from the inside. I haven't even got halfway. I wanted to get as far as the wall, I wanted to dig all the way to there. I position the spade, push it into the ground, each cut next to the one before, black moist clumps, a long paragraph of excavated words. I plunge my earth-encrusted hands into the churned-up ground.

Chapter Seven

Do you want to come with me, my grandmother asks, I'm going to visit Aunt Ruchla and Aunt Olga, Betty too if she's there, and of course Wilma and Emilie are always there.

I do want to come, but my mother wants to do dictation with me; she's supposed to be doing the books but she just doesn't fancy it. When we do dictation I sit where she's sitting now, at my father's desk. She pushes his papers and her own papers to one side and I put my exercise book on the dark-green desk pad, my mother and her bed are behind me, I can feel her breath on the nape of my neck and drops of her saliva on my ear, she is spitting the words into my head, she enunciates them letter by letter to ensure that I write them down correctly, and I strain every sinew to get the words out of me and onto the page. I always start on a fresh page. The page must be pure and unsullied, it awaits my agonised words like a freshly made hospital bed. His minuscule embarrassment at this weird occurrence was superseded by irresistible ecstasy when he inadvertently found separate accommodation near the cemetery.

Everything's right, oyoyoy, my mother beams with delight and kisses me, except for one word, Fania, you spelt one of the easiest words wrong, I don't get it, sep*e*rate instead of sep*a*rate.

Because that's how you said it.

Because that's how I said it, so how did I say it. She tries out all the different ways she could and couldn't have said it, she twists the words between her teeth, she stands up, she's not certain any more, it *sounds* like seperate but I'm quite sure it's spelt with an a, she looks in the dictionary, she comes over and shows me the word. Separate. I think it looks boring and so does she. That's just the way it is, Fania, a not e, she sings a pop song that my father sometimes hums, perhaps to help me remember. Turn around just one more time, she sings, before we part for ever. She dances slowly towards me, the way she does with her husband, instead of going off like it says in the song. It would be better to spell separate with an e in the middle, I tell her. 'Hurt' as well. Hurt cries out for an e, a curled up, frightened little e, I know hurt is spelt with a u, it's no good with a u, it's a very sully hurt instead of a wild, berning hert. She tries it out, she agrees with me: hurt with a u – impossible.

My grandmother wants to take a pair of glasses with her from my father's old sample-collection, she wants to give them to Aunt Ruchla for Carola.

Best take three or four, says my mother, she'll definitely want one pair and she might want two, then you'll have enough with you.

We take five frames for men with us, Carola only wears men's glasses. My grandmother wants to know what she's to say when Ruchla asks about the price, and after a brief pause for thought my mother says Fifty marks a pair, forty at the very least.

She doesn't see us off at the door, she stays in the bedroom seated at my father's desk which is covered with invoices, delivery notes and carbon copies of reminder notices, blue for the first reminder, pink for the second. When people still fail to pay and my father is in agonies of unspoken impatience my mother intervenes: don't you think I ought to give this customer a quick ring, Paul, I'll be very nice and friendly, then he'll pay up like a shot, believe you me.

Just as we're standing by the bedroom door on the way out she looks over her shoulder at my grandmother and me, her slender hands resting on the arms of the chair.

We'll be off then, says my grandmother. My mother nods. Do you want us back at any particular time, asks my grandmother. My mother shrugs her shoulders. We'll certainly be back by supper-time, says my grandmother.

I'm impatient. I want to be off. I want to be out, out on the street.

My mother gets up from the desk, her daughter's keen to leave, and without a kiss, she comes over to us, she adjusts my beret, she kisses me, she kisses her mother. Off you go then, be careful, my regards to everyone. We can leave at last, we could have left without the kisses, we'd have lifted our feet, bent and straightened our knees, our legs would have carried us to the front door – and we would have been distraught. We have to touch one another again first, and I know in my bones that even I can't do it differently any more. Perhaps I've never been able to do it any differently.

My grandmother is pleased that I'm going to the Jewish Old People's Home with her. Aunt Wilma will be sitting on her rubber ring in front of the TV in the lounge arguing with the other residents about which channel to watch, fat Aunt Ruchla will be with thin Aunt Olga whose room is next door to hers, and Aunt Emilie with a nappy in her trousers will be having her palm read by Aunt Betty, whose mouth is a gold mine. Aunt Betty has her reparation money in her mouth so that no one can steal it from her. I asked Vera whether Aunt

Betty uses metal polish on her teeth and Vera said You're a donkey, Fania, Aunt Betty doesn't have to clean her teeth at all, gold glitters all the time. Vera hates cleaning her teeth, especially at night.

My grandmother doesn't like going there on her own, she prefers to have me with her, I'm her connection with the outside world. She doesn't want to live in the old people's home, Aunt Lotti doesn't live there either, she has her jewellery shop on the Reeperbahn. Except for her and my grandmother the entire Theresienstadt Circle lives in the home and that's too much of a good thing for my grandmother, she doesn't want to live in a kille consisting only of Jews, she wants to be among the young, the Jews there are all old, only the Germans have young people. She goes to the pictures with Elisabeth, Elsa Kupsch's daughter. Elisabeth is just as fat as her mother and a bit older than Vera; my grandmother likes going to the pictures with Elisabeth Kupsch, she pays, and Elisabeth is delighted – Elisabeth would never get out otherwise, says my grandmother, she's so fat and she feels so ashamed. They go to film premières together, my grandmother always brings the programme back for Vera; Vera studies the photos intently and after a while starts looking like the female lead.

Why don't you live in the old people's home like all your friends, my mother screamed once. My grandmother cried and screamed back that Ruchla and Olga and Emilie and Wilma and Betty were always telling her how well off she was; Hedwig, they say, you live with your daughter and your wonderful son-in-law, what a good man he is. She could count herself lucky to be living with such a daughter and son-in-law, and what would it look like if that were no longer the case. My mother clenched her teeth and clutched at her hair. Everything is so cramped and constricting, she said, not the flat, that's big enough, but everything else. Everything, do you hear, everything. And then she added: I can't cope for much longer.

Whenever things get to this point Vera and I get anxious about our mother who can't cope for much longer but *has* to cope, and anxious about our grandmother who we feel terribly sorry for, and we get enraged at our mother, what sort of a daughter is she, how can she scream at her mother like that. Whenever we invite friends round, she screams, you simply come and join in, why don't you stay in your room, please do stay in your room, we don't want a mother sitting with us all the time, we want to chat, we want to talk to each other, and we can't do that if you're always sitting there.

What about? I ask, interposing myself between mother and daughter, they're to stop, my mother has to stop, my heart is thumping in my ears, I haven't got a temperature, I do this sometimes, I start a temperature when things get too much, I get burning hot and go out like a light, then when I come to everything is alright again, they're standing round my bed smiling down at me and they're delighted I've come to and my grandmother gives thanks to Adonai.

Vera treads on my foot: shut your trap. It's quite normal in our family for our mother to scream at her mother, Vera and I scream at our mother too. But this is a different sort of screaming. My mother wants them to split up, she wants her mother to leave, how can she, a mother can't leave her daughter, it's the daughter who has to go, the mother stays put, the daughter has to take her things and go and not look back. This isn't possible any more for Hedwig and Alma, they revolve round each other.

Why, what am I doing wrong, wails my grandmother, you can talk about anything you like, I never intrude, I never say a

209

word. My mother yells and wriggles and then brings herself to explain calmly and quietly to her mother that everything is different now, everything is normal now, we can live a normal life now, just like everyone else. My mother never abandoned her mother. She could have done. She could have taken the train to Italy, on her own. While that was still possible. A one-way ticket was eighty marks and she carried the money on her all the time, hidden away in a special little pocket in her knickers, the whole lot held in place with a safety pin because the elastic in her knickers had usually lost all its stretch and without a safety pin they would have slipped down beneath her skirt and ended up round her feet, shoe size 35. That looks terrible, moaned Hedwig Glitzer, what if anything happens to you, and she put in new elastic and removed the safety pin, what on earth would people think, and Alma said Once things get to that stage I really won't care, and she got herself a new safety pin just in case and for the sake of the eighty marks that would get her to Italy. But Alma couldn't leave. She couldn't abandon her mother or the old folk, her mother's parents. The men had gone, Leon and Julius, and she stayed – but now at last this had to stop. Don't you understand, we want to be on our own for a change, I want to be able to live with my husband and my children just like everyone else.

But Vera and I don't want this, and nor does our grand-mother, she's a woman without a husband, she was as good as dead but has been restored to life, all she has left is the married state of her daughter, it is her daughter who has a husband, this wonderful son-in-law who is a real human being and just the kind of husband any woman would wish for – and who is too soft-hearted for her daughter and sometimes too kind, too forbearing.

I'll never abandon Mummy, I'll never leave her no matter

what happens, if you love me you have to stick by us, if you stick by me then you have to stick by her as well. He was a soft sort of man. And one night when he failed to turn up because his sister had stopped him – he'd be signing his own death warrant if he got involved with that Jewess, it wasn't too late to pull out – and Alma was sitting at the kitchen table waiting vainly for him to arrive, Hedwig said to her daughter You must give him up, he won't stand by us, we're Jews, it's too dangerous for him and he'll put us in danger, we can't rely on him, he's too weak. And the following morning Alma got up from the kitchen table and went straight out with her high heels and silk stockings and a touch of fresh lipstick right down Osterstrasse until she got to Heussweg and the offices of the furniture company Klamme & Co. where he arrived at his desk every morning at eight, and there he was coming up the street on his sister Mimi's arm, a man sick in spirit who needed watching. Mimi ignored Alma and Alma noticed this and shrugged it off, that's how things were now, it hurt her, but things *were* that way now and it didn't matter, what mattered was him. His sister looked straight through her but she simply stood in his path: You have to make up your mind now, Paul, either for us or against us, I'll expect you this evening, or we're finished for ever. She went home and told her mother Let me wait for him until this evening, then if he doesn't come – she couldn't bring herself to say that it would all be over and done with. Hedwig, a woman who had been abandoned by her husband, remained calm and strong, her daughter should stick with her, we'll have to get through this on our own, she said, he won't come. Alma whimpered and wept and seemed ready to bow to her mother and her bitter prediction when suddenly the doorbell rang: weak enough and strong enough, he had come after all.

We know everything, my sister and me, we weren't there but we know all the same. Sometimes details emerge that we didn't yet know and then we realise once again that we don't know everything after all, although my mother maintains that she's so often told us every last detail.

We know from Aunt Ruchla what it looked like when Hedwig Glitzer went rushing off to her clients with scissors, comb and curling tongs in her pocket, through Henriettenstrasse, along Eichenstrasse, down Unnastrasse, to give hairdos to Frau Dr Braun and the vicar's wife, dress the wig of the rabbi's wife, mop the floors and empty the spittoons of Uncle Martin Loewe Nehemias's cigar shop. And trotting along behind her was always Alma, my mother, just four or five years old in those days. And fat Aunt Ruchla stood in the cellar doorway leading to the cobbler's shop of her parents, Bette and Jakob Fisch, Ruchla wasn't fat in those days, just a little bit plump, and the same age as Hedwig, early twenties. She watched her friend go hurrying past, her head bent forward in her haste like a pious Yid, where are you rushing off to, she called after her, is the rabbi doing a wedding, and as Hedwig neither stopped nor heard Ruchla shouted Oy vey Hedwig, your little one, nebbish, with her tiny feet. Hedwig Glitzer didn't have eyes for her little daughter, she was conducting imaginary conversations with Julius, her former husband. She was a divorced woman; this wouldn't have been apparent had she been on her own, having a child but no husband made it very apparent, and a child without a father, what a disgrace, things would have been easier without a child. But the child, her child, her little girl smoothed Hedwig Glitzer's difficult path; despite always trotting along behind, the child nonetheless ran ahead of her mother, who put her in pretty dresses she made herself and dolled her up, so her clients looked forward to Alma's

212

arrival, recite a poem, Alma, give us a dance, Alma. What was needed in addition to her daughter was a man, and her daughter found the right man, and he saved the lives of both mother and daughter.

We walk down the driveway, my grandmother wobbling slightly on her bandy legs, she's wearing a bright-coloured cloth coat, a little hat with a veil, and thin gloves. She asks me whether her hair is alright, how can I possibly know as she's wearing a hat, so I say Yes, it's fine, but you've put a bit too much rouge on. She opens the snap fastening on her voluminous handbag and hands me a lace hanky scented with eau de Cologne, we stand still full in the sun, she holds her face towards me, I dab the soft wrinkly skin on her high-boned cheeks. Once we're on Mittelweg we get into the tram that takes us right to the door of the Jewish Old People's Home, the tram stop is directly in front of it, the Mayor of Hamburg will have ordained this because the Jews are all in such poor condition. As we get out the thought suddenly occurs to me that people will now know we're Jews. My grandmother and I are the only people to get out.

The home is newly built in yellow clinker brick and looks ugly. We go up a couple of steps, my grandmother rings the bell and peers through the giant panes of glass trying to see if anyone is coming to open the door. She presses her forehead against the glass dislodging her hat and uses both hands to screen her eyes from the glare of the sun. That's bulletproof glass, I tap my finger against the door, that's just how I imagine bulletproof glass. Bulletproof glass: the term cropped up in one of our new magazines, a black limousine with bulletproof glass, made specially for the Shah of Persia and his wife Farah Diba. An intercom crackles next to my ear. Say your name, orders a woman in a hoarse voice.

My grandmother positions herself in front of the

loudspeaker, her face is agitated. Yes, Fräulein Tannenbaum, she shouts, it's me, it's us, my granddaughter's come with me.

Say your name, rasps the voice.

Hedwig Glitzer and Fania Schiefer, I yell, and my grandmother, watchful as ever, looks over my shoulder at the street to see if anyone heard me, apart of course from Fräulein Tannenbaum.

The crackling of the intercom stops abruptly. We wait. After a while I make to ring the bell again.

No, no, says my grandmother, she can't move all that quickly with that leg of hers, you remember surely. And in due course Fräulein Tannenbaum comes flailing along towards us, she's younger than my mother and walks with the aid of a crutch, at each step swinging one leg in a semi-circle while lifting the shoulder on her other side as far as her ear. She opens the door without a word of greeting. No sooner are we past her than I want to know what happened to her.

We're going to see Hermine Kleingeld down in the basement first, says my grandmother, I think Hermine Kleingeld has been looking for a new pair of glasses for ages.

I've told you a hundred times, Fania, she whispers on the stairs down to the library, in the concentration camp they repeatedly broke her leg.

But why. I ask because asking is what you do when a woman has had her leg repeatedly broken.

Why indeed. My grandmother, who has told me the story a hundred times already, carries on down the stairs, be careful, Fania, they've been polished, you'll break your neck. You can only break your neck once, better to have your leg broken repeatedly than to get your neck broken, in the latter event Fräulein Tannenbaum would have been dead straightaway, as it is she's still alive and can give us lots of trouble.

214

Down in the basement Hermine Kleingeld sits behind rows of tall bookshelves, she looks after the Jewish Community's book holdings having taken over from Mottl Kummer two years earlier, he was found dead one morning lying on the floor amongst the bookshelves. A lovely death, said my grandmother, a lovely death, said the Theresienstadt Circle, he met the Almighty in the midst of his books. Mottl Kummer had had a lovely death, they all thought, especially considering the life he'd had. As well as having a lovely death Mottl Kummer also had extremely lovely handwriting, with a blue indelible pencil he entered the name of every book and every reader on a file card in Gothic script.

Hermine Kleingeld gets up from her desk to say hello to us, she has a typewriter that is almost as old as Mottl Kummer was when he died – forty-seven. At least this Erika is an improvement on what was here before, says Hermine Kleingeld. The Erika is made of cast iron and doesn't have an ß, words with ß in them have to be written with ss, but it does have an extra key with the two italic letters *RM* on it, the abbreviation for Reichsmark – that's how old the Erika is; next to it are Hermine Kleingeld's spectacles, one wing of which has sticking plaster on it.

I'll be sixty-five on the sixth of June, says my grandmother, but that's as far as she gets: Hermine Kleingeld professes not to believe it, you look so young, Frau Glitzer, just like a young girl we always say, my grandmother flushes with delight. I also think my grandmother is like a young girl, she's quick to blush and she never understands dirty jokes, it must be because she's been without a man for such a long time.

I'd like to invite you to my birthday party, my son-in-law will be there too, my grandmother emphasises. Hermine Kleingeld would love to come. Does she have a nice lot of work to do, enquires my grandmother, can the Russians read our books at all, so many Russians and Poles have come to see them, I hope that doesn't do us any harm in the eyes of the Germans.

Six of them from Russia, says Hermine Kleingeld, and my grandmother breaks in: And I hear one of them is a man. He is from the third aliya, says Hermine Kleingeld portentously, and I wait patiently to find out something about this word aliya that I've never heard before, and gather that the five women apparently came out with the fourth. Is that a ship, I ask, and why didn't they come by land. It's the Hebrew word for immigration to Israel, says Hermine Kleingeld. I feel ashamed as I blindly suppose that within my body all things Jewish are stored up in readiness for me and that in a Jewish environment the entire vocabulary will be instantly accessible. Aliya means ascent, says Hermine Kleingeld, and my head is burning hot and ringing, yes, yes, I know, I say quickly, and hungrily devour Jewish lore that has been denied me up to now without my realising it. Hermine Kleingeld is not the least bit bothered by my shamefaced hunger for information. Ascent to the Promised Land, she tells me, and if you want to you can make it too, Fania, later on once you're a young woman. My grandmother laughs and reaches for my hand, go on, talk her into it – as if my daughter would ever allow it; and is he fairly elderly, this gentleman, she asks.

He made the ascent in 1919 so he told me, Frau Glitzer, an old kibbutz man, so why did he come here, I ask you, why didn't he stay over there.

And why, asks my grandmother.

Because of the reparations, and who can blame him, and the five women too, and on top of everything else they've got rheumatism as well here in wet Hamburg. Yesterday he nearly

216

fell down the stairs on his way down here, I'm always telling Fräulein Tannenbaum not to have them put polish on the stairs, and what do you think she does, Frau Glitzer.

And my grandmother raises her hands and eyebrows, lowers her voice and utters a meaningful Aha.

Exactly, whispers Hermine Kleingeld.

She's cussed, that Tannenbaum, oy vey, nebbish, her leg.

Just what I say, Frau Glitzer.

I go off into the book stacks and stick my hands in amongst the books that stand in their hundreds and thousands on the shelves wrapped in browny-grey covers with a number on the spine and distinctly unappealing in appearance. The dust makes my fingertips dull and dirty.

Our Jews, I hear Hermine Kleingeld saying at her desk at the far end of the room, well I can't complain, but as for those from the East, Frau Glitzer, Poles have come to the Federal Republic as well now, in the GDR they let the Jews go straightaway, the sooner the better so far as they're concerned, and several families have come from Romania via Israel, five months in the Promised Land and from there straight to America, and if they're not welcome there then we take them. I have to be careful with the books and make quite sure I get them back, there's some valuable stuff, first editions, family heirlooms, get a fortune if you sold them. I'm always telling Herr Blättner that we ought to be insured, but you know what he's like, it's no use talking to him, and those people from the East, some of them get grease-marks on the books, but fortunately I've put them all in brown-paper covers, and it's true, Frau Glitzer, the people from the East adore German literature, they reel off long ballads by Friedrich Schiller, in German. How about Heine, asks my grandmother. But of course, says Hermine Kleingeld, Heine too, good old Heine, and only recently one of the

217

women recited *Faust* from beginning to end, though only Part One.

The phone rings.

My grandmother studies the inside of her handbag, she doesn't want to look as if she's listening, but as she happens to be standing there she listens all the same. So do I.

Da. Da, da, says Hermine Kleingeld to whoever is on the phone; she says it repeatedly. It sounds as if she's stammering. Da means 'there' in German and 'yes' in Russian. I know this thanks to Aunt Betty. The foreign words go slithering past my ear, soft, moist sounds. Probably the Russian from Israel, it'll be about the book.

That was my father, I hear Hermine Kleingeld say to my grandmother, he rings every day from Munich, always at around this time. He never says his name, I just listen to his breathing and I know it's him. I ask him How are you, and he says Fine. Then I ask him if everything is okay, and he says Yes. Then I say Me too, and he says Good. I ask if he's had any excitements, he says No. And I say Good. Talk to you tomorrow then, and he says Yes, look after yourself, and I say Yes, you too. In Russian. As you heard. My father is from Russia, Boris, Boris Kleingeld.

And the same every day, I hear my grandmother ask, and Hermine Kleingeld says Yes, Frau Glitzer, every day at around this time, that's why I can never be away from here at this time of day. He's been ringing me ever since my mother died, nearly twenty years ago now. I'd just left home, I was twenty-six. He stood at the edge of her grave and said After all that she'd survived did she really have to be run over by a milk float; a young man was driving it, two years after the liberation.

Standing behind the tall book stacks with all their old books I'm racking my brains trying to work out why Hermine

Kleingeld, a fully fledged adult, has the same name as her father and I realise all of a sudden that I just can't think straight, that I must have fallen out of the kitchen window and landed on my head on the iron stairs: Hermine Kleingeld obviously isn't married to her father, she isn't married at all. Like Carola, Ruchla's daughter, she's not married either, even though she's completely adult. I'll be the same. I can think straight again, I didn't fall on my head, I don't have to leave the family via the kitchen window. With my forehead resting against the dusty books I swear I'll do things like Hermine and Carola and not like Vera with that dirty swine of hers.

You're a good daughter, I hear my grandmother say, I've brought you some spectacles, just choose yourself a pair, the price tags are still on them so you can see how expensive they are, my daughter thought fifty marks, that's only a third of the normal price, but I want you to have them as a present, Ruchla's daughter can pay, she has plenty of money or so I'm told, keyn aynore, touch wood, cross your fingers.

Upstairs in the residents' lounge we meet Aunt Ruchla and Aunt Olga, they've been waiting for us, and there at the far end of the room in the sitting area by the window are the Russian women, five fat, heavily built creatures in scuffed, tightly laced shoes, chattering away in Yiddish and Russian in raspy, twittery, squelchy voices and very poorly dressed – they're no match for my Theresienstadt aunts.

Aunt Ruchla and Aunt Olga are all agitated, oy Hedwig, oh dear; I get a kiss, and throwing an abjectly mournful glance at Olga Aunt Ruchla says You must help, Hedwig, it's Fritzi, we've got to have Fritzi put down. Olga puts her hands over her face, you must do it, Hedwig, please do it for me, I can't, it's breaking my heart, she'll go with *you*, and Aunt Ruchla says It's all his doing, the 'house rules' – *his* house rules. He's just not open to reason; and because she's talking about him, Aunt Ruchla speaks normal German for a change.

Who is 'he', I want to know, and all three women silently nod their heads towards the back of the room and give me a knowing look. They mean Heinrich Blättner, Director of the home and President of the Jewish Community. What's he got against dogs, I ask, Fritzi may be an ugly, stinky dachshund bitch but she's completely harmless.

My Fritzi doesn't stink, says Aunt Olga.

Hmm, says Aunt Ruchla, oy vey she farts, but she's old, when Olga arrived at the home with her four years ago that was, no just three, says Olga interrupting her, leave off says Aunt Ruchla, three years ago, Mottl Kummer God rest his soul wasn't dead yet and everyone thought Fritzi would die first, that's what everyone thought, and look what happened, Mottl Kummer died God rest his soul – but He doesn't want our Fritzi.

And now Heinrich Blättner has found out about her, you ought to have seen it, Hedwig, he made such a terrible fuss, the house rules, the house rules, yet he's known for ages that I live with the dog, all of a sudden it doesn't suit him, he took fright at her, at Fritzi, she's in his bad books, the poor creature, it's not her fault.

It's all because of what happened to him, says my grandmother.

What happened to him, don't talk to me about what happened to him, things happened to all of us, to Ruchla, to you, to me; he's afraid of dogs, my Fritzi's afraid of him the second she gets the scent of him. You get rid of your dog, he snarled at me, or else I have to leave the home, who'll want Fritzi, no one will want Fritzi, she's old, she's got heart problems, and she's used to me.

Close by, just a few houses along, says Aunt Ruchla, there's a doctor, a real gent, down on your right as soon as you've gone out of the door.

Taking Fritzi to be put down was certainly not on my grandmother's agenda. I've come to invite you to my sixty-fifth birthday party, and here – she digs around in her handbag – I've brought you five, no four pairs of glasses for Carola, she's to choose herself a pair, fifty marks each, the prices are still on them, we're more or less giving them away.

Aunt Ruchla takes the glasses from my grandmother. Hedwig, you've got Fania with you, there are two of you, do poor Olga a tojwe.

Yes do me a kindness, says Olga, her face twitching.

Alright then. My grandmother has let herself be persuaded. So let's go upstairs to Fritzi.

They're Russians, says Aunt Olga as we walk past the five women. My grandmother clicks her tongue: meshugge, what baloney, they're just old Israelis. On the way to see Fritzi I want to know what's up with Heinrich Blättner, what makes him so afraid of dogs, and Aunt Ruchla tells me that the Germans treated him like a dog.

Literally or just in a manner of speaking, I ask.

Literally, she says, they shut him in a dog pen, they truly did. The brutes nipped him and bit him and he had to clean out their muck, he wasn't even allowed to share their food. He was in clover compared to us, says Aunt Olga.

I like animals and I'd like to have a big dog, I'd have trained the dogs in secret and one fine morning I'd have given the order and they'd have bitten the Nazis to death. I know about the concentration camps, I'm not sure where from. A fence and beyond it people in stripes, just thin pyjamas.

We're afraid of him, continues Aunt Ruchla, we call him the

221

Prussian; have you ever seen him, asks Aunt Olga, he has a sharp, high-pitched voice and his desk's all neat and tidy, have you ever been in his office. Aunt Ruchla clicks her tongue, what would our Fania be doing in his office, and Aunt Olga says Well, just to see what he's like, and Aunt Ruchla says Why on earth would the child be interested in the director of an old people's home, she's got plenty of time, another sixty or seventy years. He'd have made a good trusty, says Aunt Olga. Aunt Ruchla stops in her tracks and remonstrates with Aunt Olga, How can you say such a thing, the Prussian was a boy not a trusty, and the German men bullied and tormented him in his dog pen there. She's getting really worked up, remember your blood pressure, my grandmother warns her, remember my blood pressure, shrieks Aunt Ruchla, how can I when Olga's going on about trusties, and I ask Did trusties wear pyjamas too or did they wear proper clothes. What does the child mean, asks Aunt Olga; I don't know, says my grandmother. My darling, says Aunt Ruchla, tell us what you mean, what's this about pyjamas. They wore pyjamas in the camp, I say, I think that was a really dirty trick because you couldn't escape if you'd been able to escape in the first place, I mean you couldn't walk down the street in pyjamas could you, all the Germans would have known straightaway that you were from the concentration camp.

Three pairs of eyes focus in on my face, Aunt Ruchla sinks back against the wall of the poorly lit corridor, the vast bulk of her body heaving and wobbling, and in a staccato succession of shrieks she says Tell me, Hedwig, what sort of pyjamas does your son-in-law wear.

My Pappy, I say, wears striped ones of course.

They have a good laugh about husbands and their striped pyjamas. Stop it all of you, says Aunt Olga, you're hurting the poor child's feelings, and she strokes my burning face.

222

It was me. Me that didn't know it right. It really was me. I *must* know it right. It must come out of me right. Not wrong, like just now, so that people can see that I don't know and that I'm separated from them by a gulf, a huge gulf, there must be no gulf between us and no expanse of grey coldness that burns like hot ice.

For this child here, says Aunt Olga stroking my cheek, we weren't prisoners in prison clothing, but people in pyjamas who'd been snatched from their beds in the middle of the night, and isn't that just how it was.

She opens the door of her room. Fritzi thuds her rat's tail against the floor and rolls her eyes. I take her lead from the hook on the back of the door and put her collar on, Fritzi licks my hand and stays in her basket.

Look, she knows, she won't come out of her basket, she knows. Aunt Olga is crying.

Aunt Ruchla, my grandmother and I all know that Fritzi always stays lying down whenever she is due to be taken out on her lead. She doesn't like walking. There's too much for her to schlepp around on her four short legs. I pick her up. Olga kisses Fritzi between her eyes. Off you go now, be quick.

We go out of the room, my grandmother and I, I turn round again in the doorway, Aunt Ruchla has her arm round Aunt Olga and signals to us to leave.

We walk silently along the poorly lit corridor, turn the corner at the end of it, another corridor opens up in front of us, long and gloomy, beyond this is the stairwell.

Ruchla could have taken Fritzi, she really could, says my grandmother, and I could have looked after Olga.

Fritzi stinks incessantly, I put her on the floor and make her trot along behind us on her lead.

I hope we get seen by the vet straightaway, my grandmother

continues, I wanted to talk to them about whether they can lend Paul some money for buying the house. What did Alma say, she said fifty-six thousand marks. If Ruchla, Olga, Wilma and Betty – not Emilie, she's poor, and Lotti's too mean – but Ruchla, Olga, Wilma, Betty, my grandmother counts off four fingers on her right hand with the index finger of her left, they could give ten thousand marks each, oy, wouldn't that be lovely. We'd certainly scrape the other sixteen thousand together.

The door is opened at the end of the corridor, sunlight shines through for a moment or two, a man comes through the door which closes behind him and shuts off the light. He's holding a briefcase in one hand, he walks fast, feeling his way along the wall with the fingers of the other hand, he's coming towards us.

I'll give notice on my special savings account, muses my grandmother, they can't all give ten thousand, Ruchla can't and Wilma can't either, they might be able to give five thousand, then at least we'd have thirty thousand. Someone's coming, I say. Fritzi has lain down flat on the floor and simply won't budge.

Come on now, says my grandmother to the dog, you need to give a really good pull, Fania.

I suddenly realise it's Heinrich Blättner, the Director. He's recognised us too and in his ringing, high-pitched voice calls out Good day Frau Glitzer, and Fritzi, flat on the floor, growls. Oh my goodness, whispers my grandmother. Why doesn't he run away, ah of course, he can't. He presses himself against the wall and bares his teeth, he snarls at me with his piercing voice, he's holding his briefcase pressed against the front of his body, his face is wet with sweat, Fritzi can smell his fear, she's bared her sharp teeth, and he screams, he roars. This is an order. Right now. We're taking her to be put down, Herr

Blättner, it's me, my grandmother screams back at him. Yes, he says, his voice is hoarse, yes, Frau Glitzer. And then I start running, I race, I sprint, I yank Fritzi's lead and still flat on her stomach she slides over the polished linoleum to the end of the corridor, just before we get to the stairwell I snatch her into my arms, she can't manage the stairs, she's not up to it any more.

My grandmother follows me. How unpleasant, she says, the poor man, how unpleasant.

In the street, on the way to the vet that's supposed to be putting Fritzi down, I spot Sirena's red hair in the distance, and walking beside her is a woman with exactly the same red hair. That's bound to be her mother, they'll think fat smelly Fritzi is my dog – if only Fritzi were already dead and not puffing and panting along behind me.

Do you know that girl, asks my grandmother, is she in your class, I'm sure that'll be her mother, say hello to her really nicely and do a curtsy, perhaps we'd best go up to them and say hello. I'd much rather not but they come up to us instead and Sirena introduces me to her mother who then offers my grandmother her hand and says her name, Thea Bechler, I'm Sirena's mother, and you must be Fania Schiefer's grand-mother, and my grandmother says Yes, her face is all sweaty and her hat askew, I notice that she doesn't reveal her name, as if she too were called Schiefer and not Glitzer, she's pretending to share my name, the name of my father. Thea Bechler offers me her hand which is clad in a white kid glove and asks me if I can give her daughter extra tuition in maths. Sirena standing next to her gives me a smile, oh yes, Fania, that would be fantastic. We'd pay you of course, and my grandmother says My granddaughter will be delighted to do it.

Are you happy with twenty marks an hour, Sirena's mother asks me.

I nod. It's a lot of money, too much, ten marks is the going rate, I'm dumbstruck, a nod is all I can manage. Sirena hugs me and gives me a kiss on the cheek.

When can you start, asks Frau Bechler.

Thursday next week, says my grandmother.

Could you manage Friday, Friday would be better.

No, say my grandmother and I as though from one mouth. Sirena and her mother yield to our chorus. After all my son-in-law does get back home on Fridays, says my grandmother as though Frau Bechler had simply forgotten this self-evident fact, and the family's always together then.

Alright then, says Sirena's mother, if Friday's out then you'll just have to come on Thursday at three. Sirena smiles.

We have to wait quite a while at the vet's but once it's our turn it all happens very quickly. I hold Fritzi on my lap, the man in the white coat inserts his syringe behind her ear. After a while I ask him how long it will take her to die and he says She's already dead. I hadn't noticed. Her body is just as warm as before. What will happen to her now, I want to know, and the man promises to bury her in his garden. This tells me at once that Fritzi's corpse will go into the rubbish bin.

What do I owe you, asks my grandmother, fifteen marks, he replies, and could she make a quick telephone call. He says nothing but points at his desk where there's a white telephone, a brand-new one, our telephone is black.

My grandmother rings the Old People's Home. Fräulein Tannenbaum answers. Could she speak to Ruchla Fisch please. There's a long delay. Fräulein Tannenbaum is crippled, my grandmother explains to the vet holding her hand over the mouthpiece. The man nods and turns away. He looks nice with his grave eyes and his beard. I'm still holding dead Fritzi on my lap. Suddenly my grandmother's voice, sounding loud and unfamiliar, rings out through the animal treatment room.

Ruchla is that you, yes, it's all over, I'm going home with Fania now, Alma will be waiting for us. No, it was very quick. Fritzi didn't suffer at all. You're coming to my sixty-fifth. Good. We'll talk on the telephone again next week. Of course, Wilma, Betty and Emilie as well, Lotti's already said yes. I'll ring you, no, not much, fifteen marks, a splendid man, an excellent vet, I can't talk now, he's ever so busy I'm sure, she died straightaway, he's going to bury Fritzi in his garden.

My grandmother unlocks our front door. The door to the living room is open. The living room is empty. The door to the bedroom is open. My sister is leaning against the door frame with her back to us, my mother is still sitting at the desk, and my sister says She's having you on, she's completely barmy. Ah there you are, was it nice, asks my mother ignoring Vera. I've such a lot to tell you, Alma, says my grandmother. It's not the time for that right now, there's something important going on between my mother and my sister.

Just now when I was coming up from the larder in the cellar Frau Hainichen stopped me in the stairwell and said she needed to talk to me about my daughter, I asked her which one and she said The oldest, Frau Schiefer, and I said As you wish, and my mother demonstrates by her tone of voice exactly what was implied by her 'As you wish', namely that she, Alma Schiefer, was not prepared to have anything said about one of her daughters by anyone outside the family unless it was something good. She twiddles a pencil between her fingers. Then she says to me, right there in the stairwell, that she suspects – and my mother looks at each of us in turn – that my daughter Vera is having an affair with her husband.

My sister bursts out laughing. Her laughter is patently fake

227

and dripping with fear, and it amazes me that my mother doesn't notice. She puts a pencil into the opening of the sharpener on my father's desk and turns the handle. Amidst the noise of grinding teeth, paper-thin shavings of wood and lead fall into a special receptacle. Vera darts a glance at me. My mother checks the pencil point. My grandmother follows Vera's glance all the way to me.

My daughter is still under-age, I said to her, and if this were to be true then your husband would be having an affair with my under-age daughter, Frau Hainichen, and that is a criminal offence, what's more my daughter would never do such a thing, hand on my heart, *both* hands on my heart. And she holds up both her hands, in one of which is the freshly sharpened pencil. And with that SS swine of all people, you'd never do that to me would you, says my mother fixing Vera with a beady, pleading, penetrating gaze.

Oh nonsense, Mammy, never, never. Vera says this with all seriousness, she wants to reassure that beady, pleading, penetrating eye, even I believe her at this particular moment, and she believes herself too.

If that were true I'd leave at once, I couldn't stay here another day under the same roof as these people if my daughter, my own daughter, did such a thing to me.

Calm down, says Vera. She goes to the desk and reaches out over my mother's head for the cigarette packet. Don't take my last cigarette, says my mother; it *is* the last one, says Vera lighting it, Pappy's bound to have some in his desk.

I've already looked, says my mother.

And right at the back, asks Vera, behind the envelopes, under the carbon paper.

So you've even found out about that, says my mother hesitantly, our absolute last-ditch emergency reserves.

My father's family are coming for lunch on Sunday. My father has his own family, they're not Jews. We're the Jews, my mother, my grandmother, my sister and me, although my sister and I carry the other part in us as well, the part we get from him. You get that from your father, my mother says to me; she must know, she saw it in me, and I'm immediately a little less Jewish. The attributes she thinks I've got from him are never as good as the ones I got from her. My shortsightedness comes from him; my habit of apologising all the time comes from him. He apologises far too often. Sorry, Alma, he says, sorry, I take it back, you know far better than I do, sorry I ever said anything on the subject, sorry I was ever born. And the more he apologises the more enraged she becomes. She never apologises, any assertion she ever makes she defends to the hilt. How do you know, screams Vera, I just do, she says, sticking to her guns.

In Nazi days you'd have been half-Jews; she divides the kilo of butter down the middle, one half will go into the larder down in the cellar, the other half will go into the butter dish; your children would be one-quarter Jews, their children one-eighth Jews and so on. The big carving knife hovers over the remaining piece of golden-yellow butter. She takes it as read that Vera and I won't find any Jews to marry. Where could we. Certainly not in Hamburg. All wiped out, and any that were left have gone elsewhere.

And if I marry a Jew, I ask. Well in that case, says my mother looking at the half piece of butter, then they'd be a half plus a quarter. And if my three-quarters Jewish daughter marries a Jew, I say playing around with the figures, then her children will be seven-eighths Jews, and if *they* marry a Jew then their children, my grandchildren, would be fifteen-sixteenths Jews. Vera stamps her feet. She wants me to stop. It's just because she's no good at maths.

According to Halacha you're Jews anyway, says my grandmother. If the mother's a Jew, the children are Jews.

Vera has forgotten that I told her this quite recently when she read me a bit of *Joseph and his Brothers*, I told her when we were alone in our room that we're Jewish and that our mother can't do anything about it. Vera has forgotten that she knows this because of me, that I knew before she did, that I shared my knowledge with her.

She stands still and looks at herself. So we can forget all this stupid stuff about fractions. So we two, me and Fania – she glances at me – we two – she looks past our mother at our grandmother – are just as Jewish as she is – and she nods her head in the direction of Hedwig Glitzer's daughter, who is our mother.

According to Jewish law that's how it is, confirms my grandmother, despite the fact that Alma married your father and not a Jew.

What did I tell you, I say to Vera, what *did* you tell me, my sweet little one, she says, obliterating me from her field of vision, it's the first I've heard of it, it's a good thing to know about, she bellows in an attempt to shout me down as I still haven't given up trying to prove to her that it was me who first told her, and my mother's screaming at her mother demanding to know if she has any good reason to complain about her son-in-law.

My grandmother shrugs her shoulders, the children asked me, she says pushing her glasses from her forehead down onto her nose and returning to her perusal of one of the new magazines.

I look over the top of the magazine at the pictures. It's that man again. His black hair falls at an angle across his forehead and onto his face. They've photographed him just as he's pushing out a razor-sharp word through bared teeth. He's wearing a leather jacket. There are other young men with him, they look more respectable than he does with their conventional suits and neatly parted hair. I've heard his voice on the radio. A high-pitched voice, hurried and strained. I didn't understand what he said even though it was German. Lots of razor-sharp words. 'Class' was one of them, repeated again and again. That's Dutschke, says Vera, Rudi Dutschke. She takes the magazine from my grandmother; you can't just take that away from your grandmother, says my mother, can't you at least ask her whether you can have it. Vera gives the magazine back to her grandmother and my mother takes it straight off her, I just want to have a quick look.

He's great, says Vera.

I don't like this man. My mother is suspicious of men in leather jackets and never misses an opportunity to say so. Only in the case of taxi drivers does she tacitly accept leather jackets, the sole function of taxi drivers being to get my mother home when her husband's out on the road.

Vera points at the others, the respectable-looking young men, students all of them.

Ah just look, says my grandmother with a smile of delight, they're students, so nice and so smart.

Vera turns over a few more pages and points to an elderly man, and even though he has no jacket or tie but just a white shirt with the top button undone it's obvious that this man with his fine-featured face is highly educated. He's standing in the midst of two or three thousand students, listening to what they have to say, I spot some young women and assume they're girlfriends of the students, I expect they've been allowed to tag along just for once on the occasion of this important and highly interesting encounter with this jacketless, tieless old man, it's just the same with the Shah of Persia, he's bringing his wife Farah Diba along with him to Bonn and Berlin, Farah Diba's invented a brilliant hairstyle, the students' girlfriends don't have their hair piled up quite so high on their heads as the Empress of Persia; my sister even has a little purple bow fastened to the top of hers. Vera taps her finger vigorously on the tieless, jacketless but distinguished-looking man. He's a Jew as well.

My mother immediately wants to know how she knows. Not from you, says Vera, and my grandmother takes the magazine and reads out the caption underneath the picture, it says, Amongst the students in the lecture theatre, right foreground, and she pauses and takes a breath, here's his name now, she says, come on come on, says my mother, and my grandmother reads out the name Ludwig Marcuse then looks up and over the rim of her glasses at her daughter Alma.

That's not a Jewish name, maintains my mother.

Why not, says my grandmother, the surname of her headmistress at the Israelite School for Girls in the Karolinen Quarter was Markus.

I know that, Mummy, says my mother, who is not very pleased.

The man *looks* Jewish, says my grandmother, I'm certain he's Jewish, such a clever man, and she carries on leafing through the magazine. A photo right across two pages, that's unusual, a huge photo like that. Something must have happened. The students and their girlfriends have linked arms. There are police standing in front of them with batons.

I don't like him. My mother scratches away at the plastered-down strand of hair across Rudi Dutschke's angular face.

He's looking straight out of the photograph, despite the turmoil he knew perfectly well that he was being photographed.

Come on, Fania, look over here, look at the lens, and stop pulling that face, be my cheeky little Fania, do you want some chocolate, wrinkle your nose for me, your father wants to photograph you, what for, for later, for all eternity.

Come off it, says Vera indignantly, the students are against the old Nazis.

I know, says my mother, but I don't like this sort of thing, they form mobs in the street, they cause brawls, and as for him – and this time she makes the point of not touching Dutschke's face – he's got such a fanatical look about him.

What's happened to make them go out on the street, asks my grandmother. My sister reads out something about a fire in a Brussels department store, three hundred people lost their lives. Leaflets have apparently been circulated in Berlin asking when Berlin's stores are going to go up in flames.

They're meshugge, grumbles my mother, we've already had that once, I don't need a second dose, one Kristallnacht is quite enough for me.

The poor souls, says my grandmother, they go out shopping, and look what happens.

You don't know anything, says Vera all worked up, it's meant symbolically, because of Vietnam and what the Yanks did – Vera deliberately says 'Yanks' and not 'Americans' because it was the Yanks and the Tommies that actually liberated us – they dropped napalm bombs on completely harmless people, the Yanks did. Look. She turns back the pages of the magazine, and there's that girl again running along the road naked and screaming in terror, she can't feel the pain of her skin because she's so terrified of suddenly being dead.

I wouldn't put anything past them.

Me neither.

I mean your students.

And I mean your Yanks, says Vera.

But what about the music of my Yanks, says my mother triumphantly, you like that well enough, and their films, and their chewing gum that you're continually chewing on like a cow chewing the cud.

What about the women, I ask, what are they doing in amongst the students.

Oh them, they're the students' girlfriends, says my mother.

Vera takes her chewing gum out of her mouth and sticks it under the table edge for later use. Nonsense, Alma, she laughs, what rubbish you're telling your little girl. They're at university as well, Fania, they're female students.

Are you calling me Alma now, asks my mother with a brittle laugh. Is that the fashion now, and remove that chewing gum of yours, Frau Kupsch has found three of those revolting lumps of stuff recently while she was doing the dusting.

Perhaps I'm too grown-up now to be saying Mammy, says Vera.

My mother pulls me into her arms and hugs me. But my baby still says Mammy to me, doesn't she. She purses her red lips and plants a kiss on my mouth, my back hurts, she bends me almost double to make me fit under her wing.

Your father wouldn't think much of your new opinions, she says to Vera. It's her last chance of stopping Vera's passage to the world outside.

I'm not so sure about that, says Vera coldly.

The imminent visit of Harald Schiefer and the Old Nazi make a shopping trip necessary. Harald Schiefer is my father's elder brother, and his wife is the Old Nazi; her name is Gudrun Ellerhausen, but my mother calls her the Old Nazi. Actually she's called Schiefer, Gudrun Schiefer. She's married to my father's brother and so has the same name as us, but that's simply not on. For my mother it's unthinkable and unspeakable. It's eight years since Harald Schiefer and the Old Nazi came here for a meal, says my mother. Mimi, my father's younger sister, is coming as well. My father is the brother in the middle. I'm really looking forward to seeing my father as a brother.

What are we supposed to call her, asks Vera, Aunt Gudrun, Frau Schiefer, Old Nazi, or just Gudrun, perhaps it would be best just to call her Gudrun.

If at all possible I won't call her anything, muses my mother, if I absolutely have to I'll call her Gudrun, for me she's always been and always will be the Old Nazi.

For me too, I say. My mother throws me a grateful glance, Vera's look tells me that for her I am cowardly and twisted, the very lowest of the low. This doesn't bother me; for the very first time it doesn't bother me. You're different from me anyway, dear sister, you and your Hainichen, the dirty swine. I don't flinch from her gaze. I'm cowardly and twisted, more twisted, most twisted, I'm more Jewish than you. I hold Vera's gaze for a long time and quietly savour my triumph. A smile flickers across Vera's mouth, not a malicious smile. She signals to me with her eyelids. We've fought a secret battle but it hasn't destroyed her, I haven't destroyed her, it hasn't destroyed us.

The meal is to look good but cost as little as possible. On the one hand my mother wants to offer the Old Nazi nothing special, on the other hand she wants her to see just how good a hostess Alma Schiefer née Glitzer is. My grandmother is baking a Madeira cake to follow the roast. The roast is actually a fish, a large steamed fish: it's not very expensive, and while you're eating it you can't do much talking because you have to watch out for bones all the time and that makes matters easier, so my father reckons.

Your brother, says my mother to her husband, your brother could help you out for once, Paul. So far as he and the Old Nazi were concerned – and I hope she chokes on the bones – you might as well have died like a dog. Perhaps we should do a roast after all so that your brother can see for a change what it's like being married to a woman who can cook.

Hidden in the roast that's actually a fish is my mother's hope that Harald Schiefer might possibly give his brother some money to help him buy the house, an interest-free loan perhaps. Your brother really could do something like that for you just for a change, she says, not for me, just for you. My father smiles. He doesn't think it will happen, and my mother is determined to discover yet again that it's not going to happen. My father could do without all this, but he lets her get on with it all the same. His breath smells of liquorice, he's been sucking stomach pills for the last half an hour. There's a ring at the doorbell.

Are you going, my mother says to her mother.

Why me, asks my grandmother, I'm going into the kitchen to see to the potatoes, they need to come off.

My father goes to the door.

My mother holds fast to her beautifully laid table and checks her appearance in the large mirror that hangs on the wall. She's wearing a skin-tight red dress.

Out in the hall I hear the pure, silvery-trumpet tones of my father's voice. Hello Harald, so there you are again after all this time the pair of you, and on foot again I see, all the way from Barmbek to save the tram fare, well I never, so you still haven't got a car then, do come in.

The living-room door, already ajar, is suddenly thrust open and Harald Schiefer, tall, gaunt and with a crooked smile, enters and stretches out his arms – at the ends of which hang

236

two enormous red hands – towards his brother's wife. Hello my dear sister-in-law, he says before adding in English Very nice to see you, whereupon Aunt Mimi, following close behind, explains to Vera and me that our uncle Harald was a prisoner of war in England. Ha ha, Harald, you with the Tommies eh; my father laughs. Clutching his arm is the Old Nazi, Gudrun Ellerhausen, she's scraggy and coarse featured, her neck stiff, her shoulders hunched, her pale lashless eyes awash with moisture, her hair grey, her dress grey, her lace-up shoes flat and brown; her pallid mouth is twisted into a frivolous smile and shapes itself into my mother's name. Alma, she murmurs. Nothing more.

My mother has let go of the tabletop. She's standing in the middle of the room in her skin-tight red dress. She is The Jewess. From her deep black hair to her black suede high-heeled shoes she is every inch the proud Jewess, flaring her nostrils and half closing her eyelids over her dark-coloured eyes. After a pause she greets her mortal enemy by reaching out her hands with their red-painted fingernails, two of which were still hanging off a short while before but have now been glued back on, while the two brothers, despite years of estrangement, are soon exchanging warm fraternal glances.

Why don't you open the wine, Paul, says my mother seeing the alien hand of the Old Nazi resting on his arm. Let me have him for a bit longer, says the Old Nazi on my father's arm to my mother, the proud Jewess. You've hidden him from us for so many years. And I know that later on my mother will say She said that to humiliate me, and my father will say Go on, you're making too much of it, Alma, did she really say that, I certainly didn't hear it, and my mother will say But I did, Paul, I did, and she said it to humiliate me, and she clawed at your arm as she said it, and my father will say Perhaps she really was

237

just pleased to see me, how can you know for sure. But my mother knows, and I saw it all.

Do sit down all of you, she wants to pop into the kitchen for a moment, would you look after the guests, she says to Vera with a wink, and Vera swings into motion. My sister starts flirting with her Uncle Harald, getting him to light her cigarette, crossing her legs and lifting her skirt above her knee. My mother watches her daughter from the living-room doorway with great satisfaction. She nods her head in the direction of the Old Nazi who is staring fixedly at Vera, and Vera smiles and lifts her skirt even higher. My father opens the wine.

In the kitchen my mother uses the fish stock to make a second sauce to accompany the butter sauce. She mashes together soft-boiled carrots, shallots, celery, tangy-smelling juniper berries and two garlic cloves, then adds the stock and and cream. My grandmother drains the potatoes, transfers the fish onto a large serving plate, and places slices of lemon and tiny bunches of dill all round its resplendent bulk.

So what's she like, she asks her daughter.

What do you think she's like, a vile ponim just the same as she was back then when she chased you away from her door.

I stand in the doorway. The kitchen is Jewish country. It's warm and cosy here. In the living room the air is poisoned. Old Nazi is far too nice a term.

The meal is a mixture of words and fishbones. The Old Nazi talks about her three men, meaning her husband and her two sons, neither of whom has come with them. Vera asks about the sons, how old they are and whether they're tall.

Taller and older than you, says Gudrun Ellerhausen, my oldest is nearly two metres tall, and Vera immediately wants to meet these two sons, she desperately wants to get to know them.

238

Just come and visit us, says Gudrun Ellerhausen, but ask your mother first whether she'll allow it.

My mother's just spitting some bones out onto her fork and can't reply, my father chews and swallows in silence, his brother chews and swallows in silence, and Aunt Mimi refrains from talking while eating fish on account of the bones. Vera's not bothered by the bones, she eats fish like a cat does. Are your sons well and truly related to us, she asks, To you, yes, says Gudrun Ellerhausen looking the fish in the eye and taking herself another chunk of its flesh and another two potatoes and some butter sauce – she doesn't like the other sauce, it smells of garlic, she says, screwing up her pointed nose and lifting her fork to her narrow little mouth. I can see a bone in the white flesh that she's about to eat, a bone the size of a pitchfork, and I'm curious to see what will become of it.

How are we related to these two sons, Vera wants to know, and Gudrun Ellerhausen gives a shrill laugh causing the fishbone to tremble on her fork; has your mother hidden all that from you, she asks.

Dolf and Charlie are your cousins, says my mother, you've played table tennis with them, don't you remember, Vera, here in our garden, eight years ago now.

Dolf and Charlie, repeats Vera in a positively rapt tone of voice, Dolf and Charlie, I don't have the faintest recollection unfortunately. Needless to say the Old Nazi doesn't realise that Vera and I in fact remember precious little of our own slender past, whereas we can recount our parents' lives in great detail, we know the backgrounds and names of people we never knew because we didn't yet exist. What sort of a name is Dolf, Vera wants to know, it sounds so Dutch.

Mimi laughs hoarsely, Dutch, that's good, and my grandmother makes her presence felt: nebbish, she giggles, poor boy, and her reward is to get her toe trodden on under the table by my mother. There's something funny about the name. Even Vera notices this despite her blithe but blind enthusiasm regarding her two tall cousins: I thought because of Delft, delft tiles, that sort of thing. The Old Nazi pretends not to have been listening and asks me whether I would like to come and visit her as well in order to meet my two big cousins. She's talking to me directly and this makes me jump. I stare at the fishbone on her fork that could choke her to death, I'm not going to speak, my pounding heart is almost leaping out of my mouth. I know that my grandmother stood at her front door when my father was in jail charged with defiling the German race and asked her for money for a lawyer so that his trial could take place and then perhaps he would be released by the Gestapo instead of being shot. The woman sitting opposite me at our table slammed the door in my grandmother's face. My grandmother, sitting right next to me. The fishbone is dangling in mid-air. All of a sudden the man who is my uncle and my father's brother puts down his knife and fork and reaches across the table with his large red hand to help himself to some more wine, and my father looks up from his plate, sorry, Harald, he says, do help yourself. I no longer need to reply to the Old Nazi, I've lost sight of the fishbone, and Gudrun Ellerhausen remains alive.

As we sit round the coffee table having coffee and Madeira cake my mother remarks that her mother baked the cake, and my grandmother nods vigorously, do take another slice, Frau Schiefer, I used nothing but best butter. I suddenly take in the fact that my grandmother calls my father's sister-in-law by her surname. She does the same with my father's brother. Please, do have some more, Frau Schiefer, she passes her Madeira cake to this woman with her hard grey face, she pushes the little jug across to her, here's some cream for you, for your husband too, for Herr Schiefer, it's real cream, not tinned. Gudrun Ellerhausen rejects all my grandmother's offers, the real cream is too much for her, the cake is too much for her. Nothing, thank you. My grandmother is too much for her and also for her husband.

A door slams shut. Is the kitchen window open, Alma asks her mother. The kitchen window, Mummy. Hedwig doesn't answer. Mummy, are you dreaming. She puts her hand on the hand of her mother.

Well you *are* well set up, Paul, says Gudrun Ellerhausen, you've such a lot to be grateful for, living in this lovely house in this lovely area, you really are well set up.

We'd like to buy the house, sighs my father. My mother isn't happy about the way he's tackling things, she's not happy about the fact that these people are still here, she wants an end to it all before too long, she casts a worried glance at her mother, she wants to get it over with right here and now. We're having to leave this place, she says, we don't have the money, the house is being sold, they've offered it to us, and we were wondering whether perhaps you – and at this point the man who is my uncle suddenly starts telling us about his attack of shingles. I got it just like that, right out of the blue, and *so* painful.

Not out of the blue, Daddy, says Gudrun Ellerhausen, poor Daddy was sent to a camp, wasn't he, these things are the long-term after-effects of his time in the camp.

You mean your husband was a prisoner of war as a member of the Wehrmacht, says my mother.

My God, Harald, is it painful, asks Mimi with a grimace. She's not only my aunt and my father's sister and my mother's sister-in-law, she's also related to these people. She puts her left hand with its two diamond rings on Harald's enormous red hand. What beautiful rings, says Gudrun Ellerhausen taking Mimi's hand from Harald's and inspecting the two rings; she could never afford such things, she remarks, her sons were her jewels, her two lovely men.

What were their names again, asks Vera. Adolf and Karl-Hinrich, replies Gudrun Ellerhausen, Adolf is the older one, but Daddy calls his two sons Dolf and Charlie, and Dolf looks just like an American, would you like to see some photos. Vera immediately wants to see the photos and is immediately bowled over by this Adolf with his smarmy quiff, just like a real American. My mother remarks that to her mind the diamond rings on Aunt Mimi's hand are too bulky, and Mimi explains that her boyfriend had lent her the rings, so sweet of him, she thought, they'd been his dead mother's and she was allowed to wear them but only as a loan because they were his mother's though it gave him such pleasure to see them once again on the hand of a woman he adored. And now Mimi wants cognac, Paul, would you pour me one, and my father pours her one. My Aunt Mimi is already a bit tipsy thanks to the wine; even when she arrived and greeted me with a kiss her breath had the familiar reek of cognac. Harald also takes a cognac, then sticks a fat cigar in his mouth. Or will the smoke bother you, he asks my mother, who hates cigar smoke. Not at all, she lies, and he's pleased, he says, because Gudrun doesn't let him do it at home on account of the net curtains. You can do it here, minces my mother.

Contracting her hard mouth into the ghost of a smile Gudrun Ellerhausen remarks that her husband smokes his cigars at his sister Mimi's house. That being so then Harald must be a frequent visitor at Mimi's. This is not lost on my mother whose eyes – closely followed by Gudrun Ellerhausen's icy gaze – dart from Mimi to her husband. My father seems to have already known this fact.

Anyway, says Harald Schiefer, he hadn't noticed anything to begin with then all of a sudden there were these tiny blisters on his skin. It was me that noticed the blisters, Daddy, says Gudrun Ellerhausen, d'you remember, I knew what it was as soon as I saw them; central nervous system, the doctor thinks, he doesn't know how long it might last, it can just keep coming back. You can't exterminate something like that. The doctor gave Daddy the name of a woman who cures things with magic spells and he went to see her didn't you, Daddy.

Harald sucks on his long fat cigar and enjoys the attention, he takes his time, he gazes around at his select little audience – his little brother, his even littler sister, his attractive sister-in-law, my mother, and my grandmother, her face glistening with sweat – and puffs his smoke into the air. Meanwhile Gudrun Ellerhausen quickly grabs a third slice of cake and pours masses of cream into her coffee. My grandmother notices this and nods her head encouragingly.

The woman took me into a little room with nothing in it except for a bed, a table and a chair. I stripped off down to the waist of course, didn't I, and she came up close to me, really close, had a good look at what I've got down there, then mumbled something and passed her hands over it. For about three minutes, perhaps even four or five. The second time she'd touched him and felt him. She'd pressed him against her body and mumbled something. She didn't say how much she wanted. He puffs away at his cigar. I gave her ten marks.

We on our side all have the same thought. It wasn't enough. He's mean, and that won't help.

Mimi wants to know whether the woman was a gypsy.

Perhaps not a gypsy, but jet-black hair and black eyes just

243

like you, Alma, says Harald Schiefer, and I bet she earns a tidy sum with those tricks of hers, she had a whole mouth full of gold teeth, enough to buy this house here, he says, thus returning unprompted and completely out of the blue to the topic closest to my parents' heart. My father, who meanwhile has turned yellow in the face and loosened his waistband because his stomach's hurting, pulls himself together in his armchair: Yes, ha ha ha, how about that for an idea, Harald, perhaps we should get our wives to do the same thing so we can get hold of some money, what d'you reckon, Alma, we urgently need a loan, you see, if we're going to buy this house.

Although it's been said it hasn't been clearly enunciated: we need money. We need fifty-six thousand marks. Surely they must have got the message. His big brother and his big brother's wife and Aunt Mimi with her rich boyfriend. My father pulls his large white handkerchief from his trouser pocket, removes his glasses and wipes the sweat from his face. He doesn't know what to say next.

They all know how to get hold of money, so does that gypsy woman, says Gudrun Ellerhausen, and us poor devils in Germany, we've only ever earned a bare few crumbs, the houses in the best areas, this one included I'm sure, all owned by Jews, and it's just the same again today, and prices are rocketing. I'm not complaining and what's happened has happened, the war and all that, then the Russians arrived, now we're all quits.

The word has been spoken. Jews. It's a good word, I like it, Jews, in our house and our garden the word enjoys total freedom of movement. But the way it comes slithering out of the mouth of this woman is ghastly to behold. No, Gudrun, says Harald Schiefer, that's not the way it is, what's happened has happened. Huge sums have been paid out in reparations, and we doubtless have little right to complain about that. Just as I say, Daddy, says his wife, then the Russians arrived, and now we're all quits. He wraps his lips round his cigar, leans back in his chair, and puffs away.

Give me a cigarette, Paul, my mother grabs the packet before he can pass it to her, three cigarettes fall to the floor, she takes the fourth, and he bends down from his armchair and picks up the fallen cigarettes, she sticks hers between her red lips that have suffered somewhat from eating and are trembling slightly. Vera gives her a light, don't upset yourself, Mammy, she whispers, like a trainer talking to a boxer between rounds, and my mother sizes up her challenger, gives a quick nod of the head, and takes a hurried drag at her cigarette, she wants to know whether there's more to come, she's the family type, she'd love to have a big family around her, she had been prepared to establish friendly relations with this family here, but things have turned out differently, just as they did back then.

People who joined in thirty-three, says Harald to his brother, can't be blamed, Paul, don't you think, they just didn't know. People who joined in thirty-eight knew alright. Not in thirty-three though, don't you think.

And you joined in thirty-three, says my mother, and my father sits up in his chair, stubs out his freshly lit cigarette in the ashtray, refastens the waistband of his trousers.

Yes, sister-in-law, says Harald grinning and puffing on his cigar. I obeyed the laws in force at the time.

Look, says my father – and he has firmed up his voice as well as his waistband, and my mother, who was just starting to say something, falls silent – look, that's precisely the difference between you and me. I didn't obey those laws, I flouted them, and I'm proud of it, and now we're going to put a stop to this encounter and perhaps try again in a few years' time.

245

My father stands up. They stand up. We all stand up. Harald Schiefer carefully deposits his cigar in the ashtray next to the squashed-up cigarette of his younger brother, he holds out his enormous red hand and with a bow and a handshake says goodbye to everyone in turn, first the old Jewess, then the young Jewess, his little brother's pretty wife, and finally us two daughters, though not without running his greedy eye over Vera. He bows repeatedly, keen to demonstrate his perfect manners. His wife watches him throughout, Gudrun Ellerhausen keeps her small brown handbag pressed tightly to her body with both hands, her husband's goodbyes are on behalf of them both.

I'm so sorry, says Mimi to my parents, I'm sure you'll understand that I'd rather like to leave as well.

Of course, says my mother with a sickly sweet smile, you'll ring us of course, as usual.

She wants the Old Nazi to know that Mimi will tell us everything. My father escorts them to the door. When he comes back into the room we're all still standing by the coffee table, motionless but keyed up ready to leap to his defence or run for our lives.

He looks at us and laughs, what's the matter all of you, we can breathe properly now, I'm going to have a piece of cake at long last, and come to think of it where's the champagne. Oh dear, the champagne, says my mother, I clean forgot it, Paul. She flings her arms round his neck and sobs; I'm so happy, exclaims my father, isn't it wonderful that we can afford to do such a thing, and we'll always be able to afford to do it.

How are we meant to buy the house. The ground's caving in beneath our feet and we dance blissfully on. Hainichen will throw us out so that he can get a better price for the house.

That night I wake up feeling infinitely hungry for chocolate. My craving for the sweet, creamy balm drives me from my slumbers, I can think of nothing but chocolate. I put the light on and wake Vera. I need chocolate, I say, and Vera struggles out of bed still half asleep, staggers across to our clothes cupboard, opens it and takes out the Prange shoebox. The box is empty. They were my last reserves I was going to give you, she says turning her tired, pale face towards me, her eyes half closed. I know, I say, I needed some the other day after school. She nods. That's just the way she is: she can touch me for money and never give it back and she can tell me lies, but at the same time she doesn't take it amiss when I secretly eat her chocolate. She gets back into bed and looks at the clock. Just gone midnight. Perhaps they're still awake, she says, perhaps there's something wrong with Pappy. You go, I ask. There's nothing Vera detests more than being rudely awoken in the middle of the night and sent off somewhere, but she gets up without a word, puts her slippers on and goes across the hall and through the living room. I hear her knock on the bedroom door. I can't go, all I can do is sit here in my bed hoping that someone will bring me chocolate. I hear her talking. My grandmother appears in the doorway. She hasn't got any chocolate either, would I like her to do me some bread and jam or some hot milk and honey. No, nothing. Only chocolate. My mother comes in in her dressing gown and sits on my bed. She tries to persuade me that I'm perfectly capable of going back to sleep without chocolate. But I need it. This convinces her. But where on earth is she supposed to get chocolate from. She has a brainwave: cocoa. Chocolate, I say. Not cocoa. My father appears in his pyjamas.

I've looked everywhere, Fania, I usually have some Cadbury's in my bedside cabinet, but not today of all days. What about the car, my mother asks hopefully. None there either, he says, I know that for a fact.

Oh Paul, she sighs, what are we going to do with Fania, could I have a cigarette please. My father shuffles back into the living room and we can hear him rummaging around. Did you have a bad dream perhaps, she asks and puts her hand on my forehead, have you got a temperature, no, you haven't got a temperature.

My father comes back. I can't find any cigarettes.

What, my mother looks at him, incredulous, no cigarettes either, that's impossible, we've run out of life's most basic necessities. Vera roots through her handbag. Nothing. Then I'd better go and get us some, says my father.

I know there's a cigarette machine up in Milchstrasse by Finke's grocery shop, says my mother, there's probably one for chocolate as well.

I've already undressed, says my father looking down at his baggy striped pyjama trousers. I'll just put my mac on over my pyjamas, it's pitch-black outside.

He goes out of the room and returns wearing a mac and tennis shoes and carrying a torch in his right hand.

What are you up to, asks my mother with a laugh, you're not meant to be going on a burgling spree.

Good point, says my father, I'll take an umbrella as well, you never know what kind of shady characters are lurking around here at this time of night.

Half past twelve, says my grandmother, holding an alarm clock in her hand. Why've you got the alarm clock in your hand, asks my mother. I was just going to set it, says my grandmother. We can all have a lie-in in the morning can't we, says Vera. We all look at my father. His help is needed. I'd better get going then, he says, holding the torch in his right hand and the rolled umbrella in his left. Have you got enough change on you, my mother asks. He nods, she accompanies him to the front door and comes back to my bedside. My grandmother has sat down on Vera's bed. We all wait silently for his return.

If anyone were to see us like this, says Vera all of a sudden, just sitting here in the middle of the night waiting. The three of them giggle. My mother starts laughing so much she can barely speak. I was just thinking about the fact that he had the torch in his right hand and the umbrella in his left. She doubles up with laughter, scarcely able to breathe. After all, she hisses, he's not left-handed. My sister laughs helplessly, my grandmother wipes tears of laughter from her cheeks. I can't join in the laughter, I feel so weak, so utterly given up to this craving within me. Chocolate. I need chocolate in order to stop thinking about chocolate. I don't find it odd that they're sitting around my bed waiting with me or that it's because of me that he's gone out into the night looking for chocolate. They're busy imagining him coming face to face with a thief or robber or mugger of some sort and helplessly shining the torch in his face instead of knocking him to the ground, all because he's holding his umbrella in the wrong hand. But my father is incapable of knocking anyone down anyway. He'd want to introduce himself first, squawks Vera, and my mother nods and gasps for breath, she holds her stomach, she tries to speak, stop scratching yourself, she manages to say. I can't stop. My arms are itching as though covered with thousands of ants. I scream. I flail around with my arms. Stay calm, really calm, my mother calls out to me. It shoots right up my body, my legs aren't mine any more, they're mere attachments, attachments in the form of body parts, my mother tears my pyjamas from my body, a sensation of heat engulfs me like wildfire. He promised. He'll bring me the chocolate. Quick, quick. That's my mother's voice. Fever. They're holding tight to my feet. They're holding

249

tight to my hands. They're holding tight to my eyes. They're coming. Millions of whirring dots. I can't do it. I can't count them. Too fast. Too many. Quick, quick. Whiteness suddenly strikes my body.

I open my eyes, and my father is sitting by my bed with a tentative smile on his face and his hand resting on my forehead. I'm wet, they've wrapped me in a wet sheet, even my hair is wet, my teeth are chattering, and I feel like a new being; lying on my stomach are two bars of Cadbury's chocolate, Dairy Milk and Dairy Milk with Nuts, and the squawking, cackling women have retreated to the end of the bed and are standing there in a row all silent and demure gazing down at me with solemn, frightened faces.

Chapter Eight

The nougat man is standing outside the school. I can hear him
calling out, I can see white overalls on his rounded back and
the round white cap on his bald head. He's calling his wares.
Nougat, nougat. His broad-bladed knife scrapes and scratches
the sticky substance from the pink-and-white-layered sugary
block. Ten pfennigs for a handful of sticky shavings. I've
walked the whole way to school without looking up, past all
the front gardens, I know the whitewashed houses sitting on
their cellars at the other end of these gardens with their
jutting-out sun rooms and topped in some cases by little towers;
generations of Hamburg merchants have lived beneath their
roofs with their wives and children, shipowners, exporters,
financiers, senators. They don't buy their bread and potatoes
themselves, or their fruit and Sunday roast. Frau Kupsch does
that for them or Frau Kupsch's daughter Elisabeth, or else her
son Wolfram has to run an errand and earn ten pfennigs for his
pains. But not always.

There are shipowners' wives and exporters' wives and
financiers' wives and senators' wives who didn't say hello when
my mother said hello. And now my mother walks straight past
them, her blood-red lips pressed tightly together, her pace fast,
our journey punctuated by the click of her heels. Come on,

Fania, she grabs my arm and pulls me close to her, I stumble, we rush on past. That went off alright again. You know who they are, don't you.

I do. But I ask all the same, Who are they. Because her face is on fire. And she's holding her breath. Frau Blechmann. Frau Schlenk. Frau Schulze-Edel. Saying their names makes her feel better. She says them with contempt in her voice, and she can breathe again.

If I'm on my own I say hello to Frau Blechmann, hello to Frau Schlenk, hello to Frau Schulze-Edel. Good day, I whisper, quietly and without saying their name. I don't do a curtsy, there's no time for a curtsy, I rush past, they don't want a hello from me, they just want to check that I've seen them. That's all. We don't belong here. But my father thinks that this is exactly where we do belong given the loveliness of the street and the area and that we're more entitled than anyone to a lovely life.

I've got something round my neck. A strip of red. I'm wearing his bow-tie under my chin. This morning I crept into my parents' bedroom. My mother was in the kitchen, my father's on the road. I opened the clothes cupboard. On the top shelf, next to the neatly ironed handkerchiefs, I saw the slender cardboard box. I took the lid off and commandeered the bow-tie. I didn't want an ordinary tie, I know how to fasten one, Wolfram showed me, I didn't want a tie dangling down there between them. Not that you'd be able to see anything yet. I'm supposed to splash cold water onto my flat chest with cupped hands three times every morning according to my grandmother. Vera uses warm water though. She says cold water makes her breasts shrink back into her body. She thinks her breasts are small enough already without that. She's wearing a bra now to make them look bigger. I think it's

252

because of Hainichen. She stands in front of the mirror and stuffs handkerchiefs into the cups. They both have to look the same, and there mustn't be any creases. It's better if you use cotton wool, my mother showed her how to do it.

I can see old Frau Schmalstück coming towards me in the distance, hobbling along all black and gaunt in her skinflinty body. I cross to the other side of the street. I'm to say hello to her. The house isn't ours yet. So long as she lives in the same house as us you're to be polite to Frau Schmalstück. Do you hear, Fania, I don't want this woman to have *any* grounds for complaint. I don't want to have to say hello to Frau Schmalstück. She denounced my father. For defiling the German race. He went to prison. Here in this city. For months and months. And here she is as free as a bird hobbling down the street that I've just walked along. My father, my poor father round my neck. Oops. Look straight in front of you all the time, Fania. I've walked straight into a woman. Men are worse than women. Only my father. My father. My poor father. To my mother women are just as dodgy as men – differently so, but just as dodgy all the same. It was Frau Hainichen. I ran straight into her. Three, five, seven. I'm already well past, the paving stones are rapidly receding beneath my feet. Seven is my father's lucky number. Because he was born on the seventh. He's not shy. A lot of people think he's shy, he looks shy. He's polite. He just doesn't want anyone to do him any harm. That's all.

I *can* write. The fact that I can't write is due to the mess. The mess invades me from outside and piles up within me, I'll never be able to sort it out, behind it somewhere there's me. The fact that I can't write properly is the most embarrassing thing in the entire world, even more embarrassing than the fact that I've just run bang into Frau Hainichen. I'd turned round to look at old Frau Schmalstück and all of a sudden there was Frau Hainichen, and I bumped right into her. She'll think I'm meshugge, no she won't think I'm meshugge, she'll think I'm plain mad. I'm not mad. I just don't concentrate hard enough, you don't concentrate hard enough, when am I *ever* going to concentrate hard enough for it to stop, for me to be able to do it at last. If I, if you concentrated hard enough, you'd be able to write properly, I'd be able to write properly. At your age people can write their own language, at your age, I *can* write my own language. It's not true, I do concentrate. At my age everybody can write properly, except for me. It's precisely when I *don't* concentrate so much, when I don't have to think about every single word, that I write best, I write everything correctly, every word, the letters stand there next to one another in a row, in numerous rows, with every so often a breathing space between them. I chew over every word with my eyes. Give me your lips. Careful, Mammy's already put her lipstick on. Give me your lips. Be really careful. I want you to give me a proper kiss. On the mouth. Make my mouth red. I find your lips on my pillow in the morning. During the night a huge mouth was roaring within me. Tiny bones were forcing their way through its gullet, they were shattered words, shattered letters. There were bits of chicken. Chunks of bread. Garlic mixed with olive oil. And last of all, chocolate. He brought it for me in the night. Something's knocking against my eyes from the inside. It's a migraine. She leant over me. Her hands and arms were covered by long black silk gloves, a second skin reaching above her elbow, and just at the point where my mother's pulse throbs and throbs three small buttons were undone. She wanted to do them up on the way out, stooping over her upraised pulse. Light-coloured flesh, heavily scented, in the gap where the buttons were still undone. They

254

wanted to go out into the night. She leant over me and with her black-gloved hand brushed the damp hair from my forehead. Her lips came closer, then just before her red mouth reached my lips it veered away to one side. Kiss me properly, you're to kiss me properly. She pursed her lips and kissed me on the cheek. That wasn't a proper kiss. Kiss me properly, on the mouth. So we can find each other again. My father was standing behind my mother, the car keys were jumping around in his hand. Later, when I was asleep, there was a man standing there. In uniform. He was shooting at a woman. The woman was holding a child in her arms, pressing it against her body. They were only a rifle-length apart. He couldn't have got any nearer. He could have not shot her, he could have pointed the barrel up or down and shot the sky or the earth. He raised the rifle to his cheek below his soldier's helmet. The woman pressed the child to her body. He pressed the rifle to his body and leant forward. The woman turned the girl's face towards her own chest. She didn't want the child to see her killer as she died. The woman watched him as he finished the job. He fired the bullet through the girl into the woman. The woman fell to her knees. She held her child and fell with the child, her dead body falling on top of her daughter. She held up her outstretched arm towards the man. Paul, could you do my buttons for me. My father put the car keys in his trouser pocket and fastened the three buttons on my mother's glove. He stooped over her pulse.

To avoid thinking about things you need to be doing something. My mother is knitting a red woollen blanket. She knits squares. Sixty-five rows of sixty-five stitches. Later on the squares are sewn together. I count the paving stones and run ahead of myself, I estimate the number of stones up to the corner, I lose count, I stop and look around, I don't know where I started counting and I can't go back, lessons will be starting any minute, the nougat man is calling out. My mother told me the way she used to do it as a child: anyone stepping on a join had to stand still as if they were dead. Yes, I thought to myself, that's how it was for you back then: you'd have been dead. I'll have to watch out that I don't tread anyone to death, and that I don't swallow any letters or lose any words. No sooner has a word come into my mouth than some of its consonants are all awry and I listen to them with my tongue, I follow them right along my teeth, the roof of my mouth arches up, the wind wafts through the sails of my vocal cords. Meanwhile there's creeping and crawling in every join. Dark abysses gape between the paving stones. Holding my hand in hers she leaps over lines, she's taking me with her. Legs wide apart. Vera and I have reflected on the fact that we could bring numerous children into the world. I'd produced a large family, they're all sitting at a round table eating a meal, each at their own particular place, and of course Vera immediately had staff whereas I was trying to work out what diameter saucepan I would need to make chicken broth for ten children, what's the ratio of the circumference to the diameter, Pi equals 3·1415926536. The Buddenbrooks had staff too. Vera's reading *Buddenbrooks* for the third or fourth time. She's been moody recently. No one's allowed to talk to her. She's not feeling good so she's reading a book that she already knows like the back of her hand: from page nine to page seven hundred and twenty-eight everything in *Buddenbrooks* is just the same as it ever was. To be absolutely precise, the novel has one page more: it finishes on page seven hundred and twenty-nine. It closes with the words The End. Without a full stop. It floats off into infinitude. No book commences on page one. The story's up to page five or seven or nine by the time you start reading.

Something has invariably already happened when you begin a book, something has invariably already taken place on the preceding pages that are counted even though they're not there. My father brought *Buddenbrooks* back with him, he'd got it from the lending library on Mittelweg. An old book. Gothic script. Published in 1903, when my grandmother was a year old. In a few days' time we'll be celebrating her sixty-fifth birthday. My father put the book down. We're keeping that, he said solemnly.

Who knows where it came from, my mother wondered, from complete strangers I'd imagine, who did it belong to before, perhaps there's a name in it, it looks very well thumbed, what's more Elli Dingeldey will spot it.

Do you think the books used to belong to a family, asked Vera.

Why not, the stuff must all have ended up somewhere.

My father didn't want to return the book, he preferred to hang on to it. My father enjoys having a beer with Elli Dingeldey, the Mittelweg librarian. Once or twice a year he really fancies a nice fresh beer straight from the barrel. He doesn't like pubs and he doesn't like the men in pubs but with Elli Dingeldey it's a different matter, with her he'll happily visit Hamburg's bars. My mother has no objections to Elli Dingeldey. A woman who spends her whole life with books can't be bad, and my mother is magnanimous: her husband can go off and have a beer without her and in the company of another woman provided she's as unattractive as Elli Dingeldey.

She didn't record the loan, said my father. Give it back all the same, retorted my mother. Vera thought we should keep it: we had a right to it, it might have belonged to a Jewish family. My mother looked at the book, a family saga that had plainly meant a lot to numerous hands. Well anyway, said my father, it's in the possession of Jews now.

My sister and I write our names in our books, right at the front on the first or second page. For me it's a huge pleasure writing my name in a book that henceforth belongs to me. It makes me happy to look at my books, my very own books. There they stand, bursting with stories that they keep to themselves. I write my name on the inside of the front cover, even though it would be nicer if I wrote it on paper instead of on the cover. But the first few pages before the book actually starts might be torn out and my name would go with them. Vera doesn't even bother to do this when she pinches a book. What's more she's interested in my parents' books rather than mine. She simply crosses out my father's name and writes hers above it. She claims he gave her the book as a present and although my mother knows this is untrue she doesn't put up much of a fight, it's still in the family after all, it simply migrates across the hallway from my parents' book cabinet to my sister's bookcase. I can see it from my bed. More and more grown-up books are appearing on Vera's shelves. The spines are cloth-covered, some have gold or silver lettering. *Buddenbrooks* is bound in pale linen. The signature is in italic as though written by hand, and the lettering is as blue as the waters of the River Trave. In our *Buddenbrooks* the novel begins immediately after the front cover. The blank pages in between are all missing. They disappeared before we got it. The novel begins on page nine. Vera had put *Buddenbrooks* in amongst her own books, but my mother took it away from her and put it back where it normally lived, just before *Rebecca* and *Gone with the Wind*. If Fania ever wants to read the book, she said, I want her to be able to get it from her parents' book cabinet, just the same as you.

Fania can't even begin to read the words, said Vera indignantly, it's in Gothic script, you can't read Gothic.

Yes I can, I retorted.

That's new, I didn't know that, and Thomas Mann's long sentences, you hate that sort of thing for goodness' sake.

I didn't reply. Vera objects to long sentences, but I don't. She's been going on to us for weeks about Adalbert Stifter and his long sentences. In a word, said my mother, *Buddenbrooks* belongs to me.

You mean it belongs to you and Pappy, said Vera.

It makes no difference, whatever belongs to your father also belongs to me.

When Vera took the book and sank into my absent father's armchair with *Buddenbrooks* in her hand and a gloomy look on her face I immediately felt anxious and of course she noticed this and hugged the book tightly to her chest and settled more deeply into his chair. It troubled me the way she was hugging the book to her chest. She has to leave something for me. Perhaps there's only enough for one of us. Perhaps not even that.

Vera's waiting for her period to start. I'm wearing his red bow-tie. The nougat man is standing by his sugary block scraping and sweating. He's erected an awning over his nougat and his fat body, pink and white like the nougat. The man does everything with his left hand. The fingers of his right hand have been chopped off right up to the middle joint, only the thumb is still fully intact. With his left hand he pushes the sticky shavings onto a bit of greaseproof paper held in place by his four stumps. On his left hand there are five fingers each with three joints and a fingernail. Every finger present and correct. As if they had experienced nothing of what had happened on the other side. All of this on one man. The nougat man.

Ten pfennigs' worth, he asks, I nod silently, in the process my chin touches the silky knot in the middle of the bow-tie that I have purloined from my father. The man holds out my helping of nougat, I gaze at his stumps, and with his narrowed eyes he watches me watching his stumps. My blouse is as white as a man's shirt and its collar as stiff as a shirt collar. I smuggled my father's bow-tie out of the house in my school bag and put it round my neck in the street, right in the middle of the street where no one could see me, no one in my family anyway. I don't like nougat but I do enjoy buying myself a little something before entering the school building, I ask a stranger for something and he gives it to me and I pay for it. That's the right way to do things. I'm doing it right.

Do you want some more, he asks.

This makes me jump. I wasn't expecting it.

In the classroom the other girls look at my father's bow-tie beneath my chin, I'm different from them. Today I let them see it. I'd very much like to know whether the bow-tie beneath my chin is straight or crooked; I don't want my father's bow-tie to be crooked, but I don't want to feel for it with my hands right there in front of everybody.

What *do* you look like, says Annegret, what *do* you look like.

I don't look Jewish, not in the least, unfortunately. When it came to your face, says my mother, your father won out for once. I do speak with my hands though, and I do use Yiddish words, often without realising. Leave her be, says my grandmother, and my mother says Better not to do it, you know what people are like. In the classroom I put the greaseproof paper containing the nougat on the desk in front of Annegret.

Here, you can have it.

Really, do you really mean that, and she stuffs it into her mouth with her fingers. I watch, and I take hold of the bow-tie

260

beneath my chin and give a little tug at both ends. To make it sit straight. None of the girls laugh. Bow-ties are a man's thing. None of them laugh about that. Sirena's seat next to me is empty even though the bell has already rung. Herr Bobbenberg comes into the classroom. He's not wearing a tie today. He's put on a bow-tie today, or his wife has put it on for him, how about a bow-tie today, Wilhelm, or doesn't he always wear a bow-tie, never a necktie, Bobbenberg always with a bow-tie, I'm not sure any more. Better not to look at all. He puts his heavily scuffed briefcase on the desk, leafs through the register and calls out our names one by one, each pupil answering Here. I say Yes. I don't want to say Here. I want to say something different from all the others. The girl after me also calls out Yes. He doesn't call Sirena's name. Perhaps Sirena doesn't exist any more, the Bechler family have moved away from Hamburg, how can I find out whether the invitation still stands or whether they've long since cleared off and no longer expect me, wouldn't I look funny standing there at their front door with my bow-tie beneath my chin if they'd long since departed. I'm as red as if someone's tipped a bucket of fire all over me. The other girls laugh. That looks good, says Wilhelm Bobbenberg tugging at his bow-tie, stand up would you, Fania. We face each other bow-tie to bow-tie, he isn't very tall, shorter than Vera I would guess, he's making squelchy noises with his grinning lips. I hold my ground.

At Finke's grocery I turn the corner into our street and catch sight of something happening a fair way away, a lump of some kind writhing around on the pavement. My glasses aren't clear enough. I need new lenses and I'd like a new frame, one called Gigi, I came across it in my father's sample collection when we were cleaning all the spectacles. Gigi is expensive, black, slender, square-cornered and brand new. He can only give me a model from his old collection. I push my round-framed specs closer to my eyes and hold my hand over the lenses. By looking along the lines of my fingers I can focus more clearly. The writhing lump is a dog with six legs and two heads. I rush towards it. I want to see nothing and everything and I don't want to be seen myself, the houses are staring from their windows. I dash up to the dogs. It's already over. Tassi the poodle bitch belonging to Katjenka Nohke – Katjenka Nohke who comes from Russia and married one Alfred Nohke of Nohke Bros, the clothiers in Mönckebergstrasse, formerly Silbermann & Co., and is having an affair with Admiral (ret'd) Friedhelm Stierich, a boozer ever since he lost the war – Tassi the poodle bitch is panting her way along the street dragging a blackish-brown mongrel behind her. The mongrel's ears are standing up, its eyes are rolling as it hops and slides its way across the cobbles on its hind legs while its front legs are firmly clamped around Tassi's wasp waist. She appears to have completely forgotten his presence, she's trotting along with him firmly stuck inside her, wailing. I'm burning. I'm frothing. They're to stop before someone comes and grins their leering grin and I won't be able to raise my hand to wipe the grin off their face. I rush into the garden, throw my school bag aside, turn on the tap, fill a bucket with ice-cold water, lug the bucket back with me, water slops over my feet, I dash out into the street again, they're bound to have gone. They haven't gone, they've followed me into our driveway. I tip the water over their jerking bodies. He falls out of her. She skips away. He sits down in front of me and licks his red dick. I give him a kick up the backside. He jumps up with a yowl and snaps at me. I'm afraid of being bitten but my hatred is stronger, he can smell it and backs off. He runs into Katjenka Nohke's garden. He hides himself in the bushes to await Tassi's return.

Vera opens the door to me. Where've you been, I ask, I didn't see you at school, how come you're already back home. Interrupting me and etching every word into my face she tells me Yes I was at school and you saw me there and Bobbi's ill and that's why I didn't have the last two lessons and why on earth – she laughs and grabs my throat – why on earth have you got this ridiculous thing round your neck.

I take my father's bow-tie off. Vera's been with Hainichen. What *do* you look like, she says stepping closer to me, your face is flaming red and your feet are wet. I can smell his breath, it stinks of cigarettes and wine. Unfortunately you're standing too close for me to be able to quarrel with you, I say, otherwise I'd want to hit you, right in the middle of your grinning face. You're so close to me that I can't even bear the sight of you any longer. Vera recoils in astonishment. You must be off your head. She's breathing heavily through her nose, she's outraged, she doesn't frighten me any more, I push her aside without a further word and go into my parents' bedroom to put the bow-tie back in my father's clothes cupboard. The room is dark, the shutters have been pulled across the windows. My mother's lying on her bed half undressed and without any covers on. The straps of her suspenders disappear into her white trousers. Vera didn't tell me our mother was lying here in half-darkness trying to cope with one of her migraines. Come in, come in, I hear her say in a slurred voice. I sit on her bed. I feel so rotten, Fania. She's yellowish-green in the face, her face is circled with black. On her bedside table is a letter from the Reparations Office.

What do they want from you, I ask.

I want something from them, she says smiling cautiously and holding her hand over her eye. I'm going to fight them all over again to get them to pay me something: no school leaving certificate, no proper job training, thrown into prison, then years spent in hiding. Perhaps it'll be enough for the house. I've got an appointment with their expert next week, here, read it for yourself, she touches the letter with her limp hand, a psychiatrist by the name of Ehrlichmann, Professor Siegfried Ehrlichmann.

Sounds Jewish, I say, he won't make difficulties for you.

She presses her fist against her closed eye. Don't say that, my little one, she says. It's because the whole business is too big for her that she calls me her little one. Some Jews have to prove to the Germans that they're even better Germans.

Don't talk so much. I kiss her hand, her head's too fragile for a kiss, I get up from her bed and walk over to my father's clothes cupboard, I give him back his bow-tie and take out one of his big white handkerchiefs as if that's why I'd gone to his cupboard. I go to the washbasin, wet the small square of ironed and folded handkerchief with cold water, and lay the compress over my mother's forehead and temples.

Is Vera home, she asks.

Yes, she's been back for ages, Bobbi's ill, I lie, so Vera's classes were cancelled.

And why weren't yours, her words are long drawn out, you had him today as well.

Someone else filled in for him.

My grandmother appears in the doorway wondering whether she shouldn't perhaps bring Alma some chicken broth. She's worried about her daughter, who shudders at the mention of the words chicken broth. No broth, Mummy, much too fatty. All she wants to drink is hot water. Go and have something to eat, both of you, she says, your grandmother has made you semolina dumplings, Fania, a whole thirty.

As from today I'm too big for semolina dumplings. It's

264

suddenly dawned on me that in fact I've already known this for ages. But that being so I might as well eat them, as I still like them as much as I always did. The three of us sit at the table in the kitchen spooning up chicken broth with semolina dumplings. Vera's thumbing through a magazine as she eats.

Reading at the table, tut tut, says my grandmother disapprovingly.

Vera looks up briefly. We've no business telling her anything. She's not in the least bit interested in talking to us.

My grandmother's getting agitated. What kind of behaviour is that, is that what they teach you at school. I go shopping, buy good food, wear myself out, stand in the kitchen all day, just so that you can have nice meals, such a waste of money, now put that magazine away and eat with us properly.

Don't start making trouble, says Vera without looking up.

Trouble, trouble, I've every right to be cross, hisses my grandmother, but you're enjoying it, my little bird, my little treasure, and she puts a few more dumplings on my plate. We eat. Vera eats and reads.

Look. She holds up the open magazine for my grandmother to see, you're just as interested as I am.

Big photos, three or more pages of them, in colour too, Farah Diba and the Shah – and a few drops of chicken broth as well. Horror of horrors. I doubt if anything could horrify my grandmother more. Chicken broth on the Persian emperor and his wife, and broth made according to an ancient Jewish recipe at that. Oyoyoy, quick, get it off, she yells, think of the people who get the magazine after us, what an awful sight.

Anything else, says Vera flicking the pages over and eating.

It'll soak in, I say trying to calm my grandmother down. She doesn't calm down, she wants a sheet of blotting paper from my school exercise book. I give her a pale-blue one still free of

265

ink blots. She clears a corner of the table, fetches the iron from the bottom kitchen cupboard, puts it on a saucer, plugs it in, spits on the sole plate, taps it with her fingers, winces with pain even though it didn't actually hurt, but all of a sudden it's hot enough and with the help of the blotting paper she irons the chicken broth out of the Persian emperor.

Vera shoves her spoon between her lips and chews and swallows, keen to clear her plate and be rid of it. She asks whether the price for the house has been settled yet.

Why are you asking, I want to know.

Why are you asking why I'm asking, she asks me. Hainichen has come between us. I can smell him on her. If I had a room of my own I wouldn't have to get into bed next to her tonight and every other night. I'm going to Sirena's as you know, I say to my grandmother, hoping she still remembers our encounter with Frau Bechler and her daughter in the street outside the old people's home: I don't want to have to explain anything, I want to keep it secret from Vera, I don't want to share everything with my sister any more. What's hers can stay hers. My grandmother's face slowly lights up: she has remembered. Are my fingernails clean, I'm to comb my hair and put on a fresh blouse, shall I go over it again as the iron's still hot so you make a good impression on these people.

Vera wants to know who I'm going to see. None of your business, I say.

Sirena. Vera drags the name through her teeth, Sirena, do I know this Sirena, and when are you coming back from this Sirena of yours.

None of your business, I say flaring my nostrils. That's what my mother does when she wants to look arrogant.

Have it your own way, says Vera flaring her nostrils as well, and we sit there face to face flaring our nostrils at each other, belligerent hippos, except that hippos open up their mouths not their nostrils, bull hippos in the Congo, I read about it in one of the magazines, they pretend to yawn so that their opponent can marvel at their teeth and their powerful jaws. Whether female hippos do this too remains entirely unreported.

I just need to know, says Vera, in case Mammy wakes up later and wonders where you are.

I hadn't thought of that. I look at my watch. I'm the owner of a watch, so my time belongs to me. I see it's half past two. At five, in two hours or so; Sirena won't be able to cope with more than a couple of hours of maths, and I aim to leave their house before they start thinking I might want to stay for supper. I'll be back around five, I say.

Otherwise you're to give us a ring, they're bound to have a phone, says my grandmother rubbing her thumb and index finger together approvingly, well-heeled woman, she is.

If only she'd shut up so that Vera doesn't find out too much.

The posh lady's presumably Sirena's mother, Vera guesses. She wants me to feel that I can't escape her. She's touchy and cross, she must be pretty deeply in the shit with that Hainichen, that swine, that Nazi swine, and Sirena's parents will have played their part in the war too. We never use this phrase. We say before the war or after the war, and if it's anything to do with Jews we say during the Nazi period – and with us it's always to do with Jews. Thea Bechler. Sirena's mother. Theodora probably. I'd like to ask Vera whether Theodora is a Germanic name, but I won't. I'm meant to ask her everything, you can ask me anything you like, what do you want to know, in the dark, in bed, did I want to know how to do it with a man. I don't have the feeling that I don't already know.

Right then, I'm off, I say.

First I leaf through our lexicon, a book that contains everything from A to Z. On quite a few pages Vera has cut out little pictures with a pair of nail scissors, the head of Julius Caesar, the head of Johann Wolfgang von Goethe, they're hers now, and she couldn't care less that something was written on the back of their heads. I leaf my way to Theodor. There's a hole under Theatre too, a fairly large one. Theodor comes after Theatre. Theodor, Grk, gift of God. Theology. My God I'm so stupid. Greek. Not Aryan. Theodora's listed too. Theodora. 1. Byzantine empress, born Constantinople *c.* 497, died 28 June 548, daughter of a circus attendant, did I read that right, yes I did, a circus attendant in a uniform with gold buttons who tears the bits off the tickets and sells juice and nougat and checks the cables and the cages in readiness for the lion and tiger acts, daughter of an overseer who drives prisoners to their deaths as lion and tiger fodder, married to Justinian I before 527, heavily influenced his policies through her energy and political talent, and saved his throne in the Nika rebellion (*q.v.*), not now, I have to go, 2. Citizen of Rome, wife of consul and senator Theophylactus, dominated Rome and the papacy during the early years of the tenth century, as did her daughters Marozia and Theodora later on. Another Theodora. Why haven't I heard anything about these women in our history lessons. And it's a girls' school for heaven's sake.

I walk down the driveway right to the end and enter the grounds via the underground garage in which there's a Mercedes convertible and a large black saloon, a French car, a Citroën. I go through the big kitchen garden and on into the house through the back door, it's a white house, then climb the stairs to the second floor. Sirena told me that she and her mother live on the first and second floors while her father has his office and living quarters on the upper ground floor. She was embarrassed. Her father was a diplomat, she explained, the government owned the house because he often had to invite lots of people, I wasn't to get the idea that they were filthy rich. The house used to belong to Esther's parents. The Fingerhuts have gone. They emigrated to Brazil. Esther's father, Simon Fingerhut, has family there, his mother's sister got away from Lübeck in time. Aunt Ruchla told my grandmother. No one in the other family survived except Recha Fingerhut, Esther's mother. Simon found Recha. In a train. Frau Fingerhut is fat nowadays but back then she was as thin as a rake and very young, about the same age as I am now, Recha, thirteen and a half years old. In a train, where. In a train, why. In a sleeping car, they said. Recha lay in a bed, a freshly made bed beneath the smooth-painted ceiling. It looked as if no one was lying there, and that's where Simon found her. What incredible stories they tell us. Can that be true. The wagons weren't sleeping cars. But everything they tell us is a miracle. Esther's mother, a girl then, not yet Esther's mother, was pretending to be a corpse. And Simon found her. Just like that. A miracle. I played with Esther in this house, her little sister Miriam lay in her cradle and we rocked her gently. Frau Fingerhut hung a mosquito net over it. You couldn't get at Miriam all that easily, not even if you were a tiny gnat. On the door of the flat on the second floor there's a large piece of paper with writing on it. Back soon, key under doormat, love and kisses, Mummy. This information was not meant for me, it wasn't meant for me any more than it was for any other outsider. I cautiously lift the corner of the doormat. There indeed is the key to the Bechler family's flat. A silver-coloured Yale key, flat and jagged-edged, lying there in a pool of dust from people's shoes. We haven't got a Yale lock on the door of our flat. We do have a door chain though, screwed into the crumbling plaster. I've stuffed used matches into the wall plug to stop the screw being pulled out of the masonry by the weight of the chain.

I sit down on the top step and wait and think. Perhaps it isn't even the right day today, it's completely the wrong day. My mind rushes through the preceding weekdays. If today *isn't* the right day then Sirena and her mother and her mother's husband might turn up any moment now. They won't recognise me, I once opened our front door, I opened it just like that, I was certain my father would be standing outside, he'd gone down to the cellar to get a file of business papers from our cellar, from the room just before you get to the locked and bolted bathroom beyond the air-raid shelter doors, and it wasn't my father, it was Hainichen from upstairs, I'd torn the door open and stretched out my hand, I'd touched this man who wasn't my father at all, my eyes had had my father in them, his image, his body, his smile, and I had transferred his image, his body, his smile onto someone else, onto Hainichen, and I hadn't recognised Hainichen as Hainichen. As soon as I did I slammed the door shut. I was inside, he was outside, there was silence both sides of the door. I wanted to creep away down the hall. The doorbell rang again. My mother appeared, Fania why aren't you opening the door, and she opened it herself, Hainichen was standing there laughing, his arms were hanging down on both sides of his body, he was swinging them back and forth, as if they were wet and he needed to dry them.

It will look as if I couldn't wait to come, or else it *is* the right day and Frau Bechler has simply forgotten that she asked me to come over today to give her daughter Sirena extra tuition in maths, I get paid for it, and they've simply forgotten all about me. When Sirena's father brought his daughter into the classroom that morning he looked nice, rolling in it, as Frau

Kupsch always puts it. Well heeled. And height-wise just right for Vera, a good two heads taller than she is, perhaps even as tall as Hainichen – just as tall and just as old.

I could creep away and then come back as though I'd only just arrived, because today is definitely the right day, I've not got it wrong, it's them who've got it wrong, and I'll act as if I haven't noticed that they've simply forgotten about me. Tomorrow my father's coming back, if today was tomorrow I couldn't be here anyway. Vera's now told me why she's only interested in men the same age as our father. Giving me a sympathetic look as if I were her and she were our mother, she said it was because she'd never be able to have our father. Mammy's got him already, she added, and cried. I tried to console her but she shouted at me that I didn't have a clue. That's not true, I said, I do have a clue, Pappy would be too lethargic for me, my mother says that to him sometimes, Paul, stop being so lethargic, and it's true, he's sometimes so lethargic, and often *too* lethargic for me, but not the other night, the other night when he went out into the dark just for me. To fetch chocolate. For me.

You find Pappy too lethargic because you're like Mammy, said Vera. That was fine by me, I'm more Jewish than you are, that's all. She'd make a better wife for him right across the board, Vera claimed emphatically, and he'd said so himself, not in so many words, but she felt whenever my mother and I found him too lethargic, she sensed that she alone understood him, only she really understood him. I feel myself to be more on his side than yours and Mammy's. Vera looked at me defiantly. I said nothing. Sometimes he complains about being the only man amongst four females, my grandmother, my mother, my sister and then me as well. I arrived last. He hasn't enough energy left to cope with me. He loves me too, but he can't do

271

anything for me, I can read it in his eyes. He'll leave me, the youngest, in the lurch. I get up from the steps. I'll walk back down the stairs and through the garden and the underground garage into our drive and go home. Sirena's standing in front of me. She's carrying a box full of cakes in her hand.

Oh dear, Fania, sorry I'm a bit late, there was a huge queue at the baker's, why didn't you ring the bell. She sees the notice on the door and pulls it off, my mother, typical, she's even more illogical than I am. Can you pick the key up please, or why don't you hold the cakes.

I've already bent down and lifted up the doormat and I can see the key, we're already acquainted with one another.

I walk into the Bechler family's home behind Sirena and take stock of everything we don't have. Everything. By comparison we don't have anything at all. Heirlooms. Antique furniture, paintings, silverware, expensively bound books, heavy rugs, and on one of these heavy rugs a piano. Not an upright. A small black grand piano. A shiny black baby grand. Such a beautiful thing.

Most of it doesn't belong to us, Sirena assures me, it belongs to the government, my father's a diplomat, but of course I've already told you that, but the baby grand, that does belong to my mother, and, you know, a few other bits and pieces and the silverware, she inherited that from her parents, but we're not rich really so far as I know, she says.

Are fifty-six thousand marks a lot of money to you, I want to know.

It all depends, says Sirena diplomatically.

What does a diplomat do.

Travels. Goes abroad a lot and negotiates with politicians.

My father travels a lot as well and does negotiating. He's a salesman. He sells spectacles and negotiates with opticians.

Mummy and I are often alone, says Sirena getting ready to make us some tea. You've got a sister, haven't you. I nod. Do you like green tea. I nod again. I've never drunk green tea, but I do have a sister.

You're not supposed to drink green tea after two in the afternoon, Sirena informs me, otherwise you can't get to sleep at night. We giggle: it's already long past two in the afternoon.

When my father's away my mother gets bored and then she spies on me or makes me go to operas and concerts with her. I don't like music. Not that sort anyway. Did I like that sort of music, she asks turning the tap on, water gushes noisily into the kettle.

My parents love music like that, I shouted against the din of the water, we often listen to operatic arias, we've got a gramophone, anyone except Wagner.

Did I like the Beatles.

The Beatles, I don't know, could be. I've seen them in magazines, the girls scream, their faces are distorted, they all sob and scream together, they stretch out their hands towards the young men on the stage. Completely crazy, the adults say, everywhere you go adult heads are being shaken in bewilderment, adult heads just can't understand how such a thing could ever happen, masses of people in a hysterical rapture over four crazy men, these adults have never experienced anything so unnatural or degenerate as this hysteria about four men.

Sirena throws her arms in the air, I *love* the Beatles, yeah, yeah, yeah, she screams, and my mother loves Wagner, hojotojo.

I discover that Sirena's grandfather sang Wotan at Bayreuth and as Daddy's darling Sirena's mother was always allowed to go along with him. Nazi stuff. I interrupt her: where are we going to do the maths. Don't tell me things, telling me things

273

is dangerous. I want Sirena as a friend, not an enemy, and I need her money too, her parents' money, twenty marks for each hour of extra tuition. I'd have to give her maths lessons once a week for fifty-four years to be able to buy the house. Perhaps I can persuade her to have *two* lessons each week.

So your mother spies on you then, I ask.

Mothers do that all the time don't they. Sirena pours us both some green tea, which isn't green at all but brownish, almost reddish. Doesn't yours?

This is not good. Sirena is asking too many questions. I'll simply repeat what my mother always says. My mother always says that her daughters can leave everything open, letters, diaries, she'd never read it, she trusts her daughters, her daughters would tell her everything anyway.

Sirena laughs.

I didn't know that was funny.

You haven't got a boyfriend yet. She can tell just by looking at me. My sister has to have a boyfriend first before I can have one. If I ever find one I'll give him to her.

What about you, I ask.

You bet, she says nodding, that's why my mother keeps spying on me. Rüdiger is so sweet. She doesn't know about him at all. You mustn't ever say anything to her. He's already twenty-eight. If she knew she'd go completely bananas. Rüdiger's so grown-up, a proper man.

He might be right for Vera. Vera's already seventeen. How can a twenty-eight-year-old man be sweet. All I'm interested in is whether he's tall and if so how tall.

About the same as me, says Sirena, a bit taller.

He wouldn't suit Vera in that case and I won't have to take Sirena's boyfriend off her. Does he have an older brother.

No, why, asks Sirena.

274

I don't reply. And what does his father do, I ask, just as my mother would. His father's dead, he was killed in the war, it causes Rüdiger a lot of heartache. He grew up without a father, just him and his mother, they had to flee. Sirena puts on a tragic face. How awful, I lie: I think it's quite right that these people had to flee, at least they had the chance to flee.

His father was in the war, he was a soldier and he had a really tough time, it must have been terrible, he was the same age back then as Rüdiger is now. Sirena the war widow. My eyes have turned cold. Where was he, I ask.

In the east somewhere, he was killed over there.

Where was that exactly.

No idea, she says, just in the east.

Near Auschwitz or in the Theresienstadt area, perhaps Riga or Babi Yar. I'm juggling, I'm battering her with clubs, I want her to be flabbergasted and collapse onto the floor.

She's not flabbergasted, she doesn't fall down, and she's blissfully ignorant of the blows raining down on her.

No idea. Was your father there?

My father. How can she ask me such a thing. My father. As a soldier, she means. She has no idea. We have to get away from here. We must get on with the maths, I say.

Sirena stands up. She leaves the kitchen, she's fetching her school bag.

I stay where I am. Alone. The objects all around me are hostile, I examine them meticulously. So they hadn't been Jewish property. I'll take them on all on my own. With my mother not here I am the Jew and I must fight our corner.

Sirena comes back, and behind her someone opens the front door. Thea Bechler comes in wearing a large blue hat, she kisses Sirena on the cheek and also pulls her in under the brim of her hat and under a blue horizon.

275

She offers me her hand, a white, soft hand with strong fingers and short nails, not long and not red.

Because, says my mother, German women don't smoke, don't use lipstick and don't paint their nails either, well as you can imagine that was quite something for your mother, I always had lip rouge with me, even for the first few days in Fuhlsbüttel jail, I didn't let them take that from me. In bed at night Vera asked me how she reckoned she'd managed that, there were body searches, they were all thoroughly checked, how can she claim that she smuggled her lip rouge through. Frau Bechler plays the piano, that's why she has short nails, and she smells lovely, a cloud of perfume surrounds her. My mother sometimes dabs a little behind my ear lobes, she'll be going to a parents' evening, first she dabs some of her golden-yellow Je reviens behind her own ears, then behind mine, then on her wrists. Sirena's mother asks whether we've finished the extra tuition. We haven't even started yet.

Yes we've finished. Sirena treads on my toe under the kitchen table. Good, says her mother, in that case we can have a cup of tea together, I've bought us some petits fours. Sirena's box of cakes stands unopened on the kitchen table, Frau Bechler pushes it aside and unwraps her own package: tiny tartlets in fancy paper baking cases. Sirena hands me an envelope. Here, your fee for the first maths lesson.

I blush. I haven't done anything to earn it.

Take it, she says.

I take the envelope, it isn't stuck down, I can feel the two ten-mark notes inside, I make a resolution to give Sirena two hours of tuition next time.

Sirena's not there the next time. Her mother opens the door. Come in, Fania, didn't I know that Sirena had a Spanish lesson this afternoon. Probably Rüdiger, I think to myself.

276

Sirena must have forgotten to tell you, come in, do come in, and Thea Bechler carries on talking while taking the maths book out of my hand, my husband's being posted to Madrid next year.

She's wearing something red and long, it's not a nightie, it might be a loose-fitting long red dress, she couldn't go out in the street in it though, and below it she has bare feet. My mother says that red-headed women shouldn't wear red, red and red clash, red suits women with black hair best, really black, like hers. My mother gives me lots of things in blue, blue blouses, blue pullovers, blue dresses, blue skirts. My father wears blue a lot as well, blue shirts, blue pullovers, a dark blue suit, even though he doesn't have red hair, his is earth-brown. He is a man. Men don't wear red, except perhaps for a dark-red tie or a wine-red bow-tie. I don't have red hair, my hair sometimes has a shimmer of red, sometimes dark brown, sometimes blonde, and sometimes no shimmer at all. I could wear red. Vera wears red. Her hair is dark brown these days. She used to be golden-haired, but it went dark, and you're mousy-blonde, Vera said to me. My mother was cross. Fania's my blonde little Jew. She gave me a hug. I'm not blonde. I can't decide *what* colour my hair is. Yesterday I sat at my mother's dressing table, looked in the three-fold mirror and pulled out a hair at random. It was black, jet black. A Jewish hair, and from my head.

There's no clash in Sirena's mother's case. Her red hair and her red dress go perfectly together.

I must go. Where's my maths book. She's holding it in her hand. Do stay, she says, keep me company for a little while. I stay put, I stay embarrassed, I just stand there in the hallway, and she's holding my maths book pressed to her chest. The door to the living room is open, I can see the piano, music lies open on the rugs in between. At the opposite end of the room

277

there are large windows. They look out on the Alster. And there is the Alster itself, its waters shimmering quietly away. I've never seen it like this, from so high up, right across the tops of the trees and Harvestehuder Weg and the park and all the people.

Did you know that music and maths are closely related, she asks me. No I didn't know that. Closely related, even though they belong to different worlds. Do you play.

No, I can't play.

I could teach you. She takes hold of my hands and examines them. She lifts my fingers, she lifts each finger in turn and pulls on it. My fingers crack quietly. They're not supposed to do that. It embarrasses me. They crack all the same.

Good, says Frau Bechler, there's energy in there. Would you like to hear something?

I follow her, her bare feet going ahead of me below her red dress, which I think is probably a nightie after all. She sits down at the piano, lays her hands on the keys, and the little black grand is instantly festooned with rippling garlands of sound. Make yourself comfortable, she calls to me through the tumbling cascades of music.

I don't know where to put myself and step out of the window onto the Alster. Behind me a crashing torrent of notes. I'd love to be able to play the piano like that, I'm already too old to learn to play the piano, it's too late once you're over thirteen. Esther played the piano in this house, she started when she was five.

Come and sit next to me, says Sirena's mother, here on the piano stool. There isn't much room for both of us on the rectangular leather seat. I can feel her thigh against my leg.

You can come more often if you like. I'm often on my own here.

She must be able to feel my leg, my left leg against her right leg, like two warm animals nestling up to each other. She carries on playing, and her leg dances away from me, it dances around in the music, her foot has to press the golden tongue sticking out beneath the piano. Up above, her hands pull forth an infinite stream of longing, and the longing runs away only to return disguised as a dancer in colourful clothes who wants to know nothing of longing. Her red locks tumble over her face and hide my gaze from her. Beneath her red dress her bosom leaps, throws itself about between her hands, bounds up and down with her leg, with the golden tongue beneath her foot. Then suddenly the dance is over.

You're all hot, Thea. I've actually said that. Thea. To Frau Bechler. I want to die. I'm going to die anyway. Perhaps now is the moment. It'd be best.

It's hard work playing the piano. Yes, call me Thea.

I can't call you Thea, you're Sirena's mother. It slipped out, I was lost in thought.

What kind of thoughts.

As I haven't in fact died I'd sooner keep it to myself, lots can still happen to me. I was thinking about whether I prefer to think bosom or think breasts. I like both words. Bosom is when there's material covering them; naked, and you think breasts.

She doesn't laugh. She gives me a searching look, she reads my face page by page.

Do you prefer language or do you prefer music.

Both, I say to be on the safe side, because I can never get enough, I want music *and* language, but language doesn't like me, the way I write it it just won't cooperate.

Sirena calls me Thea, and so do all her friends.

That's meant to reassure me. I'm full of disappointment.

It won't seem in the least out of the ordinary if you call me

Thea. She looks at her gold wristwatch. Sirena will be here soon, it's just gone five.

Just gone five or long gone five, what does she mean, just gone five, it shouldn't be gone five at all and certainly not long gone five. I said getting on for five, and at our house getting on for five means *before* five. I must go, straightaway. I jump up. I've forgotten my leg, it has to tear itself away from Thea's leg.

I have to go home, I'll be late.

Don't you live very close by, she asks, she talks slowly, much too slowly, how can she sit and speak so slowly. I rush to the door, every second is valuable. Goodbye, Frau Bechler, I say calling over to her from the door, she's still sitting there at the piano where only moments ago my thigh was secretly warming itself against hers. This time I didn't say Thea.

Your maths book, she calls, jumping up and bringing it to me at the door. Valuable seconds. I bound down the stairs. Shall I ring and say you'll be home any second, she shouts after me, I'm holding onto the banister with my right hand, my feet are taking the stairs five steps, ten steps, a whole flight at a time, I've done it in dreams, lots of times, I tear down through the floors in whirling circles, down, down. No, no, I shout up. That's all I need, her talking to my mother on the telephone.

I'm coming, I'm on the way, I'm getting closer, I'm back.

Vera yawns. Did you have a nice time.

No one's missed me at home.

How's Mammy.

I massaged her head for an hour, she's asleep now.

My grandmother's ironing shirts. Did I have any homework to do, she asks. Her daughter has been having migraines for a week. So now she's the housewife and she's ironing the shirts of a husband who isn't her own husband.

I won't tell Vera anything, not even tonight in bed.

My father comes back early because it's the appointment tomorrow. Professor Siegfried Ehrlichmann will be undertaking a psychiatric examination so that he can confirm to the Reparations Office that my mother is entitled to lots of money.

How did we angle our story, she asks. Her face is still a yellowy-green. We mustn't make any mistakes, Paul. He'll have everything in front of him, the papers concerning Frau Schmalstück's trial, the reports of the other psychiatrists.

Loss of occupational training opportunities.

Before that. I had to leave school, you always forget about school, Paul.

Yes of course, school, I do apologise, school.

I stood in the corner of the playground. Every single morning. I wasn't allowed to join in the singing or raise my arm. Not that that bothered me, mind you. I wasn't allowed to join in anything. I was a child. What d'you think that does to a child. This man Ehrlichmann, we have to tell him. Not that I wanted any part of it. Hitler Youth, League of German Girls – it made me sick even as a child. We'll have to put it differently to this Ehrlichmann. Being excluded from everything. As a child. They threw me out of the school. I was the best in my class.

Yes, Alma.

If this Ehrlichmann doesn't ask me you must mention it so that he does get round to asking me. They're so young sometimes and haven't a clue what it was like. I didn't get an education and nor did you, Paul. All because of me. You can claim for loss of career opportunities as well, Paul.

Lost for love of you. They don't pay out for that, Alma.

We mustn't go on about love, Paul. Otherwise this Professor Ehrlichmann will think it was a bed of roses for us the whole time.

He takes her hand.

Compensation for wrongful imprisonment. My God, my God, what luck we had surviving that.

Then we went to Poland. First you. Then me with Mummy. Your migraines.

Even at school. Even now. Just look at me.

He'll ask whether it's periodic.

The last expert caught me out with that one. All because of my periods. All because of my time in the concentration camp more like. I didn't *have* any periods in the camp. But I did have migraines.

Don't upset yourself, Alma.

What was his name now, something with B. B or P or both. A double-barrelled name I think. Already a top dog in his field under the Nazis.

She's trying to make light of it. She reaches for his hand.

We'll get there, Paul.

We will, together.

Friday morning. My mother changes her outfit three times in succession. Chic first, then drab, then chic. She paints her lips. If it all comes to nothing because of my high heels and my smart black suit then they can all get stuffed. One of her eyes still looks as if someone has hit her. She looks in the mirror, then tells her reflection Right, let's go. Masl un broche. She turns to us. Wish your mother good luck and God bless. Vera and I both take her in our arms and kiss her and say Masl un broche.

My father's standing by the door with the car keys in his hand.

Is my tie alright, Alma.

Vera says Yes, it's fine.

Why not wear your red bow-tie, I say.

They laugh. I'm perfectly serious.

*

He was wearing a bow-tie was Professor Siegfried Ehrlichmann, a check bow-tie in green tartan. So ludicrous. My father is holding his undone trousers with both hands. He immediately needs a hot-water bottle and a warm compress on his stomach. She looks tear-stained. Her lips are smudged, her red lipstick has run, tiny wrinkles have suddenly appeared round my mother's mouth, I've never noticed them before, she must have cried a lot. She kicks her high heels off.

My feet hurt so. He sinks into his wingback chair. She collapses onto the sofa.

How did it go, asks my grandmother. She has folded her hands so that she can keep a tight grip on herself.

Ask me something easier, Mummy. My mother is pushing her mother away in order not to cry. Vera comes back with the hot-water bottle and the compress. I go into the kitchen to put the kettle on for some tea and make bread and honey for my father, all cut up into bite-sized pieces, and bread roll with prawns in mayonnaise for my mother – my grandmother popped out to Herta Tolle the fish lady, she's provided for her daughter – my mother wolfs the prawn roll, the rich fatty yellow of the mayonnaise mingles with the tear-stained red around her mouth.

Has Paul got anything to eat, she asks looking at her mother, who is still standing in front of the couch with her hands folded. Her daughter's lying stretched out on the couch. My grandmother nods.

Bread and honey, says my father with his mouth full. He's sitting in the armchair, behind his wife's head.

Oh my God, there you are, she says and reaches for his hand and bursts out crying and bites her lip and stems her tears. Vera sits at her feet and starts to sob uncontrollably. She is now her mother's little tear-girl, I could be it too, but it is she who sits

283

in the shadow of the darkness that my mother has brought into our life. The tears flooding from my sister's eyes are my mother's tears.

Next morning I come back from school an hour early. Bobbi is ill, and Fräulein Brunhilde Kahl is also ill, or so we gathered from the headmistress, Dr Liselotte Schmidt. Otherwise we'd have had Fräulein Kahl in place of Bobbi. Thank goodness she's ill. I've realised that Fräulein Brunhilde Kahl is an old Nazi, she looks like Gudrun Ellerhausen, my father's sister-in-law, it's odd that this has never struck my mother. Our headmistress sat herself down on the teacher's desk to make her little speech. She always gets agitated when she has to announce something. She couldn't look after us herself, she told us, because she had things to do, so she was sending us home an hour early. She giggled, and the girls laughed. I like her. She's damaged in some way. It's the damaged part of her that I like.

I'm home earlier than expected and walk straight past our front door without my family realising I'm there. I want to see what it looks like above us and what happens when you carry on right to the top. Above us are the Hainichens, and above the Hainichens are old Frau Schmalstück and Sturmius Fraasch with his wooden leg. They go past our door on the way upstairs, and as I go up I try to see how they see us when they walk past our door, I climb the steps, the stairs bend round slightly. It gets lighter the further you go. I've never been up here before, I've never ventured so far up in our house, a whole floor higher. There's a large window in the stairwell, where on earth is this window when you look from outside, I've never spotted it before. I go up to the window and look out. I've never seen the driveway from above; it's so familiar to me, but so foreign from up here.

I turn round with a start. Behind me is a spyhole. Hainichen's front entrance, a snow-white double door. I rush down the stairs and ring our doorbell.

It's my mother. You're back early, my darling, has something happened, give me a kiss, lovely that you're back, did you eat your sandwich, how was school, lunch isn't ready yet, go and wash your hands, we're having a macaroni bake with Parmesan topping and then stewed fruit with, guess what, kugel: Granny's made bread pudding.

Early in the evening – Vera and I are already in bed because it's so cosy and we want to read – our mother comes into our room to say goodnight, she wants to get off to bed with her husband. My grandmother's at the cinema with Elisabeth Kupsch, she won't get home until nearly midnight. They're seeing How I Learned to Love Women. The terrace door is open, it's still light outside, warm summer rain is falling, strings of pearls drip down from the clouds in perfect straight lines. A bird is singing. Birds fall silent when it rains. For this particular one the rain has probably gone on too long.

My mother sits on the edge of my bed and talks about some other people with a daughter who have thrown her out of the house. And there she sits, banished from her own home. I don't know, says my mother, they've no humanity. If either of you ever get pregnant you needn't be scared. I'll do my bit to bring the child up.

Perhaps Vera's already pregnant and is lying there pregnant beside me, my mother has no idea how close to the truth she is. What makes her think that her daughter will be dumped by a Jew, or that the father of her grandchild is the son of Nazis and that her daughter would sooner dump him than introduce him to her. We wouldn't consort in any way with the man's Nazi parents. My mother would entertain them as they'd never have been entertained before and after that they wouldn't dare try to return the compliment, that would be curtains for the man's whole family, we'd make the child kosher sooner or later, then years later we'd say that these people don't even wonder what's become of their own grandchild, can you understand such a thing, no I can't understand such a thing, isn't that just typical.

Have you got a problem, my mother asks.

No, not me. Vera has.

You're hiding something from me, Fania, out with it, don't bottle it up.

Vera and I wanted to read in bed, we wanted to have a nice cosy time, summer rain outside, us under the bedcovers inside, the terrace door open, books from the local library, a whole bag full, Vera and I are always allowed to borrow more than the official limit because we read so quickly, the limit is only three books, we get through those in a couple of days. And now my mother's poking away at me. Everything's ruined, she's ruined everything, such a lovely atmosphere, I feel bulldozed.

Leave me in peace, just leave me in peace for once.

She flinches visibly, she'll be crying in a moment, I don't want her to cry. Tears come into my eyes.

What on earth's the matter, Fania. She examines my face, she concentrates her eyes on my mouth, she's looking for an opportunity to slip in, to look around inside me. Vera's lying next to me, she's erected an invisible wall between us, my mother is desperately staring at my lips which refuse to open, and she enumerates all the things she knows about me and I say, no, it's not that. I'd do better to say yes to something or other, yes, yes, that's what it is, to stop her chancing on the real thing, the thing Vera's schlepping around inside her, the thing she's burdened me with.

Is it because of your periods, because you've not started your periods yet, is it that, Fania, or is it something to do with school, have you written a bad test, it doesn't matter, are the girls in your class bothering you, that Annegret and the other one, what's her name again, should I go down there and give them both an earful. No that's the last thing I want. That's fine, Fania, if you don't want me to, but it'd be best if I did so they'd leave you alone for a change. So she knows that too, she's heard it from Vera, Vera's let on that I'm letting myself be bullied by Annegret and Gerda. My mother keeps on at me. We don't have any secrets from each other do we, I don't want to pester you, don't go to sleep angry, it's not good, you have to make up before you go to sleep, please make it up with me, give me a kiss, she offers me her mouth, she needs my kiss or else she won't get to sleep later on. Alma, calls my father from their bedroom, where are you, what's the matter, is anything the matter, not right now, Paul, she shouts back, I'm on my way, please give me a kiss, Fania, tears come pouring from my eyes, she's ground me down, I cry, pent-up rage suddenly comes pouring out of me in floods, she's not to die during the night, I don't want it to be my fault. I kiss her. Is everything alright again, she asks, and I nod, and she smiles, I throw my arms round her neck, I press her body to my body, I press until I can't press any more, then sink back exhausted onto the pillow.

She walks round the bed onto Vera's side, she leans over Vera and gives Vera a kiss. Everything's alright with you presumably, she says; she knows Vera's lying to her, I can tell by her tone of voice. Vera smiles a sugar-sweet smile, everything's alright, Mammy. They look at each other and I lie there weak as can be. It's not an unpleasant feeling being no longer capable of doing anything. My mother walks to the door, in a moment she'll shut the door behind her and leave us to ourselves for the night, she looks back one last time at Vera and me lying there.

I love you both so much. We love you both so much. Her husband can't be excluded from these ritual expressions of love and farewell that are meant to see us through the night.

We love you too, says Vera. I can't say anything any more, I'm breathing so heavily that I can't maintain the smile on my lips.

She's gone, says Vera. We listen. We faintly hear my mother shut the door of her bedroom.

Sorry, Fania, I couldn't help you out, last thing I needed was for her to ask me whether I'm pregnant.

Are you pregnant. I just don't want to ask. It makes me sick the way she said that, she's showing off, that's all she's doing. None of it's true, all this stuff she's told me. About her and Hainichen. The whole thing's just a novel that she's reading in her own head.

Well anyway I've been waiting for my period for three days now.

I've been waiting for a period for months.

That's not quite the same thing, my little lamb.

She can't fool me. Something's turned bad in her, turned sour or rotten. I won't say anything. I simply won't say anything.

Do you know who this house belonged to.

I still don't say anything.

I mean before Hainichen, says Vera.

It's very nice just not saying anything. I'm on the down end of the seesaw and she's stuck at the other end with her feet dangling in mid-air. Vera gets giddy very easily. Alright then, tell me, I say.

So you're talking to me again, I thought you weren't going

to talk to me ever again. She sits up and turns towards me. The Fingerhuts used to own this house, Esther's grandparents.

Esther's grandparents. Esther's father's parents. My Esther. Esther Fingerhut.

Yes, her grandparents, Simon Fingerhut's parents.

Then we can buy it from the Fingerhuts.

It doesn't belong to them any more, Hainichen bought it from them.

Stole it you mean.

No, Fania, bought. The Fingerhuts wanted to get out, and he, well, not him, he was too young then, so how old is he, I cut in, I can scarcely hear her there's such a howl of rage within me, about Mammy's age, says Vera, impossible, that man can't have anything in common with my mother, not even age, his uncle bought it, Vera continues, he bought it off the Fingerhuts, they needed money, they wanted to go to Brazil, but they didn't get away in time.

And how much did Hainichen's uncle give them.

I don't know, I imagine pretty much the same amount that he wants from us.

You're an idiot, such an idiot. My sister is taken aback to hear this coming from my mouth. You're the biggest idiot I've ever known.

Stop shouting at me like that. She's offended. Anyway Hainichen says it all went back and forth for ages between his uncle, the Fingerhuts and the authorities. Apparently the Fingerhuts had to make an inventory of their entire property right down to the last drawing pin, he says there was a huge file of papers, he thinks the whole lot was destroyed by his uncle, his mother's older brother, he was called Menkel, I think he said Menkel.

Menkel, I repeat, like Jürgen's mother in the house next

door, right at the top, the woman who's always lying in the sun on her roof terrace.

Menkel's not an unusual name though. Vera's talking as if Hainichen had specially asked her to cover things up. But what's much more important, just listen to this, Fania, I think all those papers are in the bathroom, beyond the air-raid shelter, but I didn't tell him that, could be that the papers weren't destroyed after all.

I'm willing to believe Vera. Perhaps despite everything she'll stick by us. And what use is that to us.

I don't know, says Vera. Probably none at all.

If it's no use to us, it might be useful to the Fingerhuts. We could write to the Fingerhuts in Brazil.

Vera bridles. Don't you dare.

What if I do, what then. They'll be thrilled to get their stuff back.

I don't think it's fair on him, says Vera, let me talk to him first, he won't do us any harm, and he trusts me, after all we do want to buy the house, if it comes to the point the Fingerhuts will want more money than he does.

If the house belongs to the Fingerhuts, I say, then we don't have to buy it any more.

We both fall silent. It's stopped raining. We both look from our beds into the garden, the top of the pear tree is turning red in the light of the setting sun.

Do you know that feeling, she asks me, and I immediately know that I know it. Do you know that feeling that all those other people out there don't know we exist. They simply assume that we *can't* exist. And if we ever tell them, they immediately blot it out again. We wouldn't need to hide it from them, as Mammy always insists we should. We could tell them as often as we liked that we're Jewish. No one would be listening.

290

I nod silently.

And do you, asks Vera lying back on her big pillow and tucking her little baby pillow under her head, do you sometimes do like me and turn the toilet into a little home for yourself when you're sitting there completely alone. Just for yourself.

Yes.

No more is said.

Chapter Nine

The day before my grandmother's sixty-fifth birthday we talk about this new war. My father's staying at home even though it's a Monday, he wouldn't have gone off anyway as it's his mother-in-law's special birthday tomorrow, but now there's war and that's another reason for him to stay with his family, he's not even taking his cases of samples and scouting and touting in Hamburg today. My father's a scout, he goes out into the world offering his customers his wares and in the process he discovers what they're thinking and what they're complaining about. He tells us later what it was like. My father enters the shop with a case in each hand and a smile on his face, and at first his customers aren't interested in buying at all and his cases stay shut. They moan about politics, about the most recent tax increase, about their competitors and their customers, their customers aren't fashion-conscious enough, they complain, people want their glasses to last a whole lifetime; they grumble about the car dealer who hasn't got them their new car, workmen who haven't turned up to build their little place in the country, the son who doesn't want to come and work in the business, the daughter who married far too early; buried under their mountain of sorrows they look to my father, and he says Oh dear and nods his head and wonders whether there's any chance at all of him leaving here today with an order in his pocket.

Alright then, Herr Schiefer, let's see what you've got in your case. And my father sits himself down on a little chair facing his customer, sticks his burning cigarette in the corner of his mouth, lifts the first case onto his knees, opens the snap fasteners, turns the case round to the customer and flaps the lid up against his chest and a shirt freshly ironed by my mother. Take your time and have a good look, he says, you don't have to buy anything. His customers don't need anything at all really, their shelves are groaning, they've barely touched their stocks, and a rep from the spectacle company ClearSight has been in touch, so they claim, he'll be arriving shortly, he's due in twenty minutes or so, very good prices, does Herr Schiefer happen to know the ClearSight rep and their current range. My father makes no reply to any of this, he keeps his knees together under his case, and looks steadily down at his samples to encourage the customer to do likewise. With pursed lips and narrowed eyes the customer bends over the open case on my father's lap, making a humming noise as he does so. Hm-hm-hm. He ponders at length before deciding which gleaming sample to pick up first from the four rows of five, then the customer picks all of them up in turn leaving fingermarks on each one, and my father wipes them over right in front of him, he rubs the customer's fingers away, he enfolds them in a bright yellow leather cloth, he touches them only with the cloth, runs the cloth carefully along their extended wings, closes the wings with the tip of his finger, then returns them to their beds.

The customer is quite happy about this, he knows that once he has left his shop Herr Schiefer will call on his competitors, so it's worth considering whether the frame that my father is polishing so carefully and that the customer has just been so unenthusiastic about might be the very frame to attract the possibly quite justified interest of the optician two streets away, so the customer has to hold the frame in his hands once again, this might do, would this do, what do you think, will it sell, will it sell well, I'll take three of those, let's make it four. At this point my father gets his order book out of the pocket in the lid of the case, the customer's name is already written at the top of the page, all that needs to be entered are the model number and the quantity required, model nineteen slash forty-two, how many must I buy to get a discount, a dozen, says my father, twelve pairs, and the customer laughs, Schiefer you old rogue, and had Herr Schiefer heard that joke, not a joke really, more a riddle, really funny, his son had brought this joke, well riddle, back from school, how did it go now, Turks, that's exactly it, a dozen of them, how do a dozen Turks fit into a German Volkswagen, come on then, what d'you think, you'll never guess, Herr Schiefer, nor did I, a dozen Turks in one of our Volkswagens, well there are four in the back and three in the front, that makes seven, and bang! our Volkswagen bursts apart at the seams, but what about the other five, where are they, they're in the ashtray, that's the sort of joke children tell each other at school these days, but why in the ashtray, I asked my son, and he said, well they're ash, but what do you mean they're ash, well the other seven have put them in their pipe and smoked them, I ask you, Herr Schiefer, how do children get such ideas, right could you give me ten of that one with the paste gems on it, I'll give one pair to my wife, she might like it, you can let me have that one half price don't you think, between friends, Herr Schiefer, bearing the same cross as we do, wives want finery and don't care where the likes of us are supposed to get the money from, inflation, tax increases and then reparations, millions' and millions' worth, doesn't half run away with the money, our money, the Jews were certainly rich, but surely there weren't *that* many rich Jews. Tell me, am I wrong.

He'd be staying at home the next couple of days as well, my father tells us, best stay the whole week. My mother throws her arms round his neck, oh Paul, can we afford it, of course, he says, we can always afford it, in this sort of situation I can't possibly go visiting customers. Vera and I hug him and kiss him on his stubbly cheeks, he hasn't even shaved yet, and my grandmother gives her son-in-law a kiss, such a good man, she says. Vera and I aren't going to school. All because of this war that is so ominous and makes us huddle closer together. My mother's ringing all the customers of my father who are expecting a visit from him, she apologises on her husband's behalf and tells them he's suffering from a stomach upset and will get in touch again very soon.

My father wants to wait and see how things turn out with Israel. We're afraid for Israel. All of a sudden Israel is in our home, Israel is unexpectedly sitting at our table, we have a brother, his name is Israel, and my mother is anxious for this brother and so proud of this brother that the world has abandoned to his fate, but we shall stick by him. The Arabs want to destroy Israel, they want to wipe Israel from the map, that's what it says in the paper, they hate Israel, and we're praying that we'll win and we *shall* win, there's no alternative. Israel must survive. We're going to give blood for Israel, all necessary arrangements have been made at the Israelite Hospital to send stored blood to Israel, we want to do our bit, my mother means to go with us straight away this afternoon or early tomorrow, she hates having injections, the very thought of a needle going into her flesh through one of her pores makes her ill, her entire body tenses up when a nurse comes near her wearing a starched apron and brandishing a loaded syringe, Israel's victory isn't going to depend on whether or not she subjects herself to such agonies. And so we don't go.

Should she celebrate her birthday at all while the war's on, wonders my grandmother, will anybody even come tomorrow seeing that everyone's turning on the radio every hour on the hour to find out – Goteinu protect us – whether Israel – keyn aynore – we'd know what she meant, she tells us, she's not going to utter the words, Israel has only existed for nineteen years, since the calamity, let's not paint the devil on the wall, what do any of us know about anything, and the inexpressible Almighty comes tumbling from her lips: oh God oh God oh God oh God.

My mother puts an abrupt end to her lamentations. Of course we're going to celebrate your birthday, you wait and see, we'll have good reason to celebrate.

There were good omens. The name came from outside, with ever greater frequency and urgency. From outside. That was a surprise. Everyone on the outside is fully cognisant of what we on the inside have always kept secret. Israel. Israel exists, and Israel means Jews. Everyone knows this. The news on the radio begins with Israel, morning after morning Israel lies there by our front door. We have never discussed Israel with anyone outside. Israel, our carefully hidden relative, our secretly adored brother, is on the front page of the newspaper. My mother bends down every morning and collects Israel from our doormat and brings Israel in to us, all in large letters, the I as big as my little finger. Everyone can read it. Hainichen and his wife, old Frau Schmalstück and Sturmius Fraasch with his wooden leg, he works for the paper, he's a news editor. All the women in our street will know about it, they'll say hello to my mother. They'll talk about Israel at school, and Thea Bechler,

I wonder whether she reads the papers, she buys large hats and small cakes and plays the piano. Her husband can tell her all about it, he has to read the papers, he's a diplomat after all.

There are two trees growing somewhere in Israel planted on behalf of my father and of all of us, donated by Paul Schiefer for Max and Marianne Wasserstrahl née Nehemias, the parents of his mother-in-law Hedwig Glitzer. My father keeps the certificate in his desk and I'll get it when I'm grown up, he's promised me. A slender tree is depicted on it going from top to bottom, beside its supple trunk two younger trees are shooting up, they're all having children down in Israel, behind the tree is a distant landscape covered with dense legions of trees, black and silent they jostle with each other as they march up hill and down dale, like the dark pieces of furniture on the crumpled photograph, the huge sofa, the big round table, the heavy sideboard, black and silent, my great-grandfather Max Wasserstrahl is leaning against the sofa, he hasn't any hair, he's small, in his hairless head are two dark, round eyes, a large nose protrudes from his sunken face, next to him, slender and delicate, is Marianne Wasserstrahl, née Nehemias, she's sitting on the sofa so that she doesn't tower over her short husband, neither in the photograph for all eternity nor as the tree in the Judaean Desert. There they are, the two of them, lying in a shoebox from Prange's on Jungfernstieg, and there are other photos in the box, most of them dating from the era that followed. A photograph taken in Poland. A photograph from that era. In the middle of a street somewhere. A young woman. My mother's face. Peering anxiously over her shoulder. She's holding tight with both hands onto the arm of her mother, who is wearing a hat with a veil. Someone has shouted out. Stop. Stay where you are. Outdoors, in a street in Poland. No idea who took the picture, no idea at all, she doesn't know any more, someone or other, and why do you look so frightened and why are you clinging onto your mother, no idea, someone or other who happened to know us, a Pole, he was playing a joke on us, Bogdan I should think, Bogdan Balschowski, we've told you about him, do you remember, the little fat man, yes I remember, we were having a meal at his house once when all of a sudden black clouds start rising into the air and I jump up and say There's a fire and he says as calmly as anything That's the ghetto, there you see, I do remember, and I say What, the ghetto, and Paul gives me a look and I quickly drop my napkin on the floor, we couldn't afford to arouse any suspicions, Bogdan didn't know the truth about us. Yes, I do remember.

The border of the tree certificate is made up of Hebrew letters, leaping links in a dancing chain. The Zionist organisation Keren Kayemet Le-Israel, it says in English on the certificate, 'reafforests the heels of the land of Israel in memory of Theodor Herzl, founder of the Zionist organisation'. I think every time that the English must be German that's gone wrong. Why isn't it written properly, in German I mean. My mother expels her breath, pfff, she's dousing a fire with the blast of air from her lungs. In German. My father can read the English text, Vera and I can read it, my mother can decipher it only with difficulty, my grandmother knows no English at all, she reads the Hebrew words, the decorative garland round the edge, words that none of us can read except her, though I can manage a few of them, if they were in German we'd all be able to read them equally well, why aren't they in German. All of a sudden they're arguing about German. Something precious and much loved has been ruined. Impossible in German. My spelling is impossible in German. Perhaps I spell correctly, but correctly in the wrong way. According to some book or other,

298

says my grandmother, she can't remember which one, she learnt it from Fräulein Krumm, Ida Krumm, at the Israelite Girls' School in Karolinenstrasse, according to this book there's a letter missing from the aleph-bet, the Hebrew alphabet, so it was claimed in cabbalist circles, and cabbalists duly recorded this, but the record about the missing letter was itself written without the letter, and thus enshrined the missing element, for the missing element is a presence, we have it within ourselves, the letter will come and will be found, it will not be a sweet-sounding vowel but a grating consonant, strong, deep and dark – something along those lines anyway, but one couldn't know for sure. Every split, every crack, every stain was supposed to mark those places where the letter was not yet manifest. Nothing in the world was complete without this letter, and every scar in lieu of it meant life and survival and meaning and interpretation.

This soothes my inner sense of shame and ignominy. Misspelt German is a precious vessel, within it is something of great significance, a letter like a pointing finger.

Then why am I of all people supposed to be able to spell German correctly, I say triumphantly to no one in particular.

My grandmother kisses the tips of her fingers and stretches them out towards me, gebensht, she says. When I was younger she used to lay her hand on my head, grandmother to grandchild: be blessed, gebensht, endowed with talents. Now that I'm already a bit taller than her she sends her blessing across the table with a kiss.

Before Israel I read Cisco and Poncho on the back page of the newspaper. Before Israel the front page never interested me at all. Cisco is a slim young cowboy in a black shirt and tight black trousers and a broad black leather belt and a revolver dangling from it; beneath the leather belt is the curve of

Cisco's backside, a round backside just like my mother's, and the heels on his boots are as high as the ones on her shoes. Poncho is Cisco's trusty sidekick, a short, fat man, both simple and kind, they're a duo, just as my mother and Elsa Kupsch are a duo, they have adventures in which Cisco rescues Poncho within the space of three frames, every single day except Sundays, when the newspaper doesn't come out. Let me have a quick look at Cisco, I was still saying that only a few days ago, and Vera wanted a quick look at Cisco as well, together we sat hunched over Cisco before anyone else could read the paper. There wasn't a lot to read. A few speech bubbles. Since Israel I've only glanced at Cisco and Poncho, everything's the same as always, Poncho does something stupid that lands him in hot water and Cisco rescues him, always the same formula. I fold up the front page and put everything to do with Israel into a red folder along with all the other front pages from previous days.

The Magic Flute, by Wolfgang Amadeus Mozart, was put on at the Deutsche Oper in Berlin for the Persian royal couple, and they broadcast the performance for us on the radio. We thought the bass voices were boring, they just ground away at each other and my mother treadled the sewing machine really quickly, but she did it slowly and quietly whenever Pamina and Tamino and the Queen of the Night were on. Beneath the dancing needle lay a dark-red dressing gown, a birthday present for my grandmother which we pretended was for Aunt Mimi, and my grandmother also pretended that it was for the sister of her son-in-law, she even tried it on, pretending that she was pretending to be Mimi. Every page of the paper the next morning showed the Shah and his beautiful young wife with her black hair, all combed up into a great heap and topped off with a rich diadem, oy, said my mother without ceremony, oy, worth a fortune, completely priceless, I'd like just one of the stones off that and we'd be able to buy a house very different from this one here.

I don't want a different house. I want to stay in this old, sick house and our two gardens, I don't want to have to leave the pear tree next to the old wooden shed, I don't want to be separated from the lime tree in the front garden, and next to the fence beneath the overgrown bushes there are all my little graves. Don't touch it, says Vera standing next to me, I'm sure it's poisonous. I drop it. She jumps aside. It's lying between my bare knees. Its head has fallen right back, its neck is broken. Hold it with this. Vera has pulled a large leaf off the lime tree. She gives it to me. The body is warm. The bones are soft. The skin is a bluish purple and still featherless. I wrap the body up in the leaf, the head slips out again, two huge eyeballs and the yellow triangular beak. The eyes are closed. They had never been open. Because it's so young, says Vera. Fill up the hole. I push the earth into a mound with both hands. Me now; Vera holds her outstretched hands over the bird's grave. I don't know what she's whispering, an incantation of some kind so that the dead bird can escape from our garden. He dared to reach out and died for his pains, he is one of us, a comrade of Vera's and mine, and that's why we're helping him to get out of here.

In the newspaper photographs the streets outside the opera house are thronged with people, the sky is dark, and the solemnity of the occasion is under attack from a barrage of shouts: Murderer! Murderer! Young voices, the voices of men and women alike. A man is dead. Shot in the head at point-blank range according to the newspaper. A student with a surname like a prophecy. Ohnesorg. Is he a Jew, he could be, with a name like that, no, impossible, my mother shakes her

301

head, she doesn't think so, he was one of the demonstrators after all, and Jews don't demonstrate, not in Germany.

Vera, hunched over the newspaper, says Bloody pigs the police are. She wants to find out whether the language of the demonstrators fits in our kitchen – one of them might be her future husband. Bloody pigs. None of us protests. Bloody pigs, she says again, and the mountainous Farah Diba hairdo on the top of her head vigorously nods agreement. My father's bothered by the word 'pigs'; he doesn't mind 'bloody', but pigs – pigs, he says, reek of the lascivious filth of the battlefield. His words reflect his loathing for armies of every sort. But everything is different in Israel. My father has never seen such appealing soldiers, the Jewish soldiers in the desert look thoroughly slovenly, even the officers and generals, their shirts are unbuttoned, their trousers are crumpled and baggy, and the belts of the more overweight men constrict their bulging hips. I've seen German soldiers in newsreels at the cinema. They stood in a dead straight line and at precisely the same moment all shouted Good morning, Herr Bundeskanzler. They'd no doubt been practising for ages. I thought it was pathetic. Then they showed GDR soldiers, they looked like a gigantic cube with a hundred legs and were marching past a clutch of little men in winter coats and grey hats. I don't like men. Poor Vera. But everything is drowned out by blaring headlines. War in the Near East. Arabs Call for Holy War against Israel. Turn the radio on will you. A man's voice is talking about the possibility of a third world war and about panic buying. There's a sudden racket in the stairwell outside. Something slams against our front door. My mother jumps to her feet.

You are not to go out there. My father gives his wife a stern look.

I want to go with you.

Fania, stay where you are. Vera makes a face like my father's.

Her face as white as a sheet, my grandmother looks at her daughter. As always with her in moments of terror, her mouth tightens into a smile, as though you could avert disaster at the very last moment by adopting a more friendly expression.

I'm going out there. My mother's already on her way to the door. Wait, Alma, hold on a second, shouts my father, he has to do up his trousers first. I stand behind my mother, she opens our front door. Frau Schmalstück is lying on our doormat surrounded by tins, packets of noodles, bags of rice and coffee beans, a foraging hamster dressed in black. She's trying with much moaning and groaning to struggle to her feet but sinks back down again at the sight of my mother. My father joins us, what's up, Alma, my mother is looking at Hildegard Schmalstück lying there amidst her hoard of food and squinting up from beneath her wonky felt hat at Alma Schiefer, née Glitzer. Nothing, says my mother in an icily calm voice, nothing at all, Paul. He nods. He has seen everything and understood everything. She shuts our door and double-locks it.

On my grandmother's birthday the headline in the newspaper is Israel Wins Air Supremacy. Within twenty-four hours of the start of the war Israel had destroyed altogether three hundred and seventy-four Arab warplanes on all fronts and lost nineteen of its own. We dance with delight. Our Israel. Our beloved David, victor over greatly superior forces. And we grieve for the dead, nineteen of them, the same as the number of years that the country has existed. Israel, youthful Israel, was nineteen in May of this year. The phone never stops ringing, everyone's calling us, their lungs bursting with joy and sorrow and fear. Masl un broche, good luck and God bless for Hedwig and for all of us and for Israel, masl un broche for

Hedwig until she's one hundred and twenty, for Israel for all eternity, come to the birthday party, of course we're having it, what a question, have you seen the papers, what a question, we're winning, and the Americans landed in Normandy on the very same day twenty-three years ago, my grandmother keeps telling us this, that has to be a good omen for sure, fingers crossed, keyn aynore, and this several times during every telephone conversation, could I perhaps make some phone calls as well today, Paul has to ring his accountant, my son-in-law has to make a business call right now, my grandmother shouts down the telephone, it's very important, talk to you this afternoon, go easy now.

You have to go easy with joy: who knows whether people will be pleased about Israel winning the war. You have to go easy with joy all the time: there's no joy without fear for us Jews. My mother says this to Vera and to me and to her mother, and glances at her husband. He is not a Jew.

Our whole life is rooted in the pain occasioned by this divide. Because Israel, a Jewish man, is in our house right now I can bear the moment of separation from my father. Not every separation is death. I look at my father and see him fully for the very first time. He is the man that he is. And it is because of him that I exist and Vera exists. We come from him too. He stands before us, albeit separately, he is not an enemy.

Vera goes over to him, cuddles up to him, puts her arm round his waist. It's exactly the same for Pappy as it is for us, she says. It's a tender trap. He's embarrassed. I kick the table leg. Vera wants him for herself. She means well, says Paul to Alma. My mother knows differently and says nothing. Vera has moved away from us. We Jewesses stare at her cuddling up to this man. He is the only man we have.

The sun shines in the afternoon and it's really warm, we

bring out wicker chairs, ordinary chairs, stools, the little club chair from our bedroom and the sofa from the sun room and put them on the front lawn underneath the acacia with its masses of flowers. My mother gives her mother the most beautiful bouquet of wild flowers, and in honour of the occasion it is quite fabulously beautiful: peonies with heavy round heads in pink and dark purple, deep-blue cornflowers, in amongst them ears of rye with stiff, sticky hairs, white marguerites, red poppies, marsh marigolds the colour of egg yolks, blue and reddish campanulas, white hellebores – my grandmother's two arms are full of summer and riotous colour. The aroma of Madeira cake, strawberry cake, streusel cake and chocolate cake wafts out through the open windows, in the evening there's to be a cold buffet with sour pickled herring, marinaded matje herring, sour gherkins in dill and garlic, challah with egg and onion topping, chicken broth with matzo dumplings, cheese croissants, beef rissoles.

Really pure minced beef, Alma.

Yes, Mummy.

Has to be kosher, because of Lotti, it matters to her.

Yes, Mummy.

And you're not telling me fibs are you.

No, Mummy.

Lotti notices if there's pork mixed in with it.

How *could* she notice it, she's never eaten pork. I'll tell you what, Lotti eats kosher meat at other people's houses because beef mince is the most expensive kind. But don't worry. It's pure beef.

Look me in the eye, Alma, I'm paying for it after all.

My grandmother decides to believe her daughter, and since the decision could have gone either way her doubts stay with her, she examines the mound of red mincemeat in its pink

305

wrapping paper and is satisfied that it doesn't look like pork. She herself has a relaxed attitude to the food rules but draws the line at pork, though if she unwittingly eats pork then that's not a sin in the eyes of the Almighty, so she says, that's the Almighty for you.

Rissoles made of allegedly pure beef mince sizzle in the pan with a little garlic and lots of onion, we eat the first few before they have a chance to cool down, Vera's lips glisten with fat, my tongue and the roof of my mouth are tingling with desire for these hot, spicy morsels: Vera, my father and I have to try everything out in advance. There's supposed to be Silesian potato salad with the rissoles, Elsa Kupsch is donating it as a birthday present from the Kupsch family, but without any bacon or ham in it, Frau Kupsch would you do me a big favour and not put anything pork in it, some of my mother's guests, you know how it is. As though it had nothing at all to do with us. And Elsa Kupsch jerks her ponderous head up and down several times but doesn't know what to do next as her Silesian potato salad isn't Silesian if it doesn't have lightly browned cubes of bacon in it. The best thing, says my father who is salivating at the very thought of it, would be if you made two separate lots, Frau Kupsch, a nice big Silesian one for me, I'll come down to your flat later to have a little taste, and a small kosher one for my womenfolk up here.

And could Frau Kupsch perhaps help out in the kitchen with the washing up, but of course, Frau Schiefer, and if required Elisabeth could lay the table, pour the coffee, and no, Elsa Kupsch didn't want to be paid any money, we wouldn't hear of such a thing. And in addition to the envelope containing two banknotes, one for the mother, one for the daughter, my father has spread out a white napkin on a stool next to the coat rack in the hall and placed a large china plate on it decorated with motifs from the Harz mountains. For tips. Where on earth had he got that dreadful object from, my mother asks. The Old Nazi had brought the display plate as a present on her recent visit, explains my father, and I quickly hid it from you. On the birthday morning there are lots of ten-pfennig pieces on it for messengers delivering flowers and telegrams. By late evening the Harz motifs have disappeared beneath fifty-pfennig and one-mark pieces, tips for the Kupsches, mother and daughter.

A hamper arrives from the Jewish Community with masl tov and m'ea v'esrim, may you live to be one hundred and twenty. Goodness gracious, says my mother approvingly, the kille have certainly done it in style. In the hamper are two tins of pâté de foie gras, two bottles of kosher red wine from Carmel in Israel, oranges and grapefruit from Israel, all to wish yom holedet to Hedwig Glitzer. A large bunch of tea roses arrives, sent by the Hamburg Savings Bank. The first telegram of the day is from Leopold Ketteler, spectacle-frame manufacturer. My father turns deathly pale, tears the telegram open, hastily scans the first few words and laughs, what an idiot, for a moment I thought . . . then he reads it out, In honour of the birthday of your esteemed mother-in-law, and hands my grandmother the yellow piece of paper with its glued-on strip bearing a string of letters. Ketteler hasn't even run to a greetings telegram. Are you expecting bad news from him, asked my mother, and my father laughs his silvery trumpet laugh, absolutely nothing, everything's fine, he embraces his wife, he kisses her, and between the hug and the kiss she manages to gasp You know you can tell me everything, Paul.

Our neighbour to the left, Adolfine Küting, sends her housekeeper Susi Brätzig around with a huge round box of chocolates adorned with a huge red bow, just look at that, says my mother in rapt tones. Later on she will bite into every single chocolate, and any she doesn't like she will squeeze back into shape and return to the box. My grandmother is familiar with this habit of her daughter's. From Magda Stierich and her husband Admiral (ret'd) Friedhelm Stierich there is a congratulations card with a glittery golden cross and 'God's Blessing'; mother Hedwig and daughter Alma wrinkle their Jewish noses, what silly nonsense.

Vera has taken on the job of going to the door, she's playing the role of Lady of the House and handing out tips. I'm going to be an actress, Fania, don't let on to anyone. She can do whatever she likes as far as I'm concerned so long as she stops this business with Hainichen. A special-priority telegram arrives from Rio de Janeiro, signed by Recha, Simon, Esther and Miriam Fingerhut, and standing there in our sun room all of a sudden are Katjenka Nohke and her husband Alfred Nohke, of Nohke Bros, formerly Silbermann & Co., under his arm two bottles of Crimean champagne, in her hands a large tin of caviar, an extremely large tin. My mother yelps with delight, genuine Russian caviar, she has never tasted real caviar. None of us has ever tasted real caviar. Caviar isn't kosher, my grandmother hands the tin on to her daughter. This is no problem for my mother. In Hollywood films Russian bigwigs eat caviar with blonde-haired American secret agents, and now she can do the same.

Everyone sends something, flowers, chocolates – Finke the grocer, Mackelberg the milkman, Bohn the vegetable man, Herta Tolle our fish lady. Elli Dingeldey from the lending library has turned up and brought a bottle of Lübecker Rotspon wine and a box of marzipan bread, because actually I'm from Lübeck myself, she says. How on earth do all these people know that despite numerous adversities my grandmother

Hedwig Glitzer, neé Wasserstrahl, has managed to stay alive for exactly sixty-five years to the day, and if they found out from Elsa Kupsch, who cleans for them all, then what's the explanation for their warmth and affability. Israel is the explanation, they're all in raptures about Israel.

Alfred Nohke is full of praise, fantastic the way the Israelis have done it, he says, if they go on winning victory after victory they'll save us from an oil crisis, Herr Schiefer, Germany simply can't afford an economic collapse of that sort right now, the Israelis should seize the oil fields down there seeing as how we've shelled out so much since the war, don't you think, Herr Schiefer, fantastic the way those lads have sent the Arabs packing, they'll have been shitting their pants, bloody wogs, and the Russians are just playing games, I'm sure of that, they don't want to lose face in the eyes of the Americans and the Jews, the Russians'll do nothing, don't you worry, my wife has relatives in Moscow, they're saying the same, the Russians want to flog their old weapons to the Arabs at an inflated price, that's all, and everyone can see how good *they* are.

Chatting amiably, Vera escorts the Nohkes and Elli Dingeldey into the garden in order to offer them one of the chairs put out there in readiness, and my father heaves a sigh of relief. Do they realise we're Jews, wonders my mother, but she doesn't want a reply, I'm not going to let them spoil my caviar, it's a big enough tin so Nohke can say what he likes.

Vera's doing that really well, says my grandmother nodding contentedly and gazing out into the garden at her granddaughter. She's sitting in her son-in-law's wingback chair, we've carried the heavy thing from the living room into the sun room for her and put it next to the gift table, she's crossed her hands on top of her stomach. Such a beautiful day, the windows are open, the air in the garden is silky-soft and holds the promise of a warm summer. There's another ring at the doorbell, no one takes fright, the bell has a different sound today, voices fill the hall, the Theresienstadt Circle has arrived, my grandmother immediately hauls herself up from the armchair, and my father seizes the opportunity to sink into his own special seat next to his mother-in-law's gift table, he crosses his legs with a deep sigh, and makes some room for his cigarettes, lighter and ashtray beneath the large bouquet of sweet-scented summer flowers, some of whose colourful fronds hang down over the dark-red dressing gown. Padded out with tissue paper, the soft towelling material flows across the table, invisibly supported by an upturned saucepan, in its dark-red folds the seven delicate white cambric handkerchiefs that I've edged with white lace for my grandmother, my mother has arranged the hankies in the shape of a rose; the pot of fingernail powder and accompanying sausage-shaped pad in suede leather are from Vera, they're the tools my grandmother needs to polish her fingernails, and Vera has also started polishing her fingernails recently. My mother has bought a little bottle of 4711, some face cream, a fat book of crossword puzzles, a slender black propelling pencil, a white India rubber in the shape of a car that portends a trip to the Baltic coast, a new horn comb and some perfumed soap. My mother needs these little side-presents to decorate the birthday table, and a birthday table arranged by my mother can hold its own against the finest shop windows on Jungfernstieg.

Ruchla, Betty, Wilma, Emilie, Olga and Lotti schlepp their bent and damaged bodies from the hall into the living room, the floor groaning under their heavy tread. Their loud squawking voices precede them into the sun room, Wilma has her rubber ring over her arm as well as her handbag, Emilie with her weak bladder smells slightly of wee, they all laugh and shout together except for Lotti, who neither shouts nor laughs, Betty has baked a shtrudl in true Jewish Mamma style, lying on top of it is a tichl for the sabbath bread, a lustrous silk cloth in varying colours from whitish yellow through orange to a bluish purple, the colours of Israel's deserts; the cloth is from Carola, Ruchla's daughter, she bought it in Israel. Will Carola be coming later, asks my grandmother, and Ruchla shakes her head. Her daughter is over there and hasn't been in touch yet, Ruchla has tried to ring but the line to Tel Aviv is either down or blocked. We look aghast at Ruchla. Israel at war is suddenly different. Its skin and flesh are dropping off.

Lotti places a slender box in Hedwig's hands. Tall and gaunt, she looks at her diminutive friend and kisses her on the forehead, she herself is moved by her generosity, everyone is moved by Lotti's generosity, a piece of jewellery, something precious from her shop, a necklace perhaps or a bracelet.

Whoever would have thought in Theresienstadt back then that we'd live so long, open it, Hedwig.

A gold wristband for a watch lies inside on black velvet, the delicately wrought object, made from spun gold as fine as linen, is passed from hand to hand, that's no fool's gold, says Wilma, I should think not, says Olga, more carats than my teeth, says Betty, Emilie wants to know how many carats, fourteen, eighteen, more than you can afford, says Olga. It's pure gold, twenty-four carats, Lotti takes a pair of silver pliers from her black circular handbag in patterned black leather.

Should I put it on your watch straightaway or would you like to exchange it, you're welcome to exchange it, whatever you prefer, it needs to be something you really like.

Not for the world, exclaims my grandmother, I wouldn't exchange it for the world, it's *so* beautiful.

But if you want to you can, says Lotti.

No, put it on for me.

But tell me honestly, you really do need to like it. Lotti keeps her piercing gaze fixed on my grandmother and waits with the pliers suspended in mid-air.

Go on, just put it on for her, you're sending us all meshugge with your but but but, says Olga.

But what if she doesn't like it after all.

You heard what she said, she likes it.

Ruchla squeezes her fat hips into a small wicker armchair, turns her round, kind face towards the sun and calls out Maybe Hedwig wants platinum, maybe she wants jewels, diamonds.

Alright then, says Lotti, I'll put it on your watch. Though her fingers are crooked she handles the pliers with deftness. As I watch her I think of ordinary pliers. I know about it through Vera, and Vera knows about it through Ruchla's daughter Carola, she told Vera the whole story. About Lotti's gold teeth being torn from her mouth. I'm afraid of my thoughts betraying me, I'm so close to Lotti that she might sense that I know and that I'm thinking about it; being so close I try to read the numbers on her wrist as she juggles with the pliers, the watch and the wristband, they're half visible, half hidden by the dark-green silk of her sleeve, forty thousand something or other I tell Vera later, just think, there were already more than forty thousand people in the camp when she arrived, it must have been such a squash. Lambkin, Vera takes my hand, we cross the grass and stand under the maple tree where no one can hear us. Most of them had already been murdered. I'm shocked and startled at not having thought of that, in my mind they were all still alive. The way I imagine it, says Vera, the worst part must have been going to the toilet. I know it's stupid to think of that but it's what I always think of first, just look at

312

Lotti, that stiff old lady, okay we don't like her all that much, we're fonder of Ruchla and Olga and Emilie and Betty and Wilma, but just imagine Lotti in Auschwitz and she suddenly gets diarrhoea, you'd want to be on your own then.

Elsa Kupsch and her daughter Elisabeth come down the steps from the sun room into the front garden, they've put white aprons on and are bringing out the cakes, my father pours the coffee, Vera hands round plates, pastry forks and paper napkins.

Rosa arrives, Rosa Freundlich, she comes through the dark passageway into the front garden, she must have entered through the back garden gate, I must go round there very soon and check whether she shut the gate behind her, we don't want anyone simply walking in through the back. Walking alongside Rosa and half hidden by her is Hermine Kleingeld. Rosa, whose ample frame advances only slowly, is an educated lady, says my grandmother, a highly educated lady. She belongs to our family but doesn't figure very large as she so rarely gets in touch. My mother goes up to the women, she makes to embrace Rosa and I hear Rosa say to my mother No, Alma, your mother's the star today; she kisses my grandmother on both cheeks, my mother stands to one side like a scolded child. Rosa is a secret envoy from Julius Glitzer, my mother's father, Hedwig divorced him, he cheated on her and gambled all their money away playing poker. His sister was Rosa's mother, Fanny, my grandmother's sister-in-law, my mother's aunt, Fanny Freundlich. I know the whole background. There's something in Rosa of Julius Glitzer, this man who disappeared and forgot his daughter, simply forgot her. I wish him no ill, says my mother whenever she talks about her father, and she's thinking of the gas that did for Rosa's mother and perhaps did for him as well as for his sister, we don't know.

There's my sister, my father exclaims. We can hear Mimi's tobacco- and cognac-laden voice in the driveway, we hear her laughing hoarsely behind the tall bushes and the thick foliage of the trees, hello there, I've brought someone along with me. Vera runs through the garden, up the stone steps to the sun room, through the living room, she can't wait to see who Mimi's brought with her, obviously a man, bound to be her married boyfriend, it's Tuesday today, he doesn't have to be with his wife, my grandmother explains to her Theresienstadt Circle friends; they all lean back in their chairs and await the arrival of my aunt and her married lover. We've never seen him before, ah there he is, he only reaches up to Aunt Mimi's shoulder, Vera notes this with great pleasure. He's fat and puffs and pants a lot and his head is red and round. He comes down to the sun room, steps into the garden at amazing speed and introduces himself to all and sundry, Hubert Arnold Zinselmayer, he says, chartered engineer, from the jolly old Rhineland, his limpid blue eyes flash in the pink bulk of his face, he makes a bow to no one in particular, his eyes light on the elderly Jewesses who are leaning back in their chairs giving him a good going-over, standing there on our lawn amidst the dandelions and daisies he brings the heels of his shoes together, he's holding sixty-five pink roses in his hand, his trouser leg is as wide as one of my mother's tight skirts, he steps up to my grandmother and kisses her hand, he steps up to each of the other women in turn and kisses her hand, afternoon, madam, he says to Lotti, to Betty, to Emilie, to Ruchla, to Wilma, to Olga, and then to Katjenka Nohke and Elli Dingeldey, only then does he greet Alfred Nohke of Nohke Bros. To do all this he has to dart repeatedly to and fro. The entire procedure is exactly *comme il faut.*

My mother is still standing near Rosa and Hermine

Kleingeld, Aunt Mimi takes him over to them, Hubert Arnold Zinselmayer kisses their hands too. Ah, the lady of the house, he says to my mother, and when kissing her hand he lays his spare hand on her wrist, something he hadn't done with any of the others. Aunt Mimi doesn't take her eyes off Alma, it's important to her to know whether my mother likes him. Vera sticks her hand right into his hairless face, just below his snub nose, she's desperate for him to acknowledge her. Just above her hand his pointed lips draw apart slightly, he emits a panting little laugh, he kisses Vera's right hand and then her left hand, he asks whether he can kiss her on the mouth, he was more or less her uncle after all, Aunt Mimi quickly intervenes and gives Vera a stern look. He's mine. And she takes hold of Vera's arm, on her fingers are the oversized diamond rings that belonged to Hubert Arnold Zinselmayer's dead mother, they're keeping watch as well, they're now stationed on Vera's arm radiating shafts of green and blue. Vera laughs and shakes her hair. Vera needs to watch out. I must watch over her, I can't watch over her, no one can watch over Vera any more.

There are the Hainichens standing in the garden, they want to wish my grandmother happy returns. They'd seen what was happening from up on the balcony and they'd thought, well. I look up at the balcony, it's immediately above my parents' bedroom. And where's Vera. She was there a moment ago and now she's gone. I run through the dark passageway into the back garden. Rosa came through this passageway just now, there are people everywhere today, Vera's not in the back garden, the gate is open a crack, I shut it and fasten it with the rope.

Vera's standing at the kitchen window. I run up the iron steps and into the kitchen. There's no one there except her.

315

She puts a small brown bottle down. Leave me alone, she hisses. I just want to know whether she's crying, whether she needs help, whether she can cope on her own. You don't need to worry, she says. This worries me. I go out of the kitchen. What was that small brown bottle, I don't remember seeing that before, yes I do, it was cooking rum, what does she want with cooking rum, she's surely not drinking cooking rum. I run through our bedroom, across the hall, through the big room, into the sun room, and out into the bright daylight. From the sun room steps I can see who's talking to who. The men are standing in a group under the maple tree, all the men except for my father, who has sat himself down amongst his mother-in-law's band of old friends, Rosa Freundlich and Hermine Kleingeld are sitting with Elli Dingeldey and Katjenka Nohke, Eva Hainichen has positioned herself close to them, my mother and Aunt Mimi go past me into the house, where are you off to, I ask because of Vera, they want to fetch two chairs from the kitchen. Let me get them, I say. My mother has already gone on past me, Paul needs to make some more coffee, she calls from within.

I tell him. He nods, and although he doesn't stay there long enough to make his wife impatient, he does stay sitting in his chair for quite a while amidst the elderly Jewesses who heap praise and flattery on him, Hedwig's son-in-law, what a good man he is, your father. I jump across the sandy path, I want to hear what the rest of the men are talking about, they're standing under our maple tree with cigars in their mouths.

Fantastic lads, says Hainichen, I said to my wife, with soldiers like that we'd have won the war.

Alfred Nohke laughs and chokes on his cigar smoke, he holds his glass in the air so that the cognac doesn't spill out. Hainichen pats him on the back, and Alfred Nohke of Nohke

Bros, formerly Silbermann & Co., stands with hands raised and says thank you, thank you. Chartered engineer Zinselmayer looks down at the toes of his shoes.

My mother and Aunt Mimi return from the kitchen, each carrying a chair, the three men, cigar in mouth and cognac in hand, rush across, but the two women have already successfully negotiated the steps without them.

How's Vera.

Vera's washing up in the kitchen, my mother calls over to me, isn't that sweet of her. Elsa Kupsch takes a plate of cakes out of her daughter Elisabeth's hands and sends her off to help Vera in the kitchen. That's good. Then Vera's not alone, at least she can enjoy the cooking rum with someone else and I can go over to Rosa, I want to sit with Rosa, I want to listen to Rosa. Elli Dingeldey and Katjenka Nohke are also sitting with Rosa and listening to Rosa, Frau Hainichen is standing, my mother brings her a chair, Eva Hainichen doesn't want the chair, Aunt Mimi sits down, she signals to my mother, my mother shrugs her shoulders and looks at Frau Hainichen, then she sits down next to Hermine Kleingeld who's sitting next to Rosa, she's been sitting next to Rosa the entire time, as though she were Rosa's wife, as though she had to protect Rosa.

Do you want to hear a secret. That's Vera's cooking rum breath on the back of my neck. Why isn't she in the kitchen, she pulls me over to the sun room stairs then up a few steps.

Elisabeth is pregnant, her mother doesn't know, nobody knows, and guess who the father is.

Hainichen.

Shh, says Vera.

She could have an abortion, I suggest. After all Frau Kupsch had an abortion.

It's illegal, no doctor would do it for her. Vera's not looking at me, we're standing together talking to each other but to stop people listening to us we don't look at one another, we both look at the adults down in the garden.

Elisabeth is young and healthy, somebody would only do it for her for lots of money and she doesn't have any money, the Kupsches are poor, you know that.

Vera is putting on a grave and solemn air as though she were talking about herself. She could ruin us, we haven't got any money, money wouldn't help us anyway, if Vera were pregnant by that man it would poison our whole family.

She's hoping it will somehow just go away on its own, says Vera.

My father walks past us carrying two pots of coffee down into the garden, he gives all the women a refill, first the women around Rosa, then the Theresienstadt Circle, where he settles back down into his chair. He forgets to do the men.

Elisabeth's saying special prayers at church, I hear Vera say, she wants the baby to shrivel up inside her, just imagine, Fania, Elisabeth wants to give it to the Mother of God, she's to take it and turn it into an angel.

The mother of God, who on earth is that.

Mary, says Vera, the mother of Jesus.

Oh him, I say.

Elisabeth said her son's to be called Pilate if he doesn't turn into an angel, and if the angel's a girl she hasn't got a name for it yet.

Why doesn't Elisabeth go to Frau Hainichen and tell her, that would be the best solution, right here in front of all these people, she can stand on the steps here and shout it down into the garden. I could do it. For Elisabeth. Right now. For me. Because of Vera. That can't be true, says someone with my mother's voice, yes the voice is my mother's, she has jumped up

318

from her seat, only moments earlier she had been sitting under the jasmine next to Hermine Kleingeld, who has put her hand on Rosa's arm.

I just don't believe it. It's my mother's voice, it pervades the entire garden. The three men give the women an irritated glance, what's the matter over there. They wait to see. For the time being they carry on puffing their cigar smoke into the summer air. My father gets up and leaves the elderly Jewesses, once he's gone the elderly Jewesses all put their heads together, he walks across to his wife who has jumped up from her chair with incredulity, he wants to calm her down, he wants to see what he can do to help her – and to hinder everyone else should that prove necessary.

With their cigars between their fingers the three men stir themselves and cross the narrow sandy path between the two areas of lawn, they look down at their shiny shoes and watch them accompany them as they walk over to the women where something must have happened as Rosa is smiling and my mother has jumped up and is holding onto the arm of the chair. My father goes up to his wife, he wants to touch her, she rushes away from the little circle of women, hurries up the sun room steps, dashes past Vera and me, Mammy, what's the matter, I shout after her; oh Fania, that Rosa, she replies with a dismissive wave of the hand, she's completely meshugge. She has already disappeared in the summery darkness within the flat, I'm just going to put some more lipstick on, she shouts. What did Rosa say. My mother is standing by the bedroom door with her hand on the door handle. Go and hear it for yourself, Israel's an imperialist aggressor, that's what she said in front of everybody, in my garden.

The lot of you should let Israel get on with it, I think to myself, what has Rosa got against Israel, let Israel be aggressive for goodness' sake, Israel on his chariot with his muscular, sunburnt thighs, his short leather skirt does look a bit ridiculous though and I don't like the dimple on his chin, the six horses out in front of him are wild and beautiful, it's Ben Hur, the handsome aggressor with his golden helmet. The cinema had extended its white screen and drawn back the curtains extra far specially for him and all his splendour. I almost didn't go in with them. Row seven, said my father at the cashier's window, three seats including one on the aisle. Seven is his lucky number and he needs an aisle seat because of his long legs. Take your daughters to the pictures, Paul, my mother had said. They're showing *Ben Hur* at the Gondola in colour and widescreen. He gave a groan and laboriously did up his waistband, eventually we went off in his car, Vera sat next to him, as though she were his wife. You always sit next to him, I complained from the back hoping he'd do something to help, but he just said Don't you two start squabbling. He paid for three tickets at the window, then the woman taking the money looked at me. Not her, she's too young. Vera was already standing by the usherette on the other side of the foyer, and I wasn't going to be allowed in, I was always involved in everything, but now they were going to go in without me, Vera and my father together, and what would become of me then. Come on, hurry up, the usherette whispered to Vera. Either both or neither, said my father. Vera pulled a face and gave a condescending sigh, alright then, let's not bother.

My father turned to the woman in charge, a woman in a grey suit with a grey cap on top of her permed hair bearing the word 'Gondola' in gold letters. Did he have any proof of his younger daughter's age, she asked in a cold voice; not on him unfortunately, he had a friendly air, she didn't, he caressed her with his eyes and said We all look young in our family, and she wagged her finger at him with an impish smile. He grabbed me by the shoulders and propelled me past her, we went side by side up the steps into the darkened auditorium.

I walk down the steps into the garden. Rosa is smiling. My mother thinks Rosa is arrogant, according to her she has the arrogance typical of many intellectual Jewesses, you can all regard me as anti-Semitic if you like, but I know what I'm saying. Although it usually looks as if Rosa is simply asleep behind her veiled smile, she's wide awake inside, and this deceptive tranquillity riles my mother, this deceptive tranquillity makes her want to tear her hair out, while Rosa sits there calmly stroking her own with her soft, white, plump-fingered hand and the folds of her skirt give off a gentle aroma of tea and tobacco. Alma's father smelt the same, claims my grandmother, she says this to Rosa, your Uncle Julius smelt of tea and tobacco just like you, and as for your hair, this lovely thick hair, Fania's inherited that too.

A fragment of memory, a tiny piece of mosaic from a once large whole, a salvaged remnant of a Jewish family. Rosa alone came out of it alive. Her cousin Alma, who was never there, comes across the lawn with freshly painted lips and sits back down on her chair, no one has taken it, as though it were out of bounds. My mother has redone all her make-up, a cloud of perfume surrounds her, Rosa looks at her, and there is a warning darkness in my mother's eyes. Rosa smiles. My mother smiles too, she has shaped her plucked eyebrows into beautiful arcs. I'd like to be like Rosa, I'd like to be as free as her. Rosa is free. Nothing more can happen to her.

Rosa speaks so quietly that her fellow guests have to get close to her in order to hear what she is saying. Except for the old Jewesses everyone has gathered round her, Vera and my father have brought chairs over, he wants it to have the air of a relaxed and happy circle, my father offers everyone cigarettes, the old Jewesses are sitting nearby, they look at one another, what are they supposed to say, they could say a lot, they say nothing. Rosa smiles. The others look at her smiling mouth. Aggressive expansionist campaigns undertaken by Zionists in Arab territories, says Rosa's mouth. My ears photograph every word, later I'll have to try to undress them.

What was that, whispers Aunt Mimi, what's that you're saying.

Yes, says Rosa with a nod directed at Aunt Mimi who doesn't have a clue about anything but is taken just as seriously by Rosa as my father or Hermine Kleingeld or the three men standing there silhouetted against the blue sky smoking their cigars. You heard right, she says to Aunt Mimi, and Aunt Mimi, startled, says What, me, I never said a word. Several thousand US specialists with experience in Vietnam are already working with the Israeli army as military advisers. In my mother's head every one of these words is accompanied by the ring of a cash register. And I understand nothing but need to remember everything. It's not the time for questions, Rosa's hands are jittery, all these strangers, men and women alike, are looking at Rosa's hands. Rosa's hands are always jittery, they tremble ceaselessly, it started back then and has never stopped, it has nothing to do with here and now, but these other people don't know that.

Hubert Arnold Zinselmayer steps forward a pace, so do you really believe that, madam, you really think they'll drop napalm on the Arabs.

Missiles come shooting out of Rosa's mouth, she's looking at the three men but she hits my mother, she hits us. Billions from the Federal Republic for Israel's armaments, disguised as reparations.

Hainichen gives a low whistle, my dear lady, he says, my dear lady, he doesn't know Rosa's name, Rosa Freundlich, you can call me Rosa, my dear lady, says Hainichen, you really are going a bit too far if I may say so, my dear lady, you're going much too far with all this stuff you're telling us, these Zionists are communists for God's sake.

Rosa smiles. She thinks Hainichen is stupid, I can see it on her face, and this does me good, oh it does me so much good. Vera sees it too, and she smiles just like Rosa, my sister is a chameleon, she'll be a great actress and Hainichen never goes to the theatre, everything will turn out fine.

Zionists aren't communists, says Hermine Kleingeld shaking her head.

Alright then, socialists, growls Hainichen, not much difference between them so far as I'm concerned.

No communist or socialist would ever regard a Zionist as one of them, explains Hermine Kleingeld, and now she's smiling as well as Rosa.

Zionists aren't communists, repeats Hainichen incredulously.

You heard what she said, Hermann, says his wife. Rosa looks across at Eva Hainichen, her heavy eyelids are half closed, just half a look for this woman, not a whole one. I want to be able to do that too, one really mustn't allow such people completely into one's eyes.

Surely if you're a, erm, Hainichen says to Rosa puffing heavily on his cigar, I mean aren't you, erm, and Rosa says Yes, I'm a Jew. Exactly, says Hainichen, from Israel, just what I was going to say. No, says Rosa. Really, Hainichen asks, so you're not one after all, he says, disappointed. Yes I am, says Rosa. Just as I thought, says Hainichen, happy again. I look at my

323

mother. Jew. The word reverberates through her garden, my mother puts her head back without a word, her eyes are closed. I'm a Jew, says Rosa, but not from Israel. I come from Germany, just like you.

Ah well yes, obviously, of course, yes, of course, if that's the case, if these Zionists aren't commies, madam, and they aren't socialists either, I'm all for them, I'm telling you.

Alfred Nohke of Nohke Bros, formerly Silbermann & Co., announces that he'd heard earlier on the radio that Israel was on the verge of taking Gaza, and Gaza was Egyptian territory wasn't it, and he looked enquiringly at Rosa to see if he'd got that right. Rabbi Rosa nods her heavy head, it is Egyptian territory, she confirms. Alfred Nohke feels encouraged to travel on into the Sinai desert, where the Israelis have just captured numerous prisoners and massive quantities of arms and munitions, all of it Russian, all of it rubbish.

'Rubbish' does not go down well with Rosa. The Russians, she says, are quite correctly demanding that Israel withdraw unconditionally behind the armistice line. They *must* do that, she says.

No. Absolutely not. My mother has decided to make her voice heard again, she has decided to be not only a hostess but also a Jew. My cousin Rosa may see things differently, she says, but for me, and I'm a Jew as well, for me there can be absolutely no question of a withdrawal.

How strange, says Elli Dingeldey, to hear that biblical name mentioned in conjunction with war, Sinai, in Mount Sinai, her voice becomes resonant, I'm thinking here of something different you know, she says to all and sundry, I'm a librarian you see, books are my world, and it is written that thou shalt not kill.

That only seems to apply to Jews, says my mother sharply,

and a flash of lightning bursts through Rosa's smile. Rosa loves my mother, I can see it in her face, she loves this anger in her, an anger that transcends all fears and barriers. The sharpness of my mother's voice has completely silenced the guests. My father looks anxiously at Elli Dingeldey, he holds the librarian in such esteem.

After everything that's happened, Vera whispers to me, the Germans are *so* touchy; she grins, and I bet Elli Dingeldey is too.

Katjenka Nohke announces that she saw pictures from there on the TV last night. From the crisis area, she says. In Cairo a furious mob had sacked the American and British consulates, in Tunis they'd looted Jewish businesses and set fire to the Jewish church.

Synagogue, says my mother correcting her, they set fire to the synagogue.

Yes, of course, says Katjenka Nohke. But no one takes up the word. No one. No one moves. Even the importunate pigeons on the roof remain silent.

Ah, so that's why the police drove through here earlier, says Vera all of a sudden.

Where, my mother wants to know straightaway, where and when; when, she wants to know that straightaway as well.

Earlier, says Vera drawing out the word, they drove to the British Consulate down our driveway.

Have you got a radio, Hainichen asks my father.

Yes of course, says my father with a start, why do you ask.

The news is on in a minute.

My pleasure, says my father. He stands up and goes off with the other men. He's not very happy to do so, and the glance he leaves with his wife is full of anxiety. I want to listen to the news as well and go along with him. I don't want to leave him alone with the three men right now. We stand round the radio, our heads bowed. The newsreader announces that Cairo has closed the Suez Canal to all international shipping.

It's only applied to the Jews up to now, Hainichen says to my father. My father keeps a mask in front of his face.

We go back into the garden.

The Suez Canal is closed, soon there won't be any petrol left, announces chartered engineer Hubert Arnold Zinselmayer.

Then we'll have to walk, says my father.

But I run a freight business, says Hainichen. My father co-opts the Israeli Foreign Minister onto his side, the one with the patch over his eye; the Lion of Sinai, he says enthusiastically, he'll do the job, just you wait and see. My mother gives my father a warning look, he's not to enthuse vociferously about a Jew in front of other people. But my father's not the only enthusiast, all the women, Jewish or not, like this gaunt Jew with his one eye and his crooked smile. He's sexy, says Aunt Mimi.

She'd been rung up the previous evening by a friend in Israel, recounts Hermine Kleingeld, who immediately shoots up in the estimation of the men. Nohke, Hainichen and Zinselmayer move even closer. Her friend lives in Tel Aviv, she'd heard the sirens blaring over the telephone.

Do tell us all about it, says Hainichen.

My child, my little girl. The wailing voice of Aunt Ruchla shatters the silence of the huddle of old Jewesses. Her daughter's in Tel Aviv, explains Olga taking Ruchla's hand. Everything's fine, says Hermine Kleingeld, her friend had said everything's fine. The Egyptian officers had slipped away as soon as things turned serious. The Arabs in the PLO had fought bravely, the poor devils hadn't even had proper footwear, just battered trainers, she knew that because her friend had told her.

And what's happening to our people, cries Ruchla, tell us what's happening to our people.

Schools and kindergartens were closed, Hermine Kleingeld continues, Radio Kol Israel was calling for all reservists in the entire country to report for duty, there were groups of young men everywhere trying to hitchhike to their units, everything was working like a well-oiled machine, as always when Israel's at war there was no in-fighting, everyone could depend on everyone else. The old Jewesses are triumphant, it's what we all share, it's our Jewish inheritance. My mother chimes in, she exults in the catastrophe, she rejoices at her enemies whose teeth and claws serve only to bring the family of Jews closer together. What's more, says Hermine Kleingeld, the Wailing Wall is back in our hands, and that means that a two-thousand-year-old dream has become a reality for us, for us Jews.

Displeasure is written across my mother's face, this euphoric declaration of faith is not what she wants to hear. Myself, I don't believe in God, she says, I have other dreams, but you go ahead if that's what matters to you.

What do you believe in then, asks Rosa.

I believe in me and my husband. My mother lights a cigarette. She gives a sudden laugh. And I believe in the miracles that have happened to us, to Paul and to me and to my mother, they were miracles born of our love for each other, not miracles sent by God.

Lotti levers herself out of her wicker chair, her voice trembles, Lord Rothschild, she says in tones full of respect, the London banker Lord Rothschild has pledged at a charity dinner to give Israel a donation of seventy-seven million marks. How did she know, my grandmother asks re-emerging from her long silence. I have my contacts, says Lotti with an artful smile.

327

Let's drink to that, exclaims my father, to him Lord Rothschild is manna from heaven, it makes him squirm to hear his wife having a go at God, for my father God is an ally, a father-like older brother, he sends his voice rolling out across the garden like a ship under full sail, and in its wake he retrieves God from wherever his wife had banished him to, seventy-seven million marks, seven is our lucky number, he dashes into the house and comes back with champagne.

Corks pop. We drink to Israel's health, and we drink to my grandmother's health while she sits in her chair and lets everyone kiss her. She's surrounded by a cheerful throng, from which Rosa is the first to emerge. She looks around in all directions, are you looking for something, I ask, I want to attract her attention, I'd like to ask her a really telling question, but nothing occurs to me, and Rosa carries on looking around. Then Rosa steps up to Eva Hainichen, why her of all people, aren't we far more important, aren't I more important for instance, but I can't stop Rosa, heavy rocks drop from her mouth onto blonde Eva Hainichen, who's standing under our acacia sipping champagne. Atrocities are one such rock. At this Eva Hainichen puts her glass to one side. Torture. Israeli prisons. It's too much for Eva Hainichen. She tries to turn away.

Rosa doesn't stop. Gestapo methods.

I don't know anything about that, says Eva Hainichen looking around for her husband. He's standing with the other men. Have you heard about the fire bomb, she asks Rosa, it was the anarchists, it said so in the paper. Rosa's not listening. She's bombarding Eva Hainichen with words. Torture. Gestapo methods. Israeli prisons. Witnesses. Gestapo methods. I'm afraid for Rosa and for me. If Rosa carries on like this I shall lose her.

They threw a fire bomb at the Jewish Centre in Berlin, says Eva Hainichen, these lefties, these students, they're all anarchists.

Rosa shakes her head. It's just certain newspapers, she exclaims.

Get away, snaps Eva Hainichen, it was the students, they defaced the memorial, I read it in the paper myself.

That's the Springer press for you.

Nonsense. It was your lefties, they defaced the memorial to the deported Jews.

Rosa shakes her head. Just let me explain things to you. The Springer press, all these newspapers, they're turning Moshe Dayan into a folk hero à la Rommel.

Shalom and napalm, interjects Eva Hainichen. That's what these lefties daubed on the memorial to the deported Jews, shalom and napalm.

I was deported. Rosa has her arms pressed tightly to her body.

Eva Hainichen turns away. She pushes back the left sleeve of her dress and looks at the time on her wristwatch. Hermann, I think we need to go.

My mother suddenly erupts from the gaggle downing champagne and drinking to the health of Israel and Hedwig Glitzer. She has heard every word that Rosa has spewed out against Israel. You're meshugge, you're completely meshugge. She doesn't shout, the words that come marching from her mouth to confront Rosa are deathly pale. You're meshugge in your hatred of everyone. Just go over there for goodness' sake, go to the GDR. Even today that lot look just like the Nazis used to.

Herr and Frau Hainichen say their goodbyes. The Nohkes leave at the same time.

You can't simply go off now, Aunt Mimi says to her married lover. He goes all the same. Shall I see you tomorrow, she asks. I'll ring you, he says, then he asks Nohke whether he'd like a lift, not knowing that the Nohkes live in our street, just a few houses along. He can give Frau Dingeldey a lift. Vera shows him the way out. Aunt Mimi needs a cognac.

All the others have gone. There's just us.

My mother casts her eye around. Pick up the pieces, such as they are. Rosa. The house.

I'm going to go, says Rosa remaining firmly in her chair.

My mother freezes.

They need doctors in the GDR, says Rosa, I can become the head of a hospital, as a woman I'd never get the chance here in the West.

Is that the reason, asks my mother.

In the GDR, says Rosa, being a Jew is not an issue.

So that's the reason.

She lights a cigarette.

Rosa wants a cigarette too. My mother lights it for her.

I can't bear it here, the wealth, the sheer surfeit of everything.

I can count the Jewish members of my family on the fingers of one hand, my mother, Rosa, my grandmother, my sister, and then Leon as well, Leon Wasserstrahl in Israel, he probably wouldn't even recognise my mother, his niece Alma, if they met in the street.

So you want to leave us, says my mother to Rosa. But if Jews are not an issue in the GDR, why go there. Still seated in her chair she stacks a few plates on top of one another, very meticulously, no clinking, no clanking, she shakes the crumbs onto the grass before putting each plate onto the heap, she does it one-handed in her chair, her cigarette in the other hand, her legs crossed. And she carries on speaking. Communists and Poles were the only ones to be gassed, that's what they say over there don't they, and there are Nazis only here in West Germany, and the Jews in the GDR stay mum, I just don't understand it, over there they don't want to be Jews and they do exactly what's been typically Jewish for generations, they keep their heads down.

And you, Alma, do you talk to other people about it.

No.

Exactly.

If you go to the GDR you'll be as good as dead so far as I'm concerned, and we'll be as good as dead for you. She presses her lips together. She has severed her ties with Rosa before Rosa can do it herself.

So that's what happens if you quit on my mother. I've never experienced it before. I must keep an eye on how things go, how Rosa does it, how she survives being separated from my mother.

Alma spits something out, a shred of tobacco. A last remnant of the tie that bound her to Rosa. We all watch, totally dumbstruck. Does anyone want to say anything, does anyone want to intervene, my father perhaps. He has screwed his mouth up, he can taste the full pungency of his wife's implacable stance. My grandmother feels that it's not her responsibility any more, her daughter is an adult, and in any case she wouldn't dare to speak out against her.

Rosa stands up. That's something she can do. She heaves herself across the lawn on her fat legs. Her dark-coloured skirt billows in the breeze. I've only ever seen her in this pleated skirt. She leaves without a hug or a kiss. Without a goodbye. See you soon, au revoir: she doesn't say it. She doesn't say anything. Without turning round one final time she disappears into the dark passageway.

331

Someone else is standing up, does someone else want to leave for ever and break irrevocably with my mother, does someone else want to follow Rosa and go along with her to the other side of the Wall. It's Hermine Kleingeld, she hastily shakes everyone's hand and rushes after Rosa.

Wonder if she'll go to the GDR as well, says Betty.

Why would she go, says my mother, they can't both be that stupid.

But they're a pair, says Olga, they love each other.

Elsa Kupsch appears out of the dark passageway followed by Erich Kupsch and then their three sons, first Kurt, the eldest, then Michael and finally Wolfram, accompanied by daughter Elisabeth with a little angel in her stomach. Erich Kupsch and his three sons have come to wish my grandmother a happy birthday, and Elsa Kupsch wants to tell us that everything's all done upstairs, the cold buffet's ready and waiting, Frau Schiefer.

It's late, it's already nearly nine. There'll be news on the radio again in a little while. She always feels terribly hungry after she's eaten cakes, declares my mother, and would the Kupsches please stay and be our guests, the children too. They decline. They can't do this to my mother, she's going to be stuck with all her food as she's driven the neighbours away and Rosa's gone too, we'll be eating kosher rissoles, pickled gherkins, herrings and egg and onion for weeks. But Kurt Kupsch has to get back to his books, he's doing the school leaving certificate he should have done years ago, and Michael, Elisabeth and Wolfram want to go to the pictures.

Just you wait, remonstrates Elsa Kupsch, pictures my eye, there's washin'-up to be done.

No, no washing-up, says my mother; we'll do that tomorrow morning, Frau Kupsch, we'll leave everything for tonight.

The Kupsch children leave. Wolfram and Michael get some cakes to take with them, but Elisabeth doesn't fancy anything, which is unusual; Kurt's to have something from the cold buffet before he goes back down to his books. My grandmother fills a large plate for him, a little bit of everything.

Vera and I watch the Kupsch children as they leave. What's on, shouts Vera with longing in her voice. A trip to the pictures. Just like that, and all on their own, without their parents, at night, the late show even. We'd never be allowed to do that.

Michael turns round in the doorway to our living room, *Winnetou and the Half-Breed*, what's 'is name again, and Elisabeth calls out *Apanatschi*.

Israel has taken Gaza, reports the newsreader on the radio. We sit there in silence and listen. Our joy at Israel's successes is muted. Rosa has gone for ever.

Now tell us, Herr Schiefer, says Erich Kupsch as he sits there with a heavily laden plate in front of him and dips his kosher rissole in his Silesian potato salad, now tell us, where's things with the 'ouse.

Ah yes, Herr Kupsch, laughs my father, that's one topic we haven't touched on today. Fifty-six thousand marks if we're lucky, better say sixty thousand marks, or just to be on the safe side sixty-five thousand marks.

Let's say, Herr Kupsch nods, let's say seventy thahsand marks all up, got to be renovated regular the house 'as, top to bottom, cost a bomb that will, no one'll do it fer yer fer free, well me, us, me and me Elsa 'ere, we'll lend yer, sure as I sit 'ere we'll give yer ten thahsand marks towards it an' me labour on tick and Kurt's labour an' all, 'e'll 'elp as well, 'e's a site foreman now, 'e is. What abaht all these other ladies and gents, says Erich Kupsch gazing around the room. He takes it for granted

333

that everyone present is fully in the picture and that we're all gathered round the table eating egg and onion on challah and chicken broth and all the rest of it for the specific purpose of discussing the matter. Besides him and my father there are no gents present at all, but lots of old ladies.

Silence and embarrassment engulf us.

My father isn't the property-owning type, he doesn't want the house, he wants his peace and quiet, his aim is to be content with little so that the little he has continues to be his. My mother wants the house, she wants us to have security. There are so many things my father has to force himself to do, the life of a sales rep doesn't suit him at all, the house would bring security, bricks and mortar increase in value, you can sell up and then you've got money and you've got ready cash for a life elsewhere if you have to get out at some point – but getting out, going elsewhere, that's not really my father's cup of tea, no matter whether it's Israel or anywhere else.

Or should I 'ave . . . Erich Kupsch looks around him with a hangdog expression and smacks his hand against his mouth. Yes, screams Elsa Kupsch, yer should've kept yer trap shut, an' all this on poor Frau Glitzer's birthday.

Wife, says Erich Kupsch. That's all he says. He's as red as a beetroot. The whole thing is just too embarrassing for him. Especially in front of the old ladies.

We're sitting at the dining table, it's been extended today to form a large oval, an elegant tablecloth has been spread over it, the cloth has already been soiled by me, by Aunt Wilma and Aunt Emilie who are both a bit shaky with a knife and fork, and by my mother as she pours the wine and serves the food. A long piece of ash drops from my father's cigarette and lands on the white linen; Vera wets the tip of her finger, dabs it on the ash and precariously transfers it to a flower vase.

Oh dear, says my father, recognising that something needs to be said at long last, and anyway he likes the people sitting round our table, the old Jewesses who have witnessed the end of civilisation, and the Kupsches, decent people as we well know, oh dear, sighs my father, so far as the house is concerned, I think – but he gets no further: Aunt Wilma next to him puts her ancient little hand on his arm, he's to listen to Ruchla, she's got something to say.

Toches on the table, Herr Kupsch, says Aunt Ruchla with great deliberateness in her coarse, croaky voice. Toches on the table.

What's that, asks Erich Kupsch disconcertedly, what d'yer want me ter put on the table.

Your toches, squawks Aunt Wilma who has had a good few and is a little bit tipsy. Your backside, Herr Kupsch, she adds, turning red.

Ah yes, says Erich Kupsch, yes, if that's 'ow it is.

Aunt Ruchla nods, that's just how it is, 'cos for the son-in-law of our Hedwig, good woman that she is, we'll do anything, let's not make a big tsimmes for eppes.

A what for what, laughs Erich Kupsch.

Make mountains out of mole hills, says Aunt Ruchla gravely, got any dosh, Herr Kupsch, got any money, me neither, we've all got dalles.

Money worries, ventures Erich Kupsch.

Dalles, says Aunt Ruchla nodding to him, you're a man with seichl.

A man with what.

A man with lots up here, says Aunt Olga tapping her forehead.

Ah yes, says Erich Kupsch.

Aunt Ruchla smacks her lips contentedly.

It's a tricky business, says Betty, maybe it's not on, but it's worth talking about, there's plenty of goodwill on Herr Kupsch's part, give a bit of help without forgetting your own interests, that's what I reckon, might be a bit of profit in it, then we'd all get something out of it, let's wait and see, bricks and mortar are worth a penny or two. Let Ruchla speak, says Olga to Betty. What you interfering for, says Betty to Olga. Me, says Olga to Wilma, me interfering, you tell me, just tell me honestly, Wilma, was I interfering, and Wilma says Ruchla's got something to say, then let her say it, says Olga, meshuggene, says Betty, and Emilie strokes Erich Kupsch's burly arm, because he's such a lovely strong man, she says to Elsa Kupsch with a nod and a giggle, it really gets us old women going.

Don't listen to her, says Aunt Ruchla, listen to me. Buying this house here, it's not money down the drain, so what I says is buy it, problem is though, Herr Schiefer here has got to buy the house from a paskudniak.

Too right, says Erich Kupsch, paskudniak, learned that from the Russkis I did, it's someone what's really bad, you can't trust 'im, Herr Schiefer, not as far as you can throw 'im you can't.

This sparks great animation round the table, my father is warned from all sides that he can't trust Hainichen as far as he can throw him, even Lotti starts wagging her finger.

So what's his wife, Vera wants to know, if he's a paskudniak.

A paskudniashka, says Aunt Ruchla patting Vera's hand.

We slump in our chairs exhausted, cheerful, sated and without any solution to our money worries.

Two taxis arrive. We all go out into the driveway.

I'm going to walk, no need to drive me, says Mimi squeezing her brother's arm. It's not far from our house to hers, a quarter of an hour's walk to Heimhuder Strasse. She kisses my mother, don't get all worked up about Rosa, she presumably knows what she's doing.

Me, says my mother in complete astonishment, I never get worked up.

Mimi walks off down the driveway, her high heels click-clicking in the dark, she crosses the street and is gone.

Ruchla, Olga and Betty climb into one of the taxis, the driver of the second – a young man in jeans and a black leather jacket – has a rather trickier job, he has to lift one of his three old ladies onto the front passenger seat complete with her rubber ring as Wilma declares that with her rubber ring she can only sit in the front next to the driver. No sooner has the gum-chewing driver managed to install one little old lady in the front seat than the other starts whining that she can't possibly sit in the back, sitting in the back makes her feel sick. He smooths his well-greased hair on both sides of his head, a carefully shaped quiff arches up over his forehead. As Emilie won't stop whining, Wilma gets the young man to lift her out again and deposit her and her rubber ring on the back seat. Emilie won't give us any peace otherwise, Wilma says to the driver, you don't know Emilie but I do know Emilie.

It's the same thing every time, Lotti whispers to my father, old women, really, it's enough to make you feel ashamed, but what I wanted to say to you, Herr Schiefer – she takes him by the arm and leads him off under the overhanging jasmine bushes between the garden and the driveway, Lotti is nearly as tall as my father, but being so scrawny she almost looks taller.

I'm a businesswoman myself, as you know, and you won't spurn a bit of good advice. Talk to your bank, have the house and land valued, there's a lot of money here, I can smell it. She taps her finger against her black-veiled nose, take your confidence in both hands and you will make a profit. But it's

337

you that has to make this courageous step, no one can do it for you.

Lotti gets into the back of the taxi, next to Wilma. Little Emilie in the front has almost disappeared in the seat cushions. The taxi driver shuts Lotti's door and gets into the driving seat. Lotti, sitting in the back next to the window, lifts her gloved hand and almost gives a wave.

She could have lent you something, says my mother as we gather up the crockery in the kitchen, Lotti's got money.

My father stands eating the last rissole. He walks over to the window. My sister Mimi said nothing, she kept completely quiet. Why should Lotti lend me anything when my own flesh and blood don't, neither my brother nor my sister. Mimi's boyfriend, that Hubert Arnold Zinselmayer, he's stinking with money, she could ask him, she doesn't dare, I just have to accept the situation. I fully respect the fact that Lotti doesn't want to lend us anything. I'm not at all sure I would have accepted it anyway.

My mother looks at her husband. Paul, you're *too* good sometimes. She lifts a saucepan to her lips and noisily drinks what's left of the chicken broth.

My father looks at his wife. Alma, perhaps we shouldn't buy anything at all in Germany.

At least go and talk to the bank, Paul. My grandmother rarely says her son-in-law's name, and very rarely says it straight to his face like this. She works it all out for him, carefully adding the various amounts together, ten thousand from Erich Kupsch, fifteen thousand from her, that's already twenty-five thousand, so we need another forty-five thousand at most. Alma's expecting some reparations money.

Quite right, my mother slaps her hand against her forehead, how did we manage to forget about that, the lawyer said ten thousand, at least ten thousand he said, and it might be as much as thirty or forty thousand if they accept the full claim, wrongful imprisonment, denial of career opportunities, no school leaving certificate, house set on fire, persecution, somewhere between twenty and forty thousand he said, you heard him yourself, Paul, but let's not assume it'll be forty thousand, let's just say thirty-five thousand, no let's say thirty thousand, that leaves us needing fifteen thousand, that's nothing, the bank'll throw it at us, a small mortgage on the house, with this size plot and in this area, it's a gift.

What do you reckon, I ask Vera in bed later on, do you think Rosa really will go over to the GDR. If she does we'll never see her again. We won't be able to visit her and she won't be able to visit us. She'll be living behind a wall, in a gigantic prison surrounded by watchtowers. We'll be able to send her parcels with coffee beans and chocolate.

Shall I show you what Rosa gave me, Vera asks.

I'm burning with jealousy, why did Rosa bring something for her and not for me, then I immediately realise that it's a birthday present for my grandmother, I'm furious at Vera for grabbing something for herself, and grabbing it from under my nose, but in fact it doesn't belong to either of us. I snarl, I kick at my bedcovers.

I'm allowed to keep it, Fania, I swear. Vera holds her face towards me, her eyes are full of specious promise, she has shaped her lips into the semblance of a smile, I could strangle her, and she pulls a slender book from under the pillow, a book bound in red linen with *Rosa Luxemburg, Letters* written on it in gold. It's a very old edition, says Vera, do you know who she was, there you are you see, you don't know.

I can't speak. I'd like to grab her by the throat, and I'm choking with rage.

Rosa Luxemburg was a Jew, like us.

But Vera doesn't want to be a Jew.

I'm so cross with my sister I could kill her, then we turn out the light and lie close to each other in our double bed to await the night.

Not a pretty woman, Rosa Luxemburg. Vera carries on talking, oblivious of the fact that I am murdering her in my mind. A small, plump woman with large breasts and large hats, Fania, she walked with a limp and wasn't married and had no children, she was a revolutionary, she made speeches in the streets and public squares, in halls and even in the Reichstag in Berlin, just imagine, Fania, a woman in front of thousands of men.

Before or after, I ask curtly. I want to join in just a little bit at least.

Before, it was all before. She was murdered before the Nazi period even started. She was put in prison first, and those are the letters she wrote from her cell. Vera opens the red book. There it is: Letters. And where they were sent from: Prison.

Read me a bit. I roll over onto my side with my face towards Vera, I pull my cold legs up under my stomach that is still burning with rage. I wait for the words that Rosa Luxemburg wrote in her cell, a kindly warder gave her paper and pencil, no, she stole the paper, she had to glue paper bags just like my mother. You have to fold the square reddish-brown sheet of paper on the diagonal, but not exactly corner to corner, you have to make sure one edge sticks out a little beyond the other, then you daub bone glue from a large bucket along the short edge, let it dry off for a short while and pass it on to the next woman, talking is forbidden, she presses the two sides of the bag together along the glue line, the bags are exactly the same today, Herr Bohn has them hanging on a hook in his vegetable shop and uses them for weighing grapes, tomatoes and onions.

Why aren't you reading out loud, read me some of it, you're gobbling up Rosa Luxemburg's sentences all for yourself.

Listen, Vera giggles, it says here the book was published by the Executive Committee of the Communist Youth International, Berlin 1927. I bet you don't know what an executive committee is.

I know what execution means. It's a word that dogged my father. Next to his cell was the condemned cell. The people in it used to sob and scream at night. He could hear them from his own cell. And in the morning they would tap out a message through the wall, they wanted to go to their death with their head held high. He was in solitary confinement for months. A warder brought his food, and never uttered a word. Do you think they beat him.

What on earth's made you think of that, asks Vera leafing through the book.

When they interrogated him.

Why are you asking.

I want you to answer. Go on, answer.

Do *you* think so.

He doesn't like men.

What about you, Vera retorts, you don't like men either.

Just read, I say.

She looks at the book, she's put her little cushion on her chest and rested the book against it. She can start.

I'll read you what Rosa, our Rosa, wrote in the book as a dedication, it's a quotation from one of Rosa Luxemburg's letters. Vera takes a preparatory breath, inaudibly re-reads what she had already glanced through moments earlier, my whole head's about to burst, get on with it, I can hardly bear the wait,

341

when will it be, the tapping on the wall, when, I'm waiting, I'm waiting.

19 April 1917 – Life has always been like this, it's all part of it: sorrow and suffering and longing. You just have to accept it along with all the rest and take the view that everything is fine and good.

Vera strokes her hand across the pages as if the letter had been written to us.

Chapter Ten

That's the bin men, outside by the rubbish bins beneath the toilet window, they're pushing and shoving the bins. Vera's got a dancing lesson this evening, she won't be back until late because of the lesson, it'll be getting on for half past ten, it's already dark by that time, young girls need to have dancing lessons, women need to be able to dance, they have to be able to let a man lead, he goes forwards, she goes backwards. I could nudge the open sash of the toilet window with my index finger. Then it would shut. They'll have gone soon. Vera went off this evening in high-heeled shoes, she twirled round in front of the mirror, she lifted her skirt, she gazed at her calves, a flat shoe on her right foot, a stiletto on her left, her leg looks more attractive the higher the heel is, she'll have found a pair big enough, my mother and my grandmother exchanged expectant glances, they didn't say anything but they thought it: a tall young man for Vera, at last. I'll have to have dancing lessons as well. When the time comes my mother will enrol me, we'll travel into town and buy me a dress and nylon stockings and suspenders, perhaps a bra, and I'll go off to the classes in flats or in heels, depending on whether I grow any taller. I hope it'll be heels.

We laughed ourselves half to death. They've got TV,

Sirena's parents have. Qualifiers they're called, for the international dance championships in Lucerne. There were the Sauers, a man-and-wife team from Germany, he looked like Jürgen Menkel next door but grown up and without binoculars, he had thick glasses and a heavily greased quiff. They were exactly the same height the two of them, I particularly noticed that. Probably a good thing when you're dancing. She was thrusting her thumb and index finger against his shoulder and keeping her elbow stuck out horizontally. We laughed ourselves half to death, we were on our own one afternoon, Sirena and me, it was our extra tuition hour, she was Frau Sauer and I was Herr Sauer, we held each other tight and did long strides and snatched our heads back and forth, all at breakneck speed, and we laughed ourselves half to death, Sirena laughed so much she wet herself a bit and so did I. Her knickers were wet, have a feel, she said. Like Jürgen Menkel from next door. It can't have been his father. Everyone says Jürgen's father is dead, he was killed in the war. And Frau Menkel gets a big fat pension. Vera did say that the man's name was Menkel and that he took everything belonging to the Fingerhuts. Those papers in the cellar, beyond the air-raid shelter door. It isn't very far from here, down the cellars, turn right, follow the passage to the air-raid shelter doors. Not now. A torch would be a good idea, a large torch, and I'd take some drink with me, just in case. The air-raid shelter doors could slam shut behind me. It must be lovely being able to dance. But like my mother, not the breakneck way the Sauers do it.

Why didn't you pass *that* on to me, said Vera in a fit of pique, you passed quite a lot of things on to me, why not that as well, it's exactly what I could have done with. My mother gave a brief laugh. She can't decide what gets passed on to us. But Vera behaved as if she could. She screamed and sobbed. I can't dance and it's all your fault. She slammed the door behind her. Think yourselves lucky that *you* can go to dancing classes, says my mother. She never went to dancing classes but she dances better than all the other women. She just knows how to do it. Move with the music, she says, that's all, come on, I'll show you, look, like this, and she moves to the music, she shuts her eyes, smiles, snaps her fingers and rolls her hips, her feet whirl and leap, her lips part, her heels clatter, she dips her head to the rhythm, her hair falls across her face, and we watch her, my grandmother is proud of her dancing daughter. My grandmother danced with Aunt Ruchla once, a pair of old ladies. My mother dances with wild abandon. She is completely absorbed in herself. She's forgotten us. And Vera becomes stiff and rigid.

I've no desire to dance, I don't want to suffer the way Vera does. And if I try it and it turns out that I can do it like my mother, Vera will suffer twice over. It must be wonderful being able to dance, Vera and I can see it in our mother. Vera collapses into my father's armchair and sobs. Don't touch me, she yells, and my mother sighs and stops dancing.

It's dark outside. My father is away. The moon is rising over the Fingerhuts' house. I say Fingerhuts' house even though they don't live there any more. If that house over there belonged to them, why did this one. Perhaps both did, or just this one and not that one, perhaps they lived there just so that they could see this one, their house, the house that belonged to Simon Fingerhut's parents, Esther's grandparents, and we live in it now and I never knew, Esther and I used to play together in our garden that was actually her garden, and we didn't know. Now Sirena lives there with her parents. They know nothing about anything, absolutely nothing.

My father's out on the road. Vera always has her dancing

lessons on Wednesdays. Wouldn't you sooner go and meet her, says my grandmother looking up from her magazine and glancing across over the top of her reading glasses at my mother who has repeatedly looked anxiously at the clock. Last Wednesday. I'm not you, says my mother to her mother, because that's what her mother said to her when my mother was the same age as Vera is now, seventeen, I've worked it out, it was just under three years before she was arrested, in fact my mother was still only sixteen, and she, a Jew, went dancing with a friend, Jews weren't allowed to go dancing, there were Nazis everywhere, but she did it all the same, and we're not allowed to do anything.

It's a good thing Paul's not here, said my mother, otherwise her father would go and collect her, and how is Vera supposed to meet anyone if she can never let a young man bring her home because she's afraid her mother will come rushing up to her out of the darkness in a totally distraught state. In saying this my mother was thinking of her own mother, my grandmother didn't let on that she'd noticed this, she saw the anxiety on my mother's face, an anxiety she well knows herself.

Vera should already have turned up really or at any rate she ought to arrive any second, she could well get here any second now. That can't be the bin men pushing and shoving the bins beneath the toilet window, it's been dark for ages and there's all this clattering and squealing, the bin men come early in the morning, perhaps it's rats, the Alster's so close, it's rats, they come through the sewers, a rat can come up through the soil pipe and leap straight inside me, I'm sitting on the loo completely agape, I'm sitting in the dark, I'm not going to turn the light on, the moon is shining in through the open toilet window, it's not full yet, I can see it clearly, I can see everything, the bushes out there in the back garden and a bit

346

of the driveway, I can't see the bins, they're right under the open window and really close to me. I'd like to turn the light on because of the rats so that they'll run away and stop their shoving and squealing, unless it's not rats at all, rats squeak rather than squeal and they don't giggle and push and grunt. I'd prefer to put the light on, but then anyone outside could see me standing up to reach the switch and the light from the bulb will fall on me as well, better not, I'll lean forward and stretch my arm up to the switch, my knickers are dangling round my knees.

There's a man there. He's come through the barred window of the toilet. Right into my ear. He's by the rubbish bin beneath the window, the window's open, it's open so the moon can shine in on me, his face has bars across it, it's only a short distance from here to the ground, from the outside anyone can just hoist themself up and they're in, there are the bars on the window, but they shut you in rather than protect you from whatever's outside, the man isn't on his own, he's got something with him, a squealing something or other, he's poking and pushing it. I mustn't move. It's jumping up at me. I can't get away. I'm part of it. I'm stuck fast. They're pulling me along with them. I don't want to be part of it. It's a woman. It's not a woman. It's my sister. I can't get down to her. I can't get away. It's happening right now. My sister. It's happening right now. I want to get out of here. He's to stop. My sister. Stop, please stop. Listen to me. He's to stop. It's you. Let me out of here the pair of you. I'll have to wait. Has he finished. Stop it both of you. My mother. I'll be the only one to know. It'll be my burden alone. Behind the bars of your hair. I'll have to wait. He's finished. I'll have to wait. For the footsteps. There are the footsteps. On the stairs. There's a light on. In the stairwell. Through the crack. Her footsteps. In front of the door. Through the crack. His footsteps. In front of the door. I want darkness. Where's the darkness. It's dark now. It's quiet now. I stand up. It's me. I wipe myself. I pull my knickers up. I straighten my skirt. I undo the latch and sidle out into the velvety darkness of the stairwell. A few steps below me our front door is thrust open. A light goes on. A voice says Fania.

Yes, it's me.

What are you doing in the dark out here. Vera's standing behind me. I drop the key to the toilet. I bend down, pick it up, insert it in the lock, I'm about to turn it when I ask Vera whether I pressed the flush.

How should I know, giggles Vera.

Was it her or was it Elisabeth, it was Vera's voice wasn't it, perhaps it was Elisabeth, by the bins just now. With him. It was him.

What was it like, I ask.

Tedious, says Vera, I hate dancing.

Most men don't know how to lead, says my mother when we're back in the flat, that's why. She hangs Vera's raincoat on the coat rack.

Your father doesn't know how to lead, I lead him instead, and your father can only dance the waltz. Then she asks Vera what she's learnt at her class this evening, foxtrot, says Vera, show me the steps, says my mother, I don't think I can do the foxtrot, Vera and I know she *will* be able to do it, Vera will just need to demonstrate a couple of steps, and she'll do the rest off her own bat, by pure intuition, while Vera trips over her own feet and forgets everything she learnt at her class and it will look as if she never went at all.

Something ought to be arriving quite soon, my mother had said, and the very next afternoon the special delivery postman rings the bell, bringing my grandmother her monthly reparations payment, and giving my mother a large brown envelope that she has to sign for. Something important. My mother signs, shuts the front door, looks to see who sent the envelope, and says This is it. She has to sit down. A somewhat smaller envelope, also brown, falls out of the big one, together with a white letter, signed p.p. Professor Siegfried Ehrlichmann.

I can't bear to read it, says my mother and begins to read it. Vera lights her a cigarette and puts it between her lips. Re your claim in accordance with paragraphs twenty-eight to forty-two of the Federal Indemnification Act: damage suffered to body or health, file number, oblique, register number, three hundred and twenty-six thousand etc. etc. who cares, Dear Frau Schiefer. She reads on in an inaudible murmur with narrowed eyes and pursed lips, my insides are churned up all the way from my stomach to my tongue. Read it out loud, why aren't you reading it aloud, what does he say, Alma, my grandmother's feet and hands are twitching like mad.

What a nerve, says my mother. This eases the tension a bit. He says nothing at all. I'm to hand the enclosed envelope unopened to the Reparations Office at my next interview. Even as she says this her red-varnished fingernails make their way into the sealed brown envelope and tear it open.

Don't do that, Alma, my grandmother puts both hands over her mouth, it's forbidden.

What absolute nonsense, her voice is cold and calm, she isn't trembling at all, she isn't afraid. It's about me after all, she says, why shouldn't I know what this man says about me in his report to the Reparations people, those days are gone for good, and anyway did I obey their rules even then, no I did not, I especially didn't back then, and I'm not going to do any different today, do you remember when Paul got his decision letter from the Military Exemption Board, I steamed it open then glued it carefully back down again, I don't need to go to those lengths today, what could possibly happen to me, they can't arrest me for it, and back then when Paul went and reported in to those filthy swine he already knew he'd been certified unfit because of his stomach ulcers when he gave them the letter that I'd so beautifully stuck back down again. We already know all that, says Vera, just get on and read what they've written. Paul had to stand there in front of them and wait while they read the letter, unfit for war service, then this swine, this SS swine with his white coat and his high black boots underneath, he got up from his chair and said to Paul, please, Mammy, stop it, read out what it says about you, no, you shush, he said Congratulations, Herr Schiefer, you have been cleared to go and fight for our beloved Führer, that's what he said, and if I hadn't carefully steamed the letter open before he was due to report, Paul wouldn't have known he'd been certified UWS, unfit for war service, and that this swine, this filthy SS swine, was telling him a pack of lies.

I've forgotten what my father told the SS swine, but I'll be reminded any second now, my mother will spit the words out, I want to fix it in my mind this time, I want to fix it in my mind *every* time, I don't want to forget it, but it'll slip my mind all the same, I must manage it this time, I won't manage it, I *have* to manage it, they managed it, why can't I manage it, they tell us about their great triumph and Vera and I put our heads back and watch them as they ascend into the mists that then descend on us, the entire story is wreathed in mist. What did he say to the SS swine, she's just told us, I didn't catch it, something or other ingratiating and necessarily polite, something or other exceedingly cunning with an undertone of submissiveness and of fear, fear that they might sniff out his

Jewish lover's fingerprints on the Nazi document, because of the race laws, with Jewish finesse she had steamed open the Nazi envelope in the Jewish kitchen of her Jewish mother, he didn't have to go off to war, he had a duodenal ulcer thank God, they cried, they laughed, a duodenal ulcer, there he was before the Hamburg Exemption Board, and there's the SS doctor in his white coat and shiny boots, they tumble on top of each other, she's hacked all their heads off, dead they fall in a tangled heap, the men come up the stairs and knock on the door, bang bang, there are several of them, she's standing in the kitchen clinging to her mother, we're not going to the door, they can break it down, we aren't going to open it, she goes to the door hand in hand with her mother, there are two armed soldiers outside the door with Soldier Paul Schiefer slumped between them, they ask where they're to put him, here on this bench in the kitchen, they look at each other, don't say a word, wait until the front door snaps shut at the bottom of the stairs.

We fell into each other's arms, sobs my mother, my God we were lucky, he'd been exempted. And as the curtains go swishing across the screen to the sound of the final crashing chords she adds The Gestapo came later on and arrested us, Mummy, Paul and me. But we survived.

This all floods back into her mind now, they pulled through together, her husband's not here today, he's out on the road and we're alone with her faced with this psychiatric report that she hasn't yet read. This is all about her. It is she who has been put to the test.

Go on, read it now, says Vera sitting down by her side so that she too can see the report to the Reparations Office concerning the claimant Alma Schiefer, née Glitzer. The hopeful waiting is over. Our joy at receiving the official missive is all gone. Anything and everything can descend upon us. She doesn't understand a thing, every word that leaps off the page at her is like a blow rendering her more and more dazed. Is that her, is that my mother, this is about her, camp-induced amenorrhoea. Sounds like diarrhoea, says Vera. Vera always thinks of diarrhoea whenever there's any mention of concentration camps.

Where's the dictionary, quick, give me the dictionary.

Vera fetches her the dictionary. I hope Vera hasn't cut something out anywhere near the entry for amenorrhoea. Every letter of the alphabet could make a crucial difference to whether we can buy the house or not, this is the big moment that will decide whether we can stay or not, you look it up, Vera, she says, I can't see straight any more. Vera hunts through the first few pages, A for amenorrhoea, absence or suppression of the menstrual discharge. Menstrual discharge. A bodiless term. That can't possibly mean our periods. I've got camp-induced amenorrhoea, my poor periods are held prisoner within me. Vera writhes with pain every month and has to stay in bed until her blood starts seeping out, my mother claims to have no problems at all with her periods, when the time comes it just comes flooding out of her, she never keeps track of it, she says, it's her husband who knows what's what, he always knows when she's due, she never does herself. We all know, we all run for cover, every month just before her period starts she goes on a cleaning binge, she tidies cupboards, ours as well as her own, she throws things away, mucking out she calls it, she rearranges the flat, she suddenly feels driven to clean the windows even though Frau Kupsch cleaned them the previous week. We look at one another, she's getting her period, we whisper, she hears and flies into a rage, what rubbish, she exclaims throwing herself head first into the bottom kitchen cupboard, pots and pans clank and rattle, all of a sudden she has this tight feeling in her stomach, it's your period, Alma, says my grandmother, she protests, yesterday's green peppers hadn't agreed with her, they're lying on my tummy, she says, my father creeps around her, he wants to put a hot-water bottle on his wife's abdomen, she doesn't want it, he wants to calm her down, the warmth would soothe your stomach, he knows that from his own stomach, he says, and she flies off the handle, you know that, you know everything, you understand everything, you'd say you knew all about it if I were having a period but I'm not having a period.

Give it to me. Vera wants to carry on reading.

No. My mother's not surrendering the report. No proof of any link between claimant's amenorrhoea and her subsequent miscarriages and premature births. She lets her hand drop down, the sheet of paper slips from her grasp, Vera catches it. I slipped out of her body, and others had slipped out before me, they weren't fully formed, they arrived too soon. But I was fully formed, I hadn't just dropped out of her, every year on my birthday she sobs, for joy, Fania, for joy, and I calm her down, you're a good mother.

Endogenous depression, says Vera carrying on reading, that sounds pretty good, Vera's become interested in psychology recently, we're all hoping for enlightenment from her, but in the meantime another alien word comes creeping along: constitutional.

What do they mean by constitutional.

They mean it's not the Nazis' fault.

There's something else here. Vera hasn't given up, she's come across something else, deprivation of liberty: – but the excitement goes out of her voice – insignificant; loss of life: not indicated; reduction in ability to earn a living: twenty-five per

353

cent, at least there's that, Mammy, you're bound to get something on that score, and look, there's something here about your migraines: exhaustion syndrome, it says.

Just leave it.

No, wait, can be attributed to claimant's sensitive asthenic nature and pre-menopausal condition, rather than to any persecution she may have suffered. My mother hits out at the sheet of paper and knocks it from Vera's hand.

There'll be no money for that.

It wasn't enough. It wasn't bad enough.

I can't touch her. None of us can. She'd hit me if I tried to touch her. We're all in the same room yet isolated from each other, I'm isolated from Vera and my grandmother as well, and they are isolated from me and from her.

At some point one of us laid Alma's rigid body on the sofa. At some point one of us crushed up some tablets on a plate, turned them into a runny paste with a little water and fed her the paste. Later one of us held the dish into which she vomited all her bitter gall.

At some point darkness fell.

We hear my father through the walls of the house. Outside. His car horn is our signal. He wasn't supposed to get back until tomorrow. Tomorrow is Friday. He's found us today instead. My grandmother gets up, goes to the door and opens it for her son-in-law. He slips into our darkness. He grasps the situation at once. He sits down on Alma's makeshift bed. I've failed, Paul, her body becomes all hunched up and she tells Vera and me that she's so sorry that after all our father has done for her she's not going to be able to contribute any money for him to buy the house, and now she starts crying and at last I begin to get warm again.

And now Vera has gone.

She's gone on a school trip to the Lüneburger Heide. She wasn't really meant to go on the trip, Vera and I have never been allowed to go on a school trip, our parents are too anxious. But all of a sudden my mother took the view that Vera should indeed go, no matter what, it'll be good, for all of us, and although it was supposed to be good for all of us my mother was furious with Vera, so furious that I was scared for Vera.

Vera had wanted to go when my mother, as usual, didn't want her to go, and nor did my father. Much too dangerous. Vera's form-master, Wilhelm Bobbenberg, had wanted to take the class to London for a week, but now Bobbi's got a slipped disc and has gone to Bad Pyrmont to recuperate, so Fräulein Kahl and Fräulein Hahn have taken over from him, but instead of a week in London they're spending a fortnight in Kakenstorf, somewhere in the Lüneburger Heide, and taking two classes, not only Vera's class of twenty seventeen-year-olds, but also twenty-nine fourteen-year-olds as well. Vera doesn't like Fräulein Kahl and Fräulein Hahn, a view I share, and she detests the Lüneburger Heide, a view my mother shares, but she was made to go all the same. I'm not going to Kakenstorf under any circumstances, she screamed, and my mother said You're going. Her voice was made of armoured glass.

When my father intervened wondering why school trips were on the agenda in the first place, after all neither of his daughters had ever gone away on their own either to London or to Kakenstorf, and especially not to Kakenstorf in the Lüneburger Heide, why was it such a good idea all of a sudden, and my mother said She's not going away on her own, Paul, she's going with two teachers and all the girls in her class, and when Vera said That's been the case with all the other school trips you've forbidden us to go on, and when my father laughed and said She's quite right, Alma, why's she to go to Kakenstorf all of a sudden, just let her stay here – my mother simply yanked him off into the bedroom. He stumbled in alongside her throwing us a look over her shoulder, and she locked the door from the inside. I've heard her lock the bedroom door when she's packing up presents for us, I've never heard her lock the door simply to shut us out.

My grandmother disappeared into the kitchen, Vera stayed where she was and lit a cigarette.

Why not just go, I'm sure it won't be all that bad, I said. She bit her way clean through me with her eyes. Leave me alone. Her voice was snapping at me like a dog. Then she forgot all about me. I stayed sitting in front of her. In our years of sharing a room we have learned how to be simultaneously together yet on our own. Murmurings and angry whisperings were audible from behind the door. Vera smoked. I watched her. This was not the Vera I knew, she had become a stranger to me. A row was going on behind the door. Have to leave the house at once, I heard my mother say. If you. If he. If she. If he. My daughter. Never. That was my father, and Vera raised her head.

The door opened.

Where's Pappy, asked Vera, she had shrunk all of a sudden, she was smaller than me, she seemed to have withdrawn from the life she had lived thus far. The cigarette stuck between her index and middle fingers seemed completely out of place.

Your father's in bed, his stomach hurts, said my mother.

Can I go and see him.

Not now.

Do I have to go to Kakenstorf.

Yes.

I expected an outburst – tears, screams, something like that. Vera swallowed and said that every girl was supposed to take forty marks pocket money with them, would she be getting the money.

Of course, said my mother coldly. And both of them left the room to go and pack Vera's suitcase. Vera's cigarette end lay in the ashtray giving off clouds of smoke. I put it out.

Fräulein Brunhilde Kahl, Geography, and Fräulein Regula Hahn, Music, both in Tyrolean hats and loden suits, were waiting outside Dammtor station with forty-eight girls when my mother and my father and Vera and I drove up in our car. We got out.

I'm not coming to the train though, said my mother, she had tears in her eyes, she gave Vera a hasty kiss on the cheek, turned round and walked off a little way, and Vera was crying, and my father took Vera in his arms, I ran after my mother and took her in my arms.

The fact that Vera is on a school trip in Kakenstorf has a lot to do with Pilatus Kupsch. He was born to Elisabeth Kupsch. She was sitting astride the wash bowl washing her lower bits when Pilatus suddenly dropped out into the water. I know from Vera that for a moment Elisabeth wondered whether it wouldn't be better to let him drown. Frau Kupsch got into a terrible state about it, now she's a grandmother and Wolfram's already an uncle even though he's a year younger than me, though what upset Frau Kupsch the most was the fact that she'd never noticed that her daughter was pregnant. But then Elisabeth is fat, as fat as her mother, and it just didn't show.

You surely must have noticed, Frau Kupsch, said my mother, she was positively indignant. She just couldn't understand it, she said, you as a mother, Frau Kupsch, you surely must have noticed. Nah, nah, Frau Schiefer, God's honour, nah. Erich Kupsch gave his daughter a couple of clips round the ear and Elsa Kupsch planted herself in front of her daughter and screamed at her husband that you don't go around hitting young mothers. Erich Kupsch went off to the pub to get drunk and bought a round to drink to the health of his grandson Pilatus Kupsch. Everyone knows who the father is. Elisabeth told her mother, and Frau Kupsch came to my mother asking her to go with her to see Frau Hainichen and tell her all about it.

'Cos of the money, Frau Schiefer, reckon 'e's got to pay up seeing as what 'e's the father.

A shadow flitted across my mother's face, she hesitated a moment, she took Frau Kupsch to the door, Frau Kupsch was to go down to her flat and wait there for my mother, she just had to sort something out first. Frau Kupsch left, and my mother went looking for her daughter Vera and found Vera sitting in the armchair with a book. She wasn't reading.

Have you been having it off with that man, you just tell me the truth now, I won't do anything to you if you tell me the truth right now, but if you lie to me heaven knows what I'll do to you. Have you had an affair with him, my God, I'll go mad, my own daughter with an SS man.

At this there were signs of movement in Vera. She had turned white, and her face was like a sheet of paper on which her blue, trembling lips inscribed the two words Not that.

What do you mean, not that, screamed my mother.

Not that. Vera's voice was firm.

I want to believe you, said my mother. I want to believe you.

Then she sent Vera on her school trip, and once Vera had left she went with Elsa Kupsch to see Frau Hainichen. Hainichen was out on a job with his truck, Herr Kupsch was at the shipyard and my father was away on his weekly sales trip. This was a women's thing, my mother said. I watched them as they went up the stairs, Cisco in front with his pistol at the ready, Poncho lumbering along behind. I went back into the sitting room and waited. Above my head I could hear Frau Hainichen's footsteps. I knew which door was now opening for my mother. More footsteps on the floor above. Stilettos. My mother. In the stillness I could see her gaze travelling around the Hainichens' flat, the wallpaper with no signs of mould, the expensive furnishings, not at all to our taste, but money, such a lot of money, where did it come from. Chairs rasping on the floor above the ceiling rose in our big room, I was waiting right underneath it, suddenly the loud voice of a woman above me. Eva Hainichen. Then my mother. Then loud sobs and cascades of tears. Elsa Kupsch. Footsteps coming down the stairs.

Do come in a moment. My mother to Frau Kupsch. He has to pay, maintenance claim, dead cert, blood test.

That's all very well, Frau Kupsch wailed, but it ain't so easy, Frau Schiefer, you want to buy the 'ouse.

Maybe, I heard my mother say, maybe not, maybe my husband and I should steer well clear of a property like this.

Now Vera's away for two weeks, and my mother and my father are standing in the sun room and he's reading a letter out to her. From the Tax Office. They're going to audit his accounts. She laughs, whatever next, Paul, he lights two cigarettes at once, one for her, one for himself. Was she up to date with the bookkeeping, he wonders. Almost, very nearly. What did that actually mean, he wants to know. Roughly up to date, sort of more or less, it was just the current year she hadn't quite got around to. When do they want to come, she asks, and he says In five days.

I'll manage it.

But how will you manage it. The very thought of how much there is for her to manage makes him ill.

Just let me get on with it, she says, you know how I get things done when the pressure's really on.

First of all the sun room is completely rearranged and becomes our office, the office of Paul Schiefer, Sales Representative. My father buys a lockable cash box and a petty cash book. I sort out a year's worth of carbon copies on the floor, receipts, payments, reminders, pink, white, blue, in date order. My mother sits at my father's desk which we've schlepped from my parents' bedroom into the sun room office, a cushion against her back, a cushion under her bum, a cushion beneath her feet. My father and I go down into the cellar to bring up the old roll-front cabinet that must be lurking down there somewhere, we need it to give the office the right ambience, we go down the wooden stairs, he goes first, carefully planting his flat feet down sideways and warning me with every step to be careful. When we get to the Kupsches' flat we go round the dark corner into the narrow passageway leading to the first air-raid shelter door, behind that you turn left to get to our cellar area, but if you go straight on you come to the second air-raid shelter door, beyond which lies the bathroom. Keen to seize the opportunity I ask whether we couldn't just pop through into the bathroom at the back now that we're down here. He bends down in front of the first air-raid shelter door, I stand behind his crouching body, he pulls the lower iron lever up then, reaching above his head, he pulls the upper iron lever down, the door swings open, some other time, Fania, certainly, my darling, we've got more important things to do right now.

I feel like shoving him forward into the dark corridor, I want to get to the bottom of it at long last.

I hope the cabinet isn't too full of stuff, he says. He undoes the cellar door, the cabinet is stuffed full, we have to clear it out, crates and cardboard boxes crammed with bundles of old bank statements, old unsold goods, a batch of spectacles from twelve years ago, you'd just turned two, he said tenderly, the washing basket full of Christmas tree decorations, two galvanised washtubs full of holes, old wooden chairs, old winter shoes.

My grandmother wipes the cabinet clean, it smells dank and dusty, a mixture of mould and crumbling plaster, my father and I label the file-pockets that are going to go into it. Business correspondence, reminders, receipts, payments. Don't make the labels too smart, says my mother over her shoulder, everything must look as if it's been in use for years. We're not practising a deceit, Fania, says my father apologetically, it's just that none of it's in any order at the moment and if they see it in that state they'll simply estimate my tax and that would cost us dear.

You'd do better to go and buy some cigarettes, says my mother without looking up, and don't bother giving any eytzes, your daughter knows what's what.

I look up at him aghast, he must have been hurt by that, he laughs to try to reassure me, so it *did* hurt him. Without standing up she has a good stretch, folding her hands and raising them high above her head.

The office needs a stock of cigarettes for visitors, Paul, and get a receipt, and buy a receipt book, and don't forget chocolate for Fania.

My grandmother makes prawn rolls, salmon rolls, egg rolls, cheese rolls, she brews coffee, she silently places everything on the desk next to her daughter, she takes the full ashtray and replaces it with an empty one, she doesn't speak to her daughter, to me she whispers Your mother smokes too much, and it's only when she's in the kitchen that she unbuttons her mouth and I hear her wailing Oy vey, the tax inspectors, nebbish, I feel so sorry for the poor man, and he's such a good man.

My mother enters columns and columns of figures in a large account book, her back is bent, she has crossed her legs and entwined them round each other, her slender nose hovers above her writing hand, her head bobs back and forth between orders, letters, delivery notes, invoices. My grandmother's nose is fleshier than her daughter's, mine is somewhere in between. She smokes too much, it's true, the smoke comes out of her beautiful nostrils.

What lessons have you got at school tomorrow.

I want to know whether she needs me.

If there's nothing important at school, Fania, then yes, I need you to help with the adding up, I'll do the adding and you can check it through.

This is real life here, why go to school, my mother needs me for something really important. Where am I to sit.

Facing me at the desk, she says, and makes me some room. My grandmother comes in, she's made me some cocoa. Fania can have coffee if she wants some, says my mother. I'm pleased, I'm pleased about the cocoa and pleased about the coffee that I can have if I want some, I'm suddenly so rich despite our lack of money. The Reparations Office is not giving us money, and money's being taken from us by the Tax Office. I dunk my cheese roll in the cocoa and look at my mother's head bent over her account book. I can see a white hair amongst her black locks. Then another one. I only tell her about one of them.

Not again. She looks up briefly. I pulled one out only yesterday. Your mother's getting old.

At gone ten in the evening when it's already dark she sends me to bed. Sleep, you have to go to sleep, I need you in the morning. She stays sitting at the desk, my father steps round behind her chair and massages her shoulders, her head, don't you want to call it a day, soon, Paul, would you make me some coffee. He goes into the kitchen, he makes some coffee, he sighs, he puts his head round my door, I'm already in bed. There's no Vera next to me. I've never before spent any part of my life without my sister Vera. This is already the second night.

I hope Vera's coping alright, he says, he's thinking about her too.

We put little messages for her everywhere, in amongst her spare clothes, in her skirt pockets, in her shoes, hugs and kisses, cigarettes, money. I look across to see Vera, she isn't there, she's taken her little pillow with her.

The next day Vera rings up, everything's awful, she says, she's terribly homesick, they sleep on straw mattresses in a dormitory and the food's vile. Where are you phoning from, my mother shouts down the phone, write it down, Fania. The Heidekrug Inn. Not today, tomorrow, I promise, now go back, be careful, my darling. Do your teachers know you're out, will you get back in again.

The accounts will have to wait a day or let's say half a day, my mother draws me close to her, we'll manage alright, I say, she has a little relax snuggled against my chest, we've already entered up seven months' worth, we've still got three days, no, two days, we'll go and see Vera tomorrow, let's say two and a half days, and I want to come with you. Good, my mother's happy with that.

We drive through the Lüneburger Heide. I'm going to see my first school-trip hostel. My mother looks out of the side window. Dreadful place. My father pats her hand. Punishment battalion. Concentration camp. Their memories churn away even here, I know. Being the daughter of these parents I will never be able to go on a school trip. At least once in my life I want to see inside the sort of places they stay at on such trips.

What's that. My mother stares out through the windscreen. Is that it. It can't be it.

Just hang on until we've actually got there, Alma. My father is on edge. We drive along a sandy road.

Paul, my mother bursts into tears, there's Vera, there she is.

We get out.

Vera pushes her way out through a narrow gap between the hostel's double gates. She looks pale and bloated. After just four days and three nights. Are you taking me home with you. These are her first words.

Are you hungry, asks my mother, are you ill.

Vera says yes, she says yes to anything that might help to get her away from here.

Where's this inn, this Heidekrug place, asks my father.

We can drive there, says Vera, it's quicker.

She gets into the front, next to my father, my mother and I sit in the back. There's something different about Vera. I don't know what it is. I think she's lost our smell, she doesn't smell the same as us any more.

My father drops us in front of the inn. He wants to visit a customer in the area, he'll pick us up in two hours, he says, my mother's quite happy with this, it's what he prefers, he's running away from Vera's misery, he would have taken her home there and then.

My mother goes inside with us. The air within is dank and cold. There's a man behind the bar in the yellowish-brown gloom, behind him again beer glasses dangling from hooks. He stares at us and says nothing. My mother grits her teeth and says Good day to you.

Vera giggles, we're not in a posh hotel, Mammy, and she

leads us between oilcloth-covered tables into the garden. A dog starts barking and tugging at its chain. Quiet, Harass, shouts the man who has followed us out.

We sit down at a wooden table. The sun pokes out from behind a cloud. Chickens cluck.

Apart from Quiet, Harass the man still hasn't spoken.

My mother blinks into the sunlight and her puckered lipstick-red mouth says to the male face looming above her We'd like a drink and some food please.

The man nods.

What have you got today.

Spicy schnitzel with fried potaters.

Three of that please, says my mother, and could you bring us some citron pressé as well, how do you make it, freshly squeezed lemons topped off with a little water, or how do you make it, don't you make it like that.

No, he says, transfixed by the froth of words emanating from my mother's mouth.

What's citron pressé in these parts then, she asks, not freshly squeezed lemons topped off with water, how *do* you make it, no sugar for me by the way, quenches your thirst better if there's no sugar in it.

Lemonade, he says. In bottles. That or nothin'.

Right, my mother smiles and shakes her hair and flutters her eyelids, three of your lemonades then.

He goes off.

Now tell me, Vera, is it really as bad as all that. Vera hangs on her mother's every word, she soaks it all up. The loo's the worst part apparently, she can't go to the loo, she waits until the middle of the night when all the other girls are asleep.

That won't do, my mother is worried, you'll get constipated and you'll be ill, everyone goes to the loo, it's no big deal.

I've had diarrhoea, Vera's crying, she sobs and gasps and wipes both hands across her face, my mother hasn't got a hanky on her, she never has a hanky on her, we give Vera the paper napkins that the man has just brought us.

Excuse me, landlord, my mother calls after him, could you bring us some more napkins please.

He stares at her. I just did, he grunts.

Yes I know, she tells him, but I'm sure you can spare us another three. He goes inside, then comes back carrying three spicy schnitzels with fried potatoes, three bottles of lemonade, three glasses, and no paper napkins. Either he's mean, says my mother, or else it's beyond him and he thinks we're going to eat his napkins. Vera laughs through her tears, that's better, says my mother and squeezes her hand.

Vera gobbles up her schnitzel in huge chunks. We watch her. We can't eat anything ourselves. It's worst at night in the dormitory, she says, and when you wash, nothing but cold water, and always ten girls side by side at one long washbasin. She sobs and she eats, she eats our two schnitzels as well, wordlessly we'd pushed our plates across to her, she stuffs it all in to keep her going later on, unasked for the landlord brings three little bowls of dessert, all included in the price, Vera piles them in on top of the schnitzels, green blancmange with vanilla sauce, anything she can lay her hands on, anything that will prolong her stay in this place before she has to return to the hostel.

My father arrives back, he has four trays of plum streusel in his car, they're for the other girls at the hostel so that they'll like Vera.

You're not taking me back with you are you, says Vera staring at the plum streusel. My parents don't reply. They don't look at Vera. They don't look at each other. Vera doesn't ask

366

again. The four of us go through the gate. There's the hostel. A woman comes towards us with a blue apron flapping out in front of her, she has plaited her ash-blonde hair into a chaplet. She tells us she's the house mother, she doesn't tell us her name.

My mother runs her hand through her black hair, she forces a smile, she holds out her right hand with its red-varnished fingernails, the house mother wipes her hands on her apron, reaches for the trays of streusel and takes them off my father, all four at once.

No need fer all this, that baker's much too expensive, she says in her broad country dialect. My father rubs his arms which are hurting from the weight. It doesn't bother her. Off we go then. Her voice is truculent. She speaks like that all the time, Vera tells me in a whisper. The women, the teachers, they're waitin' in the dining 'all, they've rehearsed summat fer yer visit. She walks ahead of us along a creaky corridor and through a door into a large ground-floor room with six windows looking out onto the courtyard. Rustic tables have been pushed together to form one long table at which forty-eight girls are seated. The two teachers get up, Fräulein Brunhilde Kahl comes striding over to us with outstretched arms, she greets my father as though he were a mere adjunct, albeit a useful one, then turns to my mother with fulsome smiles, for my mother is on the PTA.

You've already met our house mummy, says Fräulein Kahl.

My father nods. But you haven't yet told us your name, says my mother turning to the house mummy. The woman is visibly embarrassed. This is our wonderful Irmgart Knerk, says Fräulein Kahl jubilantly, but we're all allowed to call her House Mummy, then lowering her voice she hastily tells the woman not to cut such big slices of streusel, that's much too big, even

367

smaller than that, give that top row to the adults not the children, and with that she turns round and calls out Right, dear girls, we're ready, isn't that lovely, we're ready.

My parents are invited to take a seat. I sit next to Vera. The four of us sit alone at the long line of wooden tables. The girls have all stood up and with a quiet tip-tap of shuffling feet assembled themselves into a phalanx of neat rows, in front of them stands Fräulein Regula Hahn, her hair gathered at the back into a coiled plait. She raises her hands. A delicately hummed note reverberates through the room, and at a given signal forty-eight mouths take in a great gulp of air – air that smells of streusel, chicken droppings and floor cleaner. They have divided themselves into two groups of sixteen. A canon. Sixteen girls' voices sing C-O-F-F-E-E.

Ah how lovely, laughs my father, I couldn't half do with some of that.

Ne'er drink so much coffee, the words come floating over his head from sixteen girls, then another sixteen girls' voices sing exactly the same, then another sixteen. Not meant for babes this Turkish brew. Wrecks your nerves and makes you spew, No Muslim you that can't stay off it, sings the first group, hotly pursued by the second with their brew and spew, chased in turn by the third, so much coffee.

And after the bunfight, says Fräulein Kahl, we'll all go for a nice walk over our lovely Lüneburger Heide, though I must say, she adds with a glance at my mother's red high heels, alas alack, Frau Schiefer, you won't be able to come with us in those. Such a pity, *such* a pity. My mother can't go on walks, it's not because of her shoes, it's because she gets nervous within minutes when she goes for a walk, she needs to have a destination, and in any group of people she always needs to overtake everyone, in the street, on an escalator, she has to

368

hurry ahead on her bouncy little high-heeled feet to ensure sufficient distance between her and those behind her. And yet my mother is determined to join in this walk. Vera's school friend Dörte Lückenhausen, the girl with the big heavy breasts, has two pairs of tennis shoes with her and wonders whether Frau Schiefer would like to borrow a pair. My mother slips into them, and everyone admires her tiny feet, both of which would fit into one of Dörte's shoes.

On the journey home in the car without Vera we can't get Vera out of our minds. She stood behind the gate and waved and waved. My mother hasn't stopped crying ever since. She lights one cigarette after another. My father drives and smokes and sniffs noisily. He tries cracking a joke, it works, my mother laughs, tears come flying off her face, her cigarette falls from her mouth. She is unbridled in tears, unbridled in laughter.

We don't get much sleep when night comes. My mother needs sleep. Only one more day until the tax audit. Our doors are ill-fitting. Scraps of memory squeeze through the cracks. My father is afraid that we won't pull it off, that he'll be arrested, that the dodgy dealings of Ketteler his supplier will redound on him. He sits by my bed in the middle of the night. Nothing can happen to us, Fania, he says, what matters is that we love each other. He gives me a kiss and stands up and his kind face looks down at me.

A lot can happen to us. Once they come a good deal can happen to us. My mother and I have been adding up columns of figures until just a little while ago, my father sat in his armchair drinking cognac and sighing that he couldn't help us. He's just no good at figures, so we get on better without him. We'd have to redo all his calculations, twice as much work, said my mother, be better if you massaged my shoulders, Paul. He did so, then his feet started hurting and he had to sit down, he was being made giddy by all the figures and the rapidity with which we were adding them up, my mother and I were whispering the figures to ourselves, three, eight, seventeen, count more quietly, I said to my mother and she giggled. A pair of children at school. It was late, we were almost done, my mother just had to fiddle the petty cash a bit.

I lie in bed and nod to my father to tell him not to worry. He looks at me pensively and goes into the kitchen, his shoulders drooping, I can hear him, he blows his nose, he lights the gas, he wants to warm himself some milk and make a nightcap cup of tea for his wife, he's turned the radio on and left the kitchen door open, there's the sudden sound of an orchestra, a piano joins in, it's dark in my room, he tiptoes into the illuminated doorway and leans the back of his head against the woodwork, he is completely lost to the music. I want to know how the music sounds to him, I want to understand what he loves about it, I want the very sounds of it to lead me to him.

Beautiful, isn't it, he whispers from the light of the kitchen to me in my darkness, he has lifted his hand, the orchestra recedes, the piano ventures out on its own, dances, frolics on a meadow, is rejoined by the orchestra, runs away, returns, gets chased, and suddenly there he is, the music floods all over me and carries me away, I didn't hear him coming, he's sitting by the side of my bed and he bends right over me and lays his head on my chest and cries. I can't stroke his hair, my hands are buried underneath him.

At night I run through unfamiliar flats, I'm looking for something, I can't find my way around, I begin to settle, I feel uncomfortable, too much unfamiliar furniture, the walls are damp and crumbling. I can't possibly stay, I stay nonetheless, I have to stay. My mother speaks a woman's name, it drops from her mouth, a poisoned fruit, my father laughs up at the ceiling, he's ashamed, he's naked, he's sitting naked on the sofa in our sitting room, I can see him, someone's stolen his things. My mother's cross, her words run by me through a burning aura of hidden guilt. Something's concealed in her voice, they've buried it where I can't see it and are growing over it together. Has he betrayed her, or have I betrayed him. Something's weighing heavily upon me. That red bow-tie, I took it from him, I took it behind his back and returned it behind his back. I robbed him and he doesn't know, how on earth can he prove himself when he's faced by these men.

As I wake up I can hear my parents' voices from the other side of the hall, and the bed next to me is completely empty. Vera, when are we going to fetch Vera. I leap out of bed, my bare feet know the terrain: floorboards, threshold, lino, threshold, carpet. My mother's already back at her desk, my father's wandering back and forth, back and forth.

Fania, you're going to school again today. My mother pushes a green twenty-mark note across the desktop, here, have this for all the work you've done, I've already entered it under Fee-based Out-of-house Office Services, you've even given me a receipt.

You've faked my signature, let me have a look. It's her handwriting, but not my name. I put the money in my skirt pocket. Just in case you need me, all we have first lesson is Religion.

For God's sake, she says, go in time for second lesson.

The doorbell rings.

I'm on my way, says my father, and my mother gets up from the desk and surveys the sun room as though it were a stage on which she will soon make her entrance.

All of a sudden Tax Consultant Friedreich Hasenpusch, a small, assiduous man with shiny jacket sleeves, is standing in our living room with two inspectors from the Tax Office.

371

On account of the tax audit, as you know, Frau Schiefer.

My mother smiles her good-hostess smile. The men shake hands. My father retreats to the kitchen. I'll make some coffee, my wife is much more au fait with everything than I am. The men laugh briefly, they're not in the least bit interested, they just want to stick their noses into our files.

This way. My mother leads the men into the sun room. This is our office.

My word, yes, you've picked the very best part of the flat, says one of the tax inspectors. He's the older of the two, and he's showing his younger colleague how it is possible to be maliciously insinuating whilst remaining simultaneously polite. The front garden is bathed in sunshine, the leaves on the maple are beginning to change colour.

Not *too* big though, parries Tax Consultant Hasenpusch, in fact quite modest for an office, less than thirty square metres I'd say, and with long strides he paces out the long side with the windows and the short side by the door.

My mother's standing by the entrance to the sun room, she runs her hand over her forehead and through her hair, then putting both hands behind her head lifts her mass of black locks a little and gives them a shake. She will sit all day with these three men, two are older than her, the younger of the two tax inspectors will have been a schoolboy back then. She quickly leads the way to the desk. Yesterday evening she dipped cotton-wool balls in acetone and removed the dark-red varnish from her fingernails. That sort of thing was too much for German tax inspectors, she said.

During the afternoon there's a phone call from Fräulein Kahl who asks to speak to my mother. My mother's not available at present, I say, taking great pleasure in rebuffing a teacher. She tells me my sister's not faring very well. I call my father to the phone. We'll come and fetch her, he says, and puts the receiver down. Vera is ill with homesickness.

Where's Mammy. This is Vera's opening sentence. She's standing in front of the door with her little suitcase.

Was it really as bad as all that, my father asks.

I don't know any more, says Vera, it's over now.

Vera doesn't ask what I've been up to. As if I'd ceased to exist while she was away. She tells me about her final night in Kakenstorf. She slept in the same room as Fräulein Kahl. I almost suffocated in that dormitory with all the other girls, Fania. And do you know how Fräulein Kahl takes her nylons off, she stretches out her fingers and rolls them down her leg, first the right one then the left, each stocking looks like a round sausage on Fräulein Kahl's big toe by the end; she lays both sausages next to her shoes, the left sausage by the left shoe and the right sausage by the right shoe, then in the morning she steps back into the sausages and rolls each stocking back up again with her outstretched fingers. And do you know why she does that, Fräulein Kahl does it because of the seam, she wants to make sure the seam is dead straight on her leg. There's nothing worse than a crooked seam, she told me, it looks slovenly. And do you know what, the seam was crooked all the same.

My sister stays at home for the following few days, my father also stays at home for the following few days, my mother tells Vera everything, and Vera devours everything.

I want to get out of here. I'm going to Sirena's, I say, and sit there waiting to see what happens. Nothing happens. I'm to be back by supper-time.

Can I have a key, I'd like to take a key with me. My grandmother offers to give me her key, she's got it in her handbag, and she always has her handbag with her, it's got her identity card in it and her purse and a hanky and a little bottle of 4711 and her house key. Whenever she goes from her own room into our living room she always has everything with her in her handbag.

It's high time we gave Fania a key of her own, says my father, and why hasn't she got one already, says my mother letting her gaze wander over me, she is pleased with me, she's proud of her big daughter, except that I'm *not* her big daughter, my sister is her big daughter, and she's sitting slumped on her chair. My grandmother opens her bag and pulls out her key ring. I take it, and she's very happy to give it to me. She doesn't need a key, she says, she could use Alma's if she needed a house key.

My key, my mother is aghast, I need it myself.

But I'm always at home, says my grandmother, I'm always here. I scarcely ever go out these days, I really don't need a key any more.

Have *you* got a key of your own, asks my mother looking at Vera. No, Vera shakes her head, what's the point of me having my own key, I'd only lose it, you always open the door for me. My father has his own key, he has to have one, he comes and goes a lot, his key hangs on a slender silver chain, his car ignition key is on it as well together with a small key for the boot and a little leather pouch containing Vera's first tooth, and because my first tooth got lost, Vera's first tooth is swathed in a reddish-blonde lock of my hair from when I was a baby: my father is devoutly superstitious.

I get up from the table and take my grandmother's key. Before shutting the living-room door behind me I look at my big sister. My father's just giving her a cigarette. Had I started smoking yet, Vera wants to know, giving me a searching glance. No, I say, and my mother is indignant, why on earth should Fania have started smoking. Vera puts her cigarette between her lips and draws on it. I turn away. I shut the door. I leave my family behind.

I was always the one who could have gone first.

Where do I go now though. I can't go to Sirena's, I can't stand about in the driveway, it's not the day for extra tuition, where else can I go, I'm afraid of going off anywhere, afraid of getting in a train on my own, going into town on my own, I've never ever done it, people will be able to tell that I don't belong there, and I won't be able to find my way back, they'll have to come and collect me, I don't know anyone, I've never been to anyone's house on my own except for Esther Fingerhut's and Sirena Bechler's, and one of these two lives where the other used to but doesn't any more. I follow the route I know, to the house at the end of the driveway, this is fine, I'm quite happy with this route, fear and pleasure follow close behind and quickly overtake me. I hope she's there. I want to see her. I ring the bell. She opens the door for me. She's there. Sirena isn't there.

Come in, says Thea Bechler, I'm on my own and I'm bored.

Her husband could have been here, I don't even want to think about her husband, she holds my hand, I hold her hand, we have to let go of each other so that I can pass through the door, our hands stroke one another as they separate, and she lets me walk ahead of her into the room with the piano. Her steps follow me, what do I actually look like from behind, when do you have to leave, she asks, I have to laugh, she's on the ball, I show her my house key.

Congratulations, she says.

I can stay until eight this evening.

What shall we start with, music or reading aloud. Her hand is already resting on the piano.

Reading, I say. Not music. She's not to play the piano now.

I don't want to sit there and watch what she does to the piano and what the piano does to her and I just sit there and watch and drown in the music of my longing.

Then follow me.

We walk along a corridor, there are pictures on both sides, I can make out colours but nothing else, perhaps I ought to stop at every picture and ask her to explain it to me, perhaps I'd make a good impression if I did, better not ask whether they're valuable, that *wouldn't* make a good impression, she might think I think about money, I'm not thinking about money, I'm thinking about her husband, I need to know where her husband is, I need to know whether he's on the way here. She opens a door, this is my bedroom, she says, the book she wants to read to me from is in here. Sit down, Fania, do sit down.

I'm to sit down, where am I to sit down, there are cushions on the floor, I'm wearing a blue woollen skirt, I choose a round cushion in dark-red velvet, the blue wool of my skirt goes well with the red velvet, what's more the cushion looks quite firm, and much less soft than the other ones, I don't want to sink right down, I should have worn trousers, and the velvet cushion is softer than I'd thought, the blue woollen skirt suits me, my mother says, together with the blue jumper it looks as if I'm wearing a woollen dress, very pretty, Fania, really feminine, I pull a face and my mother quickly corrects herself, no, not that, not feminine, more sporty, really sporty, I pull another face, I don't want to look really sporty, I don't want to look anything like what my mother considers best for me, I shouldn't have worn it, what am I supposed to do with my legs, if I stick them out straight in front of me I'll look gawky, if I have my knees up Thea Bechler will be able to look up my skirt, perhaps I should dash back home and change, I could say I've forgotten something, but what; I have to ring someone, I could do that from here; I don't have the phone number with me, she's got a phone book.

I haven't read it for a very long time, I expect you won't know it.

She's standing on a little ladder in front of a ceiling-height bookcase holding a much-thumbed book in her hand.

I'm sure I will, I say, at least I might.

You already know it, she asks, incredulous, from the top of her ladder.

I don't want to be taken for a little girl, I might easily know the book, after all my sister has read me loads of things, novels and plays, even this one perhaps that she's holding in her hand and leafing through as my eyes glide up her legs.

What's it called, I ask.

I'm not telling you. She presses the book to her chest so that I can't read the title, I can't read anything at all, I'm looking at her and the book, she's pressing it to her chest, what is she actually wearing, not that red nightdress that's really a housecoat, she's wearing dark-green trousers and a dark-green rollneck jumper, she's completely enveloped from top to toe and she's wearing trousers and I'm not.

Are you sitting comfortably, Fania, if not then you could sit over there, she says pointing to a piece of furniture the like of which I've never seen before, a cross between a bed and a sofa, a couch that's had one armrest and half its backrest taken away, like a stretched-out armchair.

That's my chaise longue.

She pursues me with her eyes, she looks at me to see where I'm looking. Are you thirsty, very possibly, am I thirsty; do make yourself comfortable, how can I; I'll be straight back, she goes out shutting the door behind her, shutting the door on me. I stay sitting on the cushion listening to her footsteps, I want them to have carried her far away before I dare to extricate myself from this cushion. Where am I going to sit, I want to have found myself a seat before she gets back, I want it to look as if I've always been sitting wherever it is I eventually sit, the question is where, I don't want to be standing about. Perhaps after all I *should* sit on the sofa that's almost a bed, that's where she'll sit, I can hear her footsteps coming back, I dart over to the bookshelves, I stand with my back to the door and with my head on one side start deciphering the titles of the books and the names of their authors, all of them men, surnames without first names are always men. I pretend not to have heard her come in.

Could you help me a second.

She needs my help. She's holding a silver tray in her hands, and her hands are poking out of two dark-green silk sleeves, and that's actually a dark-green silk coatdress she's wearing, was I wrong, didn't she have trousers on at all, isn't she always dressed as if she spends all her time either in bed or at the piano. She is a woman abandoned. But I'm there now.

I felt so cold before, she says, but not any more, now that you're here. Help yourself. Smoked trout with horseradish sauce and toast and a few little cakes and that's Parmesan, Wilhelm held a small reception here yesterday.

I take the tray.

Wilhelm's my husband, Sirena's father, you know that already, anyway this is left over from yesterday and I haven't eaten anything yet today.

There, he's so close, her husband and his small reception and loads of guests, beautiful women with their husbands, all of them in high positions, according to Sirena he's not her father, not her real father. Sirena's mother sits down, she pats the seat cushion, I'm to sit next to her. I'm still holding the tray, I sit

378

down next to her with the tray in my hands, she takes a small cake decorated with hundreds and thousands and takes a bite, and what shall I do with the tray.

Give it to me. She puts the whole lot on a small round table. If you don't want to drink any wine, Fania, she says taking a sip of wine, I've got some tonic water here.

I take the tonic water, I don't take anything to eat, I can't sit next to her and open my mouth and bite into something and chew and swallow and digest.

She's hungry. I'm really enjoying this, she says, since you're here perhaps you'd like to have something to eat with me later, we've plenty of time, Wilhelm is in Bonn for three days.

Is her husband away that long, I can't stay that long, it would be nice though I think to myself and look at her.

She's carried on talking. About Sirena.

She's staying with a girlfriend tonight; actually, Fania, I know she's with her boyfriend, I don't ask, she doesn't like being asked, and I think she's old enough.

Sirena's the same age as me, in that case I'm old enough too. Sirena's with Rüdiger, Thea's husband is with the old Nazis in Bonn. They're back again with their fingers in every pie, says my mother, they've been there all the time, my father retorts. I want to touch this woman. She's chewing and talking, her lips are moist and unfamiliar. Her teeth tear at the fillet of trout. Doing it in front of me doesn't bother her. I try her wine. The women in Vera's stories say the men do wild things to them. What sort of things, I asked Vera, and she said they lift the women up, they throw themselves on top of them, they drag the women away with them, that's what it says anyway. And the women are off and away. Vera showed me some sample passages. In her books.

Start reading. In my longing I chase after her until I'm right underneath her green silk. Her breasts are moving beneath it. Start reading. I don't say her name, I can't say her name, I'd like to say her name. I daren't even try the sound of her in my mouth, and she's blithely pulling the trout through her teeth. I don't even say 'you'. I don't have any idea of myself. How will I be, why do I exist. And she dabs her mouth with her napkin and shoots a glance right into my stomach. What a wonderful fright.

She picks up the book and leans right back on the sofa that's actually a bed and opens it in the middle and leafs through the pages. She looks at me.

Are you comfortable.

I read the title of the book. *Elective Affinities*. I don't know it. I'd like to know what I look like sitting there. Terrible I should think. Like a visitor. No, I'm not comfortable. I want to be with her. With her. Her breasts. Right there, with her.

Lie down with me.

She makes room for me, pushing herself up against the back rest.

If I lie down I'll have to take my glasses off.

Take them off.

If I take them off I won't be able to see as well.

Then you'll just have to come closer.

I lie down on my side facing her, close enough to stop me falling backwards off the sofa, far enough for there to be the slenderest zone of thrilling unfamiliarity between us. I lay my head next to her shoulder beneath her outstretched arm, her unfamiliar arm, white and soft in its green silk, I'm so close to her that her red hair tickles my forehead, I've never lain like this with a woman outside my family. She takes a breath, her chest lifts, she runs the tip of her tongue over her lips and I study her earlobes.

The first name she reads is the name of a man, he's to leave, he stays, he stands outside his wife's bedroom door, I'm lying behind it, my fur's standing on end, and she strokes me. He's listening at the door. My little pet, she says, and continues reading. A woman's crying inside, his wife, she's talking to her chambermaid. The man outside the locked door hears his wife ask for a young girl, he hears her name, she's called Ottilie, he's instantly electrified, he wants to go to her and not to his wife but he can't because he mustn't, he eavesdrops on his wife, she dismisses her maid, I wish to go to bed by myself, I hear Thea's voice above me, by herself, on her own. He knocks. She doesn't hear, lost in thought she paces to and fro, she takes so many steps back and forth between the wall and her bed, the sum of her steps would be enough to bring her the man she longs for. Not her husband. He knocks again and she hears. She hopes it might be the other, the stranger-friend, and not her own husband. Is there someone there? She opens the door. As he slips his way into the bedroom of his wife, Thea's right breast slips its way out of its green silken sheath. It's me. And I examine it. So unfamiliar still, yet seeming so familiar, it's completely at home on its sofa-cum-bed and droops down towards me exhaling its skin smell in the vicinity of my nose. I take it between my lips. Its owner hums quietly and carries on reading, she reads about the woman who retreats into her armchair to escape the gaze she herself has ignited, she is naked beneath her diaphanous nightgown and the gaze follows her, takes hold of her foot, kisses her shoe, her foot in her shoe, her foot without a shoe. You. That's for me. She's sending that to me. Her 'you'. Her lips on my hair, her hand, gently pressing. She wants it harder. I want her to want again, I want her to want me. Her hand presses me to her. I'm there. She holds the book a little higher, making it less comfortable for herself so that it's more comfortable for me to latch right on to her. And she reads on. This wife and this husband are deceiving each other and pandering to their lust with utter abandon, I hear her say. And all the more freely for the fact that, alas, their hearts were wholly unengaged. She takes him for the other man, he thinks solely of the girl, that's what I am to her, I am the girl, the girl is with her. He conjured up the girl for himself, and there she is with her. I am her girl. A girl with her own desire. She reads and I take what I will, I suck at her breast, she's still reading, her bud is pink, like the little French cake she left for me. She moans, and reads on. We don't kiss. She knows nothing about me. I know about her. She's not a Jewess, I'm the Jewess, she doesn't know that. I want to seduce her, I'm the seductive Jewess, I want to kiss her. And she wants to kiss me. I'm afraid. I avoid her grey-green eyes. She sees me. Where is my body. She changes position to suit both me and herself and lies there as if asleep, all on her own and not with me. I am her little nocturnal creature sniffing my way through her nooks and crannies. She smells good, smoked trout, I tell her. She has lowered the book and closed her eyes and followed me. She guides my hand, I enter. My ear on her stomach steams and glows, everything drops off me, woollen skirt, woollen jumper. My hair is wet, I'm overflowing, I'm melting away. She grabs me by the hair at the back of my head. The pain of it. I thrust myself against her, everything grows and swells. Consumed with fear and ecstasy, she throws herself on top of me, pushing her breasts right into me, I'm lying on my back, my legs are spread, I feel no shame, I want what she's giving me. She's doing what I'm greedy for, she is feeding my hunger. I wanted to play with Esther in this house in order to be near her mother, I wanted to unlock the secrets of all that lay unspoken within her, all that lay buried beneath my own

382

mother's flood of words. I sat on her lap and pressed myself against her heavy breasts, it was through me that she breathed in the notes that Esther played for us, for me, in order to feed her mother. Give. Give me what I want from you. You're from some other place. She gives me what I want. She gives me herself. I overflow and she is there, her face, the eyes of the woman, how are you feeling, oh fine, just fine, she wants to kiss me, can I still kiss and be kissed, she kisses me, and I am breathing still.

My kissing mouth wasn't mine, I think.

Don't think, she says. Her tears run down my neck.

My blue woollen jumper and my blue woollen skirt float home through the twilight. The young girl inside them is me, Fania Schiefer, bursting with inner jubilation. I have found a woman.

In bed in the evening Vera tells me about the drama school she wants to audition for. Our parents have gone out. We don't have any money, but there's something to celebrate. The audit has finished, we don't know yet how much back tax we'll have to pay, but Herr Hasenpusch thought it wouldn't be all that much, so my mother and my father are celebrating the outcome with Chérie Grell and the other gay artistes at the Bar Celona. It's dark in the room. Vera's lying next to me. She's learnt and rehearsed Gretchen's monologue and prayer, and would I like to hear it. Yes. She sits up. I stretch myself right out and rest my head on my folded hands. I have Thea with me. Vera whispers, sobs and shouts, a shiver runs down my spine, the light goes on, my grandmother's standing in the doorway of the kitchen, she's wearing her nightie and wants to know what's happened.

Nothing at all.

She'd been scared to death, and at night too.

I must have been good then, says Vera, and does the whole thing again. My grandmother and I sit on the edge of the bed and are completely carried away. Vera has to go on the stage, and we'll sit in the front row and be proud of her.

In the darkness of our room Vera makes me promise to back her up, she's going to ask our parents tomorrow whether she can join the drama school. The beam from the car's headlights glides across the ceiling and along the wall. The tyres scrunch their way through the back garden. Our guards are back, nothing has happened to them, they've returned safe and sound, we're relieved. We're already more or less like them.

During the night I wake up with my head completely clear. I've read something that I myself wrote. In my sleep. I remember every word. I was able to write without fear. Vera's asleep. With the help of my torch I find a pencil, I can't find any paper, on the inside of a book cover I note down what my sleeping hand had written: There are moments when I experience my own self, this person that is most familiar to me, as wholly alien. There are moments devoid of animation or else devoid of any thoughts of my own. I inhabit my self, then suddenly I am elsewhere, in a place where I no longer recognise myself, everything around me is mad, and the only person aware of it is the me who is no longer there.

Chapter Eleven

They could've made it a bit easier to get to, grumbles my mother, you can scarcely fight your way through any more. Stooping down with her legs apart she's scraping wet leaves from the grave with a small rake, she's skewered numerous reddish-brown leaves with her high heels, she's restoring order with hands and feet alike. We're standing there watching. We're surrounded by thick undergrowth and ancient tall trees, the Jewish calendar has been showing the year 5729 for the last few days, it is the eve of Yom Kippur, the day of reconciliation.

Leave off, Alma, please, says my grandmother. Her parents are buried here. Leave off, Hedwig, please, says my father, he's concerned about his wife. My grandmother is upset at the fuss her daughter is making, just move some of the dead twigs and clear some of the leaves, no need to overdo it. She has folded her hands across her stomach and she's moving her closed lips in and out – clear signs of dissatisfaction. My father sidles away, though not too far, and finds himself a safe vantage point. I can hear him noisily sucking in air. Such a wonderful earthy smell, he says, the air is so clear here, all these lovely old trees, he wants to pay the Jewish cemetery a compliment or two. The scratching noise continues unabated. Was your father the youngest in the family, he asks. My grandmother nods, she can't speak, she can't take her eyes off her parents' grave on which her daughter is scrabbling madly away, Marianne and Max Wasserstrahl of blessed memory lie there side by side awaiting their resurrection and their day of reckoning. Marianne went first and then he followed. Both in good time, before it all started in Germany. My mother's scrubbing doggedly at the stonework, she's determined to get the moss off it. But there's no cleaning and scouring in the house of eternal rest.

I know I'm getting on your nerves, she says between her legs with her bent-over upside-down mouth, her mouth is above her eyes, it snaps open and shut, open and shut, there are leaves entangled in her hair. It's all neat and tidy over there in the Christian bit, says her upside-down, letterbox mouth. We've just come from over there.

They've got direction signs and huge rubbish bins and maintenance staff in uniform caps over there, there's a constant bustle of people and cars and wreaths and flowers over there. All this comes spouting forth from her. And the crematorium. She always shows it to us whenever we're over there. The slender, dark-red chimney sticks up into the sky like a church steeple. Hope the oven inside it isn't the same one, she says. My father's parents and grandparents are buried over there, my father will be buried there one day in the family grave, and my Jewish mother will want to be put next to him, she won't want to be separated from him even in death. He can't be buried here, with her grandparents, he's not a Jew. They'll let her be buried over there, they're more obliging in this respect, but they want money for it, otherwise they smash up the gravestone and put strangers on top of your bones. This little patch of ground here in the house of eternal rest will remain ours for ever and to all eternity.

Enough, Alma, says my father patting his wife's bottom, we need to go home. She stands up and purses her lips, she wants a kiss, he gives her one and gets her lipstick on his lips, she rests her head on his shoulder and inspects her handiwork. Her grandparents' grave is free of leaves. Have we found any stones yet, she wants to know. Our goy has a pebble for himself and one for his wife, we have to go and look for ourselves. My grandmother, the little old bandy-legged daughter, lays two pebbles on the gravestone, one for Mamme, one for Tatte.

I'm hungry, says my mother. Bending forward we all make our way one behind the other along the narrow path beneath overhanging bushes to the main avenue. Huge old gravestones lean at impossible angles, pensively prop each other up and arrest each other's fall. Vera and I hang back. My parents have stepped out of the tangled undergrowth, my grandmother, a few steps away from us, is busy with her lace handkerchief, her perfume mingles with the smell of rotting leaves. I go and stand with my back to my great-grandparents' grave and my legs apart and thrust my hands into the pile of leaves, Vera coughs, damp leaves flutter all over the grave of Marianne and Max Wasserstrahl, dark splotches rain down on our ancestors, some came dragging in from the East, bandy-legged and with deep-sunken eyes, others rolled in from south-western Europe, from Portugal, in magnificent coaches, dignified and pious, swathed in flowing silk and heavy perfumes. Gold ducats, spices, music, jewels, on the way they lost them all, stone by stone. Every stone is a thought, says my grandmother.

On the main avenue a young woman comes towards us with an old man on her arm. We say hello. They say hello. There are so few of us and we don't know one another, so we say hello. Quite close to the entrance an urn stands on top of a plinth with a large pale sandstone tablet inscribed with

Hebrew letters. It is the only urn in this cemetery, dead Jews are not cremated, and in the urn are ashes from Auschwitz, on the great day of reckoning all will be counted, debit and credit and every last little bone. My mother wants to hurry on past, my father makes her stop a moment, he still has a pebble on him and puts it there on the edge of the lidded pot containing the ashes. I watch him. I belong to him, and he doesn't belong to us. Sometimes I'm furious at the dead Jews for being dead and gone.

And here are the Adolfs and the Siegfrieds, says my mother. Beyond the Auschwitz urn, on the way to the exit, she draws our attention to all the dead Jewish Adolfs and Siegfrieds who fought for Kaiser and country in the First World War. She holds this against them, every single one of them. As we pass the Jewish soldiers' memorial column I notice two Adolfs, three Siegfrieds, one Wilhelm, and several names such as Jakob, Josef, Moritz.

They just wanted to be good Germans, says Vera.

Meshuggene, says my mother taking her mother's arm. My father takes his hanky off his head. We slip out through the little iron gate, on the other side of the road there are detached houses with little gardens. And this is where the beggars used to stand, says my mother lowering her voice because of the houses opposite and gesturing expansively at the whole length of the cemetery fence, Grandpa used to give something to each one of them, dear dear, oy vey, I'll soon be one of them, he used to say, d'you remember, Mummy. Of course Hedwig Glitzer remembers, he was her father, tut tut, that's all she says, she's handed the story over to her fatherless daughter. Vera and I know about the beggars as well, we've heard about them so often at the same spot that we might as well have been there ourselves.

And all of a sudden it's Christmas, and my mother enters into competition with German Christianity, and German Christian mothers in particular. Christmas is the biggest load of nonsense, it's true, but who minds nonsense when it's as lovely as Christmas can be. You have to give it to the Christians, this festival is a good idea, it could easily be a Jewish idea, but it isn't, nonetheless we celebrate it, and Alma Schiefer puts on the loveliest Christmases of all, each one lovelier than the last, but it costs money.

My father lays banknotes at her feet.

He won't have a single pfennig left, my grandmother warns her daughter, but he's giving his money to me, she says, and he laughs and raises his eyebrows and his hands. He can be wonderfully Jewish sometimes.

What's most important of all is the food, roast goose of course, two geese of course, the second to make pickled goose, it could be three really, anyway at least two, as for the bird, well we'll have to see, and stuffed goose neck on challah for Christmas Eve, that's when we'll need the first one, or should we have carp instead, and the tree, it must be really big, Paul, you sort out the tree, our ceiling's a good three metres fifty high, I'm quite sure of that, anyway we could always cut a bit off the end, stop grinning like that, why's Pappy grinning, just because I said cut a bit off the end, was Jesus circumcised by the way, how should I know, ask his mother Mary, they always drape a cloth in front of it.

What on earth can we give Mammy, groans Vera.

I've already got something.

You're mean. I'm not going to tell you what I'm giving Pappy.

In the run-up to Christmas Vera is desperately short of money, she's got to give presents to everyone all on the same day and she's broke yet again, even though she's got a walk-on part at the Thalia Theatre and gets paid for it, pin-money she calls it, but it's money all the same, and what's she done with it, there've been ten performances in December. In the second act she sits on stage at a little table and the head waiter comes in, he's the General Manager's son, the audience all know that, and the General Manager himself is an old Jew, the audience probably know that as well if they haven't decided to forget it. We don't know how he survived, in hiding probably, no one knows, and his son's a half-Jew, that's a Nazi word, how else can you put it, his mother's a Christian, Aunt Ruchla told my grandmother, apparently she's converted, they were talking about it in the Community, but she's still not Jewish in the eyes of the old Jews, what has she ever survived, said Ruchla.

On the stage of the Thalia Theatre the half-Jewish General Manager's son disguised as a head waiter magically produces three little balls from my sister's cleavage. Do you already have them down there when you walk on, I ask, and Vera gives a little squeal, that's exactly how she squeals on stage, he produces the balls from her cleavage, she squeals – and at precisely the right moment, that's the trick, and it usually gets a laugh. Vera's on display in the showcase in the foyer, they did a photo of her scene, my mother tells everyone so that they can all go and admire Vera in the showcase when they go into town to do their Christmas shopping. Vera, and next to her the half-Jewish son of the General Manager. We ought to go and see it, whispered my grandmother to my mother, they're already on about it in the Theresienstadt Circle, Lotti, Betty and Olga have already seen it twice.

Why don't you get four complimentary tickets for one of

your performances, I suggest to Vera. She smothers me with kisses. You're a genius, Fania, I'll make vouchers out for everyone, and an extra-lovely one for you.

Vera's problem is solved, I've got her off my back, good thing too, I need my brain for myself. I want to give Thea a present, Christmas is bound to be important to her, she's a Catholic, but what shall I give her, and once I've thought of something, how am I going to get it, it'll be something you can only buy in town, and I'm not allowed to go into town on my own. I'd like to ask Vera to do me a favour, she's allowed into town, she has to go to rehearsals at the theatre. I can't ask Vera for help. No one must know about it, no one must ever hear anything about it, the very thought of it, it would be a catastrophe, it would be the end of her and the end of me, the more I think about it, the less afraid I feel, oy, that would finish us, oy, if our thing together were ever to get out. Such trains of thought are very familiar to me.

I'd like to give Thea some hair combs, perhaps green or blue ones to go with her red hair, I like it when she puts her hair up, all those tiny hairs on the nape of her neck that won't do as they're told and stand out in little curls that catch the light. I ring Aunt Ruchla, Carola can help me, they're bound to have such combs in Israel, she'll do me a good price. I'm going to visit Aunt Ruchla, what on earth do you want of Aunt Ruchla, that's the good thing about Christmas, it's a pretext for everything.

Be careful though, says my mother, all I need just before Christmas is for something to happen to you, do you even know the way.

I don't remember it any more.

You take the tram, you get in the tram at the stop where you've got your back to the bank, do you know where I mean.

Yes, it's where you've got Herta Tolle's facing you on the other side.

Not quite, her fish shop's a bit further up, now who's right opposite just there, wait a second, you go down Böttgerstrasse, the first shop on the other side is the baker's, or is it the flower shop first, anyway more or less between the cigar man or let's say between the stationer's and just opposite our fish lady, that's where the stop is. For goodness' sake, Fania, you've been there so often with your grandmother, I just don't understand why you can't remember the way, and me I've got such a good sense of direction, why haven't my daughters inherited it, I can't come with you right now, I've got so much to do, I don't know whether I'm coming or going.

We don't *have* to celebrate Christmas you know.

Get away, the geese are already ordered.

By the time I get to Aunt Ruchla's I'm sweating like a pig, she's waiting downstairs by the entrance and hustles me past Frau Tannenbaum who has come hobbling up and is eyeing me suspiciously.

What's up now, Frau Tannenbaum, Aunt Ruchla says crossly, the little Schiefer girl, our Fania, you know her, you do. She takes me into her room, my precious, got the loveliest combs in the world, I have, won't half be pleased, your Mamma will, for Christmas is it, ooh, what am I saying, is it for Christmas.

Take a look at the combs first and buy some, the price for my mother's bound to be less than the price for a goy lover.

When I get home with three sparkling green combs in my school bag I'm still dripping with sweat. I've achieved what I wanted to achieve, I've done everything right, I found the way there and I found the way back.

Why are you so sweaty, it's winter out there, did you have

any money with you, asks my mother, and I'm immediately worried, surely Ruchla won't have rung up and given anything away, otherwise I'd have to give the combs to my mother.

Why do you ask.

The tram ticket, says my mother, I didn't tell you that if you get on the tram at the back you have to pay the conductor.

Quite right. I forgot. They could have arrested me.

On Christmas Eve Vera and I have always stayed in bed until the evening. Not this year. I'm too old now. If we don't stay in bed, Vera grumbled, we'll have to help, it's always been so lovely just staying in bed. That's true. We've never gone to school on Christmas Eve even when there was something on, all that stupid recorder music, said my mother, all that yacking about Jesus and Mary, nothing in it for you. So we stayed in bed. We listened to the radio for hour after hour, from early morning right through until it was time for presents, while she ran from one end of the flat to the other, rustling, crackling, whispering, giggling, her excitement came washing into our bedroom, we listened to a whole succession of radio plays, on VHF, on medium wave, on the Third Programme. Whenever there were carols we tuned in to the next station, we didn't like hearing the voices of all those enraptured children. Smells and sounds and voices reached us from the kitchen. My grandmother stood in the kitchen and stirred and chopped and kneaded and cleared things away for her daughter and passed things to her and did the washing-up. My mother, her black hair loose and powdered with flour, brought us little bits to try, a piece of goose neck roasted in goose fat and stuffed with goose liver, mince and marjoram, a pickled goose wing, a little dish of lemon posset, a piece of lightning cake with flaked almonds, a slice of poppy-seed challah, is it alright like that, is anything missing. Vera and I would sit back against our pillows and try everything out, she would watch our mouths, we'd taste a bit and sigh with delight, she would beam, we would beam, she'd roll her eyes and adopt a mysterious air, and so the day would pass, far too slowly for us, far too quickly for her, outside it would get dark.

The previous evening she'd stood on the stepladder until very late decorating the tree. Vera and I weren't allowed into the room. But afterwards she told us exactly what had gone on behind the closed door and so I know all about it as if I had been there. My father sat in his armchair and made comments from down below, you need another bauble there, that candle's too close to the branch above, Alma, if you leave it there it won't be lit under any circumstances, I won't allow it. He was drinking cognac with his sister. Aunt Mimi was drinking to numb the miseries of her love life, my father was drinking to numb the sense of giddiness he felt at the sight of his wife high above him, standing there in her tiny slippers with pink pompoms on the slender rungs of a ladder only just below the ceiling. My grandmother was sewing dolls' clothes, Aunt Mimi was crocheting dolls' shoes. Our dolls were always reclothed at Christmas time, even my old teddy bear. Needless to say they celebrated Christmas with us, all of them, every year. They sat under the Christmas tree, my mother needed them as part of the decorations, it was unthinkable that the dolls with their sweet-sad smiles should remain in our dark bedroom while His Mysterious Majesty the Christmas tree stood resplendent in the big room. We couldn't do that to them. They sat on the floor amongst the branches on Christmas blankets made of paper, they played with the red baubles and reached out with their tiny dolls' fists for chocolate pine cones wrapped in gold foil and filled with Melba cream, the Christmas room was their domain, they were very probably non-Jewish. My little naked dolls, the ones that had been trampled on, stayed hidden under my bed in their cotton-wool-lined cardboard boxes.

Don't you think you're overdoing it a bit, enquired Aunt Mimi looking up from her crocheting, her voice already somewhat thick from the cognac.

What do you mean, asked my mother from her perch near the top of the tree, if you can't see the stitches properly any more then let Mummy do it instead, the children notice if a doll hasn't got new things and I can't leave any of them out, that's just not on, can you hand me up that box of ring biscuits please and tell me if you think there needs to be more tinsel at the back there.

At Christmas time Aunt Mimi's lover Hubert Arnold Zinselmayer, chartered engineer from the jolly old Rhineland, is stuck with his Christian family. Even my mother thinks this is fair enough, though she cannot understand how a woman can allow her man to have another woman.

But his wife doesn't know anything about it, said Vera, and my mother exclaimed in astonishment His wife! I mean Mimi, how does she put up with it, I could never square it with my sense of dignity. Aunt Mimi can't square it with her sense of dignity either, which is why she drinks cognac and seeks refuge at Christmas with her Jewish sister-in-law.

When my father went to the door on the twenty-fourth of December in his dark-blue suit and winter coat to go and collect his sister, and my mother called after him Make sure you're back by six, Paul, and don't let her tempt you into having a cognac, this meant there was only an hour to go before presents were given out, and Vera and I would get out of bed and wander off into my grandmother's room to get dressed at long last. The tension grew and grew, how much longer would my mother be able to bear it, Vera and I couldn't

395

manage to beam any more, and nor could she. The final minutes of waiting were minutes where one could never know for certain whether they really were the final minutes. Then the feeling would well up that hopefully they weren't, that the moment wouldn't actually come when I have to be happy.

On Christmas Day evening the expected duly happened: she finally collapsed. She'd felt unwell the whole time, she hadn't been able to eat anything, almost no goose and very little carp. She sank onto the sofa with the words No, I don't want to lie down. My father took off her high heels and her skirt, loosened her suspenders and put the new camel-hair blanket on top of her. What can we do for you, he asked. Nothing, nothing at all, she said, and fell asleep, listen to records by all means, we heard her murmur, it won't bother me. Josef Schmidt was singing, my father loves the little Jew with the big tenor voice, he was even smaller than my mother, he'd died before he could get on the ship that was to take him to America. It was better to let him go on singing, if everything went quiet she'd wake up and in her exhausted state she'd feel frightened. A good hour before midnight she did finally wake up, refreshed and hungry for roast goose. One goose had already been eaten, the second was being pickled, so the third now made its entry, and as it had already been roasted my father carved off some pieces and served them to his recumbent wife on a tray with a bottle of champagne. We all sat around her temporary bed and watched her, Vera and me and my grandmother and my father. She gnawed carefully at the bony bits, she smeared jelly left over from the roasting onto pieces of breast and silently, pensively gobbled them up.

It *is* a Jewish festival after all, really, she said chewing away on a large mouthful of food, the mother's Jewish, the son's Jewish, it doesn't really matter who the father was. She picked up a drumstick and ate its crispy skin. And that's something else the Germans have pinched from the Jews: they celebrate the *eve* of the actual festival, because of course Christmas isn't until the following day. She tore meat off the drumstick with her teeth and washed it down with champagne. To round everything off, she produced a thunderous burp, offered her apologies, and sank back into the sofa cushions with a blissful smile.

Already on the twenty-seventh of December – our Boxing Day Plus One, introduced by us to provide extra time for getting through all our specially prepared delicacies – my mother would start prowling round the tree. It's dropping its needles, she would say, and as this was not in fact true she would give it a vigorous shake to help it along. By this stage I'd have eaten all the titbits off the tree, including a second lot of ring biscuits. Leave the tree in peace, Vera would growl. Her protests were always in vain, my mother was fed up with Christmas, Fania can use it to cover the roses in the garden, she would say, they need a few pine branches over their roots.

It was exactly the same this year. At just before eleven yesterday morning, the twenty-eighth of December, our three-metre Christmas tree went tumbling down the steps from the sun room into the front garden, even though the roses need no protection as this year's winter is abnormally mild, with no frost and no snow.

And today everything is different.

My grandmother. Hedwig Glitzer.

We weren't prepared for it, none of us were, not even her. Together with her daughter and her son-in-law she had survived death, after that dying just wasn't on the agenda, and even Vera and I are well versed in defeating death several times each day. Be careful. Look after yourself. What that actually means is Do me a favour and don't die, or I'll have to kill myself. My father left on a selling trip this morning, just to Kiel and Lübeck, to earn a bit of much-needed money, he wanted to be back by late afternoon.

When she came in through the garden gate – she'd been to buy milk – she was already harbouring death. The driveway behind her was bathed in pale winter sun. Her coat was undone. The air was too warm for December and was full of the promise of an early spring. My grandmother was carrying the milk can in her right hand, in which she was also holding her gloves. She'd taken them off, that's how hot she felt. You have to change hands when you're carrying things, she used to tell me. She often carried her handbag in her left hand, but it was now in her right hand, together with the milk can and the gloves. I stood in the doorway of the sun room with the door wide open and watched her come in from the driveway. She opened the garden gate by pushing against it with her right shoulder, her left arm hung limply down. Behind me in the sun room my mother was busy doing something or other. You could think it was spring, she said and then she went out, I'll just pop into the kitchen and peel some potatoes. And I said nothing. I watched my grandmother come and I heard my mother go.

Her face was flushed. She was upset. She was harbouring death within her and she didn't know it. She called out to me soundlessly. I could tell from her lips that she was saying my name. She was bending slightly forward against the strength of the breeze. My mother turned the little radio on in the kitchen. My grandmother came up the iron stairway, her breath was short. I feel so afraid all of a sudden, Fania. She smiled as she said it. The lenses of her glasses were smeared with sweat.

Earlier in the morning I had taken an axe to the Christmas tree and chopped it into small pieces in the front garden, first the branches and then the long thin trunk. I thought of her as I did it, she'd taught me how to handle an axe years earlier, she'd shown me down in the coal cellar under the stairs. Chopping firewood for the stove, making kindling out of orange boxes. The dull yellow light of the bulb lifted the darkness in this subterranean corner of the house. She leant over the chopping block in her light-grey skirt over which she had fastened her blue apron. With her left hand she gripped an orange box, with her right she took hold of the axe and lifted it far up until it was right behind her head. You don't need to chop any wood, Mummy. My mother was struggling to stay calm, she was standing by the wall taking the curlers out of her black hair. My grandmother was enraged, she was chopping wood because chopping wood was better than sobbing and better than turning to stone out of sheer rage. For the first time ever she wasn't to come with us, my mother wants to go on holiday in the summer just with her husband and her daughters. Like everyone else for God's sake, surely it must be possible for me as well, I can't always be having my mother with me wherever I go right up to my dying day. My father was standing on the bottom step leaning on the banister, he'd followed us into the cellar to avert the worst and calm things down, but without holding out any hope of succeeding. With his nicotine-stained fingers he fumbled around in his trouser pocket and produced a crumpled packet of cigarettes, took out a bent cigarette, the last in the packet, tapped its end to firm up the crumbling tobacco and put it between his tight, drawn-in lips, while at the same time feeling around for matches in his other pocket. He couldn't find any. The sharp axe-blade went thudding into the squealing slats of wood, my grandmother screwed up her eyes, splinters flew through the air.

Her white hair was stuck to her temples. Sweat had gathered between her breasts. I dabbed it away and settled her on the sofa.

Don't go away, she said.

I'll undo your corset so that you can breathe more easily.

I turned her onto her right side and began to unhook her corset.

We could hear my mother singing in the kitchen, the radio was singing along with her, she would lose the tune on her own. I pushed open the sun room door and the window onto the front garden. The fresh air did my grandmother good.

What's the matter with your arm, I asked.

My heart hurts, she replied.

She'd beaten her daughter with the wooden spoon or a clothes hanger. I know the story. Then with her arms dangling limply down she sank onto the kitchen chair exhausted and silent, and stayed sitting there without a word. Alma stood in front of her with blood on her lower lip where she had bitten into it, the child left the room, the door closed quietly behind her. She knew Alma was standing in the street below looking up and bobbing up and down on her feet. She'd written a little letter on the reddish-brown paper of a bag that had had fruit in it, it began My sweet Mummy and ended with a promise to be Ever yours, Peter. Written in pencil in rounded letters it was pushed through under the closed kitchen door. Down in the street in front of the house Alma waited for her mother to appear on the kitchen balcony. Hedwig sat frozen to the spot. She had to do the father's job of beating her daughter, otherwise Alma would turn out just as feckless and faithless as he had been. Alma stood on the pavement below with her hand held over her eyes to shield them from the sun and to ensure that she could see her mother at once if she emerged from her frozen immobility and appeared on the balcony. Eventually she appeared. She waved to her to come up.

My mother had gone back up the cellar steps, she desperately needed a cigarette, and my father couldn't find any matches in his trouser pocket so he went back up to the flat with her. She wasn't going to let her mind be changed by anybody this time, not by her and not by him either, we're going on holiday without Hedwig and that's that, she can go to Travemünde with Ruchla and Olga.

In the coal cellar my grandmother brought the axe whistling down, she'd tried to beat the father out of her daughter, the man who had abandoned them both, it was him she was now attacking with the axe, she watched the blade glance off the slat of wood and slice into the joint of her little finger. She dashed from the cellar up into the kitchen and stood there in front of me, the horror of it had silenced her entire body, for seconds she felt no pain but only indignation at this additional misfortune. Cradling her wounded left hand in her right hand she stood speechless, her mouth agape. I looked at her cupped right hand, it was full of blood, I pulled the neck of my jumper over my mouth and rocked back and forth over her blood-soaked hand as though in prayer. I could hear my voice screaming out of her face.

I knelt down in front of her next to the sofa. She lay there naked, naked fear in her eyes. I held her in my arms with my chest above her. She could breathe more easily. I'm thirsty. I gave her drink as she had given drink to me. And she drank as I had drunk. Alone in her wrinkled skin. Thus was I born and grew smaller day by day and my mother was driven to the verge of madness with me at her breast. They took her away.

My mother came in. She had tripped over the milk can in the hall, oh dear, all that lovely milk wasted. She saw us and yanked me away from her. My father was still in Kiel or perhaps already in Lübeck, Vera was rehearsing at the theatre, I rang 999, a man promised to send an ambulance with an emergency doctor, what's your name, madam. No one had called me madam before. I didn't know. Her daughter, my mother, knelt down by the sofa and put her arm round her mother who gave me drink and to whom I gave drink. We waited for the ambulance. And we waited for my father. The mother of the daughter with the daughter's child. Hedwig had waited for Paul. When he returned home from his selling trips of an evening he greeted a woman with a child. Mother and child.

I, daughter of your daughter, and you, mother of my mother, dreamed our dreams in the folds of the night and ate our fill in the brightness of the day. Behind you lay the night in the reflection of a million eyes, ahead of me lay the day in the shadow of its light. She came back, she returned. Your daughter, my mother. Thin from longing. She stumbled over spilt milk. She crawled to the child. I saw the daughter bend over her mother and sink into her arms. We grasped the other's hand. Then she was gone, her face was no longer inhabited.

We've written an essay. Write about a book you enjoyed reading, Wilhelm Bobbenberg said. I wrote about Goethe's *Elective Affinities*. I read the book with my torch under the bedcovers, from beginning to end, every word. Always on evenings when Vera was at the theatre.

I'd like to give it to you as a present, Thea had said.

I didn't want it given to me, I wanted to borrow it. I wanted it to be hers as I read it under the covers.

Oh Fania, oh Fania. Bobbi was funny about it in front of the whole class, Goethe's *Elective Affinities* – that's one of my favourite books, you watch your step now.

Days later we get our exercise books back. Mine was on top. As usual. I can tell by the yellow cover I wrapped it in to make sure I'm not taken by surprise by something that I already know. But he won't show me up, not all over again. He'll return my exercise book with a shake of his head and that will be that.

Yes, dear ladies, he says, chewing on his saliva, before thumping the pile of exercise books down on his desk with great zest and rubbing his hands together. Signs and miracles still occur, as the prophet might say. I'm not a prophet, I'm just an old teacher and I don't believe in miracles, I believe in willing and wanting, and so it has come to pass, the best essay is on the top.

He takes my exercise book from the top of the pile. He hands it to me, it's my book, it can't be part of the pile, the best essay must be the one after mine, it belongs to the girl behind me. I leave my book on the desk in front of me. Unopened. I don't want the disappointment of it, not now, not today, though my hope is no less painful than my disappointment. It is there now as it always is, my hope for myself. And that's how it always works with hope. In my hopes I see myself coming towards me, I know my way around in the streets of my hope, no one beats me to it, the loves and loss of those who came before me are inscribed in the streets of my hope in which I come and go, and come to my self.

Are there any questions. Bobbi's voice cuts through the murmurings of the assembled girls. As there are no questions,

I should like you all to hear the best essay: come to the front, Fania, and read out your essay.

He's in a state of some excitement, he's smacking his lips and smiling, he's sitting at his desk gripping its edge with both hands.

I leaf through my exercise book. I can't find my essay. There's something here, written in blue ink in my handwriting. That's definitely my handwriting, rounded letters, some sloping to the left a little. Nothing has been marked in red. Nothing has been demolished, not a single word. After the final sentence it says 'A+ W. Bobbenberg' in slanted writing, after that there are a few blank pages, then the back cover. Where's my essay if that's not my essay – but the penny drops at last: the best essay is mine.

How did you do it, Fania, not a single mistake, you sat here in this classroom and wrote this essay before my very eyes.

I did it the same as always, I reply, I've always had the feeling that everything was right.

He keeps me back at the end of the class. His was the last lesson for today, Music has been cancelled, Fräulein Hahn is ill, the others are leaving the classroom. I'm standing with my back to the blackboard, on which *Elective Affinities* is written in my handwriting.

Hang on just a moment, he says. We're standing next to each other by his desk, he opens my exercise book and passes his hand approvingly over what I have written.

It's no miracle, he says, it's something to do with your desire and determination, Fania, but even so I shall never understand why this breakthrough should have occurred right now and so suddenly.

I look at his hand. There's a comma missing there.

Where, he asks.

There. And this 'its' should have an apostrophe.

There you are! You know exactly what's right and what's wrong.

Oysslegen, the Yiddish word. I know it from my grandmother. I want to say it. I want it to go via my lips into the world outside, it would be lovely to quote the Yiddish word at him.

In Yiddish oysslegen means the way you write words. To write something is to tie yourself down, but not completely. You leave the vowels floating in the air somewhere while you stride along with the earth-bound consonants. There's movement in there, there are debates lurking in there, I can hear them, what is meant, what is actually written, written in this particular way or that particular way, oysslegen the laws, interpret the words, each and every one. That's what I want to say to him but I can see his smile enveloping my essay. I say nothing. Right now I don't want to alienate him. I feel his arm round my shoulder. But he's Vera's. The rough material of his suit rubs against my tear-stained face.

I go home. I run. I see myself running, carrying my essay before me, bearing it in my hands to offer it to my mother, to give my child to my mother. I run, and I run away from myself. She'll be pleased, oy won't she be pleased, she has to be pleased. For days now she has been hiding behind her face looking for her mother. I find her during the night. I walk into the room and my grandmother's sitting at the round table darning a sock with the lamp just above her head, she's stretched the sock over her darning mushroom and she's holding it close to her nose. I know she's dead, I talk to her so that she'll stay, she's no longer alive, she can't be dead, I want to fetch my mother, she's sitting right here, I want to tell her, look for yourself, she's not been destroyed, she's dead but quite normal. I go and fetch my mother, I drag her into the room behind me, look, she's sitting over there, I say, the bulb casts a circle of light on the table, and she has gone.

I catch myself up by our driveway. My knees are like jelly, it's because of all the running, it's because of my delight and fright at the miracle, I don't want to surrender my miracle, I want to keep my desire and determination for myself, for myself alone.

Inside the house the cellar door is shut. I grip the handle. The door isn't locked. The Kupsches are out. Otherwise the door would be open. I've got plenty of time. My mother doesn't expect me back yet. I wrote everything correctly, I can do anything, I shall go into the bathroom, I'll break down the door, I'll find the hoard of Nazi stuff, we'll buy the Fingerhuts' house, and Hainichen and that Schmalstück woman will go to jail. I go quietly down the wooden stairs. When I get to the first air-raid shelter door I put my school bag down so that I can use all my strength on the two levers, one above my head, the other beneath my foot. The door swings open without any trouble. I climb over the steel threshold into the narrow passageway beyond, at the end of which is the second air-raid shelter door, and beyond this again lies the bathroom. The time-switch for the light is ticking away, thumping hysterically in my ear, too loudly for me to hear anything else, such as the footsteps of anyone following me, I'm intending to enter forbidden territory, it's too late now, I'm not going to turn back, I look over my shoulder, the steel door behind me is open, what lies ahead of me, imploring letters from the Fingerhut family, demanding letters from Hainichen's uncle, threats, documents, they put my father on trial, interrogation records, the court judgment, separation for life. Darkness descends on me and stops up my ears.

The ticking of the time-switch has disappeared. My fingers

grope for the switch. I know where it is. I turn the light on and dispel the darkness. There are used matches on the stone floor. Wolfram showed me how to do it, you have to poke a matchstick into the switch mechanism to stop the light going out after three minutes. We were standing next to each other, I watched his fingers, he bit a piece of the matchstick off with his great big incisors to make it pointed, you have to stuff it in really firmly otherwise it just gets pushed out again.

The air in the passageway is damp and cold, I'm standing in front of the second steel door, the bathroom should be on the other side of it, stuffed full of documents and old bits and pieces, junk according to my father, junk and useless old papers, perhaps there are valuable paintings, precious jewellery, everything they stole from the Fingerhuts they hid down here. The levers on the door are rusty, I pull on the upper one with the whole weight of my body, it starts to move, steel grinds against steel, and the door swings open into alien darkness.

I'm afraid. There's no one else down here. It's the same cellar after all, it's only separated from our own cellar by this heavy steel door. All of a sudden our cellar seems a really homely place. I could go back there and have a sit down and give my trembly legs a rest instead of breathing in this musty, stagnant air. This door hasn't been opened for years. I go on into the darkness, behind me the time-switch ticks away like a mad thing cutting the silence into tiny little pieces, while the bulb itself casts a narrow shaft of light into the passageway, the bathroom must be at the other end of it, perhaps it has a door with a panel of frosted glass, I can't make anything out. It's deathly quiet. There'll be rats down there. There's a slight bend in the passageway. I saw a rat once, it had scrabbled up the inside of a rainwater gully and hooked itself into a gap with its two front teeth, I was standing in the garden and went to

407

see what the scratching noise was and the rat's long teeth appeared in the drain grating near the bathroom window.

The Hainichens will have nailed the door shut. They were down here, back then. They've nailed the door up and shut away all the proof for ever and ever. I need tools, I need light, a torch, there must be a switch here somewhere. The light is ticking. Perhaps it'll reach as far as the darkness along there, which may be a wall or may be the door I'm looking for. I stretch out my hands and take hesitant steps across the cold cellar floor. It's uneven. Stones with a makeshift screed on top. I'm falling. Don't fall. I'm falling into an infinite abyss.

The time-switch is ticking away at me but there's no light, it ought to be here or there, there is here or was here there. It's my heart pounding, it's you, my heart, it's me, we mustn't move. My outstretched hands find nothing. No end to it. Just nothingness. It is the end of me. The abyss is on top of me. Scream. I can't.

I'm afraid of dying, but shouting for help is too embarrassing. Is anyone coming, I don't want anyone to come, it's all fine by me, help, Mammy, oh God, Mammy, I can trust my mother, she'll miss me before I starve to death, you die of thirst before then, I could lick the walls, the cellar's damp, is there a wall anywhere, that's my head, my ribs, my stomach. My hands grab hold of me, I grope my way down myself, my knees, why are you hurting so much, you're pressing against the stones, they're cooling my skin, for ever and to all eternity. I'm thirsty. My grandmother was thirsty just before she died. So my end is near. In the beginning, B'rashit, Elohim, the eternal, created the heaven and the earth, eht ha'shamayim v'eht ha'aretz. And the earth was chaos and void.

White it was, the lovely milk, and it turned sour on the second day, and having been poured into dishes with a wet cloth over the top it turned into curds on the third day. I was sitting on the stool by the kitchen table. Beneath its lid all was chaos. The shoe-cleaning stuff is in there, old underpants heavy with shoe polish. My legs are dangling down, my face is resting on the edge of the table. My grandmother is crumbling dried-out black bread. Black stars drop into the white heaven of the curds. Sit straight. My thighs press against the stool. Press and let go. Do you need the toilet. No. Then sit nice and still. She mixes sugar and cinnamon for me in a small dish, aromas of the Orient, sniff and puff, press and let go. Take some. I take some. Not too much, think of your teeth. My teeth crunch on sugar and cinnamon. My thighs press and let go. She watches me eat. I eat with relish then slide to the floor between stool and table edge.

I dip my finger in the black-speckled realm of for ever and to all eternity. I have found my self. Do not efface yourself in my life, do not lock me away within yourself. The world of memory lies inside me. It renders me speechless. I cannot say what I want to say. I'm sitting upside down, water runs then comes in floods, I swim and bob through a space with no above and no below. That's rain. That's outside. Outside it's raining on the earth and I am beneath it and I am wet. My fingers are sticky. They taste of salt and they taste of steel. Light spills out all over me. I'm in the cellar beneath our flat. I can hear voices outside. Someone's coming. My fingers are red. Blood is running down my leg.

Outside in the garden the air thrills to the song of a thrush.